BOOK STORAGE

Weston, Michael
   The cage / by Michael Weston. -- New
York : St. Martin's, 1987.
   387 p.
   0-312-00112-6

   I. Title.

THE CAGE

THE CAGE

A PARABLE

MICHAEL WESTON

St. Martin's Press
New York

Library of Congress Cataloging in Publication Data

Weston, Michael.
  The cage.

  I. Title.
PR6073.E775C3   1987   823'.914   86-24818
ISBN 0-312-00112-6

First published in Great Britain by The Bodley Head.

First U.S. Edition

10 9 8 7 6 5 4 3 2 1

ACKNOWLEDGEMENT

A.K. Hamilton Jenkin's Book, *Cornish Miner*, provided much of the background to this work

CONTENTS

CONTENTS

THE CAGE

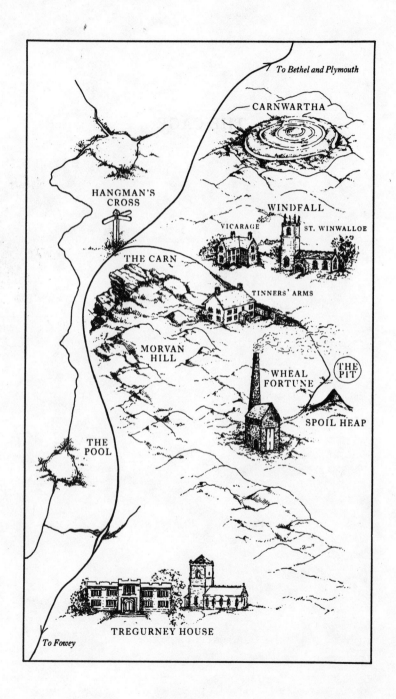

❖ I ❖

THE CARN

Ralph Fletcher never ascertained exactly what it was that made the road-mender dig in the precise spot where he came upon him that spring morning.

Jan Nicholson knelt, facing away from him on the sheep-cropped grass, so totally involved in removing the earth from his find that he failed to look up when the onlooker's shadow fell across him.

Had he been searching for Celtic gold? Or had the poor fellow merely sat down in the shade of the carn's huge rocks to eat his 'croust' as the Cornish called the snack that Jan brought with him from the old vicarage every day? Had he then noticed something man-made sticking through the grass? Or had some strange impulse, some dark intuition like a dowser's fork instructed him to cleave the overlying sod with his roadman's spade, there, in the windy emptiness between the carn and Hangman's Cross? Whatever the reason, there he crouched on hands and knees, examining the peculiar object he was bringing to sight while the disquieting nature of his find gradually percolated into his troubled brain. Ralph Fletcher was to spend years of vain surmise attempting to discover what had impelled the road-mender to choose that spot.

Hangman's Cross, the place where three roads meet, would be a disturbing locality, even without the sinister associations of its name. Even today, the twittering of summer larks cannot dispel the chill solemnity of the wide sweep of bleak moorland that forms a saddle round it. The hiss of the breeze through the stunted heather is like the whispering

7

of vicious old gossips. The cloud shadows that process across the slopes of Morvan and Carnwartha slide off like fleeting ghosts.

Close by the cross, the shattered fragments of a granite carn lie tumbled in a heap as if overturned by a petulant child. It was beside these stones that, in the Year of our Lord 1887, poor, half-mazed Jan Nicholson made the discovery that provoked Ralph Fletcher's all-consuming interest in Windfall and led to the revelation of the events that are the substance of this tale.

The fingerpost at Hangman's Cross is leaning, as though bowing to the fierceness of the west wind. One of its arms, inscribed with peeling letters, points down towards the deep combe where the grey pinnacles of a ruined house are lost among the trees. The road skirts round that mansion: Tregurney House, seat of the Gurney family which claimed descent from Sir Roger de Gourney en Bray who followed the Conqueror to win lands and honour in Britain. It winds onward down a sinuous valley to an estuary where legend has it that Tristan died. This was the Gurney domain, a land of secret woods, old manors, forgotten churches, and a race of sybarities who led wayward, careless and self-indulgent lives. Nowhere was that urge towards impossible schemes and absolute gratification stronger than among the Gurneys of Tregurney House and, ultimately, they paid the price for it.

The second arm of the cross, canted upward as though to a city in the sky, carries the name BETHEL and indicates a straighter road, running out across the heather and whin, past brook and pond, hill-fort and druid stones, to Puritan Plymouth and the world beyond. Along this road, clustered in grim villages, lie the squat, mean, comfortless homes once lived in by the tinners, close by the roofless engine houses of their abandoned mines. There are no mansions or churches here, only the unadorned chapels of a fierce, pleasure-reviling faith. For these poor miners, heirs to darkened days,

8

there were no bright valleys this side of Paradise, no mansions but those their sad Saviour was said to have prepared for them above the sky. This was the road the packmen took as they jogged in and out of Cornwall; this was the road the Gurneys' coaches took as they came swaying down from London. The pale-faced lords and ladies looked out with a vague unease at the stocky, belligerent tinners from whom they drew their wealth. In our own day, long after the tinners have passed away, the severe, classical-fronted chapel at Bethel still stands firm on its narrow faith, and the mood of renunciation of earthly joys still hangs over these Spartan uplands.

The third arm, the one that once indicated a shallow depression among the hills, is broken off short without a name. Where once it pointed, a solitary house, tall, gaunt and partly roofless, stands on a hillock to the left of the track which later loses itself in the rocky ground behind a furze-grown china-clay dump on the far side of the dip. Beside the house, the masonry of a crumbling ruin is easy to mistake for an outcrop of natural rock. This is all that remains of St Winwalloe's church which stood here for centuries and gave its name to the place until the striking of the amazing Windfall lode that brought wealth to Wheal Fortune mine. It was this lode, fabulously rich in its early stages, that called men flocking into the remote Winwalloe valley until the name Windfall supplanted that of the Breton saint who once brought the softness of Christianity to wild Cornwall.

And yet, today, nothing of that mine remains: not one stone piled upon another. The great engine houses, in which the ponderous beam-engines wheezed and clanked, have vanished more utterly than the walls and palaces of Carthage. The miners' cottages are likewise gone. So is their chapel and so is the massive Tinners' Arms. It is as if a blight, or some unreasoning fear, had struck this place and left it desolate. The hillside is patterned with patches of grass growing among the gorse and bracken. Dishevelled sheep

9

run off timorously as you approach. The track itself is disintegrating; deep pot-holes have formed and weeds are pushing up between the stones, splitting them apart. It passes within twenty yards of the sole surviving house and loses itself half a mile onward where a peculiar pyramidal, man-made hill adjoins the still waters of a circular lake.

The house is empty now; its lower windows and doors are boarded over. There are signs that someone, tramp or hippie, has tried to force an entrance, but has desisted, put off by the indefinable unease that hangs over the fast-mouldering vicarage where Jan Nicholson, Windfall's last inhabitant, lived and died. His bedroom windows have been shattered by stones. The skeleton of the gable above is open to the winds and the slates that covered it lie scattered on the grass.

In this more enlightened age, Jan Nicholson would not have been left to live out his declining, half-crazed years alone in this remote already ruinous house but, in his time, men saw nothing unreasonable in that. If anything, they found it fitting that the old road-mender should end his days wandering the hillsides where he had toiled all his working life. For much of it, he had been merely a harmless simpleton and it was only after his momentous discovery that he began to show manic tendencies. Even then, his ability to tend the roads was unimpaired. He lived mostly on rabbits he snared for the pot, making only infrequent journeys to Bethel for other supplies. The people there feared him, feared his intrusion into their humdrum lives. Mothers hustled their children indoors, afraid that they would hear him stand and swear, letting flow an interminable torrent of profanity, mumbled imprecations against God, the heavens, and the surrounding moorland.

They feared him. They knew not why exactly, for his hatred was impersonal, not directed at any of them in particular, being more of a challenge to the nature and essence of life itself.

They feared him with the kind of superstitious awe that Mohammedans reserve for the deranged, treating them as exalted, inspired mouthpieces of Allah. They regarded him through the grudging eyes with which down-to-earth people watch the forked stick jerk in the hands of a dowser.

More than anything else, it was the grisly relic that Jan Nicholson's dowser's skill unearthed and the series of revelations that sprang from it that coloured his neighbours' impressions of him. They did not thank him for disclosing what lay just below the surface of that acid soil. Jan Nicholson himself had only a confused impression of the aggrieved and guilt-laden welter of emotions he let loose with his probing spade; he was impervious to their shame and anger. Ralph Fletcher was doubtful if Jan ever managed to marshal the facts that he, a tireless researcher, gradually ferreted out from the County Archive, the ecclesiastical records, and the muniment room at Tregurney House, feeding them to the road-mender until the whole story must have been stored in his memory like a gigantic jigsaw puzzle. Jan Nicholson was probably no nearer its solution on that later evening when a benighted hiker pushed open the door to Winwalloe Vicarage and started back at the sight of a seated man, glassy-eyed and rigid in death, with his hand clenched around his glass, and the empty bottle beside it.

That had been in the Spring of 1914 and soon the preoccupations of war dimmed all interest in Jan Nicholson and the story of which he had been the unwitting harbinger. Ralph Fletcher had him borne to Tregurney and buried him in the churchyard there. Bethel would not have him, though he had claimed to be a Dissenter. There was more than a suspicion that the earnest, God-fearing chapel-goers had never forgiven him for the Pandora's box he had so carelessly opened, blighting the memory of their own forebears with implied accusations of bigotry and unchristian cruelty.

Jan Nicholson might have gone entirely forgotten to his grave had he not struck that mysterious lode of history with his spade. It was treasure trove: not gold but hidden truth; truth that would out and chose the solitary road-mender as its instrument. How else to explain why, on that spring day in 1887, he had strolled over from the finger-post at Hangman's Cross, where the three roads met that were in his own peculiar care, till he reached the granite carn and began to dig.

First came the metal ring, riveted to the top of the foot-high iron basket whose strapwork, slightly pitted with rust, but otherwise remarkably well preserved, shone with a dull purplish bloom as he wiped away the crumbs of soil with his ragged-nailed hands until, finally, the bone-white flash of whatever it was that lay trapped inside, became apparent to his ever wilder gaze.

The passing traveller found him there, kneeling by the freshly dug hole and lifting the iron cage, suspended from its ring. How long Jan had been crouching there spellbound was impossible to know, but the traveller sensed it had been a long time. The road-mender, whose face was familiar to him from his exploratory walks around the parish, did not look up, although he might have sensed someone was watching him. His whole attention was bent on one thing to the exclusion of all others; his lips moving as though addressing someone, but the sounds emerging inchoate, almost bestial. He might have been a primitive survival of Piltdown man, bemused and dazzled by an artefact of a newer, more sophisticated civilization. He knew he had discovered something of supreme importance, but knew not what. It then was and would remain beyond the grasp of his limited understanding.

But the traveller had a sharper perception of reality, a more rational, scientific mind. By a coincidence, he was none other than the Reverend Ralph Fletcher, MA, DD, rector of Tregurney parish, a Cambridge man, endued with a strong sense of antiquarian curiosity, and this led him to devote all the energy of his leisure hours to the pursuit of the facts that lay behind the simple road-mender's accidental revelation. This task was to occupy his mind with the force of a reigning passion for the next ten years as he peeled back the veils of amnesia, concealment and guilt. It was to prove a thankless task, earning him many enemies and the disapprobation of his bishop. He wasted his substance on the search, yet it gave his life a singular kind of excited purpose that would otherwise have been lacking in such a peaceful parish at the summit of the Victorian age.

The object that hung from Jan Nicholson's hand was an iron cage and in it nestled a skull. As it swung in the wind, the drying particles of soil were still dropping away from the fleshless face. The double row of teeth was still intact and the mouth grinned out through gaps in the cage as though smiling at some obscene joke. The cool breeze, wafting across the skull's nose and eye-sockets, was producing a low musical note, almost a moan, that Ralph Fletcher did not at first identify. The strangeness of the scene unnerved him, but he compelled himself to stay. Taking Jan Nicholson by the shoulders, he pulled him to his feet and led him back to the road by which he had been descending to Tregurney where he lived.

On arrival at the Tregurney Arms, where he instructed the landlord to care for Jan, he prised the cage from his hands by main force. It was as though its discoverer held it in the grip of rigor mortis, so rigid were his fingers, but the rector prevailed. He took it home to the rectory and hung it from the arm of a tall standard lamp in his study. Then, for the first of an interminable sequence of evenings, he gazed at it, seeking to fathom the meaning of its making and the equally profound mystery of its discovery. His wife Anne, who was a Gurney by birth, though only in the female line, tried to dissuade him, but he would not be diverted. That night, as he was to do time and again during the ensuing years, he shut himself up in the book-lined room and contemplated the cage and its grisly inhabitant, preparing himself for the painstaking research that was to lead him to such unpalatable conclusions at the resolution of the mystery.

While Jan Nicholson turned and groaned on his bed of straw at the inn that night, the Reverend Fletcher turned and turned about the suspended cage, trying to guess at its origin. The soft glow of the oil lamps which his unwilling wife had brought in when the maid refused, terrified at the sight of the imprisoned skull, revealed the cage to be of remarkable, even excellent workmanship. At first, he had assumed that it had held no more than a skull, but now, peering through his gold rimmed spectacles, he saw that the riveted bands had once continued down beyond the neck, where they splayed out at the level of the shoulders. Their extremities had been cut away and no amount of digging at the spot where Jan Nicholson had made his discovery, nor anywhere else in the surroundings, ever disclosed the slightest trace of the remainder of the cage or its occupant. Rector Fletcher spent many fruitless guineas persuading superstitious navvies to dig trench after trench. If the answer lay there, he failed to unearth it.

It hid elsewhere, locked in dusty documents and in the hearts of those who had observed those dreadful events which his persistence was destined to uncover. The first clue was the caged skull, but although the Reverend Fletcher was to learn several things from the headpiece, which he quickly found to be hinged on one side, and by extrapolation from the skull's dimensions, deduced it to have contained a man of slightly less than medium stature, its study proved a blind alley. The chief virtue of the cage and its reluctant occupant was to be the companionship they were to offer during Ralph Fletcher's long, unpopular search until, at the end, he was to feel as if he knew the man himself, and that to have him there, suspended from the lamp beside his desk, was an anguish-laden reminder of man's inhumanity to man and of the greatest tragedy he had ever encountered.

It is from the notebooks that Ralph Fletcher compiled

during those long nights that the tale told in the ensuing chapters has been compiled. The events that took place in and around Windfall near the Year of Our Lord 1830 are here related without the extraneous matter of his source notes and the trivia of his diary, but reorganized according to the chronology which emerges from the collection of events which he discovered severally and in confused order.

The cage and its grim occupant now hang in a small museum installed in a wing of the old Bodmin Gaol. The skull's persistent grin may well express satisfaction that, at last, the truth is out. The Rector's unwearied curiosity has uncovered all we need to know of the man in the cage, but the mystery of what impelled Jan Nicholson to dig him up remains entire. He took it to his grave.

2

THE VICARAGE

The cry the young woman heard was not the screech of owl or squeak of bat. It sounded more than half human. It halted her in her tracks and brought her heart to her mouth. She pulled her shawl more closely about her shoulders and glanced behind her. In the gathering dusk, the freshing wind plucked at her skirts and the first flying raindrops splashed her face.

Mavis Trerice was uneasy in the way all country folk were in those days, whenever they were obliged to be out after dark. Legend and folk-tale from time immemorial had peopled the darkness with malevolent beings: there were pixies to contend with, and the ghosts of giants, formless spirits lurking in the rustling hedge or waiting to spring out from behind a pile of stones. However bold she might be, there were certain places, certain stretches of lane, that made her flesh creep. Bat-squeak or owl-hoot made the hair prickle on the nape of her neck, even on quiet evenings when safe on the doorstep of her own home. Mavis Trerice was no more superstitious than any other young woman of her time, but there was no denying the ancient fears that gripped her now, alone in the silence of the night. The satchel strung across her back should have contained material for her comfort, yet it was powerless to help, less use to her than any heathen amulet. She shivered as she walked.

There was the sound again! A piteous, wailing cry that came from the black mass of the carn which loomed against the blood-red cloud a mere twenty yards from the Bethel road. Whether it was human she did not know, yet it resembled the wail of a woeful child. Perhaps it was this conviction that kept Mavis from immediate flight. Some innate maternal instinct directed her timorous, halting steps towards the object of her fear. Perhaps it was only a sheep, trapped by its fleece in a cleft in the gigantic rocks. Or it might be a treacherous pixie incarnation of a child, designed to lure and trap her. Such things were well known to happen. She hesitated a few steps from the rocks and was about to run off when the voice became audible again, first as an unintelligible whimper, but changing to the unmistakable call of a child in distress. Even then, she might have fled had not the moon shone unexpectedly through a ragged break in the clouds, illuminating the spot from which the piteous cries arose.

'I'm cold. I'm hungry. I want my mother!' the voice repeated and Mavis saw that the cries came from a frail, hunched-up figure, a child of some twelve years, whether boy or girl she could not then determine. The child seemed real enough, too real to be a pixie lure. Mavis felt a sudden urge to rush forward and comfort it, but before she could take a step, another much deeper voice sounded hollowly from between the stones.

'She's gone. 'Tis no use your calling her.'

But the child paid no attention, merely recommencing its litany of grief.

'I'm hungry, Father.'

'No use telling me, I've naught to give 'ee.'

'I'm cold, Father.'

As the child spoke, the man stepped forward, divesting himself of his coat which he placed round its shoulders with a tenderness at variance with his sharp rejoinders. In the vanishing moonglow, Mavis saw that he was a stocky, powerful man, with a shock of black, tousled hair over heavy brows and bright, angry eyes. He was not the kind of man to take misfortune kindly.

'I want to go home, I want my mother.'

For an instant, it seemed to Mavis as though the man might strike the child. His right arm twitched and she saw the muscles bulging, but he controlled himself, reaching down to stroke the child's hair and speaking with unexpected gentleness.

'There, there, little one, thou knowest thy mother's gone. Thou knowest she's gone for ever, she'll not hear your crying. As for home, 'tis here. We have no other. Try to sleep now. We'll prove another place come morning.'

There was a kind of archaic style and gentility to his speech that was like a Quaker's, almost Biblical. Mavis was re-assured by now: she felt sure these were no goblins, but real flesh and blood; strangers yes, but poor benighted travellers in need of help.

'Why don't you go down to Windfall? It's not far.'

Her voice sounded oddly thin and strangled in the night air, but it rocked the stranger back on his heels, defensive and tense. He glared at her with a wild, distraught look, and she saw his arm twitch menacingly.

'Who's there? Leave us be, we need no interfering.'

Mavis shrank back involuntarily, but stood her ground. A whimper from the child confirmed her resolve.

'There's an inn there, the Tinners' Arms. There will be rooms aplenty.'

Now that he had discovered his challenger to be a woman, the stranger softened slightly, but when he spoke his words were tinged with scorn.

'Don't think we haven't tried. They welcomed us at the Tinners' Arms – until they found out I'd no money to pay in advance. You come from down there, I suppose, don't you? Well, none of your fine neighbours would have us. "Us wants no vagrants 'ere!" they said, and barred their doors to us, one man and a child. Not one of them would give even the child shelter.'

'That's not so. They're Christian folk, but they're afraid of strangers. They could be opening their doors to a robber.

18

You don't look particularly reassuring. And what are you thinking of, dragging that poor child along with you?' Mavis was astonished at her own boldness, but the child's distress had disturbed her so much she had forgotten her self-conciousness.

'Looking for work,' the man answered belligerently, 'a chap must work.'

'There's no lack of that in Windfall,' she told him. 'Wheal Fortune always needs hands. You'll find work there and no trouble – if you're not afeared of hard labour.'

'What, me, Welland Halt, afraid of work? There's not a man this side the grave to match me at it.'

'That's something we must see. You shall speak with Mr Bolitho tomorrow. Meanwhile, bring the lad down to Windfall village. I'll see he's cared for, though I can't promise the like welcome for you. But I'll do what I can for you.'

'She's not a boy. Ruth's her name.'

Why hadn't she guessed? The child's fine, strained features, long lashes and mane of hair should have told her already. Ruth was sitting up with her father's coat clasped around her thin body, looking at Mavis hopefully.

'All the more reason you shouldn't be dragging the poor creature up hill and down dale. Come on now, follow me down to Windfall. Stop when you reach the first cottage. I'll be there having a word with Mother.'

As Mavis walked off, she was filled with a warm glow. The satisfaction of being involved in doing a good deed had dispelled all her former fears. She remembered the tale of the Good Samaritan that was so often heard from the Bethel pulpit. Every Sunday, she stood in the chapel with her mother while the minister brought the warmth of God's word to the meeting. Her mother was a strong believer, filled with the mystical exaltation that still reverberated through Cornwall years after John Wesley's celebrated tours through the half-heathen county.

So it was a surprise to discover that her mother would not

hear of sheltering the two travellers. As she stood arguing in the doorway, all Mavis's warmth and enthusiasm ebbed away and a familiar helplessness replaced them.

'I won't have no truck with him. He's a rough man, a wastrel, just like you know who I mean. I heard him swear just now: he swore at Jack Lugger when Jack refused to put them up at the Tinners' for nothing.'

'Swearing's no novelty in Windfall. If that's his only sin, there's not a man here worthy of shelter.'

'He'll not pass this threshold!'

Mavis recognized the familiar bitter tone in her mother's shrill assertion. She tried one last line of argument.

'But the girl, the young maid, she's done no harm, has she?'

'Happen she hasn't, but she's of the same brood. She'll not sleep here. Thin end of the wedge, that's what she'd be. She'd take after *him* too, I fancy.'

'Do *I* take after Father? Is that what you're saying?'

'Not yet, but you might. That's why I must be forever watching over you, to keep your steps from the Pit. Come on in, girl, and bar the door after you.' Mavis hung a moment on the threshold, her normally dutiful disposition warring with a sudden rebelliousness. 'Well, are you coming in?' her mother insisted. Mavis thought she heard the sound of footsteps approaching: a child's, pattering; a heavier set, dragging. A fresh rainstorm rattled on the slates overhead. By way of an answer, Mavis threw the contents of the satchel she was carrying across her shoulder on to the floor beyond her mother.

'There you are,' she taunted, 'those are the good books you sent me for. Minister Penrose picked them out for you special. He thinks you're his prize supporter, his prime example. Read them. Perhaps they'll teach you charity.'

'You're a wild, ungrateful child. I might've knowed this would happen. I've slaved to bring you up straight, and all for nothing. But still I pray that you'll come to repentance. I pray that God's grace will return to you and make you less of a thorn in the side of your poor old mother.'

'So you'll do nothing to help these unfortunate wayfarers?'

'No, nor will any other true believer. Mark my words, no good will come of their staying here. Nothing but ill, I promise, and you shall be the first to pay for it. If they'd been good Christian folk, they'd be still at home and paid for by the parish.'

Mavis turned away and began to walk off, gazing up the dim road for a glimpse of the arriving travellers. She stopped a few yards off and threw a parting phrase over her shoulder.

'Well, if that's all chapel will do, we'll see if church is better.' The barb struck home. She heard the hiss of her mother's incoming breath before the door was slammed shut behind her. By now, the strangers were close. Probably they had heard what she and her mother had been saying. Mavis did not care. She led them slowly down the shadowy street between the tight rows of granite cottages, glancing back to see that they were following. Most of the houses were dark now; their inhabitants exhausted after a long day's toil and reluctant to spend hard-earned pence on lamp oil. Only two buildings were lit.

The brighter of the two was the Tinners' Arms. Every window was glowing brightly, from top to bottom of its three-storey bulk. Sounds of merriment leaked out in snatches, but for Mavis they held no charm. She saw Tom Magor's great moon-face leering at a woman across a table; one of the hussies who were drifting into Windfall, scenting easy money. Poor creatures, Mavis thought, their despised trade brought them little more than a pittance and where was their future when their beauty had vanished? Yet the woman with Magor was laughing and raising her cup.

Behind Mavis, the young girl was scuffing her feet. She was drooping with dejection and fatigue. Her father too had a peculiar footfall. Looking back at them as they passed through the pool of light in front of the inn, she saw that

Welland Halt did indeed limp. It was as though he had fallen victim to some accident or been crippled by a youthful disease. Yet he had his arm round Ruth protectively, half lifting her as they went along.

The other building from which a clear light shone was fifty yards further on, perched on a knoll beside an ancient church. It was towards this house, a tall, steep-gabled construction, that Mavis directed her steps, pausing only briefly to ensure that the strangers were following her up the side road that led to it. A bright rectangle of light suffused the parlour window, revealing, when she approached, a youngish man with thinning hair, bent earnestly across an oaken desk where he wrote, paused to suck his quill, then wrote again. It was Mr Nichols, the Curate, composing the next day's sermon which he would preach, as usual, to an all but empty church, so powerless was the old, established religion to match the new Methodism's passionate enthusiasm.

He looked up almost fearfully when Mavis scratched upon the pane. The Curate was a solitary figure in Windfall: a bachelor, but lately down from Oxford, unschooled in the compromises and accommodations needful to grease the axles of the grinding wagon of life, still less to stir his parishioners' hearts with the fire and brimstone used by the Nonconformist preachers. He locked himself up with his books alone and emerged only to cross the green to the church where he performed the age-old ritual, with book and candle, bell and censer, bread and wine, murmuring of love and forgiveness – love and forgiveness he wished he himself could feel. If he hated and blamed, or despised his flock for failing to come and listen to his quiet call, he hid it well. This was his Calvary, his pilgrimage through the valley of the shadow. It was the hope of someday emerging from the nightmare of Windfall's smoky vale that kept him sane and inspired his earnest prayers. Though his parishioners did not hear him, God might. At least He seemed closer. That was how Mavis saw him, saw him and pitied him.

'Have they not tried the inn?' he demanded with defensive brusqueness when she explained her errand.

'But they are poor folk in distress. They have no money.'

All the theory of charity which he had learned at college now seemed hopelessly inapplicable in this God-forsaken place where penniless nightcomers were calculated only to add a new dimension to his own misery and perpetual unease.

'And none of your precious chapel-goers will have them, is that it? Rejected by the righteous, what makes you think they will fare better in an appeal to the old religion?'

'I've heard say – I hoped – that you were a man of heart, Mr Nichols.'

'Precious little good that'll do me,' said the Curate with a sigh.

'For the maid's sake – ' said Mavis, letting her words hang in the air. She saw the Curate stare over her shoulder at the two wayfarers who had come up with her and were hovering at the edge of the lamplight. His eyes lingered on the drooping girl, yet his expression was inscrutable. 'You can put them in my stable for the night; one stall is empty and there's hay and straw aplenty – Nay, do not thank me,' he grumbled when Mavis touched his arm impulsively, 'it is no more than my moral duty.' He shook her off with an awkward gesture. 'And now, forgive me, I have my sermon to finish.'

Mr Nichols turned back into his great empty house, with its vast kitchen, its parlour, its drawing room and its five bedrooms, designed for a large and happy family, only momentarily considering why he had consigned his guests to a stable. They were vagabonds, practically gipsies. If he had asked them indoors, his house, his castle, his refuge from the rough world, would have slipped from his grasp and taken on irremediably the status of an inn. He remained a long time with his hand on the latch, breathing heavily until the sound of dragging footsteps and low voices began to diminish. Then he threw open the door.

'Are you a Christian, Mr Halt?' he shouted challengingly into the night where three pale and dazzled faces turned round at him.

'I have tried – I am trying,' replied the man very slowly and deliberately, as though with great effort.

'And your daughter? What is her name?'

'Ruth.'

'Ruth – Well, I hope her spiritual needs are not being neglected.'

'I do the best I can,' said Welland, perplexed by the question.

'So do we all,' said Mr Nichols with relief in his voice. 'Well, good night and God bless you. I'll question her tomorrow.' His door clicked to behind him, leaving Mavis and her charges to find their way into the stable in the dark.

'Surprised you bothered to come home,' said her mother challengingly without looking up when Mavis walked in. She was crouched by the fire, reading one of the leather-bound books that still lay strewn on the floor around her. 'Satisfied, then?' she continued when Mavis failed to answer. 'As if there wasn't enough sin, evil and tribulation in Windfall without your bringing in feckless vagrants with more of it. No good will come of this. Well, answer my question, satisfied, are you?'

'No, not yet,' said Mavis, lifting the fire-blackened soup cauldron from the trivet beside her mother. 'The child must be fed. The poor creature's starving.'

'And the man too, I'll warrant. Next thing I'll hear, you'll be married to a vagrant and off on the road yourself. There's enough of your father's gipsy blood in you.'

'Marry? You must be mad, Mother, to think that I'd ever marry anyone at all, least of all some uncouth stranger.' Mavis tried unsuccessfully to remember what the stranger,

Welland Halt, had looked like. His exterior had seemed as rough as his nature. 'After all,' she went on, 'haven't I your shining example to instruct me? I never thought *you'd* dare presume to advise me about marriage.'

'Hold your tongue. You know very well how he made me suffer.'

'Why should I? Did you ever hold yours when he came home from the Tinners'? No wonder he was off again at once, drinking and whoring.'

'I won't have you using that word here, this is a Christian house.'

'And to wish him dead, I suppose that too was Christian.'

'The Lord saw fit to punish him. That wasn't my doing. That man blighted my life. Now he's gone, I've done my best to forgive him. But you didn't need to, you'd already done so, you were always full of excuses for his behaviour. You didn't have to put up with his dirty boots on the sheets, you didn't have to sleep with the vomit. You were too young to know, or you didn't want to. That's why I know you'll follow in his footsteps. You said you could see good in him. You'd see good in anything that wore trousers. That's why you'll do it. Mark my words! There's no deed so foolish a maid won't perform for love of a man, though she knows she'll repent forever. When will you repent and seek salvation in these good books? Repentance, that's all that's required, repentance. And faith. Believe only on Him and ye shall be saved. I pray for that day, Mavis when a red-hot preacher shall come from Bethel to bring the sinners of Windfall to faith and repentance, you foremost amongst them. But I've no illusions, proud they are and proud you are, too proud to hear him and be saved from the Pit of Damnation.'

It was a refrain that Mavis had heard all too many times down the years and she closed her ears to it, looking at her mother sadly, sympathetically, as if at a lunatic. She poured the soup into the old billycan her father had used to take his croust down the mine and walked out into the night.

25

3

WHEAL FORTUNE

The village into which Welland Halt and his daughter emerged next morning was an even meaner place than he had remembered it from the previous afternoon when its inhabitants had shut their doors in the travellers' faces. A Sabbath gloom had descended on the grey, straggling street. The only signs of activity came from some ragged youths playing football on a distant field and puffs of smoke from the engine house across the valley where the nodding steam-pump was unweariedly sucking water from the Windfall shaft. Close at hand, a few scrawny chickens were scratching in the dirty, stinking gutters along the unpaved street and a couple of pigs rooted among the weeds on a vacant lot.

'You'll not forget to bring Ruth to be catechised!' called Mr Nichols from the church porch where he stood in the shadows.

'First things first,' replied Welland gruffly, not much liking the way the Curate was staring at his daughter, 'a man must earn his bread.'

'Not by bread alone!' insisted the Curate. 'You know that, don't you? Surely you wouldn't deprive your daughter of the bread of the spirit?'

'We'll see about that in good time. For the present, my aim is to find Mr Bolitho.'

'You're in luck,' said the Curate, 'you won't need to walk down to his house in Tregurney. I've just seen him drive over to the count house.' He stepped out of the porch and pointed. 'That's it over there, the building across from the engine house.' Welland's eyes followed the Curate's finger to a long

26

squat shed whose slate roof glistened in the subdued light.

'What sort of a man is Bolitho?' he questioned.

'If it weren't for Hector Bolitho,' said Mr Nichols, clasping his elbows inside the sleeves of his cassock, 'there'd be no Windfall, though whether that can be judged an improvement, I'm not so certain.'

'How d'you mean, no Windfall?'

'When Hector Bolitho first came up here, this place was called Winwalloe, after the church and the saint that founded it. Hector Bolitho married the Gurney girl and his brother-in-law sent him up here to take charge of the china-clay workings. You can see the heap of spoil beside the pit on the way to Wheal Fortune. Squire Gurney was supplying the clay to Cookworthy's pottery in Plymouth. The half-dozen families that lived here then supplied the labour. Those who're still living tell me it's changed out of all recognition.'

All the time Mr Nichols was talking, he was examining the newcomers minutely. The man was of middle height, powerful about the shoulders, but not really handsome. His hips were small and he stood somewhat askew. One of his legs was bent and he dragged that foot when walking. His strong face was set off by a shock of untidy hair and his deep-set eyes were piercing. The clothes he wore were travel-stained and worn, but were too good a fit to belong to a common vagrant. The daughter was even more intriguing. She wore clothes above her apparent station. A grey serge cloak with blue facings hung over a neat dress of dark worsted. The shoes that peeped under its hem were scuffed and split. They had once been patent leather. But it was the virginal woman inside the clothes that claimed his interest. Though still slightly boyish in attitude and gesture, she was on the brink of womanhood and he relished the way her green eyes turned down when he looked into them. She was pretty already: what she would become in a few short months, he could all too easily imagine. He compelled himself to come back to her father's question.

'Bolitho was something of a geologist and in his wanderings around the pit while the navvies carted off the clay, he stumbled on a reef of gossan in a streambed. He was familiar enough with gossan to know that it usually indicated the presence of a body of ore beneath.' The Curate paused. 'Are you still listening? I do go on a bit once I get started, there's no one much to talk to in Windfall.'

'Course I am,' answered Welland, 'come to the point, won't you?'

'That *is* the point! That very day, Hector Bolitho pulled a gang of navvies out of the pit and set them to work excavating his discovery. He called it the Windfall Lode. They say it's the richest in Cornwall, richer even than the fabulous Dolcoath vein near Camborne. There was tremendous excitement: tinners came flocking in from all over the country. It was before my time, but they still talk about it.'

'So this Bolitho fellow came into a fortune,' said Welland.

'That's what you might have expected, isn't it? But it wasn't as simple as that. The Gurneys, from Tregurney House, were heirs to the mineral rights. They own all the land hereabouts, not to mention the advowson of my living. No, Hector Bolitho would hardly have seen a penny if he hadn't been married to Janet Gurney, Silverton's sister.'

'He must have been miffed at that,' Welland muttered.

'Hector Bolitho's a reasonable man. He had a name, but no fortune. He was lucky to marry a Gurney. When Silverton floated Wheal Fortune, he gave twenty per cent of the shares to his sister. Bolitho was pleased when his brother-in-law accorded him five per cent and made him purser. Silverton himself kept fifty-one; he likes to keep a grip on things.'

'That still doesn't add up to a hundred.'

'Doesn't it? Decidedly, you've a head for figures, Welland Halt, a better one than I have. From what I've heard, the remainder was sold to small adventurers who effectively put up the capital for the first workings. They've no reason to grumble. They do, of course, but Silverton Gurney isn't an easy man to get hold of.'

'You said Bolitho was reasonable.'

'Most find him so. He's middle-aged now, likes his brandy, but he's a good manager – conscientious. Wheal Fortune makes money. Hector Bolitho knows which side his bread is buttered, so don't go there expecting favours.'

'I wasn't.'

'I suppose not.' The Curate hesitated a moment. 'You can leave young Ruth with me while you seek him out. I'll give her breakfast.' He was pleased to see her look up on hearing that. She was sure to be hungry. What a waif she looked. Had her father been ill-treating her?

'Look here, Mr Nichols,' said Welland bridling, 'I know we're in your debt for a night's lodging and I'm grateful, don't think I'm not. But I won't be beholden. Ruth neither. She'll come to your church when she's a mind to, if ever. And now, good-day to you. 'Tis time I spoke with this Hector Bolitho.' Taking Ruth firmly by the hand, he led her off down the lane.

They passed the long irregular terraces of cottages. Most were thatched with marsh reed, only a few were slate-roofed like the church, the vicarage and the inn. Slate cost money, reed from the ponds was a free commodity the tinners could bring home with their own hands. Those same hands, schooled at stonecutting in the mine, had built their cottage walls with moorland granite. Small windows peered from under frowning eaves.

Beyond the last of the houses, a rutted track swung over the hummocked moor, past the stark white spoil heap and the invisible pit, over a final rise and down to the dell where Wheal Fortune's buildings stood in solemn majesty. The tall engine house with its pointing chimney presided over a huddle of lesser buildings among which Welland Halt made out the count house, a sturdy, slate-roofed granite construction, five windows to a side, over a cellar that disappeared into the hillside. There was no door on the side he first saw and it did not come into view until he rounded the end of the building and discovered it at the head of a short flight of steps. He took Ruth to the small landing at the top of these steps, knocked briefly and led her in.

Hector Bolitho looked up with a frown of annoyance from the open account book he was studying at the end of a long polished table. The other furniture in the room was a clerk's desk, a cabinet, two grey painted cupboards, and a dozen ladder-back chairs. Only one of these had arms, the one in which Bolitho sat, and he pushed down on them briskly as he stood up.

'Well?'

'I've come to ask for work.'

Bolitho cleared his throat before answering.

'Another time, wait. Knock and then wait. Don't come barging in. You'll get a better hearing.' While he spoke, he stroked his stomach through the smooth cloth of his waistcoat, weighing up the intruder's character and physical worth. 'Who sent you?'

'Mavis Trerice. She said you were in need of hands.'

'She did, did she?' The purser paused, throwing his head back and examining Welland's features through his half-glasses. 'What name do you go by?'

'Welland Halt. I expect you're Hector Bolitho.'

'What's your trade?' Bolitho tried to ignore the stranger's irreverent directness. His powerful arms and deep chest spelt the strength that was needed in the mine.

'I'm a smith.'

'We have no need of smiths. We have a smith, Tom Magor, the best in Cornwall and the strongest.'

'Be he strong as you like, he'll never have the way that Welland Halt has with iron.'

'That's as may be, you'll have no cause to show it here – and you'll do well to learn to say "sir" when you address your masters.'

'So it's to be no then, is it, "sir"? Come on, Ruth, we'd best be leaving.'

Welland took the girl by the arm and began to steer her back through the count house door. Hector was well aware of the sarcasm in his tone, but he chose to ignore it, as he ignored the man's limping walk. Tough, opinionated men, accustomed to triumph over adversity, were often the best workers.

'I said no work for a smith, I didn't say no work at all, did I? There's plenty of work underground. In this place, everyone starts at the bottom and works his way up – if he's any good, that is. There's money too, if you know what hard work is and can stomach it.' Hector Bolitho was suddenly conscious of the man's eyes, fixed on his own hands that were still massaging the distended cloth around his watch-chain, but he failed to grasp the significance of Halt's thin smile. 'Don't stand there grinning and gawking, man. There's a job for you here. Will you take it, yes or no?'

Welland Halt nodded slowly, his wide blue eyes looked straight into the purser's. He came back across the floor with hand extended. Hector Bolitho was disconcerted by the gesture and astonished at the controlled power in his grip. There was no fawning subservience about this Welland, he was a man's man, and Bolitho suspected he might grow to like him.

'You'll not regret it,' said Welland, already forgetting to use the subservient "sir" with each remark. He paused, then asked boldly, 'I'll be needing an advance on wages, not for myself, you understand, but for the maid. She must have shelter and a woman to care for her while I'm down the mine.'

'There's no need for her to sit idle,' began Bolitho, 'the village girls all work at the stamps, it'll toughen her up in no time and her wages will come in handy.'

'She'll not work here,' said Welland sharply, following the purser's glance at the frail, dejected girl. 'Life must have better to offer a child than that.'

'Suit yourself.' Bolitho hesitated a moment. It wasn't his way to be free with the adventurers' hard-won profit, but he picked a token from a pile on the desk and slid it down the table towards his new worker. 'That's good as gold here in Windfall – worth all of five shillings. I'm counting on you to earn it back quickly. Where are you lodging?'

'Last night, Curate Nichols was kind enough to give us the use of his stable.'

'Very Christian of him. I can't offer you anything much more splendid, but there's a cottage that's just reverted back to Squire Gurney, old Retallack the tenant was taken off with pneumonia. If you wait by the church, I'll point it out to you when I drive by on the way back to Tregurney. I'm leaving shortly, just so soon as I've checked Mr Farrow's accounting, so step lively.'

'We'll be there.'

'And you'll be back tomorrow morning. Work starts at five. You'll hear the hooter.'

Three-quarters of an hour later, Welland pushed open the door of the tiny cottage to which Hector Bolitho had sent them. Its thatch sagged in dark waves across the rafters. Their troughs were green with moss. Ruth gagged on the mouldy stench as she followed her father closely.

'It's dreadful. We can't live here. It's a hovel. No wonder that man, what was his name – Retallack – died here.'

'We must cut our coats to suit our cloth.' Welland's voice was close to resignation.

'But this Windfall is such a terrible place, we don't have to stop here. We could turn homeward.'

'There's no turning back. You know very well why that's impossible.'

'Oh, Father, this place will be the death of us!'

'There, there, don't cry.' He put his arms around her and pressed her to him. 'Come now, my treasure, 'tisn't half so bad as it looks, we'll soon have it bright and cheerful.' He was hard put to it to justify his optimism. 'And Windfall's the first place we've had shelter for nothing and a chance to work into the bargain.' He held her at arms' length and sought out her tear-wet eyes. 'You're a good girl, Ruth, and you're going to help your old father. Dry those eyes and off you go: take my knife and cut some broom to brush this floor with.'

After a few more sobs, she did his bidding. Alone in the bare room that was all the ground floor offered, he studied the stained and blackened table, the two rickety chairs and the rough bedstead that were its only furniture. A blackened pot lay canted over in the ashes on the hearth, still half full of some rancid liquid. He seized it up and flung the contents out through the doorway. Then he went to the window and hammered at the swollen casement until it opened. A chill draught of moorland air swept through the room. He took a deep breath that was half a sigh and crossed to the steep ladder that served as a stairway to the windowless loft under the thatch. When he poked his head through the hatchway, he discovered a pallet whose straw was bulging out of its hessian cover. A scampering from under the eaves told him that he and his daughter were not to be the only occupants. He felt helpless, hopeless. How could he expect Ruth to put up with such squalor? Tears came uninvited to his eyes in turn. What had he brought her to? Only when he heard her returning footsteps did he pull himself together. He knelt at the hearth and began to pile up furze twigs to start a fire, keeping his face averted.

The peppery smell of the broom she carried caught in his nose and made him sneeze that turned to a sob. Suddenly, she was there beside him.

'I'm sorry, Father. I'm a trial to you, aren't I? But I won't be. I'll do my best. Just watch me! And I'll work at the mine, I'll save you money.'

'No, you shan't,' he said fiercely, 'not ever.'

He clasped her to him. Both were trembling. 'You're my Ruth,' he told her. 'They'll not have you – never.' After a while, he released her and began fussing with the tinder. She sensed he was still grieving.

'What's the matter?'

'This place – it's not fit for you, Ruth. You said it yourself, it's dreadful.'

'Then we'll make it better.' She kissed his hair as she spoke and, moments later, he heard the swish of the broom on the floor. He lit the fire. Within the hour, Ruth was humming as she worked beside him. Welland grew calmer. There were provisions to buy and it was Sunday, but they would manage somehow. He had found a brush and was scrubbing the table. He looked up and saw her green eyes smiling in the firelight, for the room was dark, even in broad daylight. 'There,' she said, 'I told you so: isn't this more cheerful?' He dropped his brush and framed her young face in his wet hands. How solemn she suddenly looked, how old for her years. That was the life they were leading.

' 'Tis no life for a young girl,' he muttered, 'but then, neither was that other. I'll make it up to you, Ruth, I promise. Just give me time, a little longer.'

'Hush, Father! You shall have all the time you want. We have a house; you have work, the worst of our troubles are over.'

Welland's lips pulled back in a wan smile. It would be nice to think so.

Next morning, the mine hooter was sounding for the second time as Welland passed the count house. To his right, a range of unfamiliar machinery had just been set in motion. A row of ponderous hammers at the ends of pivoted beams were nodding and pounding. Around them the bal maidens, as the women workers were called, with a few boys to help them, were taking up their tasks under a kind of linhay. Most of the tinners had lined up at the head of the shaft and were vanishing, one by one, down the ladders.

'So you've arrived then!'

It was Hector Bolitho at the head of the count house steps. 'Come over a minute.' When Welland was close, Bolitho pointed to a man who was standing, cap in hand, on the lowest step. 'This is Curnow. He's an old hand. I've told him to show you the ropes. You'll be on tutwork, that's what we call contract labour. There's a regular wage, enough to live on if you're not extravagant.'

Welland was only half listening; he was weighing up the man who was to be his workmate. Curnow was a head taller than the general run of tinners and broad in proportion. He had an open face, pink-cheeked under piercing blue eyes that looked back at him frankly.

'Mornin',' said Curnow, bobbing his head slightly. 'We'd best get movin'.'

'Aye,' said Bolitho, 'another time be sure to arrive and be at the shaft before the second hooter. You're not paid for walking.'

'You'll be needin' an 'ard 'at and some candles,' said Curnow, setting off across the yard towards a store where other miners were clustered, 'not to mention an 'ammer and a boryer.' When Welland came up with him, Curnow bent close and murmured, ' 'Is bark is worse than 'is bite, is 'Ector Bolitho's, so long as you don't cross un.'

Welland's attention had wandered. He had just noticed Mavis Trerice among the other bal maidens. She was hardly recognizable, wrapped in kerchief and shawl over a heavy skirt and apron. He stepped towards her.

'Mavis!' he called. She looked up from the anvil on which she was beating a lump of ore with a hammer.

'What is it?' She brushed back a tendril of chestnut hair from her face with the back of her hand as she spoke.

'I just wanted to say –' He was somehow intimidated by her dark brown eyes which had flecks of gold in them. Her mouth was firm, unsmiling. 'I wanted to thank you.'

'There's no call for that.' She returned to her work.

'You're the first one that's been good to us,' he insisted,

staring at her face that was handsome rather than pretty and whose cheeks had reddened, though whether with annoyance or embarrassment he was not certain.

'Comeason, boy,' Curnow was calling and tugging at his sleeve, 'can't you see the cap'n's watchin'? You get 'er into trouble too if you 'angs about there.' Reluctantly, Welland let himself be drawn off to the store where he drew candles and other gear which was marked to his account by the clerk, Mr Farrow. All the while, Welland was wondering why Mavis was so distant. She had been friendly enough last night. What had he done to estrange her? Soon, he had no leisure for such suppositions. He was following Curnow down the first of the ladders.

With three pairs of candles strung round his neck by their wicks like the other miners, and a sack of tools across his back, he was groping for the rungs with his game leg and trying not to think of the depths into which he would tumble if he missed his footing. Alongside him, the pump rods rose and fell with a swish and a rattle. He reached one landing, changed to a new ladder, then another and another. The light faded steadily. The ladders were slimy with mud from a thousand boots, damp with continual dripping.

'Look out! Keep close!' It was Curnow warning him to press tight against the ladder while a kibble, a great iron bucket that arrived with a whoosh and a clang, swept by on its way to the bottom. It seemed to Welland he had seen a man in it.

'Bleddy fools!' complained Curnow as if in answer to his unspoken question. 'More'n wan o' they young fire-eaters 'ave got 'isself kilt that fashion.'

Another kibble rose, heavy with ore, spilling small stones into the shaft. They were a long time falling. Before he reached the level at which he and Curnow were to work, Welland's legs were tired and he was almost light-headed. How would it be on the return journey?

36

He almost passed Curnow without noticing him. His companion was stooping in the mouth of one of the levels trying to light a candle. The man's face leapt out of the shadows as he puffed the wick into flame. All around was darkness. The light at the top of the shaft was a pinhead. Curnow smiled reassuringly and showed Welland how to jam a lighted stub of his own candle into a ball of clay on the front of his hat before proceeding down the level.

They walked for what seemed like half a mile in solitude until Curnow threw down his bag and examined his surroundings. When he was satisfied, he took his hammer and his boryer from his bag and motioned to Welland to join him.

'Us'll start 'ere,' he announced. 'We're to sink a winze to the next level so's the air gets better. Fer a start off, you 'old the boryer and I'll beat un. Us'll change over later.' He planted the long-shafted drill's cutting edge on the tunnel floor and waited until Welland knelt and took it. Then he began to beat it with a lump hammer. When he tired, Welland changed places. They drove the boryer to its full depth and then, after a pause for croust, as Curnow called the snack he insisted on sharing with the newcomer, the Cornishman prepared to set off a charge of black powder.

'New to the minin' game, aren't 'ee?' he surmised aloud as he tamped the charge down deftly. 'Tes 'ard, 'arder than you bargained for, I fancy. But you'll do. Where'd you larn to use an 'ammer?'

'Here and there.'

'Don't take on. I were only askin' friendly.'

Though Curnow was a bulky man, ill at ease in the cramped tunnels, he was very cool with powder and astonishingly nimble-fingered with wadding and fuses. Welland was too intrigued to be worried, the man's easy familiarity with explosives gave him confidence.

'Move back our gear a ways,' Curnow instructed, 'then you can light un with your candle. 'Twill be the biggest squib you've ever started. You'll 'ave less than 'arf a minute to get back to safety, but 'twill give 'ee a whiff o' danger. You'll never take to this trade if you don't larn a taste fer it.'

However self-controlled he tried to be, there *was* a thrill to lighting the fuse and loping swiftly back to the shelter Curnow had contrived round a bend in the level. When the explosion came, with a flash, a thunderclap, a rattle of stones, and a blast that put out their candles, it dulled his senses. The first thing he knew was Curnow blowing on his glowing candle wick to revive it. The Cornishman was speaking, but he couldn't make out what he was saying.

'I can't hear – my ears are ringing.'

'Never mind that,' shouted Curnow as the candle flared up, disclosing a fog of fine dust that eddied slowly about the level, 'keep your mouth open next time, it won't 'urt 'ee so much.' He clapped Welland on the shoulder. 'Us'll make a tinner of 'ee yet!'

While they sat waiting for the dust to clear, Welland's senses slowly returned and he was able to discern the messages given off by the mine. There was the occasional groan from the massive timbering as the rock settled. There was the constant drip and trickle of water. There was the stifling air that made him want to rush to the surface and fill his lungs with something better. There was the loneliness. Somewhere, far off, above, beside, beneath, he knew not where, he thought he heard a tapping. Another man was chipping away at the rock.

'Do you hear that?' he asked.

'Aye, tes the boys on the two-'undred-fathom level. They'll be over'ead stopin' to meet us. Tes time us was back to work. Us'll 'ave to do more afore us goes up to grass.' He stood up, obliged to bow his head under the low roof. 'What've 'ee done with your maid? I 'eard you'd a-brought a young maid with 'ee.'

'She's at home in the cottage, waiting. I couldn't find a woman to care for her in time. I shall have to ask around this evening.'

'My Ellen'd 'elp out, if she could. She's a kind body, but she've six of 'er own to manage.' He paused. 'That's why I keeps to tutwork, can't afford to gamble my wages like a tributer.'

'What's a tributer?'

'I'll tell 'ee later. There'll be plenty o' time fer that. Now we must shift they rocks afore the underground cap'n d'catch us slackin'.'

So that first day went on. When Welland finally struggled up to grass and saw the engine house his limbs were trembling with exhaustion. The evening air made him shiver. It had been warm in the mine. The chill breeze made his bones ache. He limped off home as fast as he could travel. The exertion would warm him and he was concerned about his daughter.

When he crossed the threshold, he smelt a stew on the trivet. A candle's clear flame showed the table laid for two. In the centre stood a spray of flowers in a bottle. It took him a moment to discern his Ruth, kneeling at the hearth where she had been waiting for him, but he caught the glint of firelight in her eyes and the white flash of her smile.

'Do you like it?' she asked.

'Come here, Ruthie, let me give you a kiss. It's a real wonder.'

He caught his breath with emotion as she did his bidding. Her auburn hair shone and rippled about her shoulders. She was so beautiful, so helpful, so good. She was his daughter.

'I thought you were never coming home. The others all got back before you.'

'I'm slow on the ladders, but I'll get better. I've been fretting about you. It's so long for you to stay alone.'

'I've not been idle.'

'I can see that. The flowers are grand, where did you get them?'

'An old lady showed me where I could pick them. I think

she was Mavis's mother. She wanted to know where we came from.'

Welland stiffened.

'What did you tell her?'

'Up the country – that's what you said I should say.' She felt him relaxing.

'It's none of her business, none of anyone's business here, where we've come from. All that matters is we've come away. Now we must help each other. You know the reason.'

'I think so, Father. Will you eat your supper now?'

Only when he had washed and eaten did he realize how tired he was. He sent Ruth to bed in the loft, hoping the mice would not trouble her. Seconds after he dropped on to the corner pallet and closed his eyes, he was deep in slumber. Seconds later, it seemed, he heard the hooter. Soon, he was trudging down the track towards the mine.

And so began Welland Halt's long servitude at Wheal Fortune. Whatever his reason for coming here with his daughter, and that he told no one, he bent his body to the task. The long shadow of the engine house lay across every day of his life. The darkness of its tunnels absorbed him till his face lost all colour and the brightness went from his eye.

The peculiar form of the engine house became etched in his memory, burned by the light of those successive days. It had been built as though to last for ever, like a castle keep: thick-walled, with squared quoins, round-arched windows, a strong roof of Delabole slate fifty feet above the ground and, alongside the house, stabbing at the sky like a pointing finger, the tall chimney, always trailing smoke. All over Cornwall, similar structures were being built to hold the new engines that pumped out the water or wound ore to the surface, allowing the tinners to venture ever deeper and win metal from remoter lodes. There was a paradox in their solid construction, for most of them would outlive the excavations they were designed to serve. Timeless memorials of a hectic century of rapacious exploitation and greed, they were cheap to build; the granite lay all around, it was there for the taking, and the mason's wages were almost nothing.

Inside the engine house a Smeaton engine hissed, belched, and clanked as the beam bobbed and the pump-rod clattered up and down the shaft, bringing gush after gush of reddish water up to grass. The engine was the pulsing heart of the mine. Without its regular beat, the veins in its vast underground body would become clogged with watery spoil and it would die. But the engine was strong; its stokers piled on the sea-coal and it bowed to its task.

If the visible portion of an iceberg represents only a fraction of its true extent, so too the buildings at Wheal Fortune were a mere cipher of what lay beneath them. Plunging into the depths of the earth, down vertical shafts, creeping sideways along tortuous levels, dropping down winzes, reaching out along interminable adits, the mine extended like the roots of some gigantic plant. Every week it went further, every year a new shaft was sunk to give access and air to more distant workings. It was a maze of such complexity, caused by the blind pursuit of every twisting lode of ore, that no one, not even the underground captains, could say he carried its exact form in his head. Sometimes, as they worked in narrow stopes where a man had scarce the space to swing a hammer, the miners would pause and listen to the sound of another tinner. Close at hand, above, beside, beneath, another man was chipping.

At other times, they would think they heard the gurgle of an underground stream and stand sweating in terror at the thought of breaking through to it and drowning in the dark water.

There was never much light down the mine: guttering candles set in their hats or jammed in a crevice gave off a dim glow, burning low in the exhausted air. In the rare galleries where the lode had been thick and a great chamber had been scooped out, the roof was always lost in shade.

The heat was stifling in the lower levels and the air, never good in these workings, was particularly poisonous. Men died young in these mines. They were strong while they lived, and cheerful, or began so, but they breathed bad air. Rockfalls caught them. Some were stifled in fires. Others fell down winzes from one level to another. Some died in explosions when a charge went off prematurely. Yet it was better often to die, better then to live on: crippled, paralysed, coughing, a burden to the hale and hearty who still worked on. And notwithstanding all this, though a miner was lucky to pass his fortieth year unscathed, young men flocked down the shafts. It was better than grubbing and starving on the land. There was the chance of hitting it rich. There was pay to be had from the count house, and the Tinners' Arms to spend it in. Reckless and brave, they toiled along. A miner's life was the best they knew.

All that first year, Welland Halt was kept to contract work by Mr Bolitho. Unlike the experienced tinners who followed the lodes, he was always on tutwork, sinking the winzes that linked one level with another, allowing air or ore to pass through. It was dull work, with no hope of sudden gain even if he struck an unexpected vein of metal, but he persisted at it. The quick beat of his hammer drove the drill-bar or boryer swiftly into the rock ready for the explosive charge. Curnow set the charges and taught him words of the old Cornish language while they shared their croust together. Curnow's was always the best, for he had a wife to care for him.

' 'Twere the best thing I ever did when I wed Ellen. There's no better thing in life than to 'ave a good wife to come 'ome to. But you d'knaw that for certain – What? 'Ave I said summat to trouble 'ee? It weren't intended,' said Curnow one day as they split a pasty. 'Wouldn't it make 'ee feel better to talk about 'er? I do believe it d'make the heart more easy.'

'No,' replied Welland and lapsed into silence. After a while, Curnow continued.

'I don't mean no disrespect, but to keep quiet, to say nothin', that do naught but feed gossip. Ellen tells me the

42

women are forever talkin' about it. They say there 'as to be somethin' terrible bad to be kept so secret. They say –'

'Let 'em talk all they will,' broke in Welland. 'I've naught to offer. The past is past, and none of their business. Come on now, back to work, 'tis time we were moving.'

They cut one winze and then another. As they moved about the mine, Welland stored away its structure in his head until he could go straight to any of its levels, however convoluted the approaches.

Later, when the underground captain decided to drive a long adit under Morvan Hill to the valley above Tregurney House in order to drain off water from the lowest levels and ease the strain on the pump so they could dig deeper, he chose Welland and his mate Curnow to cut it.

It seemed an endless task. They worked alone, receding ever further from their fellow miners. The air was terrible, particularly after blasting. A candle would scarcely burn in the choking atmosphere. The tunnel was kept low-roofed to economize on the spoil they had to haul out on a small tramway, so low that Curnow never stood upright. For six months they laboured on the adit, growing more and more distant, until the other miners had almost forgotten them. They came close to each other only at the end of each working day when Welland and Curnow returned from the cutting face to find themselves at the tail-end of the long procession of tinners zig-zagging their way up the ladders to the open air. Welland Halt was always the last in that scramble up to grass, slowed by his twisted leg. More often than not, Hector Bolitho would be waiting for him there and would ask impatiently how much longer it would take them to drive the adit through.

'I hope I'm not paying you regular wages to lie about and rest there,' he chided, half-jokingly.

'Come and see for yourself, if you've a mind,' said Welland with an edge to his voice.

'I'll send Mr Angove, the underground captain, if you're

43

not through by Sunday. And you might say "sir" as I counselled, it wouldn't cost much, now would it?'

'I be the best judge of that, "sir",' muttered Welland ungraciously.

'No need to get Bolitho's back up like that,' whispered Curnow as they walked off. 'He's not such a bad old stick, not compared with the other mine captains. Hector Bolitho is brave good-'earted. You've eyes, but you won't see it.'

'If he's good-hearted, let him show it in deeds. And let him show a proper respect for a working man. The labourer is worthy of his hire, that's what your Bible says, isn't it? A man's no better, nor more respectful for tugging his forelock, Bolitho should know that.'

Occasionally, as he passed the stamps, Welland saw Mavis Trerice working late with the other bal maidens as they sorted the ore. He found it strange that, after the first night when she had gone out of her way to find shelter for himself and Ruth, she had never exchanged a word with him beyond passing the time of day. He recognized her easily now among the toiling bal maidens. Her long chestnut hair swung across her wide-set eyes as she bent over the tanks where the ore was settling. She seldom smiled; her lips were set in a serious line. Only her eyes betrayed an occasional humorous gleam, but Welland found that too ironic, too close to bitterness and wondered what sadness cast its shadow over her. But, though he purposed to talk to her when they spoke the usual 'Good morning' when they met on the road, her look was too intimidating. She stared him out and passed on swiftly. Only when she was at work under the rough lean-to that made a poor shift to protect the workers at the stamps from the rain and wind could he hover in the concealment of a weatherboarded wall and stare at her frankly. She wore a rough hessian apron over a shapeless linen dress that reached from neck to booted ankle, but her strong arms were bare and tanned by wind and sun. To see her thus smothered Welland found it hard to imagine the handsome young woman he had sometimes encountered on Sundays, walking beside her mother towards the chapel at Bethel. On those occasions, she had looked away, avoiding a greeting, and he had seen old Mrs Trerice's hand clutching at her elbow warningly. Curiously, the mother's malevolent glare had been less inhibiting than the daughter's. With Mavis's eyes staring resolutely ahead, avoiding his, Welland had been able to dwell on her striped gingham dress and divine the body beneath.

'Comeason, Welland!' called Curnow who had halted some way down the road. 'Comeason, boy! What're 'ee dreamin' 'bout?'

Welland started. He had not realized he had lingered so long by the stamps. He was embarrassed and his embarrassment was redoubled when Mavis looked up and caught him watching her. Straightening, she set her hands on her hips, faced him stonily until he turned away. Welland pushed through the crowd of young children who, as usual, were helping their elder sisters or mothers by picking over the ore as it tumbled from the stamps or stood barefoot in the buddles, stirring the suspended mud in the water until the tin grains were precipitated out. As soon as a child could work, it came to the mine, the pennies it brought home paid for tea or some other small luxury. The youngsters seemed happy enough, sometimes they even sang at their work, but they were out in all weathers, from dawn to dusk with the bal maidens. The bal maidens did not work underground, but Welland was not sure their lot was a much better one than their menfolk's was.

Although it would have eased their poverty, Welland had refused to take his daughter Ruth to the mine, even though all other children of her age seemed to be employed there: several of Curnow's brood were around him at that very moment. Instead, he paid a woman to care for Ruth until he returned at sundown. Then they would eat together and he would play games with her at the hearth, picking out dream castles and landscapes in the flaming furze. In the ensuing

45

months he set to teaching her to read and calculate. She would be waiting for him now, pencil in hand, book on table. Curnow was already far away down the lane. Welland hurried after him.

The old wives of Windfall shook their heads and clucked their tongues over his daughter. What was the sense in depriving a maid of the taste of work? What was the use of raising her above her station? When they saw Ruth while her father was down the mine, they called her over, offering her heavy-cake or fuggan, and questioned her about her father and the life they had led before coming to Windfall. Above all, they were curious about her mother: where had she lived? What calamity had carried her off? And why had father and daughter set off on the pilgrimage that led them to Windfall? To their chagrin, they found the child as obstinate and uncommunicative as her father. They learnt nothing and, as they watched the girl grow older they muttered among themselves that it wasn't right for a man to have charge of a growing maid, even if he was her own father.

Although Welland knew all about the women's sharp tongues, for his daughter told him of their wiles and maliciousness, he said nothing. He knew that both he and Ruth were 'furriners' in the eyes of the Cornish, strange people from far away, with odd manners, not easy to take to. He had heard the gossips changing to the Cornish language as he walked down the street, and knew they were talking of him, but he smiled his inward smile and strode on. If he kept his past hidden from them, he had his reasons. Gradually, the villagers appeared to come to accept Welland and Ruth. As the months rolled by, new events, other newcomers, fresh scandals, claimed their attention and set their tongues a-shaking.

There was one woman, however, who never varied in her hostility, never wearied in her efforts to discover the history of Welland and his daughter. That woman was Hilda Trerice. From the day her daughter Mavis flung open the door to announce the arrival of two benighted strangers, she had never slackened in her search.

'One day or another I'll find out the truth, see if I don't,' she declared to Mavis as she sat in her cottage one night. 'There's summat what drove that man o' yourn to Windfall. 'Tes a woman, it must be, that Welland's wife. Why don't 'ee never mention 'er? Where's she to? Why didn' 'e bring 'er to Windfall?'

'Why ask me? What do I care? Ask him yourself. I have nothing to do with him.'

'Nothing to do with him,' mimicked her mother. 'That's what you d'say, but I know better. I've seen 'ow you looks at un. Soft on that Welland Halt, from the first you was. I've got eyes in me 'ead, I've watched 'ee.'

'How many times must I tell you? I helped him once, for the girl's sake. That's all. He means nothing to me.'

'Aye, you've told me, but tellin's one thing. Thinkin's another. I allus knowed you'd fall for a wanderin' man, a man like your feyther: a waster.'

'Welland Halt's not a waster.'

'There you go – stand up fer un. You're two of a kind, birds of a feather. I've seed 'ow you d'lead un on. I've seed 'ow 'ee d'fawn on 'ee.'

'All he's ever done is to thank me for helping him and his Ruth, that and pass the time of day, no more than what's civil. And I've done no more. Do you want to drive me to him?'

'No need o' that. Save 'ee rather. I shan't rest till I finds un out – till I've drove un from Windfall. One o' these days you'll thank me fer it. Meantime, you'd do best to 'eed the preacher over to Bethel like I do, read 'is good books, and put away frivolous livin'. I prays fer 'ee, Mavis, I do. I prays you'll turn back from your wanton ways in time and be saved. Turn back to the Lord! This Windfall's His threshing floor where 'E'll come in the day of His wrath, and the chaff shall be winnowed away!'

'You're crazy.' Mavis sighed dejectedly.

'Call your mother crazy? You know I see clearly, I can look into the future and tell – I can tell that one day someone'll come to Windfall, some coachman, some tinner, some tinker, that'll know that Welland, that'll know 'is secret. I pray 'e'll come in time, in time to save 'ee.'

'I've heard enough. I won't hear any more. I'm off out for a breath of fresh air. I'll come back when you've returned to your senses.'

'Shall I tell 'ee where to find un?' snapped her mother. ' 'Appen 'e'll treat 'ee nicer than I do.'

'Happen he would, if I wanted him to. But I know better. I've had an example to cure me of men and marriage in life – it's you and Father.' She slammed the door and walked off down the street, trying to forgive her mother for filling her with such anger.

The light from Welland Halt's window shone across the path where she walked and she looked in. Father and daughter sat side by side at the small table. His strong face was gentle now as he listened to young Ruth reading, following a pointing finger. His unruly hair was greying at the temples. His brow was furrowed, but his mouth was gentle. So this was the monster her mother was so sure she was smitten on. She sniffed with repressed amusement and moved on before either the man or his daughter looked up and remarked her. It was too soon to return home: her mother would be sitting up waiting to renew the argument. Instead, as she often did now, she trod the dark paths that climbed Carnwartha. The hilltop silence was balm to her heart and Windfall village, like her troubles, dwindled into insignificance.

And while, unknown to him, Hilda Trerice still dug into his dead past, Welland Halt burrowed into the living rock. Every day, unaware whether rain fell or sun shone on Morvan's crown, far over their heads, Welland and Curnow carved through granite. Their hair and eyebrows were white

48

with dust, their eyes were red with it, their throats were dry, and their ears rang continually with the beat of the hammer on the boryer bar. They drilled into the rock until they could remember no other kind of existence. Their days were no longer measured in hours or by the shadows thrown by the sun, but were counted in feet or yards, and punctuated by the lighting of fuse, the blast of explosive charge.

'Whatever made 'ee choose Windfall?' asked Curnow while they waited as the dust settled. 'There must be hundreds o' places out there better to live in than Windfall.'

'Windfall chose me. I wasn't looking for anywhere in particular.'

' 'Twas Mavis Trerice that brought 'ee. Were it not for she, I do believe you'd've left already. I can tell you're smitten.'

'Hold your foolish tongue,' said Welland uneasily. 'A man's a loon to make the same mistake twice in a lifetime.'

'Tiddn' always a mistake,' insisted Curnow. 'I thank the Lord 'E sent me Ellen – and the children too, they're a great comfort. It do give a man strength to keep on workin', knowin' 'e's wed to the right woman. That's the truth, if you'd eyes to see it, if you'd see the light.'

'The truth is, we're still stuck somewhere under Morvan and Angove's impatient, Bolitho's impatient. And to tell the truth, Welland Halt himself is become impatient, impatient to see the light. Up with you, Curnow, or we'll never get there.'

Then, one day, while Curnow held the boryer between a pair of tongs, Welland struck it a blow like any other, a blow identical to the thousands of times he had hit it, until its head was splayed like a flower and its tip had blunted away, but now, instead of making the hammer ring and rebound, it suddenly slipped away. Welland wiped his brow in perplexity before reaching to take hold of its head which had jammed against the tongs. The hot metal seared through the thick skin of his fingers as he pulled it back. Curnow was looking at him curiously. Their ears still rang with the beat on the boryer, though the hammering had ceased. When the boryer came clear, the candle went out.

'Dammit!' Welland swore. 'Come on, Curnow, quick, where be the tinder?'

And then, as he waited impatiently for his mate to strike fire, he felt the slightest breath of air on his face. Not for months had he sensed anything like that down in the stagnant extremity of the adit. A draught from somewhere had blown out their candle. He was about to mention it, but before he could do so, the Cornishman uttered a single word:

'Light!'

They both sat watching the dust motes dancing in the thin pencil of illumination that was coming from the hole where the bar had been. It was the slimmest of windows, but its reverberated glow was enough for them to discern one another's faces.

'Us've broke through!' exulted Curnow.

'Done it,' said Welland with a quiet satisfaction.

'Ess, us've done it all right, and you're a brave miner, even if you are a furriner,' cried Curnow, catching Welland by the hand.

'Come on then, light the candle, get a hold of the bar and let's make an end of it,' said Welland in his matter of fact way. 'That hole's too small for even a poor man like you to pass through.'

They set to work again, with Welland striking at the drill with new violence, making a fresh hole, shallower than the other so they could lay a charge. There was excitement between them now and Welland had to slow Curnow down and force him to be methodical when the time came to pour the powder down the hole and tamp it with a copper rod. For the last time, Curnow cut a length of fuse, inserted it into the opening and lit it with a candle stub before scampering off up the adit to a refuge of rough stones they had prepared a safe distance away.

They waited.

Nothing.

Perhaps the fuse had gone out.

Curnow stirred. They were both lying curled up behind the barrier, hands over their ears. Welland realized that Curnow's impatience was getting the better of him. He was getting up to go and examine the charge.

'Wait!'

Welland grabbed him by the shoulder, trying to pull him down.

At that very moment the charge went off. It threw Curnow backwards as the shock wave followed the explosion's brilliant flash and the first coils of choking smoke flew past them. The clatter of falling stones subsided and Welland loosed his grip on Curnow's arm. His own face was bleeding; he could feel a trickle of blood running down his forehead and he wondered if his companion had been badly hit.

'Are you hurt, man?' he inquired urgently.

Curnow seemed dazed and was a long time replying, but when he did, Welland let out a whistle of relief.

'Don't seem to 'ave broke nothin', Curnow said slowly. 'I shall know better when I've lit a light.'

As usual, the candle had blown out in the explosion, and Welland knew that his mate would be fumbling in his pocket for the tinder-box to light it. For a moment, he saw nothing disconcerting in this idea, but then a sneaking horror crept into his thoughts. The explosion had blown out a gaping hole at the end of the tunnel and, now that the smoke had cleared, sucked away into the bowels of the mine by a strong draught, the light of day was flooding in. He turned and stared at Curnow's face. Although it was marked by a spattering of small cuts, there was nothing to show what had happened to him.

'Come on, old feller,' said Welland gently, taking him by the arm and pulling him up and guiding him towards the entrance, 'we'll take a breath of air.'

Even then, stumbling forward, arm hooked round his head and crouching to avoid the roof, Curnow still didn't understand. Even when he stepped out into the sunlight and the open air, he knew nothing. Only when he lost his footing on the steep slope did his hand touch the grass.

'A – a – a – a – a – agh!'

And then he knew. The knowledge choked him. As Welland stood looking down at him, Curnow let out a half-throttled cry. Welland was speechless with the suffocating anguish of grief as that cry enveloped him. It was beyond words, like a hunted animal hemmed in by the pack. It swelled. It mounted in pitch. It reached out and hung over the smiling valley like a dripping sword.

Far beneath them, on the lawns of Tregurney House, a man and a woman, clad in resplendent silk, had been interrupted in their calm afternoon walk by the clap of the explosion. They stood gazing in amazement at the spot on the hillside where a sudden puff of smoke like a shellburst had gushed from the grass and sent the sheep running. They remained transfixed with amazement as two men emerged and the air was suddenly rent by that long, inhuman shout.

Welland Halt savoured the irony of it all: the shining, peaceful valley; the startled birds tumbling in the air over the trees in the park; the restrained magnificence of Tregurney House; the elegant spectators, shocked out of the even tenor of their daily stroll. It was as if he and Curnow had burst unwittingly into someone else's Paradise.

He did not know how long it took for Curnow's shout to come to an end. He did not know how long he stood in silence afterwards while the pent passion in that terrible cry echoed slowly like great hammer blows across the valley in his head.

Curnow was blind!

Welland looked down. Curnow was heaving long silent sobs, with his fingers dug deep in the grass as if to hold on to reality, pull himself back into sight.

Welland looked up at the sky. A serene tapestry of clouds

was drifting by in a succession of small, delicate puffs, like a painted awning over some royal festivity. He clenched his fist and shook it at Heaven, reaching up on his toes in a fury of reproach.

'Consider the lilies of the field as they grow,' he shouted, 'They toil not, neither do they spin.'

His words, muffled and thinned by distance, floated down to the lawns by Tregurney House. The strollers exchanged glances. Here was madness piled on mystery. The man adjusted the book under his left elbow, offered the lady his arm, and led her back towards Tregurney House.

❦ 4 ❧

THE FORGE

The red eye of the forge glared balefully, flaring at every bellows'-stroke, illuminating the line of men as it shuffled forward. Outdoors, it was not much past dawn, with a sickly sun like a pale reflection of the fire within. Welland Halt watched with unconcealed disdain when each man in turn handed his boryer to the smith who plunged its tip into the glowing coals. Ordinarily, Welland would have had Curnow beside him, to talk to while he waited, but today he stood alone, alone with a new bitterness.

While the men waited, a grimy boy tugged at the bellows, using all his puny strength until the pupil of the fire's eye shone white. The men's boryers stuck out of the furnace like arrows from a bullseye, their inner ends gradually reddening in the heat. Tom Magor, the smith, extracted the hottest one and gave it a few clumsy blows on the anvil, forming a rough tip, then quenched it in a tub of dirty water. The searing smell of steam and hot metal spread around the dark recesses of the forge while Magor held the bar aloft until its internal heat broke through its grey scaly skin. Another blow or two and he cooled it completely in the tub before handing it back to its owner.

This was a daily ritual for the miners whose boryers were soon blunted on the unyielding granite. Magor, the smith, was the mine's surgeon, repairing its broken bones, tending to the iron sinews that allowed the tinners to delve deeper than ever before into the entrails of the earth, winning riches from the adamantine rock. He was a powerful man, and yet Welland could not forbear to smile his secret, supercilious smile, watching the uncouth smith hammer at the reluctant iron. By this time, Magor was clearly aware of Welland's contempt for his skill and the knowledge made him all the more brutal and wild.

Tom Magor strove to dominate iron by sheer power, beating it into subjection by the force of his enormous right arm. He was a very tall man and, although he stooped a little, swinging his head like a puzzled bull whenever he encountered a difficulty, which happened often, his wiry black hair still brushed the cobwebs between the beams. Everything about the man was on the gigantic scale as if he were a reincarnation of one of the old Cornish giants whose bones have been preserved here and there, like the skeleton found in the chapel at St Michael's Mount. Between his hammer strokes, his deep voice rumbled around the forge like distant thunder and his hobnailed boots struck sparks from the cobbled floor.

In the forge's glare, Magor's round face shone angry red and great drops of sweat ran down his furrowed brow, through his bushy eyebrows, and streaked his blackened cheeks. The firelight picked out his hairy forearms and furrowed his huge knuckles. It played on the semicircle of waiting faces, lighting them from beneath in a grotesque version of a Dutch old master.

When Welland's turn came, he handed over his boryer without a word and stood with his hands clasped in front of him while the smith went through his routine. It was only when Magor struck his bar a glancing blow, wrenching it from his left hand and sending it clattering to the floor at Welland's feet, that Welland chuckled. Magor stared at him across the dark bulk of the anvil. He had been reaching down to pick up the boryer, but now he rose slowly.

'Laughin' at I? Laughin' at I, was 'ee?' He raised his hammer high and brought it down in a stunning blow on the anvil. 'No one do laugh at Tom Magor! Understand?'

As the ringing of the anvil died away, the tinners stared at

Welland. A deep silence fell, until they could hear their own breathing and the faint crackle of the hearth.

The two men confronted each other like statues: the one with the hammer upraised to his shoulder; the other clenching his low-slung boryer which he had snatched from the floor. The tinners caught their breath. The boy at the bellows froze and the leather bag released its air in a long lugubrious sigh. Finally, Welland spoke.

'I mocked the action, not the man.'

Tom Magor slowly blinked his eyes in puzzlement.

'Where's the difference?'

'The difference between the nature of man and the nature of iron.' Welland's voice was low, almost soft, but not once did his eyes quit the blacksmith's face.

'Tryin' to make out Tom's a fool, isn't that it?' demanded Magor blusteringly. 'Well, I'm not. I'm stronger nor you into the bargain. I've been sizing you up: you're another of them clever-dick furriners who come down 'ere and think they can learn things to us Cornish.' The hammer at his shoulder shook as he spoke and the veins in his neck stood out blue and pulsing.

'Were you ready to learn, I *could* teach you,' replied Welland, 'but you're already the smith, and smiths won't learn from strangers.'

'Think you can do better'n Tom Magor?' laughed the smith, 'Have a try then! Sharpen your own boryer! Let's see if a lame weakling can do what Tom Magor can't.' He seized a drill from the man next in line and held out his hand for Welland's. 'I'll do this one and us'll see if you can do yourn.' He took both iron shafts in the broad palm of his left hand and thrust them into the dull red heart of the fire. Then he gave the boy a cuff. 'Wake up! What's stopped you pumpin'?'

While the boy pumped and the air hissed through the coals, the tinners whispered to one another. Some of the tension had momentarily slipped away. If they had had money on them, they would have been placing bets on the outcome. It was a foregone conclusion: Tom Magor had been selected by Mr Bolitho to work the forge at Wheal Fortune. Hadn't he beaten all comers? Wasn't he able to lift a lump hammer heavier than could anyone else in the county? They studied him leaning over his anvil with his hands clasped round the haft of that hammer. They saw the immense, contained strength of the man. And they saw the short, awkward body of Welland Halt. The challenger's head was not so high as Magor's armpit. Though his arms and shoulders were better developed than the average man's, his hips and legs seemed weak and slender. They smiled at each other knowingly.

Slowly, as the two bars grew cherry red, then orange, then white, the whispering ceased. The men watched silently as Magor plucked his bar from the fire and fetched it a volley of crushing blows with his hammer, splaying out the tip into a broad edge before tempering it in the tub and giving it a final clanging stroke. He laid the boryer on the edge of the hearth, set the heavy hammer on the centre of the anvil and stood back with arms folded. It was Welland's turn.

Welland did not hurry. He turned his bar in the coals cautiously, watching for a certain change in its colour.

'Come on, man, we haven't got all day!' called Magor scornfully. 'He was all in a rush just now, wasn't he, boys! Look at 'im now. Don't know a bellows from a boryer!' Magor's shoulders shook with laughter and he covered his mouth with his hand.

When Welland was well satisfied with the look of the bar, he pulled it from the fire and crossed to the anvil. There sat the lump hammer, ponderous and challenging as Excalibur in the stone. Welland balanced his bar momentarily across the anvil and spat on his hands. All eyes followed him as he gripped the hammer's haft in his right hand. The dull lump of metal sat on the anvil as though welded there by its own mass. The tinners knew its weight: they had tried lifting it, but only the strongest could swing it upwards and even they

57

were forced to use both hands. Welland took the cool end of the boryer in his left hand and placed its glowing point at an exact spot on the flat of the anvil. Then he struck it.

The movement of his arm was so smooth and swift that no one saw the hammer move, but caught fleeting glimpses of it at the top ot its trajectory and at the moment of impact. This first blow was followed by a second ringing stroke. With equal rapidity, the bar spun in Welland's hand and its glowing head was flattened in a different direction. Each time Welland struck the iron, it altered its shape, changing into a regular cutting edge. The men forgot to be astonished by the fact that the furriner was lifting the hammer: they were fascinated by the way the iron was bending to his will.

Then he quenched and tempered it in the tub, examining it with the same concentration as before as it came out and its grey skin glowed with inner heat. He waited till the colour satisfied him, then plunged it back again. While he waited, the men murmured in the background. They did not dare to speak openly for fear of Tom Magor's anger, but it was clear what they were saying. Welland Halt had turned out to be more of a smith than his quiet manner had suggested.

'Well, you done it,' said Magor grudgingly, 'but there's more to bein' a smith than that.'

Welland nodded in reply as he removed his boryer from the tub.

'We're not done yet,' he announced. 'We have to try 'em.' He turned to the boy at the bellows. 'Can you turn the stone?'

The boy took a moment to comprehend, then scampered across to the grindstone and set his small shoulder to the handle. With a deal of squealing and creaking, it began to spin. As it turned, the lower part of its circumference dipped into a water trough which smoothed its action. Welland applied the boryer tip to its gritty surface and sharpened it swiftly. The cutting edge took on a bluish shine. He drew it back and tried it with his thumb before stepping away from the stone and gesturing to Magor to follow.

The smith shuffled across with an ill grace and set to sharpening the other bar. This was not his work and he resented it. Usually the tinners put an edge on their tools themselves. He jammed the boryer tip hard on to the wheel until the sparks flew and the metal grew hot again.

When he had finished, he looked round questioningly. Welland beckoned him back to the anvil where he had laid his own bar across the flat surface. He took Magor's from him and set it vertically on his, with the cutting edge across the rectangular shaft.

'Strike!' he commanded.

Magor took up his hammer and stood to his full height between the beams, the better to be able to bring it down. It swung up into the darkness of the roof and came whistling down on the head of his bar. There was a shattering thud and Welland lifted Magor's boryer off his own. The smith's cutting edge had shattered and the remaining fragment was blunted and splayed. All could see that the place where it had been in contact with Welland's bar was barely scored.

'Now hold my boryer for me,' said Welland, reversing their positions upon the anvil. Now that it was his turn to strike, a new problem arose. The shaft of his drill, set upright on the anvil, was too tall for a man of Welland's height to bring the hammer to bear on its top. Someone in the crowd sniggered at his embarrassment, but he pursed his lips and walked off, dragging his lame foot, into the shadows at the back of the forge where he found a baulk of timber which he dragged alongside the anvil. Perched on top, he cupped his hands, spat on them again, rubbed them together, and picked up the hammer. Once he held it, his awkwardness seemed to disappear.

When the hammer came down on the boryer head, there was not so much noise as the men expected, but they saw a sudden flash as the head of Magor's bar detached itself and spun away across the forge, narrowly missing the boy at the stone. Welland set down the hammer, took his boryer from

59

the bewildered smith's hands, and hobbled to the grindstone where he renewed its edge. Then, without turning round or speaking, he pushed past the knot of men in the doorway and stepped out of the forge.

Outdoors, the eastern sky over the count house was streaked with bold red bands, though the sun had scarcely topped the hills. To Welland's left, the stamps were already pounding the ore with their usual infernal racket and the bal maidens were bending to their task, aided by a tribe of children, most of whom ran barefoot in the soaking grass. Hector Bolitho was standing at the count house door at the top of a short flight of steps, listening to a man. When he saw Welland emerge, he beckoned him over peremptorily, while the man slunk off.

'There's a place for only one smith here at Wheal Fortune. I thought I made that clear to you at the outset,' he began as soon as Welland had crossed the twenty yards of greensward that separated them. 'Your antics are keeping the men from their work. Your provocation of Tom Magor is sowing the seeds of discontent. I'm sorry you chose this morning to do it for I had planned to say something to you that would be to your advantage.'

'If you can't tell a butcher from a smith, that's your business, Mr Bolitho,' said Welland gruffly. 'I thought you had better judgement than to believe the first tell-tale who ran over to you.'

'I know a good worker when I see one, Welland, and you're a good worker too, in your way. But you're a stranger here. Tom Magor's a Cornishman; he's the tinners' own man. They respect him. They back him in prize-fights. He wins money for 'em. They don't want some jumped-up "furriner" making a fool of him, even if he's none too clever. They won't stick it. *And neither will I*!' Hector Bolitho's voice was only slightly higher than normal, but the manner was unequivocal. Welland shrugged and turned to set off for the shaft, but Hector Bolitho reached down and took him by the sleeve.

'Not so fast, Welland. You're not using your head, are you? Isn't the adit concluded? That's what I intended to speak to you about.' As he finished, Bolitho was fumbling in his frockcoat pocket. 'You've worked well on that adit and I've decided to give you a bonus.'

Welland saw the glint of gold in the purser's hand: coin of the realm, enough to buy sea-coal for the fire, meat for the pot, books for Ruth, but he failed to reach out for it.

'Come on, Halt, what's wrong with you? Take it, you've earned it,' Bolitho insisted. Still Welland failed to take the coin. He felt that the eyes of the bal maidens were upon him, though the din was so great that they could not have heard what Bolitho was saying. One of them in particular was observing him. But his reply to Bolitho would have been the same in any case.

'What about Curnow?'

'Curnow?' repeated Bolitho, looking perplexed. 'What's Curnow got to do with it? If it'd been up to Curnow, you'd still be half way under Morvan Hill. Curnow did nothing but follow your lead. Angove told me. That's why you get the bonus.'

'Curnow gave of his best to cut the adit. He's just as deserving.'

'Then share with him.'

'I can't share my sight.'

'So that's it. Well, it wasn't my fault. You know these things happen. This is a mine. The work is dangerous. It could have been anyone. It might well have been you. But it wasn't. You're still strong, you're still healthy, and now I'm going to take you off tutwork – give you a chance to make real money.'

Welland looked at him without enthusiasm. Bolitho pressed the coin into his hand and continued.

'You can come off contract and try your hand at tribute – start stoping out with the tinners. They'll welcome a man who can cut ore as fast as you can. You'll find mates aplenty.'

'I already have one. Curnow's my mate.'

'Don't be foolish. Curnow can never go underground again. Can't you see that? And think of yourself for once, think of Ruth's best interest. If you burden yourself with a blind man, you'll be no better than any other miner.'

'How's Curnow to earn his bread? Hasn't he a wife and six children?'

'I'll speak to Mr Nichols about it. He must go upon the parish.'

'On the parish? But that's a pittance, that's slow starvation.'

'That's the way the world goes, Welland. The weak must go to the wall. Wasn't that what you were just trying to prove to Magor? Now, man, be reasonable! Down you go and clean out the mouth of that adit. You've done a fine job. We'll soon have you stoping on tribute. You must bid at the setting on Monday.'

Reluctantly, Welland bowed to the inevitability of it all. There was no other way. If there had been injustice, it had not been Bolitho's fault. *He* had not blinded Curnow. Either Curnow, by indiscretion, had reft himself of sight, or blind fate had been responsible. The money burned his palm as he limped to the shaft, but he pocketed it. What was the use of giving it back to Bolitho? It would only add to the adventurers' profit. Unenthusiastically, he began the laborious descent down the zigzag ladders. Occasionally, one of the younger miners passed him on the way down in a skip. Mining brought out a devil-may-care streak in these men. The danger was so overpowering, persistent and unpredictable that they were ready to flaunt it, pushing their luck with a fatalism that was almost Mohammedan. Perhaps it was also the daily release from this danger that sent them nightly trooping into the Tinners', so long as they had money in their pockets for ale, for gin, or wild, wanton company.

At the adit level, just beside the pump well, Welland stepped off the slimy rungs into the tunnel he and Curnow had cut. The boy that Bolitho had just sent to help him push the tramcar was waiting for him in darkness. Welland discovered him when he lit his scrap of candle and stuck it in the blob of wet clay at the front of his hat. Even at the outset of the day, the boy seemed heavy with fatigue. How old was he? Ten? It was hard to tell. Young men often ceased to grow in their early teens. They were men already. Childhood, the time when they were too young to work, was already far away. They stepped into manhood directly, scarcely knowing the romance of play and the illusion of infinite possibility. Perhaps it was as well. With no dreams, they would not be doomed to disappointment. In this world, their foreshortened horizon was never further than the longest tunnel in the mine. Here they would live, and work, and die. To be tall, to stand higher than the rest, was a handicap. What was the use of beating your brains out against the roof, their absolute, stony sky? Welland took the boy by the shoulder and shook him gently.

'Come on, lad, don't lie in that water, you'll catch an ague.'

The boy lay in a pool of the warm, rust-red water that seeped into the tunnels all over the mine. Soon, it would be running down the adit in a steady stream when the gush from the pump was diverted. For the time being, the pump-rod, rattling up and down the shaft beside them, was still forcing a heavy column of water up to the top of the Windfall shaft, but once the diversion was made into the adit, it would serve to pump out new, deeper levels and the tinners could pursue the lode further, making the adventurers all the richer.

Welland Halt thought of these things as he worked in the adit that day, clearing its mouth of the debris from the explosion that had cost Curnow his sight. All the time, Bolitho's coin weighed heavy in his pocket, and the injustice of Curnow's fate rankled in his mind. It was a still morning; the smoke from Tregurney's chimneys rose straight into a cloudy canopy, shouts from the farmhands driving their horses up the steep fields came through clear as a bell, deer were cropping slowly across Tregurney Park, the great house stood serene and handsome, flanked by church and stables. Welland ought to have enjoyed the novel experience of working in daylight, but the very beauty of the landscape soured him. He could see it: Curnow never would. Curnow had not even seen the two figures on the lawn of Tregurney House, looking up in amazement after the explosion. They had been close enough for Welland to see their expressions, yet distant, inexpressibly distant.

'It's a grand day,' said the boy beside him, sending a rock bounding down the hillside, 'more like an 'oliday.'

'I wish I could think so,' scowled Welland, then regretted his ill-humour. 'But it must be for you. You must make the most of it. Sit down and rest. Have you seen the deer in the park grazing?'

Another person was watching the deer. She stood at one of the tall casements that illuminated the dining-room in Tregurney House. Her morning gown hung decorously about her.

'They've come back,' she announced.

'Who have?' asked her husband, teacup in hand and dressing-gown clasped about him, at the fireside.

'The deer, Silverton.' Her quick eyes flitted up to the break in the hillside where a tiny figure could be seen working. 'Poor creatures, they must have been scared out of their wits by that explosion.'

'That wasn't the only ill consequence,' said her sister-in-law who was seated at the table drinking chocolate and pecking at her breakfast. 'A man lost his sight – setting the charge. Hector told me last night. The mine surgeon's examined him and it's final.'

'If only they'd stick to the rules, Janet, this sort of thing would never happen,' said her brother in a tired voice. 'It's the human element. The more we reduce it, the less annoyance we'll have.'

'Annoyance? I wouldn't call it that. A man's life's been ruined.'

'And you hold me responsible. Well, I'm not: I can't be everywhere. If you're looking for a scapegoat, you can find one at home. Hector's in charge of the mine's day-to-day running.' His long, somewhat sensual face took on a defensive expression.

'I'm not trying to blame anyone,' his sister's shoulders quivered as she spoke, 'I just think it's tragic for the man concerned, not to mention his family.'

'What a woman can't understand is that men have to take risks in that business. The tinners risk their lives: I risk my money. If I hadn't paid for that adit to be cut, they wouldn't be able to drive the shaft deeper. With the price of tin as low as it is, I might be excused for drawing in my horns and holding off on investment. But I'm not – I want Wheal Fortune to be the most up-to-date mine in the county. I'm about to engage Richard Trevithick to design and fit a new steam-pump and machinery. I shall leave for London tomorrow to discuss it. Does that sound like an exploiter?'

'You're not off already,' broke out his wife querulously, leaving the window to confront him. 'You've not been back five minutes and you're talking of leaving. Why can't you spend some time here? Do I have the plague or something?'

'My dear Diana,' murmured Silverton Gurney, 'don't get hysterical again, you know it doesn't become you. Nothing would please me more, dear lady, than to spend more time in your society, but I have business to attend to.' He set his cup on the mantel and adjusted his dressing-gown.

'Business! Business! Your toys, you mean – your damned steam-engines! They mean more to you than I do – any of us for that matter.' She encompassed Janet Bolitho with a gesture.

'I'm expected in London. However much I'd like to accommodate you, however much I'd like to stay here, and this is *my* home, remember, there are pressing matters that

65

demand my attention. The future of my steam-carriage depends on them.'

'Then take me with you. I'm weary with life in this backwater with only Rector Adams and this goody-good sister of yours for company. Take me with you!'

'Nothing, my dear Diana, would give me greater pleasure – if I weren't so preoccupied. I shall have no time to escort you to the routs and balls you pine for so desperately. You would be lonely in London. I couldn't permit you to entertain in my absence or go out unattended. You know how soon tongues start a-wagging. You'd be lonely in London. Solitude in Town is far worse than seclusion in the country.'

'Sequestration, you mean! Oh, Silverton! Silverton! *"Silver tongue"* is more like it! How you weave nets of words around me! I hate you!' She beat on his chest with her clenched fists, but he remained indifferent. She burst into tears. 'Why did I ever leave Cranworth? I was happy there. I was Lady Diana Greville, destined to become countess in my own right, with a fine estate, a host of friends about me. Why did I have to marry a Cornish nobody?'

'Because you were broke: the estate was mortgaged right up to the hilt. Because you'd soon have been the wrong side of thirty. Because I asked you before I knew your superficial nature. Let me tell you this, Lady Diana, there was a time when I found you charming, you *were* charming, but now your demands and recriminations upset me.'

'Then I'll be nice to you. I will! I will!' She clung to his collar and buried her face in his chest. 'Only take me to London.'

'Each of us has a duty. I have my duty to promote the steam-carriage in Parliament, my hopes all hinge on it. You have your wifely duty here, looking after Tregurney, preparing the future.'

'Breeding young Gurneys would be a more direct way of putting it. Well, don't count on me to indulge your wishes in that direction. Oh, Silverton, this passion of yours for steam is an impossible adversary. I should find it easy to fight against a flesh and blood mistress. If only you had one. But you're too cold a fish, too cold by half, too calculating.'

She ran out of the room. For a while, brother and sister remained in silence. Janet Bolitho, somewhat nervously, began collecting the breakfast things.

'Leave that,' said Silverton Gurney. 'I'm sorry she said that about you. She has a sharp tongue and a hard nature.'

'So have you, Silverton, though you don't see it.'

'What, is my own sister now turned against me?'

'No, Silverton, but the pursuit of your inventions is demeaning your better nature.'

'Better nature! Do you really believe I have one? Diana doesn't think so.'

'Well, *I* do! The only problem is you're too preoccupied with things. You haven't much time for people.'

'Haven't I, Janet? – Well, if you say so – ' He patted her shoulder as he crossed the room to the window. 'The deer too, I suppose they're my responsibility.' He sighed, 'What was it that man was shouting up there yesterday, after the explosion? Did Hector tell you?'

'Please, Silverton, don't bring that dreadful business up so soon. Seeing it yesterday was bad enough. Discussing it now is too painful.'

'I'll ask him myself. I must visit Wheal Fortune before I set off for London. You're too soft-hearted by far, Janet, d'you know that? You are, but I love you for it. Your husband's made of sterner stuff. At least, I hope so. It's a harsh world, Janet. We must fight to survive in it.'

When Welland topped the last of the ladders, at the end of that core, the boy was long since gone. The day was overcast, subdued, depressing. Greyness was everywhere: in the sky, in the mine buildings' granite walls, in the bal maidens' faces, in their very lives. Yet, for all its greyness, at least it was light, not the darkness that had been oppressing him, making him yearn for a life in the open air. It was light enough to show him a scene that stopped him with his head just clear of the shaft and his feet on the fourth rung of the ladder. He watched the slow, stern progress of a woman and a broken man. They moved with dream-like, painful slowness down the track towards the count house. The stern-faced woman must be Ellen, the man clutching at her arm, his feet fumbling with the loose stones and ruts in the track, had a face already softened into the bland, unresponsive mask, the face of the truly blind. It was Curnow. Yesterday Curnow had strode nimbly down this road, making Welland conscious of his own lameness. Now the tables were turned.

The lingering, tentative nature of the couple's progress contrasted plaintively with the quick, strident, purposive beat of the stamps and the pant of the pump. And yet their advance partook of an arresting, indefinable inevitability, as if each step was preordained, set down in its allotted place by an unseen hand. Welland watched and felt a tightening in his throat, a swelling in his lips and cheeks, a sudden wetness springing into his eyes. Welland watched, knowing what was to come, yet unable to turn away from the spectacle, unable to intervene. Welland watched like a man in a nightmare, seeing his brother who is walking towards a precipice, yet is unable to utter a warning shout.

It was as though Welland were seeing his mate for the first time. All their days together in close confinement down the mine seemed to have gone by without giving Curnow more depth than a shadow. He realized he knew nothing of the man; nothing of his hopes, nothing of his fears, no more of his wife than a name, of his children, nothing. Even the colour of his eyes was beyond recall. Only the voice, the deliberate, low-pitched Cornish way of speaking, and the hands, above all the hands, were what characterised Curnow in his memory. Hairy-backed, thick-skinned, broken-nailed, dirt-ingrained, it was those hands, holding the boryer, that were Curnow to Welland. Those same hands he remembered

68

lighting the fuse, those same hands fumbling with the tinder to strike fire in the daylight, and finally, those same hands hooked into the grass.

They had stopped now, Curnow and his wife, at Wheal Fortune count house door, waiting – waiting with the long-suffering patience of the poor who have never had a lever with which to push the wheel of life.

Finally, thought Welland, but no, until death, there can be no finally. Yesterday's finally was no more than a stumble on the road that is forever unfolding before you.

The door opened and Mr Bolitho stood facing them: round red face, mutton-chop whiskers, starched white collar. His lips moved, but Welland heard nothing. The pounding of the machinery was so loud that he wondered if even Curnow could hear. The lips moved: Bolitho was enunciating precisely. Welland knew the words as surely as if the purser was whispering into his inner consciousness. They were words both he and Curnow refused to hear. He was witnessing a dialogue of the deaf.

He almost sprang out of the shaft mouth to rush across and add his voice to the argument, but held himself back. Bolitho would only reproach him with cutting short his stint at the mine. And he would not be deflected from his quiet, devasting explanations that already had Ellen Curnow weeping into her apron.

Welland's brief awareness of himself brought on a fit of shivering. Up here at grass, the temperature was like winter after the heat in the deep levels. His body was still bathed in sweat from the long climb up the rickety staves of the vertical ladders. For an instant, his head reeled, but he clung on tight until the malaise passed.

When he came to himself, everything looked the same and yet, in some important way, everything was changed. Curnow and his wife were still at the foot of the count house steps, with their backs to him, hunched in coldness and grief. Hector Bolitho was still on the granite steps, peering down on them in the usual way, half apologetic, half scolding. The wind was still blowing a ragged trail of smoke away from the engine-house chimney. The empty road still curved away from the count house into the distance. Welland tried to identify the change, but it still eluded him. Apart from the wavering of the grass and the smoke's shifting pattern, the scene had all the stillness and immutability of a woodcut.

Only when he recognized the small sounds: the breeze in the grass, the soft cadence of Bolitho's voice, the insinuating pant and gasp from the beam-engine and the pump-rods' rattle in the shaft beside him, did the awareness come to him. Something had stopped. Even then, it took him time to recognize the origin of the silence.

It was the stamps. The stamps had stopped beating. The long row of wooden lifters with their two-hundredweight heads that should have been beating the ore in swift cascade, as they were wont to do from sunrise to sunset, were motionless. Beside them, the bal maidens, their sorting interrupted, stood at their recking frames, or sat, hammer in hand, at the bucking anvils, their ore-breaking interrupted. But for the fluttering of their handkerchiefs, they might have been statues. The boys also, who stood barefoot in the wooden buddles, had ceased stirring the crop-tin. The water gushed quietly over.

Every one of them had turned and was staring in the same direction, looking at the place where, her hand still grasping the lever that had just diverted the water from the stamps, stood one of their number. Defiant, her clumsily-booted feet planted wide apart on the lean-to's gravel floor, she in turn stared challengingly at Hector Bolitho.

Welland studied her hands, reddened by incessantly handling the damp rocks. He saw the trim ankles between the rough boots and her skirt's ragged hem. He saw the hessian towser or apron that protected her skirt and bodice from mud splashes. He saw her breast heave under it as she breathed deeply. He saw the flare of her nostrils, her chin's challenging set, and the anger in her eyes.

How long that frozen moment of immobility lasted, Welland never knew, but it stretched on and on until the thread of prudent reserve that held Hector Bolitho in his dignified position on the count house threshold snapped. With a certain loss of dignity, but a flash of pugnacity, he jumped down from his perch and bustled round the Curnows towards his challenger who awaited his arrival unmoved. The woman who had taken it upon herself to stop the stamps; the woman who had usurped the mine captain's authority was no stranger to Welland, though he had not expected it to be part of her reserved nature to take so drastic a step. The woman who was now defying Hector Bolitho was Mavis Trerice.

Even before he had taken the twenty strides from the count house to the stamps, Bolitho appeared to have regained control of himself. He slowed his pace to his habitual waddle. He halted, head thrown back and belly pendulous, puffing out his waistcoat like a cock's breast. When he spoke, it was deliberately and so softly that his voice was barely audible above the wheeze from the pump engine.

'The music of the stamps, Miss Trerice, that is what makes Wheal Fortune dance, and you have stopped it. Be so good as to set it to play again.'

Mavis made no move. Her fist remained clenched around the wooden lever above her head that controlled the sluice and now spilled the water uselessly beside the stamps. Bolitho swung his head sideways and raised his voice to address the silent audience of bal maidens and boys.

'Without the music of the stamps, there can be no work; without work, no pay! Reason with this woman, I pray you.'

The water trickled over the stones, the wind sighed in the roof, but no one spoke. The firemen emerged from the engine house and added their blackened faces to the ring which was forming around the green between count house and stamps. Others joined them: kibble landers, abandoning their skips in the shaft; boys from the dressing floors, leaving their dilleughing in canvas sieves; horse-minders quitting the whim-cages that wound the kibbles up the shaft; stokers from the blowing house; the grass captain, tall-hatted petty officer raised from the ranks to oversee the surface workers: all standing mute and sombre.

And, as if responding to a secret summons, the tinners began to emerge from the mine, shoving Welland ahead of them, emerging also from the cluster of other shafts and winzes that surrounded the Wheal Fortune engine house and converging deliberately on the confrontation. Welland studied their faces. None were old, though many of those in their thirties were ageing. Pale and glassy-eyed from their days underground yet muscular and, for the most part, breathing steadily after their steep climb, they pushed into the thickening ring and pressed slowly forward. Only when triggered by a quietly cleared throat, did the tinners' coughs break out in volleys, coughs like the barking of farmyard dogs, persistent, hacking, miners' coughs from which there was no escaping. When they spat in the grass, their spittle was black: black with the dust from the boryer, black with the fumes from powder. But at least they were not spitting blood. Not yet.

There were no rough gestures. The men stood almost respectfully, restrained, curious. And yet, though no fist or voice was raised, a new feeling of menace now hung in the air.

'What did he tell you, Curnow?' Mavis's voice broke through the hush like the ring of hammer on anvil. Curnow replied softly.

'The parish. He said I must go upon the parish.'

'The parish, Mr Bolitho? Doesn't he deserve better than that? Hasn't Curnow worked here since he was ten? Is he the man you want to put upon the parish? Wouldn't your old dog fare better?'

Hector Bolitho fingered the gold links of his watch-chain

72

and his eyes flicked about anxiously. Welland and the others knew that, if Windfall hadn't been so remote from the towns, he would have already sent for the constables and implored the magistrates to call out the military from Bodmin. As it was, Bolitho was trembling inwardly, but he put on the best face he could in the circumstances.

'Have you not heard of economics, Miss Trerice? Do you not know that a man must work to justify his wage? How can I explain the continued employment of a blind man to the adventurers whose capital built Wheal Fortune mine?'

'There's work he can do without eyes. Let him count the kibbles.'

Hector Bolitho affected to laugh. His laugh petered out. He was the only one to do so. 'A blind tallyman! How will he tell if the tinners are sending up ore or attle?' he demanded.

'His boy can sit beside him.'

'The man can't write.' Bolitho changed the argument.

'He can count. He can notch a stick.'

'A dead weight, a burden laid on all our shoulders, that's what he'll be.'

'Then we must bear it!' Mavis's face was flushed, her eyes shone, she was unrepentant. 'We are all one together. If your finger offend you, do you cut if off? – One and All, isn't that our Cornish motto?'

Mr Bolitho looked at all the captains in turn: the grass captain, Captain Angove and the three other underground captains. He was seeking support, but they were not wholeheartedly with him. He studied the tinners' faces: there was no softening. He looked in vain for sympathy among the bal maidens. There was none. He felt wronged. Was he not a humane, generous man, more attentive than most to the needs of his miners? Why were they all letting this slip of a girl make such an extravagant claim upon him?

'It won't work! Mark my words, it won't work! I'll lose my own position when the adventurers get to hear of it. I don't agree with this. It's a bad business, bad business. We'll all

73

lose money over it. The adventurers will lose money. The mineral lord will lose money. I'll lose money. And *you*'ll lose money, yes, all of you'll lose money for I'll be forced to dock your wages to pay for the luxury of carrying a useless body. That's what you want, is it?' Bolitho realized his voice was a trifle shrill. He waited. There was no affirmation, no denial either, but the men and women stood their ground. Mavis Trerice still held the sluice firmly shut with the handle. If he moved to take it from her, he was sure he would be swept away under a cold human tide. 'All right, then, I'll hire him to tally. But under duress, mark you, under duress.' He plucked a handkerchief from his sleeve and wiped his lips with it. 'Now then, Mavis, let's hear those stamps speak. The music of the stamps, we're all waiting to hear it.' He waited, anxious now that he had allowed her a tactical victory, not to lose his quid pro quo.

'Your hand then, your hand on it, Mr Bolitho.'

She was challenging him again already: challenging him to seal an unwilling bargain with a handshake: challenging him to pledge his word to her, a woman, a bal maiden. It almost choked him, but she still held the lever motionless in her left hand. Her right was extended towards him. Bolitho hesitated. The silence descended around them once more: not even a cough disturbed it. Then, out of the corner of his eye, it seemed to him that he saw some of the men edging forward.

Her hand was rougher than his, not a lady's hand by any account, not like those he was accustomed to pressing when he went home each evening to the tall stone house in Tregurney village. It was firm and calloused and yet not a man's hand either. He felt faintly ridiculous during the long seconds their palms remained clasped together. As soon as she released him, he turned back towards the count house. Curnow and his wife had silly looks of gratitude upon their faces and he was afraid that she too would try to shake his hand, so he gripped both ostentatiously together as he skirted round the couple. Not until he was in the act of mounting the count house steps did he hear the grumbling noise of the stamps starting up again. It was music to his ears. The stamps sang a song of money. They sang of cambric and lace, of evenings at the piano, of tea caddies and bone china, civilized conversation, and walks in the country. The bargain he had just struck, he reflected, might not turn out to be such a bad one after all. The men would soon tire of giving up hard-won money for a useless hand like Curnow, and some of them could be depended on to cheat the others, sending up poor grade ore in the knowledge the tallyman couldn't see it. Before the month was out, they'd be howling for his dismissal.

Now that he could study the circle of tinners, he doubted that they had really moved forward. That fellow Welland, whom he knew to be a troublemaker, was still in the same place and he suspected that, even if he had tried to give a lead, they would not have followed. He was still a stranger: he wasn't Cornish, and the tinners ignored him.

There was no jubilation among the tinners and bal maidens at their victory. What they said to each other as they moved off was lost in the stamps' renewed roaring. The bal maidens took up their task of spalling the large ore-lumps with their hammers and the children returned to their sieves and spillways. The miners, who had all come up to grass, set off homeward. Their core, as they called the shift, was over. Ahead of them, as if by common consent, shuffled Curnow. His wife, still weeping, held one arm. Welland Halt, who had stepped forward to join his mate, guided him as he supported the other.

When they reached the top of the first slow rise, Welland stopped and looked over his shoulder at the mine. The woman he hoped to see was lost in the crowd of working bal maidens. It had been her victory and he felt ashamed to have contributed little or nothing toward it. He wished he could tell her, but it had been too difficult and now it was all so

75

distant. Wavering smoke spilled out flat from the tall chimney and puffs of sickly vapour belched out of the burning house around which the sulphur and arsenic from smelted ore blighted the vegetation. The forge door was open, but within it the fire's dull red eye was no longer glowing. Where was Tom Magor? Lost in the crowd? For a moment, Welland imagined him crazed like Polyphemus the cyclops, one hand staunching the blood from the single blind eye in his forehead, while the other sought rocks to hurl at his puny tormentor. He knew he must watch out for Magor. Magor was like a bull he had baited, full of dumb anger. Well, he wouldn't find it easy to creep up on Welland unnoticed. If he had been in the crowd, he would have stood out, head and shoulders above the rest.

'Curnow d'look braem wisht!'

Welland felt Curnow's wife Ellen tugging at his arm. Curious, wasn't it, that some men were fated always to be called by their surnames, even by their wives? Curnow was looking pale and drawn; they must get him home quickly.

As he stepped out again on the road to the village, Welland felt a slight bump from the coin in his pocket. It had lain there forgotten since Hector Bolitho had pressed it upon him that morning. Now he took it out and was momentarily tempted by a flash of the guinea's golden shine before he folded it into Curnow's fingers. There was more than one small luxury for Ruth it would have afforded, but he knew he had no option.

'There,' he explained, ' 'tis your share of the bonus money.'

5

THE POOL

The man cupped his hands and reached down into the dark pool's still waters. He was kneeling on the smooth grass of the bank in a clearing among the gnarled alder and willow. As he reached down, he had a brief glimpse of his features, dappled with light from the cheerful morning sun. It was a broad, sunburnt face topped with a shock of tangled hair and framed with bushy sidewhiskers that looked as if he had slept in a hedge. He grinned to himself as he splashed water over his head and neck, but the reflection was broken and the mirror surface did not return until after he had stood up and begun to tie the girth under his donkey's pack-saddle.

Upstream of the pool, a rivulet sidled over brown stones and purled round tree-roots in the dense thickets that choked the valley to the south of Morvan Hill. Below the pool, it arched smoothly over a rocky weir and splashed into some shallows where minnows flickered in the current. On the weir's left bank, hidden among ferns, a roughly cut leat led off to a set of overgrown workings where the 'old men', tinners of bygone years, had worked the streambed sands for traces of ore. The trees that overhung the pool were shaggy with ancient lichen: they seemed old, immemorial, with limbs contorted like arthritic goblins. It was a quiet, numinous place, and the man had chosen it for that reason. Now, he flicked the backbone of a trout he had tickled the night before out of his frying pan, wiped the pan clean with a handful of grass and hung it alongside the saddlebags on the donkey's back. He kicked the last embers of his camp fire into the pool and prodded the donkey into motion.

'Giddup, Emma!' he instructed and she flicked her ears back and forth thoughtfully before complying. They threaded their way along a twisting path before the trees began to give way to a fringe of gorse. Here the man checked the donkey with a pull on her halter, giving himself time to scan the nearby road in both directions before either of their heads was fully visible. The road was clear, so was the distant slope of Morvan Hill. A sheep was browsing among the rocks near the summit, that was all. Foraging bees murmured in the nearby gorse blossoms. Satisfied, the man poked Emma's hindquarters with his stick and they emerged into the open, padding over the springy turf. She seemed to know her way without guidance, wheeling left and trotting up the long hill. Behind them, there was a sound of dogs barking far off and a suggestion of grey walls showing through a clump of oak and elm. Clear in the morning air, yet with a tremor induced by the rising warmth, the strokes of a clock overtook them. The man nodded to himself: his timing was good. He whistled a lively tune as he followed his donkey towards the place where moor met sky in a smooth line broken only by an isolated carn.

As he approached it, he converged with a woman coming from the Bethel direction. She was beyond middle age, as judged hereabouts, but hale and brisk in her movements. The skin on her face, which he knew all too well as she came closer, was lined and weatherstained like foxed parchment. What disconcerted him most was her ingratiating expression.

'Hello there, Johnny my lover. It d'seem like a lifetime since you was in Windfall,' she called out as they met at the fork.

She fell in step with him on the slope down to the village. 'Where've 'ee been to? The maids're all long-faced as fiddles without 'ee.'

'I've more ports of call than Windfall, Hilda Trerice,' he replied cagily. 'I never knew I was that welcome, leastways not by you in perticklar.'

'Absence do make the 'eart grow fond, they say. A man in your trade should know that better than most, I reckon. Not to mention your old calling. A girl in every port, isn't that the saying? I thought my Mavis was sweet on you once, but she's too clear-'eaded, thank goodness.'

'Aye.' He chanced a sidelong glance at Hilda Trerice. There was no sign of what she was thinking. 'Perhaps, but she never showed it.'

For a while, they walked on in silence with the donkey trotting ahead of them. Why was Hilda Trerice sharing confidences with him? Presently, when her house grew close, she spoke again.

'In your travels, you 'aven't come up with a man called Halt, Welland Halt, 'ave you?'

So this was it, this was why old mother Trerice had been pretending to be friendly with him. He scratched his head, furrowed his brow, and made a show of thinking.

' 'Alt, did you say? A name's not much to go on. A feller can 'ave a different name every twenty mile if 'e's a mind to.'

'Walks with a limp, 'e does. Travels with a maid, name o' Ruth what 'e calls 'is daughter.'

'Where is 'e?'

' 'Ere in Windfall, works down the mine, calls 'isself a smith though 'e's but a labourer.'

'So what 'as 'e done to earn your spite? Seduced your precious daughter or somethin'?' He stopped in his tracks. 'Lookee 'ere, 'Ilda Trerice, I don't care fer yer pryin'. If I knowed every last thing about this chap, I wouldn't tell 'ee. Put that in yer pipe and smoke it. I may be a drifter, but I'm not a nark.'

'I might've knawed you'd be birds of a feather. Us don't 'ave no room fer such vagrant trade 'ere in Windfall. Us shan't never rest till us sees 'ee leavin'.'

With that, she turned off to her cottage door and slammed it behind her. He walked on, bemused at the intensity of her emotion. Whoever this Welland Halt was, he had contrived to make himself at least one enemy.

'Johnny! Johnny! Johnny Fortnight!'

The village urchins had seen him coming. They recognized him instantly, knowing the familiar silhouette of donkey and burly man with the rolling gait. They snatched up their marbles from the dust and ran towards him shouting.

They saw the bulging tobacco quid in his cheek and caught the glint of the single gold ear-ring in the shade of his tarpaulin hat. Even at their age and with half an eye, they could tell him for a sailor. The way he wore his reefer jacket and the general cut of his rig were completely different from the appearance of country folk. Then there was the way he cocked his head sideways and back as though squinting for squalls. There were hearts and flowers tattooed on his right arm. And there was the little matter of the scar. A long pale welt ran down diagonally from the right side of his forehead, across his left cheek, and lost itself in the tangle of his mutton-chop whiskers. That had been a close shave, for sure. Looking up at the sharp blue eyes twinkling from a nest of wrinkles under bushy brows, the boys saw the reflected glint of the cutlass that ought to have given Johnny Fortnight his passport to Davy Jones's Locker, and imagined him plucking a pistol from his sash, felling the Frenchie before he could strike a second blow.

He walked warily, following the dainty mincing steps of his donkey. Experience had taught him he was as like to be greeted with a stone as with a smile and a shilling. For every flighty young maid, consumed with curiosity to see what he carried in his bundles, there was a sharp-tongued old termagant of a mother, or a hard-headed husband to complain that the packman was the ambassador of extravagance, the support of sin, and the harbinger of hellfire. So, despite the jaunty set of his jib, he kept a weather eye out for williwaws.

His gambolling court of urchins accompanied him down the straggling street, Windfall's sole thoroughfare. He had seen better places; even Naples had been better than this; the sun is a great redeemer. The stench of the gutters and dung-heaps made him wrinkle his nose. Even Emma picked her way delicately among the bones and other kitchen refuse that littered the unpaved road. Johnny Fortnight brought her to a halt abeam of the Tinners' Arms where the reek of vomit and stale beer was spliced on to the stink of urine. It was worse than a rancid bilge. Johnny Fortnight didn't care for Windfall; there was little to redeem it; only St Winwalloe's church retained a trace of grace, but was neglected and overwhelmed by the brash cheapness of the place. He knew a thousand prettier anchorages where he would rather be, but he had learnt that real riches were to be plundered from malodorous ports, ports that shipped the produce of factory and mine and that there was much money to be taken from untutored labourers' hands. He hung the nosebag close around Emma's muzzle and began to unlash her saddlebags.

The girls grouped around him slowly, like fawns advancing from a covert. He pretended to be busy, burying his head and arms in the saddlebags, but slyly letting a tangle of ribbons loop towards the ground. One of the urchins made a grab for it, but Johnny snatched it back, cuffing the lad for his pains. Still, he refrained from looking directly at the girls, sensing that they might be intimidated and make off despite the lure of his wares. He bided his time carefully, like a poacher watching his snare. The girls would hesitate; they would walk past arm in arm, darting secret glances into the saddlebags, feigning indifference. But they would come. Soon. He was sure of that. They always did.

Johnny Fortnight was right; he soon had a flock of maidens pressing round him, fingering fabric, giggling behind their hands at his sly suggestions. His pocket grew heavy with their coins. He was jokingly familiar with them, but retained a calculated reserve, knowing that part of his capital was his role as messenger, bearing news of places beyond Morvan Hill, Tregurney and Bethel, news of London, news of foreign wars, news of discoveries, news of scandal.

'Did I tell you about bad Lord Byron last time I was 'ere, gals? Well, it'll 'ave ter wait; first we must get down to business.'

The girls loved this, relishing his stories of lords' and ladies' peccadilloes at court, but what they loved most was his recital of Trafalgar. Although they had heard this tale so often and ought to have had serious doubts about Johnny Fortnight's claim to have been on the *Victory*'s deck when the fatal bullet struck his admiral down, there was no questioning the sincerity of his grief. There were no heroes in Windfall, but the little admiral had been one in the true English mould, having had the grace to die at the hour of his triumph and not live on like embittered Wellington. The packman always reserved his Nelson touch for the very last, confident that its anticipation would hold his audience together. He never neglected business and watched his clients closely.

'Hey there, Molly,' he called to one of them, a vain, fair-haired girl who thought she was somebody, 'don't you know what's embroidered on this bonnet?' Molly looked at him petulantly, her lower lip stuck out and one hand on her hip. Johnny waited, swinging the bonnet by one of its strings. He was well aware that the girl was incapable of reading anything that might have been written on the bonnet. ' "Don't touch me till I'm yours!" That's what it says, my lover.' When the girl stamped her foot in annoyance, he went on cajolingly, 'Now then, maid, don't take on so, but remember, you owes me three shilling already. That's all right though, and you can take this bonnet too, so long as you pays me something on account, like always. This bonnet was made for you. Come on, let me try it on you. Just find me sixpence later and you can have it along with the stuff you've bought already.' He took the bonnet and set it showily on her ash-blonde hair. 'There, ain't she handsome? If she was a year older, and her father was richer, I'd marry her meself.'

'Who says I'd 'ave you!'

'Well, if I can't have you, can I have that sixpence?'

When Molly reached into her purse and pulled out the coin, he was more than satisfied. The packman liked to be owed money; it kept his customers attached to him and what he sold in Bethel, he was paid for in Windfall and vice versa. He was pleased with the trade he was doing that morning and looking on Windfall with a less jaundiced eye.

'Come closer, girls,' he murmered confidentially, 'and I'll tell you where to meet me to hear about me little old admiral.'

With the maidens clustered about him closely, listening to his whispered instructions, he observed an auburn-haired young girl who had been hovering on the fringe of the gathering. She had now approached timidly and was standing on tiptoe peering into one of the saddlebags. He thought he knew all the children in Windfall, but this one was new to him. She had a tumbling mane of close waved hair, a high brow and wide-set green eyes. Her lips were delicately modelled, but she did not smile; her expression was enigmatically calm. Under her neat, freshly-washed dress he could see the beginnings of a woman's figure.

Sensing a chance to do new business, the packman pushed the other maidens aside in order to approach her. The village girls seemed to have no contact with the newcomer, never addressing her and pointedly ignoring her presence. He wondered what she could have done to deserve their ostracism

'Can I sell you a ribbon or a kerchief?' he inquired briskly. The girl looked up and shook her head slowly.

'She won't buy nothin',' Molly chimed in aggressively. 'She don't 'ave no money.' It was all too probably true. He had seen that look so often before on other maids' faces: the sadness of hopeless desire. Then, as he began to tie his

83

bundles, the girl took him by the wrist, gripping it hard in her small hand.

'You have a book in there. I saw it, but I couldn't reach it. Will you give me the title?'

It was true, he did have a book in there; he had forgotten it. Johnny Fortnight didn't usually carry books, but this one had come to him in lieu of payment of a small debt. He hadn't considered selling it. There was no way he could gauge its value. Now, he thought, with a little prompting, he might even give it to this pretty, wistful creature. He rummaged in the bag and pulled the book out. It was quite small, leather bound, with gold lettering on the spine. Johnny Fortnight opened it and peered inside.

'Well, what's it called?' the girl was asking and he saw the suspicion of a supercilious smile hovering round her lips. He twisted the book from side to side, chewing nervously at his tobacco quid, then finally handed it over to her, saying, 'See for yourself!'

She took the book graciously and turned it the other way up before studying the title page. The packman stole a furtive glance at the other girls in case they were laughing at him, but they hadn't noticed or understood. It wasn't as if they could read either. The auburn-haired girl was immersed in the book, turning its pages and holding it in both hands. Johnny already had an inkling of what it was that set her off from her fellows.

'What is it, then? You seem to like it,' said Johnny and waited for her answer as she dragged herself back to consciousness.

'Maria Edgeworth: *Moral Tales*,' she told him.

'*Moral Tales*?' He laughed raucously. 'You never thought Johnny Fortnight would be bringing moral tales in his saddlebag, did you, gals?' He looked round and the maidens simpered obediently.

'Well, if you've no use for them, will you sell them to me?'

'Sell them?' The packman instantly forgot his impulse to

give the book to her. She was still as pretty, still as appealing, but he suspected his book had more value than he had been putting on it. 'Next to my Bible and my hymn-book, that's my most precious possession.' The girls laughed loudly at this.

'Name your price!' the newcomer persisted. Johnny Fortnight was enjoying teasing her but he didn't want to miss the chance of a sale.

'A shilling,' he announced, 'nothing less. Look at the binding: for that alone, it's worth it.'

'I'll give you threepence,' she replied levelly.

'Threepence! She wants to rob me. How shall I feed me old mother?' he lamented tragically.

'Not to mention your wife and ten children,' the girl answered with coy malice as she took three pennies from her apron pocket. 'Here's the money, will you take it, yes or no?'

Johnny Fortnight was rather pleased at her sudden effrontery; he admired her coolness under fire. Why hadn't he seen her before, when she was younger, playing in the street with the other village children? She was a pretty one, no mistake about that!

'Give us a kiss then! You shall have it for nothing, if you give me a kiss.'

She shook her head firmly and held out the money. Well, threepence was threepence.

'Done!' he accepted after a long pause and transferred the coins to his pocket.

She was gone in a moment, skipping up the road to a house at the far end of the village. The dancing figure was suddenly younger, childish even. He tried to decide if he had made a bad bargain.

'Who is she?' he asked the other maidens.

'Ruth Halt, she d'call 'erself. She's a furriner – don't talk to no one.'

So that was it. Well, it would take her a long time to get over that drawback, Johnny Fortnight decided as he put a final lashing on Emma's saddlebags. Wasn't he a furriner himself? He knew all too well how difficult it had been to triumph over the suspicion and reserve of these Cornish. He wished her luck and wondered how she had come to be living in a place like Windfall. There was precious little call for good manners and literacy in a mining village. And her parents, who were they? What were they doing in here among the miners? Halt wasn't a Cornish name. He would find out soon enough, he decided. Sometimes it didn't pay to appear too curious. What he didn't learn now, he might discover tomorrow. He beckoned Molly over to him.

'Now, you won't forget to tell 'er the time and the place, like you did last time?' he murmured.

'I might – and then I might not,' she answered coyly.

'If I was to give you a ribbon, would it help your memory?'

'I do believe it might.' She reached out her hand to take one.

'Not so fast, young lady. You shall have it tomorrer, when I do see the person in question.'

'What if she won't come!'

'She will when you tell 'er 'tis Johnny Fortnight. She do dearly love to hear me tell o' the little old admiral.'

'You're struck on 'er, Johnny Fortnight, that's what you are.'

'Not so. But she d'owe me for somethin' – don't tell 'er I said that though, or she won't come over – and you won't see that ribbon.' If he was honest with himself, he had to confess that his interest went beyond debt collecting, but he wasn't going to admit it.

Emma's saddlebags were much lighter now than when she came. She scampered up the street as if she were just as eager as the packman to leave Windfall. Johnny had timed his visit well. The menfolk and older bal maidens were all at the mine and he had avoided the nasty scenes that occurred when they caught up with him as they did from time to time. The more daring of the bal maidens might follow the directions he had

86

given their younger sisters to find his lair and hear his Trafalgar story. If they came, he would sell them the remainder of his stock of ribbons and handkerchiefs. Tomorrow night he would return to Plymouth for a fresh load. He would see the old three-deckers moored in the Hamoaze as he took the ferry. A furtive tear sprang into his eye. God knows, he hadn't wanted to join the Andrew, but once in, it had been a different story. Shipmates, even the little admiral had been a shipmate, in a manner of speaking. Was it true that Johnny had helped them carry him below? It was just as if he could remember it.

Thud – a well-aimed potato shook him out of his reverie. Pieces of its white flesh clung to the breast of his reefer jacket and a streak of black juice from its rotten core ran down his cheek like blood. He turned in anger and saw the woman, grey-haired, bony, hatchet-faced. It was the pellar, the woman who cast the spells. They believed in her here, credulous fools.

'Damn your eyes for that, you mean old bitch!' he cried at her, unabashed. 'Is that your Christian kindness? Is that what you learn at Bethel?'

Hilda Trerice held a black book aloft in her hand, shaking it at him and shouting, 'My house shall be called of all nations the house of prayer, but ye have made it a den of thieves.'

Johnny Fortnight laughed at her. He jabbed his donkey with his stick to be off more quickly and he laughed again, over his shoulder,

'My curse on you for a sanctimonious, hypocritical witch!'

'And mine on you, you fornicating, godless usurer! I know your sort!' she ranted.

'And so you should, you were married to one, they tell me.' The packman's Parthian shot struck home. He saw her shake before the broadside; she had been holed between wind and water, but he had no taste for prolonging the engagement. Old Mother Trerice was as mean and nasty as her daughter was open and good-natured, she wasn't a good enemy. He put up his helm and bore away out of range.

On the high ground, puffing from the climb, he hove-to and looked back over the grey, charmless village. He felt relieved to have sailed out safely with his share of plunder. Windfall was a mean place: nothing was spent there for beauty beyond what the maidens gave him surreptitiously for his bright ribbons. Its inhabitants were a pirate crew, robbing and raping the land for a quick profit.

Already the miners were coming home at the end of their core. They stretched in a long line from count house to village. The youngest of them ran ahead, eager to spend their wages in the Tinners' Arms, while the older men were held up at the cottage doors along the road where their sharp-tongued wives pestered them for money. Money was all they lived for in Windfall: money and drink. There was nothing left over for beauty. Apart from St Winwalloe's church and the vicarage beside it, not one thing had been built in the village to a standard above that which was utilitarian and necessary. Johnny thought of the beautiful stone-built mining towns of the Minas Gerais in Brazil; he remembered Potosi in the high Andes: towns with gilded churches, mansions with carved and mouldering façades. Why were they so different? Was there a particular meanness in the puritanical British that led them to drain riches out of the earth with unparalleled energy and invention, only to live with their pigs in towns like this? And then he remembered that the gracious South American cities he had seen were built on the labour of slaves. These men, hurrying from Wheal Fortune mine, were they any less slaves than the black captives of the Spaniards and Portuguese? These men worked for hire or gambled their wages on 'tribute', but were they free? They were certainly not free like Johnny Fortnight. But they couldn't all be packmen.

He saw one of the stragglers pull up in the doorway of the house where he had seen the strange girl, Ruth Halt, vanish with her book. It was too far to see him clearly, but the man had a peculiar walk and an outline that was strangely familiar. Johnny Fortnight bit his lip, but couldn't place him. He liked to think he had a good eye for faces; you needed that in his profession. But although there had been something he might have recognised in her features, it was nothing he could put his finger on. Did she take after the man with the limp, presumably her father, or was it her mother she resembled?

Emma stamped her hooves. She had no interest in his speculations. She was anxious to be rid of her saddlebags and to be free to crop the grass for an hour or two. Johnny Fortnight gave her her head and she trotted away from Windfall. They would be back soon enough and time would reveal the answers to his questions.

It had been the week's last core and the men had received their subsistence money from Mr Bolitho and their share of the tribute which was paid monthly. Now, with a new access of the energy they had used in the mine, they turned to their own amusements. Some of them were trying a fall with each other at catch-as-catch-can, watched by a circle of wrestling fanciers. Others were playing a kind of rough football in an open space they had cleared of stones. Meanwhile, in the Tinners', the drinkers drank, and sang and laughed and told tall tales. They were all merry enough. Only the older men, those with many mouths to feed, wore frowns, and not a few of these ordered up another tankard or two to help themselves forget.

Welland Halt pushed open the door to his rented cottage and it creaked alarmingly. Made of a few crudely-cut elm boards, nailed to crosspieces at top and bottom, it had warped out of shape and was full of chinks that let the wind blow in.

It was dim in the room and, at first, he did not see his daughter. He felt a brief surge of annoyance that she wasn't

on the threshold to greet him as usual. There was no smell of
any dinner cooking on the hearth either. A man had a right to
expect something when he came home. But then he relented.
After all, she was only a girl, wasn't she, naught but a maid,
as they said in those parts.

When Welland saw her, curled up in the window-seat, all
his frustrations were charmed away. Still oblivious of him,
and wedged close to the window to catch the last of the light,
Ruth was reading. The sunlight glowed on the halo of hair
round her face and picked out an aureole of minute hairs on
her earnest profile. Her eyes flicked back and forth and her
breast rose and fell with her regular breathing.

'What's that, then? A new book?' he asked, leaning over
her tenderly.

'*Moral Tales*,' she replied, coming reluctantly out of her
dream. 'Maria Edgeworth – they're lovely.' She sat up
primly, with her finger in the page. 'I bought it. I knew
you'd approve. It wasn't really expensive. I bargained with
the packman.' Welland chuckled to himself and she tapped
him with the book, reprovingly. 'I really did. He wanted
lots of money, but I beat him down. You should have seen
me.'

Welland wished he had. His daughter was always surprising him. He often thought she was old before her time,
perhaps too worldly-wise, too grown-up, without the companionship of other children. And yet, on balance, he was
pleased, pleased that he had devoted all his free time to
teaching her to read and write when all her contemporaries
were playing hop-scotch in the road or begging sips from the
drinkers in the tinners' yard. So it was Maria Edgeworth
now, was it? Soon, before he could stop her, it would be
Smollett, *Tristram Shandy*, perhaps even Adam Smith. He
felt inordinately proud of her and squeezed the nape of her
neck, unwontedly ashamed at the roughness of his palm.
Suddenly she stiffened and jumped up.

'Your supper! Your supper! I forgot your supper!'

'I don't care. I'll get it myself. You must read on while the light holds. I'm ever so proud that you're such a good reader. You'll soon be ahead of your poor old father. I'm not much of a teacher.'

What he didn't tell her was how pleased he was that he hadn't sent her to learn reading from the devout and vituperative Hilda Trerice who taught the few other village children whose parents thought it worth paying her for her trouble.

'How's Curnow? Is his sight better?' she asked, putting down her book. 'I saw you walking home together.'

'There's naught to be done, poor man. I blame myself. If I hadn't hurried —'

'Hush, Father!' She put a finger to her lips. 'Don't take on so. It just happened. But what's to become of him now? Must he go on the parish?'

'Not yet.' He paused, thinking how matter of fact, how grown-up was her reaction. 'Bolitho's given him a chance as a tallyman. He didn't want to, he was pushed to it.'

'Who pushed him?'

'Mavis Trerice.'

'Mavis — is there no one else in Windfall to give lessons in charity? I suppose you helped her.'

'She didn't ask my help, she never speaks to me, she fends for herself, does Mavis.'

'Yes, she's lonely.'

'Lonely? It's you who ought to be lonely, by yourself here all day with only a book for company. But tomorrow's a holiday. We'll have an excursion, go out on the moors together. Light the candle now, while I warm the broth. A day in the sunshine will do us both good, and I'll need it. Bolitho wants to put me on tribute — more long hours in darkness.'

He did not tell her of his sudden fear that her new knowledge would distance her from him, her teacher, and carry her into a circle of minds beyond her means. He dismissed the thought. A growing plant should not be stifled because it reached towards the light.

Next day was Sunday, a day that was variously celebrated in Windfall. Drinking and sport predominated amongst the men. These were still the half-heathen tinners who had lived for centuries in isolation, panning streams on the desolate moors. They retained vestiges of freedom not enjoyed by the sedentary serf on the lord's land. The ancient Stannary Parliaments had regulated their lives, outside the margin of feudal order. They formed a corporation, proud of its customary rights and jealous of the narrowing privilege of seeking tin, as the fisherman seeks fish, wherever it lay hid. The tinner remained independent, hard-headed, often ungovernable, a gambler preferring tribute to security on tutwork.

As in work, so in religion, the tinner was ready to let the certitude on his soul's salvation go hang in return for the promise of present pleasure. Let the womenfolk nag all they would, the tinners clung to their anarchic ways. But the mines were taming them. The captains and pursers were bargaining over their share of the profit. The captains and pursers worked for the adventurers who put up the capital for the new machinery without which exploitation of the deep lodes would not be possible. And the new machinery set the pace for the mine. The beam-engines did not pause for croust, or sing a song, or rest a while. The men who ran and wrestled on the grass now found they had also to run and wrestle underground. And still they had not understood: enough of the old disorder reigned to give them the illusion of freedom. Most of them worked fiercely on in the hope of a lucky strike that would bring them the money for a farm and a few cows. The women knew better: they knew that the cards were stacked against the tributers, cutting ore for a diminishing return. They left their careless menfolk in Windfall and walked the long miles to the chapel in Bethel where the preacher assured them they could lay up treasure in heaven. They were too wise to expect to receive any on earth.

From his vicarage window, Mr Nichols watched the women file off in their best black dresses, best black boots, and best black bonnets. They gripped black Bibles in black-gloved hands and the Curate wondered what black thoughts festered behind their close-knit, darkened brows. His own church sat empty. They scorned the old mass, call it service and make it as low church as you liked. They strode off to Bethel, knowing that once past the severe, frill-free portals of their chapel, they would be treated to a show of grandilo-quent enthusiasm the like of which he could never match. They would be beaten with the stick of perdition and the Pit; lured with the carrot of faith and redemption. His own pale sermons offered nothing in comparison: the pursuit of grace and the hope of glory, ritual shaped by reason, confession and forgiveness. They passed him by, but they saw him not.

Mr Nichols watched the miners' sports with a tolerant eye, though their cock-fights sickened him. It had never been the way of holy Church to forbid frolic. Even evident pagan survivals like guise dancing and the Midsummer fires did not shock him. Was it not the way of the Church to absorb and incorporate such revels, giving them a Christian significance rather than put them under a ban? And yet, for all his tolerance, the tinners never accorded him a second glance. He felt they pitied him.

The Curate pitied himself, locked up in the flimsy citadel of the old religion, fettered by doctrine, the constraint of the cloth, enmeshed in the inadequacy of his own belief. If only he had had the interest to have been appointed to some country town living where his church would be filled with fat burghers, judges, redcoated officers, or some tranquil living on a great estate where the earl in his pew would have led the congregation of coachmen, maids and valets, foresters and gamekeepers, in the time-honoured responses. But he had been a poor, worthy scholarship boy, good at arithmetic, fair at Latin, tolerable at divinity, successful at sonnets. Ordination was easy and the Winwalloe living was vacant. That had been his sin, the sin of nonchalance, and interminably was he expiating it.

Welland Halt and his daughter Ruth were walking past: not going to chapel, the Curate would wager on that. Young Ruth was older now. How old? Old enough to make the young men turn and look at her. How much she had changed since the night Mavis had called him to the door and he had seen her in the shadows. That seemed so long ago. Time passed, even on leaden wings, time passed. How many months was it since he had offered them the shelter of his stable? Ungrateful folk, never once had they attended matins or evensong. By now, he despaired of them. That Welland was different from the other miners, not only because of his crippled leg, but by virtue of his reserve, his industry, his intellect. Mr Nichols nursed the idea that the newcomer's mind, far from mirroring the tinners' pagan animism, reached out beyond his own agnosticism to something frankly atheistical. To have put it to the test would have entailed a confrontation, and that was something Mr Nichols always dreaded. He was still trying to pluck up courage enough to visit their cottage. Now he followed young Ruth's lightfoot walk till she shrank into distance. His hand reached out to her, but he was trapped behind his window.

Father and daughter walked on, over the shoulder of Morvan, out of sight to the sad Curate. Ruth danced over the springy heather. The collar of her dress fluttered in the light breeze. She flapped her arms like a bird's wings, as though ready to fly off westwards into the turquoise, cloud-flecked sky. Under the sky, the moors extended into the haze of distance, studded, here and there, with smoking mine-chimneys that could not rest. Vivid green vales of pasture and woodland cut into the moor's brown plateau. Church steeples peered over the woods. Buzzards wheeled in the clear air.

'Look! That's where Arthur lived!' shouted Welland, pointing to the right. Ruth paused, shading her eyes from the glare, as if expecting to see the old king come riding or his sword go cartwheeling into a reed-fringed lake. Here, on the high moors, legend was reality and for her, the knights, the Round Table, Merlin, Guinevere, and the Grail were as real as the packman. They all lived in the magical world beyond the hills that her father had told her of. And he had taken her further, beyond misty Arthur's time, into ancient days when Woden walked, and Thor, and wilful Freya. She never wondered where he learnt these tales; they came to his lips as though they had been part of his own experience. All she knew was that her father was a special person, unlike any other.

They followed a sheep-run down the far slope of Morvan, among the bracken, where the sun's warmth caressed them in the sheep-cropped clearings. There were glimpses of Tregurney, cows lowing in hidden farms, fields where growing corn shimmered like wavelets on the sea.

In a quiet dell, they halted and Welland unpacked his knapsack, setting the water bottle and the slab of fuggan on a flat-topped rock, Ruth had baked the raisin fuggan cake for a Sunday treat. They ate slowly, sprawled on the turf. Ants came foraging for the crumbs and Ruth buried her face in the grass, following them into a world that was minutely small. Then she read while Welland dozed. When he woke, she was still reading, and the sun was westering. He left her buried in her book and strolled downhill, across the Tregurney road, towards the brook, aimlessly.

There was an unaccustomed pleasure in the wandering. For once, the world smiled at him. If he had looked up, he would have seen the scar on the hillside above Tregurney, where the adit had broken through, but the thought did not occur to him for his nose was full of the scent of flowers. The tender bracken-fingers were still uncurling like green feathers. Hogweed was pushing up strenuously in the hollows.

95

The air was full of the droning of flies. Welland experienced a sort of contentment, a cautious relaxation, an animal voluptuousness, a surrender to the senses, that was almost feline.

When first he heard the laughter, he doubted his ears. It must have been a trick of his imagination. He halted, listening to the moor's small sounds: the wind in the bracken, the twittering of distant larks. In the dell where he stood, the breeze scarcely penetrated and the afternoon air lay heavy and warm, soft and syrupy. The laughter, if it ever existed, had ceased. He set off again, plucking a sweet grass stem to chew. His feet crackled on last year's bracken stems. A startled rabbit bounded away.

And then he heard it again. He stopped. There was no mistaking it this time: peal upon peal of girlish laughter, the kind the superstitious Cornish associated with pixies and fairies. He moved forward again, but this time the laughter did not cease. It seemed to be coming from the long clump of trees that fringed the brook, a dense mound of stunted willow and elder, roofed so thickly with a froth of grey-green leaves and moss that to see inside was impossible.

He stood irresolute. The laughter intrigued him. He was too rational to imagine that it had a supernatural origin, but there was something faintly eerie, something compelling about those clear, bubbling cries that came filtering out of the tiny wood. To investigate would draw him further from the place where Ruth sat reading. She might have missed him already.

And yet, for all his fleeting disquiet, the laughter was too compelling to be ignored. It drew him like a silken thread into a labyrinth. Now and then, he lost it, stumbling among the head-high gorse bushes in search of a path. He became warm and flustered in his confusion. Sometimes, the twittering voices dwindled away and he had to rely on his sense of direction, pushing into the heart of the wood. Country folk said it was dangerous to seek out the little folk; much harm could come of it. They put out offerings for the pixies at their cottage doors. Down the mine, the tinners would drop crumbs from their pasties or hoggan bread for the 'knackers', the little old men they believed to live underground. If you were on good terms with the knackers, they would lead you to a profitable lode, but if you scorned them, they would trip you up or let you fall down an unlit winze.

Real or unreal, the laughter was unmistakable. Welland took care not to disturb the revellers by stepping on a dead twig. Already, he had more than half an idea of what was in store for him. Here, within the wood, the silence was deeper, the voices that flew across it more plangent, clear waves with an undertow of madness, a hint of grief beneath the joy.

A withy wand he had bent aside sprang back and lashed him across the face. He choked back the curse that followed the sudden pain. Even the slap of the branch might have been enough to betray him. He stood motionless, trying to restrain his breathing. Pieces of twig were enmeshed in his hair, burrs clung to his breeches, his hands had been stung by nettles, dust from the net of overhead branches he had disturbed was stinging his eyes.

And then he saw it: just a tiny glint at first, a flash of water. Reaching out a cautious hand, he parted the lichen strands that hung in long tufts from the interlacing boughs close to his face.

Half the pool lay in shadow, the other half gleamed in sunlight. Dragonflies hovered and flitted among the rushes along the nearby sunlit shore. Beams reflected from the gently undulating surface probed the dim undergrowth where he stood.

Welland stared unblinking into the forbidden circle. His face crumbled into a bewitched expression. White limbs sent volleys of spray dancing. He bit his nether lip.

Girls' mocking laughter broke out loudly. He froze. Had he been discovered?

A man's chuckle followed. Welland became aware of a

sunburnt torso lolling in the shadows. The man pushed himself up on his elbows and stared around him.

'Where's that Molly? – Ah, there you are, you young minx. Did you see 'er? Did you tell 'er? What did she say when you gived 'er my message?'

'Said she'd think it over,' came a simpering voice: Molly's. Welland had seen her around the Tinners'. 'She 'aven't got much time for packmen.' There was a new burst of laughing.

' 'Tisn' that,' growled the man. 'She's afeared o' Johnny Fortnight. She's afeared of 'is carronade, 'tis a devilish weapon!' He too began to laugh, but the sound died in his throat.

Welland too found himself choking. A head had emerged from the centre of the pool, fringed with long chestnut hair like seaweed. It clung to the woman's shoulders as she rose. Shining drops ran down her white skin and vanished into the water. She was still rising. She rose until she stood waist deep. She was more than half turned away from Welland, but he was sure he knew her. A jumble of anguish, bafflement and anger warred within his head.

'Hush, Johnny Fortnight! You're all bluster, no man for a close engagement. What's the matter with you, man, do your eyes droop so, is it cowardice in the face of the enemy?'

How long Welland stayed there watching that queen-like body before twisting away in dark despair, he did not know. In one way it seemed an eternity. What he was watching was unattainable, further off than the laughter of Pan and the nymphs of Arcadia. He was suddenly, hopelessly aware of his crippled body. He blundered through the trees and limped away to the edge of the covert. The shadows were lengthening and the cool evening air was rolling down Morvan. He felt unclean and longed for cold water that would cleanse the hot flush from his cheeks. He remembered Ruth and was afraid she would notice his dishevellment. He would be at a loss for an explanation. Impatiently, he brushed at the bark and lichen that was clinging to his hair and clothing.

A sudden chill came over him. Was Ruth all right? He scanned the hillside. How long had he left her alone? He began running.

As he ran, a terrible conviction overcame him. He cursed himself for his fecklessness. Scurrying up the hillside with the peculiar lolloping gait his deformed leg imposed on him, he crossed the road and plunged into the bracken. He came to a clearing. It was bare. He ran on. Another. Only a fluttering moth disturbed it. He pulled up short and clenched his hands to either side. He found he was panting. The realization had just struck him: he had lost the clearing, lost his bearings. He did not know where Ruth was.

'Ruth!' he cried, hands cupped around his mouth.

He tried to keep the panic out of his shout. She must have heard him. He scanned the hillside, waiting for her to stand and reveal herself above the sea of bracken.

'Ruth!' He ran on, blundering first into one clearing then into another. Wasn't this the one? It had to be. Look, wasn't that patch of flattened grass the place where she had sat reading?

'Ruth!' Welland looked round wildly. Down on the valley floor, a bright patch had appeared: a cluster of cotton dresses. The village girls were approaching the road. Could Ruth be among them? His harassed eyes could not see clearly. Wasn't that Mavis Trerice? She would help, wouldn't she? After all, she had helped him once before. She must have heard him shouting: they all had; they had come to a halt and were staring at him. He began to run downhill towards her.

Almost immediately, he saw a movement to the side. He slithered to a halt. It was only a sheep, blundering into the bracken. Biting his lip, he set off again.

She was sitting almost exactly as he had left her, like a human statue, so engrossed in her book that she did not look up when he dropped into the clearing. He had to call her name twice and shake her by the shoulder before she looked up with those solemn, wide-set eyes, perplexed at the change in him.

'Are you all right?'

'Of course I'm all right. Can't you see I've been reading? But what about you? You look as if you've been pulled through a hedge backwards.'

'I got lost in the wood.' Welland hoped he didn't appear to be talking evasively.

'Lost in the wood!' she laughed. 'Lucky the pixies didn't get you. I think they almost did. You're all hot and bothered.'

'I hurried back. I was worried about you.'

Suddenly she was serious.

'You needn't have been. You know I shouldn't have wandered off without you.'

Welland nodded. Everything was perfectly ordinary. He had felt an unexpected pang of fear for her, the fear that the Greeks reserved for goat-footed Pan. It was all illusion. Ruth had no enemies, how could she? She was so self-contained, so distant. Yet his agitation would not quit him so easily.

'Get up quick, Ruthie!' he told her urgently. 'You'll be catching a chill in the shade there. We must be stepping homeward.'

She made a small moue of disappointment at having to postpone the unravelling of the story, but stuck a wild flower between the pages for a bookmark. They walked home across Morvan's bald crown unspeaking, each locked in a chain of fantasy that stemmed from their respective visions. Welland was so relieved to find his daughter that he failed to look back at the village maidens. Ruth was all he wanted: his friend as well as his daughter. Isolated in Windfall, they could cling to each other.

Neither he nor his daughter glanced back to see the packman steal out of the wood with his diminutive donkey, long after the maidens had gone, and pad off into the dusk. They were both absorbed in their thoughts, she of the characters in the stories she had read, he with the new revelation of Mavis.

But the packman's eye missed nothing. When he spied out the lie of the land down in Windfall before taking the road to Bethel, he saw old Hilda Trerice, round the back of her house with a man. They were deep in conversation. He would have given a golden guinea to know what they were saying. That Hilda Trerice was a sly and a knowing old witch, though he doubted she knew her own daughter. It was her interlocutor who gave him pause: the man she held by the arm was Tom Magor. Perhaps he would never know; they were half a mile away. It took his seaman's eye to discern them. No man alive could hear their whispers. He poked Emma with his stick and set off for Bethel.

'There's a better smith in Windfall than Tom Magor, so they tell me,' Hilda Trerice was saying quietly.

'Who said that? I'll beat 'is brains out,' blustered Magor.

'More'n one 'ave said it, ever since that Welland – '

'Oh, Welland! Welland!' he broke in. 'When shall I 'ear the last of un? That man don't work iron like a natural man, 'e d'use magic. But 'e shan't 'ave the smith's job at Wheal Fortune.'

'Oh, won't 'e?'

'I've 'Ector Bolitho's promise.'

'He might change 'is mind, 'e's a soft spot fer Welland. While that man stays in Windfall, your job's not certain.'

Magor pondered. What the old woman was saying was right, it made sense, though he hadn't thought of it himself. Her small, pinched face was looking up at his, waiting for him to say something.

'There's naught I can do about it.'

'There is. Every man's got a weak point, a chink in 'is armour.'

'And Welland's?'

'Ruth – 'is daughter.'

'I don't see – Magor's head swung about like a puzzled beast.

'Do I 'ave to draw a picture?' snapped Hilda Trerice. 'You must seek 'er out, she's forever off by 'erself on Carnwartha, you'll 'ave time enough fer that, Welland'll work long hours when 'e goes on tribute.'

'She'll tell un straight off, won't she?'

'Not if you play your cards right. If you're kind and soft, she'll take your part against un.'

'If 'e d'find out, 'e'll be like a madman, I knows that Welland.' He paused and a slow smile spread acoss his features. 'You're a smart one, 'Ilda, and no mistake, no wonder folk say you're a pellar. When your Garfield fell down the mine, us thought it were witchcraft.'

'Don't be a fool, no more than you must, any'ow.'

'I may be a fool, but I'm bright enough to know you've got your knife in Welland. What's that for?'

'Be off with you now! There's Mavis coming, she mustn't see you.'

6

THE LODE

Hector Bolitho emerged from the count house and scanned the crescent of eager faces. It was setting day and the tinners who worked on tribute were on edge to know what pitches they would obtain for the coming months. They looked a desperate bunch in their rough drill trousers and jackets, frayed, worn and rust-stained, with bare feet stuck into heavy, low-quartered shoes. Some wore their hard hats pushed back on their foreheads, others held them under their arms. All of them had their croust stuck in a pocket or a bag. Day after day they ate the same thing, pasty or hoggan, food as heavy and hard as the rock they were mining. The purser recognized the leaders of the 'pares', the voluntarily constituted gangs of two to six men in which they worked. For the most part, despite their villainous appearance, they were open-faced, cheerful men, honest enough, manageable too, if you respected their old laws.

Directly below and to the right of where Mr Bolitho stood at the head of the count house steps, his clerk, sporting a crumpled white shirt collar inside his faded black coat, was poised to write in a marbled notebook. Both men were flanked by the underground captains, nearly a dozen men, somewhat better dressed than the other miners, but raised from the ranks to their positions of authority. Although unlettered men, they were wise in the ways of the mine.

The bells signalling the beginning of the first core were ringing and the last of the tutworkers, men who dug shafts, drove levels, worked pumps, transported the ore, and did a hundred other jobs for fixed pay under contract, were converging on the shafts. Hector Bolitho pulled out his gold watch and nodded to the clerk who solemnly passed him up a handful of smooth white pebbles.

'Let us proceed, Mr Farrow,' said Bolitho, 'what's the first pitch?'

The clerk held the notebook up close to his pebble lenses and read out slowly.

'Pitch from the two-hundred-fathom level, Tregurney shaft, from the kibble winze to Ivor Pellew's pitch, down to the two-hundred-and-ten-fathom level.'

To an uninformed bystander, this description would have meant little, but to the miners it was as readily understood as a set of directions from the porch to the taproom of the Tinners' Arms. It signified that the work would involve underhand stoping or cutting downwards into a lode reaching from the winze through which the buckets of ore were drawn to the next level, until arriving at Ivor Pellew's pitch ten fathoms down on the next level.

Mr Bolitho waited. There was no immediate response. The lode couldn't be terribly rich there.

'How about five shillings?' he prompted. A man at the back of the crowd laughed briefly. Welland Halt? Hector Bolitho couldn't identify him.

'Fifteen,' offered an old tinner, off to the side. Bolitho glanced at the underground captain responsible for the Tregurney shaft who shrugged expressively.

'Come on now, it must be worth better than that!' Bolitho insisted, but no one spoke up. 'Well, we haven't got all day, have we?' He was reluctant to set the pitch so high a figure which would allow the miners in the old man's pare fifteen shillings out of every twenty realized from the ore sent up from it, but there wasn't time to bargain. The setting would take all day if he persisted. 'Fifteen then.'

He took one of the pebbles and tossed it into the air as he spoke. It described a smooth arc and thudded quietly into the grass. The clerk took the old miner's name and marked it in his book before reading out the details of the next pitch. Bolitho was relieved that it was in the Windfall lode and that he had an immediate bid of only four shillings. It must be good ground. Although the downward extension of the mine had disclosed other lesser lodes, the famous Windfall vein showed no immediate sign of running out.

After a pause, another pebble flew upwards, but before it touched ground, a different miner called out,

'Three and six.'

Mr Bolitho was pleased. This meant that the second miner was ready to work the same pitch for only three shillings and sixpence in the pound. He threw another pebble and, this time, there was no counter offer. Farrow wrote down the bidder's name and went on to the next pitch.

So it continued. Pitch by pitch, the lodes were auctioned off to the lowest bidder. Each time, the miner gambled his estimation of the ore's richness and the hardness of the country rock that contained it against the ever-present possibility that, within a fathom or two, the lode would narrow to nothing and peter out. The men in each pare would discuss this together in the week preceding the setting day, pitting their experience and judgement against the sharp eyes of the underground captains and possible competition from other pares. If they were lucky and the lode got richer, they could come out of it better off by many more pounds than the tutworkers could earn in the same period. If they guessed wrong, or bid too low, they could end up excavating barren rock for weeks on end and finish up indebted to the mine owners. That was the way they liked it though. They were gamblers at heart. Secure wages only sapped their interest and slowed them down. Working on tribute made them industrious and competitive in seeking the best lodes. The mine prospered. Many a time an old shaft, worked out and ripe for closure, had been saved by a tributer's timely discovery of a new lode.

As the pitches were apportioned, the pares of miners

drifted off to the forge to sharpen their tools, to the store for candles, and to descend the long ladders to pitches where they would labour till the next settting day. Hector Bolitho was content: he liked to see rivalry between the tinners. It augured well for the Gurney family and the adventurers who had put their capital into the mine. The Gurneys gained a second benefit over and beyond the dividend on their shares: as the mineral lord, Silverton Gurney could claim mineral rights on every ounce of metal mined on his lands. Bolitho smiled: when the Gurneys were content, they often congratulated him and gave him a bonus. He looked forward to the next count house dinner, with plenty of ale and porter, brandy and rum, beef on the table and much good fellowship after examining the accounts together and dividing the profit according to their shares.

It was towards the end of the setting that Bolitho caught sight of Welland Halt, standing by himself among the knot of remaining miners. So he *was* there, after all. That Welland was such an awkward cuss that he had doubted whether he would take his own well-meant advice to come off tutwork. Despite his partnership with Curnow, he was essentially a loner and none of the other tinners appeared to have taken to him.

'So you're ready to try your hand at tribute, are you, Welland?' Bolitho called out to him with a quick scan of the remaining miners' faces. 'He's a famous hand with a hammer is this Welland; none like him at beating the boryer, but I don't need to tell you that. Who'd like to take up a pare with him?' The men shuffled their feet and looked askance. Bolitho followed their eyes and saw Tom Magor standing watching the proceedings with arms folded in the forge doorway. So that was it. He signed to the clerk to announce the next pitch. All the good ones were gone now; nothing but the parts the industrious tinners had dismissed as unrewarding remained.

'In the ground, three-hundred fathom level, eastward,'

said Farrow. 'Nineteen shillings.' Welland's voice was quiet and unhurried.

'Who's your partner? You can't work alone. Anyway, I want a better offer,' said Bolitho. The sprinkling of remaining men chuckled.

' 'Tes naught but 'ard granite,' said one of them.

'Nineteen shillings,' repeated Welland.

'Who's going to hold a boryer?' asked Bolitho.

'First I'll hold it in my left hand and hit with my right, then when I tire o' that, I'll hold it in my right and beat with my left.'

'You'll soon tire of both,' snorted Bolitho. 'Now, is there no one will do it for less?' He sensed that it was useless to persist. The underground captain responsible for that level tipped him the wink, intimating that the pitch was little more than barren country rock, devoid of minerals. He tossed a pebble in the air and watched the men's faces. There was no response before the pebble skipped across the grass. Welland registered no particular emotion, but turned away briskly giving his name to Farrow. 'Well, even if you don't win much, you won't have to share it,' Bolitho called after him.

Five minutes later, it was all over: the last couple of pitches had no takers at all and would have to go for tutwork. Some tunnelling through unproductive rock was inevitable; the workings had to be linked up with the winzes and levels. The remaining pares of miners agreed to go on contract. They were happy enough, secure in the knowledge that they would do better than Welland. No real tinner would have bid at all for such poor values.

Mr Bolitho turned to enter the count house, but paused in the doorway. Over to the east, the morning sun was shining on the white spoil pyramid beside the clay-pit. Its rays, transmuted by low-lying cloud, rimmed the two-hundred-foot hill with a golden glow, merging into stark white on the southern slope, a white that darkened through an imperceptible series of gradations to a dense blue-grey in the northern

sector. A few bracken tufts were springing out of the lower slopes. Hector Bolitho had never seen the Alps, but he imagined they must look like that: clean and pure, sparkling in the sun. The spoil heap sparkled too, not with snow but with thousand upon thousand of quartz crystals from the decayed granite that had broken down into kaolin. Now that the pit had been abandoned and the quartz sand was no longer spilling down the tip, vegetation was reclaiming it. Meanwhile, the heap stood in the purple and green expanse of the moor like an iceberg and the great pit beside it was gradually filling with water. When you looked down onto it, the pond at its centre stared up like the pupil of a blank, pale-green eye towards the heavens. Or was it the stage of a vast blanched amphitheatre, scene of titanic struggles?

Hector Bolitho shook himself. What was he doing, letting himself drift off into romantic daydreaming like that? There were accounts to be checked, letters to write, samples to go off to the smelters. He stepped into the count house.

Welland Halt had not stopped to admire the sun burning on the mountain of sand. He was already at the fifty-fathom level and descending, climbing down towards his pitch at three hundred fathom. Now that the adit was working and the pump had only to raise water to the two-hundred-fathom level, the Windfall shaft had been driven hurriedly deeper, but with little result so far. The lodes of tin showed but rarely. 'Braem wisht,' the tinners called them: thin fugitive veins that sometimes started well, but led nowhere. Welland knew this and the realization weighed heavily on him as he descended. Like the other tinners, he had become a gambler. And he was gambling with not only his own, but Ruth's future.

Beyond the two-hundred-fathom mark, the mine was quiet and grew quieter as he negotiated the slimy ladders. It was all too easy to give way to panic if you started to slip down here. No one would hear your cry for help. Even if they did, they might say it was the knackers shouting and make a

propitiatory sign to protect themselves from the little men. If they recognized Welland's voice, they would shrug and turn away. None of them had mastered the barrier of suspicion that divided them from the newcomer and they all, except Curnow, bowed to Magor the blacksmith's order for a boycott.

At the very foot of the shaft, Welland looked up. The mouth, the sole remaining scrap of daylight, had diminished to pin-head size. The only sounds were the staccato drips falling from the roof of the level that bored into the darkness beside him. His candle light penetrated only a few feet into the tunnel, beyond was complete and utter obscurity. The air was stagnant, heavy with the stale odour of black powder from yesterday's shots, and hot with the heat that emerged from the rocks. In some places down here, the rocks were as hot as the walls of an oven and hot water gushed out of the crevices. Welland adjusted his hat, checked the tinder in his pocket, and walked on.

The sound that stopped him after only half a dozen steps was unearthly: a blood-curdling, agonising wail like the death shriek of some ancient monster. There was a sharp, grinding yelp, overlaid by a prolonged hiss. Welland spun so quickly towards it that his candle went out and he had to blow on the wick to re-ignite it. Almost immediately, the scream was repeated, setting his teeth on edge with its very intensity.

The candle flared into life and, after the first dazzle, he leant against the wall of the level and began to laugh. The reason for the sound was immediately evident. It had nothing to do with knackers or subterranean monsters: it was the pump mechanism going into fork as they called it when the first few strokes began sucking water from the sump. Welland was laughing at himself for his moment of credulity and alarm. He was still chuckling when he arrived at the rock face where his pitch began and set to driving his boryer into the granite ready for the first charge of black powder.

That was the first day of the month, the first of many long months alone in the darkness, but Welland did not complain. He drove the level ahead with quiet determination, setting aside what little ore he encountered and sending it up in the kibble. He did not strike it rich, but neither did he do worse than he had as a tutworker. Until he received his share of tribute at the end of the three months' sett, he drew subsistence from the count house and chalked up expenses for his candles, tools and powder. One of the underground captains, Angove, visited him from time to time and commiserated with him over the poor quality of the ore.

'If it don't improve,' he told Welland in confidence, 'the lowest levels of the mine may 'ave to be abandoned. The adventurers won't long agree to pump water for nothing.'

For the time being, Welland worked long hours and the pump continued to suck. Its rods rattled up and down the shaft and its beam bobbed up and down in the slit on the face of the engine house. In the torrid interior, the piston rod rose and fell at the cylinder head with an unvarying gasp and hiss. The engine was mantled with an unforgettable bouquet of mechanical smells: hot oil, dry steam, hot metal, burning furze and sea-coal, sweat, and steaming cloth. On wet evenings, which were frequent, there was a great temptation for the bal maidens to crowd into the doorway, close to the boiler and firebox door. While their numbed hands revived and their soaked clothes tried to dry, the shadows lengthened outdoors and night closed in on the moor. In small groups, they drifted off into the murk and groped their way down the track to Windfall. One evening, a certain bal maiden had remained behind, musing by the fire. Finally, she too nodded goodnight to the stoker who lay sprawled across the coal heap, smoking, and stepped out into the night.

'Is that you?'

She felt an arm across her path as she cleared the doorway and shied backwards in fright.

'Who's there?' she gasped, trying to step back into the

engine house, but a hand had grasped her elbow and was preventing her.

'Don't be afeared, 'tes only I,' continued the voice, and she shrank from the set of palping fingers that landed on her throat and slid over her chin to ride over the ridges of lips, and eyes, and brows, and nose, and cheeks. ' 'Tes Mavis, innit?'

Mavis was stiff with horror. The soft, exploring fingers were like tentacles, stifling her.

'Let me go!' she hissed, and dashed the searching hand aside.

'I didn' mean no 'arm,' said the voice regretfully, and Mavis peered at the shadowy figure beside her. Now that her eyes were becoming accustomed to the gloom, she was able to make out his characteristics. Even before he spoke again, she had guessed his identity. ' 'Tes only I, 'tes only Curnow,' he was muttering.

'How did you know it was me?' she asked, her voice still shrill.

'From the way you d'walk' he explained. 'I jest wanted to get to knaw your face. And I never thanked 'ee proper, now did I? 'Twas your doin' that got me the tallyman's job and I thank 'ee.'

'I need no thanks.'

' 'Appen you don't, but I d'need to give 'em, and I d'want to knaw 'ee better. That's the reason I do need to touch your face – so's I can see un. You won't begrudge me that, now will 'ee?'

Mavis shook her head. It was a moment before she realized the futility of the gesture. Now that she was recovering from the shock of being approached in that manner, she was calming a little.

'Touch my face if you will.'

This time, the blind fingers held none of the terrors they had brought on the earlier occasion. Instead, there was something pathetic about the soft pads that scrutinized her

III

features. But for all her sympathy, there was something disquieting about a blind man's touch.

'No need for to take on so,' Curnow was murmuring reassuringly, 'a blind man can't 'urt 'ee. 'Tes a strong face you 'ave, me 'andsome. It did take someone strong to stand up to Mr Bolitho – 'Tes a pretty one too, I remembers 'ee from when you was naught but a li'l maid, prettiest in Windfall. What I can't unnerstand is why you 'aven't been snapped up by one o' they young fellers. A fine upstandin' maid like you could 'ave the 'usband she wanted for the askin'.'

'I shall never marry.'

'What kind o' talk is that? There isn' no better state for a young person – or an old one for that matter. What can be a-troublin' 'ee?' Curnow was holding both her hands firmly. She was no longer afraid. When she shivered, it was the cold night breeze that caused it. 'I knaw what 'tes,' he continued earnestly, ' 'tes that mother o' yourn, and that feyther you 'ad. 'Tiddn' no good, 'tiddn' right to believe man 'n' wife do 'ave to live in discord, not like that. You wasn't lucky, Mavis, and that's for sure: Garfield Trerice were a waster and your mother, 'Ilda, she never knawed 'ow to manage un. That Garfield, God rest 'is soul, you couldn' drive un, though 'e might be led. She never saw that there were a good side to Garfield, even if 'e did drink more'n were good for un.'

'That's as may be, but you're not going to change matters by keeping me here talking in the cold all night.'

'I'm sorry, Mavis, poor maid, you're wet leakin', I never did think to it. Comeason 'omealong, you shall sit by the fire a bit, dry out and take comfort. My Ellen will be terrible pleased to see 'ee.'

'I'll walk you back to Windfall, and pleased to, but I shan't stop. Mother'll be waiting. She sets to worrying when I'm not home by nightfall.'

The two of them set off along the track and Mavis was

astonished how confident Curnow had become; he hardly ever needed to tap with his stick. Indeed, in the darkness, he was just as surefooted as she was, until he came to loose rock on the road and stumbled. Mavis caught his arm to steady him.

'Pride goes before a fall,' he murmured ruefully. 'I were doin' ever so nicely. But I mustn' complain. The Lord 'ave dealt kindly with me and I do thank un for it. I've been better served than poor Welland 'Alt.'

'Why, what's his trouble?' Her voice sounded detached, uninterested.

'Too blamed stubborn, that's what Welland is. Too pig-headed to know when he's beat. I've been watchin' the kibbles 'e's been sendin' up to grass, there 'aven't been enough ore these past weeks to give tribute to feed a cat, much less pay rent, 'n candles, 'n' food for a man 'n' is growin' daughter.'

'What're you telling me all this for? You must have a reason.'

'Well, I remembered as 'ow 'twas you what 'elped un when 'e first comed to Windfall, and I thought, if you spoke – if you tried to persuade un to go back to tutwork, 'e might –'

' – listen to me when he won't heed what his best friend's been telling him, is that it? Well, don't count on me to do it. I don't like the way he looks at me. He's forever staring.'

'For young Ruth's sake, won't you give it a try? Poor li'l maid, she don't deserve the 'ard times she'll 'ave the way 'e's 'eadin'.'

'Here's your house,' she told him, 'your Ellen must be waiting. Why doesn't she try to persuade him?'

'She 'ave already, don't think she 'aven't, but to no good. No, Mavis, I d'knaw you'd be different. Say you'll try, for the maid's sake.'

'I'll think about it,' said Mavis doubtfully. Curnow listened to her departing footfalls with a dejected feeling.

'What a pity, Ellen, that young Mavis d'ave to waste 'er life carin' for that mischievous old mother o' hern,' he murmured as he crossed the threshold.

'You'd not change 'er, 'owever much you 'ad a mind to,' said his wife resignedly as she took his coat and pushed him towards the chimney corner. 'She's doin' the wrong thing for the right reason. 'Twill do no good to argue with 'er. Takes after 'er mother. Sit you down and eat your supper. No good'll come of meddlin' between mother an' daughter.'

Another setting day came round. Welland bid for the same pitch. Mr Bolitho was surprised; he would readily have seen him obtain a more productive one or go back on contract, but Welland didn't try. The man had his reasons, no doubt, and mistrust of his fellow miners was probably one of them. It was all too easy for an accident to happen, particularly if a man's partners took no care of him.

Curnow stood listening to the auction from his post beside the kibble landers. When Welland passed close after buying another string of candles on account from the store, he called out to him.

'Wouldn't listen to good advice then?'

'I won't be beat – I must give it a fair whack.'

'Well, if you must go on, call in and see me on the way 'ome; I've a thing or two to tell 'ee.'

From that day on, Welland would often stop at Curnow's house and talk in the evenings. Curnow was a clever tinner and knew all about different ores, though he had not one iota of book learning. It amazed Welland how easily the blind man understood his inadequate descriptions of the mineral traces he found after each explosion. He learnt how to identify arsenic, lead, wolfram, and tin. Curnow would turn a rock sample in his soft white hands, palping it while Welland gave him the colours. He would scratch it with his knife and tell Welland to describe the mark. Welland marvelled at the way he could predict which way the lode would trend and what it would contain. He felt humble at the revelation of a craft whose complexity he had never suspected. But, for all his new learning, the lodes stayed small and fickle.

After his lesson, Welland would hurry home to Ruth and they would have supper at their plain table. The early days of the tribute work had brought in enough money for better food, a new dress for his daughter, and more books from the packman who brought them specially once he discovered the market. They lived in their own small world. Windfall ignored them and they ignored Windfall. Apart from solitary walks, Ruth followed the lodes in her books. Her father spent his evenings conversing with her in their cramped cottage, emerging each dawn to pursue the streaks of metal in the mine.

But there was less and less colour in the rocks. He hewed the granite for nothing and was not even earning enough to pay for his tools and candles. One night his frustration burst forth.

'What's that, another book? Can't you see we're having bad times? What's the use of buying new novels when we can't buy bread?' Instantly he regretted it.

'I thought you liked me reading,' she sobbed. He held her close and tried to comfort her.

The daily descent into the mine became ever more dreary. The hopelessness of hewing unrewarding rock obsessed him and he had to fight the urge to approach Mr Bolitho and beg to be put on tutwork. A glimmer of hope revived each time he lit the fuse of a charge, but he was increasingly disappointed. Finally, be broke through out of the granite into a bed of killas, red and grey shale, crumpled and fused where it met the igneous rock. That night, he sat beside Curnow's hearth and showed him samples. Curnow interrogated him closely concerning the dip of the junction plane between the two rocks. Then he sat and thought, with his hands cupped over his eyes as if to see better in his imagination.

'Bear off to the right,' he advised after a long pause. 'Give over drivin' into that killas, there never was colour in killas, leastways not far. Never mind what Cap'n Angove'll say 'bout the change in direction. That cap'n don't knaw nothin'.'

The underground captain didn't often visit Welland. Nowadays, he occasionally came and stared pityingly at the small heap of ore Welland had been able to extract. As far as Angove was concerned, things were going well enough for the mine. The level was being pushed ahead quickly and soon it would be possible to drop a winze from the two-hundred-and-eighty-fathom level and use it to bring out ore from a productive seam there. He wanted Welland to cut another ten fathoms and had called to talk about it just before he had reached the killas.

'I'll recommend renewing your pitch at nineteen shillings,' he had told him confidentially. What he didn't say was that he would equally readily recommend putting the work out to contract, so unrewarding was the lode. It didn't seem necessary to point out the latter aspect; it must be obvious to even the greenest of furriners.

Next day, Welland debated whether to follow Curnow's advice and change direction. He might as well give it a try, though it would provoke the captain's displeasure if he happened to come by. It would involve setting off a couple of small charges to the side of the tunnel. After arriving at the face, he crouched on his haunches and nibbled his hoggan while he considered the question. A large crumb fell into a puddle at his feet. Well, he thought, the knackers will have their share; they ought to be on my side this time anyway.

When he fired the first charge, it brought down a slithering mass of killas that took hours to shovel way. And there was still no colour in the rock to indicate a lode. Half his core was over when he began to drive the boryer into the edge of the granite for the second charge. He was down to his last candle by the time he tamped the powder into the hole and laid the fuse.

The dust was slow to clear after the explosion. There was

absolutely no ventilation at the end of the tunnel and the mixture of gas and pulverized rock eddied about, diffusing slowly towards him. He was impatient to see the result and get on home. Not that he was at all optimistic. He had the feeling that his time as a tributer was drawing to a close. The optimism he had felt in the early days had all evaporated. He was reluctant to stir up further animosity by underbidding for another pitch at the setting and was resigned to returning to tutwork. Coughing and spitting, with smarting eyes, he broke through to the scree of loose stones and stuffed a few samples into his pockets. The fog was still too thick to see them.

The shortness of his candle stub had showed him how far the day was wearing on. He stacked his tools in a corner and hurrried off towards the shaft. If the candle gave out before he got there, he might stun himself on a projection from the roof. The level was only roughly hewn out of the rock and took the form left by the successive explosions with only indifferent attempts to straighten and smooth it. His feet splashed in the reddish stream that ran back towards the pump and heavy drops fell on his hat, making the candle flame gutter.

It was a relief to feel the wood of the first ladder and see the pin-hole of light at ground level. If his candle flame died now it did not matter, he could climb the ladders in the dark. Constant practice had taught him every step of the long climb. He knew instinctively which of the rungs were suspect and which had already broken away. The enlarging shaft mouth was no longer bright and he suspected that evening was coming on. Apart from the pump-rods' clack, there was no activity in the shaft. The levels were deserted and the kibbles were no longer rattling up and down. So much the better: a man might easily be killed by a stone spilling from an over-full kibble.

Curnow had already gone home. The count house doors were shut, but the stamps were still making an infernal racket, tended by a night core of men and boys. Bolitho must be anxious to get a shipment off to the assay office. A whiff of arsenical vapours drifted across from the burning house and made him cough. The road home was sombre and cold under a bloodstained sky. Welland shivered: the night breeze was icy after the heat of the three-hundred-fathom level and the exertion of his climb.

Ruth was waiting for him in the lee of the count house wall. He was pleased to see her, inordinately pleased, but he scolded her none the less.

'Didn't I tell you not to stay out after dark? Didn't I tell you always to go home with the bal maidens?'

'You were late,' she told him. 'I was worrried. It was too hard to sit at home waiting. You weren't at the Curnows' so I came here.'

'Hard to sit at home waiting? 'Tis harder to stay down there working – working for nothing. 'Tis a poor look out for both of us the way things are going. The lode's worked out and now I shall have to – ' He broke off suddenly and bit his lip in annoyance. 'Come on, girl, we must be making tracks, I'm starving.' As they walked, he blamed himself for having had an unguarded tongue. He was sure Tom Magor had been listening in the forge doorway. It went against the grain to disclose his feelings of defeat to the blacksmith.

Once home, he felt better. Ruth had a stew simmering on the hob and the gorse sticks she threw on the fire soon had the flames and shadows dancing. She told him about the wild flowers she had picked on Carnwartha while she was foraging for firewood. There was a bunch of them in a mug on the table.

'What're those?'

'Those are companions, and that's loosestrife. That's a bog orchid, and that one's special, it's a sundew.'

It puzzled Welland how she could know their names and characteristics: there wasn't a book in the house that described them that he knew of. Who could be identifying them for her? He studied her grave young face as she set their bowls and spoons upon the table and cut two hunks from the loaf. That was the last he could pay for. Where would the next one come from? In a few days, there would no longer be any question of worrying about who she might meet on the moor; Ruth would be up the mine, working with the bal maidens, not learning things above her station. She lifted his jacket off the chair where he had discarded it.

'What's in your pockets?'

'Only old stones,' he told her.

'Stones?'

'Samples from the last blasting.'

She reached in and drew one out, holding it close to the candle in the centre of the table.

'How pretty!' she exclaimed, 'it's all crystals, ever so shiny. Why's it so heavy!'

Her father limped across, curious now that he was reminded of the samples. He took the piece and turned it slowly. The crystals were bright gold, a colour he had never seen before. And it was heavy, heavier than any other stone he had come upon since he became a tributer. Intrigued, he pulled out the other samples and ranged them across the table. More than half of them were unlike anything else he had dug from the granite or the killas.

Ruth was ladling out his stew, but he stopped her. He was hurriedly stuffing the samples back into his pockets. She looked up in alarm as he made for the door.

'You haven't eaten!'

' 'Twill wait. I must show this lot to Curnow.'

He felt himself gripped by the tinner's fever, the excitement of a discovery that would change his fortune. His lameness annoyed him now; he wished he could run to Curnow's cottage, but had to limp with frustrating slowness. He knew he was probably making a fool of himself, but could not resist it. He had to know what Curnow would say about the strange ore he had discovered.

'Fools' gold,' sniffed Curnow when he had the first sample in his hand and heard Welland describe it.·

' 'Tis worthless then?' asked Welland, crestfallen.

' 'Tes iron pyrites, 'tiddin' worth nothin',' he paused a moment, 'but 'tes 'eavy, terrible 'eavy.' Curnow handled the stone patiently, rubbing a finger across it and touching the tip to his lips. 'Where's the knife, Ellen?' he called to his wife who was putting the younger children to bed, crammed in like piglets on the rough pallets. She passed it to him and he scraped at the crystal facets.

' 'Tis terrible 'eavy,' he muttered, 'terrible 'eavy. Tell us, Welland, the gold of these 'ere crystals, is it whitish or yellow like butter?'

'Yellow like butter.'

'And can you see a mark where I've scratched un?'

'There's a bit of a scratch.'

Curnow sat silent. The firelight played on his cheeks and brows, leaving the hollows of his sightless eyes in shadow. After a while, he nodded his head slowly.

'What day's settin' day?'

'Two days hence.'

Curnow reached back and gave him the sample.

'Will you take a piece of advice from an old tinner? – Get down to your pitch afore the cap'n comes by and tidy away all this trade. If there's much more colour like this, put it in the back o' the hole and cover it with granite. Don't go no further till you've made your bid for the pitch. Offer the same as usual.'

'But I can't. I can't afford to. I'm losing money. I have to go back to tutwork. I've Ruth to feed. You've been telling me yourself that I ought to.'

'You'll both feed better if you do as I tell 'ee'.

Welland stood up wearily. It had taken him long enough to admit to himself that he was a failure at tribute. He didn't need this complication, this last-minute decision. Oh, he understood perfectly well what Curnow was telling him to do. The tinners were always up to tricks like that. It was part of a game they played, a battle of wits with the captains and purser.

'Well, if this isn't tin, what's the point?'

'No 'tiddn' tin –' Curnow kept him waiting again as he scratched his head through his thin hair. 'No, 'tiddn' tin – but it might be copper.'

Welland slept ill that night. In his dreams, he was hacking away at the rock of a lode that would not yield or splinter. There was something in there that he had to dig out swiftly. Someone was coming soon and would stop him if he didn't succeed in breaking through the smooth glassy surface. He heard Captain Angove's footfalls approaching and burst into a cold sweat.

It was Ruth climbing down the ladder from her loft, preparing to pack up his croust and fill his bottle with water. He lay still under the blanket, letting the tension ebb out of his body before he got up. It was still dark outside, but the cocks were crowing. Soon, he was hastening to the mine.

While he worked alone that day, he kept thinking of Ruth. He imagined her sitting in the window, reading her latest book, *Castle Rackrent*, and smiling to herself as she turned the page. He saw her skipping along the moorland paths with her kerchief streaming behind her and her cheeks glowing. He had brought her this far, and she seemed to be happy. Did he have the right to gamble with her future, put at risk the small portion of security he had won in Windfall? He dug mechanically, piling up the killas into the hollow left by yesterday's blasting. In the afternoon, deciding to neglect Curnow's advice and drive straight ahead on the assumption that he would return to tutwork, he set off another charge.

The underground captain surprised him, coming up while his ears were still deafened by the explosion. They sat together and shared pieces of Welland's pasty while the dust subsided. Welland was uneasy. He felt uncomfortable about having concealed the colour from the lode. He liked Angove well enough, he wasn't a slave driver, but he wished he would go away.

Finally, the captain stood up, visibly hesitating whether to take a look at the end of the tunnel before going up to grass. There was still a lot of dust in the air.

'May as well look now I'm here,' he decided. 'You've made good progress. Pity it 'aven't paid you better.' They advanced together towards the place where the shot had gone off, the captain leading, fanning the air in front of him with his hand. 'Why didn't you tell me?' he demanded, stopping abruptly a few feet short of the face.

'Tell you what?' asked Welland, feeling guilty.

'You've broke into the killas, haven't you? – You've lost whatever lode there was for certain.' He stumbled back, coughing, into the cleared air in the level. 'If you take my advice, tomorrow, you'll go back to tutwork. As like as not, Mr Bolitho will agree to it and you'll get a proper reward for your labour.'

Next morning, Welland stood among the tinners, waiting for Hector Bolitho to appear on the platform at the top of the count house steps. He was tense, still undecided, almost desperate. The various possibilities were milling around in his head. He could chance a desperate throw and underbid one of the pares working the rich Windfall lode. If he worked it alone instead of in a pare of six men, it ought to be profitable even if he took a tribute of only three shillings. But he would have to work desperately hard to equal the output of a six-man pare. Mr Bolitho wouldn't be satisfied if there was a drop in output. He might not even accept the bid in the first place. On the other hand, he could take the sensible course and abandon tribute altogether, return to tutwork and a living wage. He was in debt to the mine for candles and subsistence, but not so much that he couldn't work it off, given enough time.

The last possibility was insane. He knew it was madness to bid for the next pitch in the three-hundred-fathom level. He had worked it out: there was no more tin. Ahead there was nothing more than barren killas. He had lain awake mulling over what Curnow had told him about the sample and more than half believed that it was copper, but that was wishful thinking. There was no copper in Wheal Fortune, never had been. There had been traces, of course, like the one he had found yesterday after Angove's departure, but they were all short-lived pockets and lodes that thinned to nothing in a few feet. Wheal Fortune was a tin mine, was and always would be.

Welland was so wrapped up in his thoughts that he failed to notice Hector Bolitho's arrival on the platform and the start of the setting. At first, even the purser's voice calling his name failed to rouse him. He shook his head like an animal rising from sleep and saw Bolitho leaning over the count house balustrade, wagging a finger at him.

'We'll not fill our pockets by dreaming, will we, Mr Halt?'

Welland became aware that he was almost alone on the patch of grass. Most of the tinners must have bid for their pitches and gone off to the mine. Only a few remained: ragged, desperate men like himself, the unwanted, the weak, the unlucky, and even these had no wish or didn't dare to make up a pare with Welland Halt.

'Welland Halt's pitch, to be carried eastward –' The clerk was reading out the description of the next pitch, extending into the killas from the end of the three-hundred-fathom level. Welland didn't know whether to laugh or cry. Farrow's dry voice told nothing of the barren uselessness of it all, it was nothing but a string of words from the book to him.

'Well, will you take it?' Bolitho was insisting.

Welland shook his head slowly. There was a long pause and Bolitho looked to the underground captain for advice. No words passed, but he understood Angove's deprecatory expression. It was barren ground.

'How about nineteen and six? I can't go better than that, can I?' Welland nodded and, before he could say anything further, a tossed pebble soared in the air. He wanted to say that he wasn't interested, even at that price. His mouth opened, but no words came. The pebble bounced on the turf. Mr Bolitho's eyes glinted behind his spectacles. He would never get a level cut that cheap on tutwork. It was a pity to see a man sinking into debt, but it was a purser's job to drive the best bargain he could in the name of the adventurers.

Heavy footed, numbed by the realization of what he had allowed to happen to him. Welland trudged to the shaft. Ahead of him was the three-hundred-fathom descent, the long stooping walk down the steamy level, and the fruitless hewing of the rock. Not just today, but every day until the next setting, and for what? A pittance of ore, if he was lucky.

'I hope to God you're right,' he called to Curnow who was at his post with his boy at his side among the kibble landers.

'Nothin' ventured, nothin' won,' replied his friend. 'A man 'as to knaw when to take 'is chances.'

As he climbed down the ladders, Welland saw the gleam of the fools' gold in the light of Curnow's fire and laughed at his folly. There was fools' gold aplenty at the back of the hole he had blasted and refilled with rubble. A broad pastel green seam liberally flecked with the gilded crystals filled the discontinuity between granite and killas. It was invisible now, hidden by the heaped-up rubble and he had determined to leave it that way. It was a will-o'-the-wisp, and a fool's errand to seek it.

What was the use of a blind prospector's advice? Curnow would have said anything to encourage him. If it hadn't been for Curnow's opinion of the ore, he would have declared roundly that he would only drive the level on contract. But he had allowed an absurd gambler's optimism to weaken his resolve. Both he and Ruth were hungry already: they would grow hungrier.

Close to the face where his tools were stacked, he saw a lump with the glint of fools' gold shining up at him. Angrily, he kicked it aside and set to work with grim determination. He vented his anger on the boryer, beating it with the heavy hammer as if beating his own brain, until its head was splayed and bent over. The hammer's clang resounded off the rocks like rolling artillery in some desperate battle that was lost before it was begun.

7

THE COUNT HOUSE

'Come on boys! Is that the last of the porter?'

Mr Farrow was checking off the supplies as they left the carter's wagon. Each time he ticked an item, he touched his pencil tip to his tongue in an unconscious gesture.

'That's four dozen we've stowed in the cellar,' said the man from the blowing house who was helping the carter with the unloading.

'Now for the brandy, there ought to be a keg there, four gallons.'

Farrow waited while the man poked around among the other merchandise until the carter laid his hand on the keg impatiently and began lugging it towards the tailboard.

'Step lively, Trevorrow,' snapped Farrow. The man from the blowing house was taking his time and the clerk knew why: he was in no hurrry to return to his usual occupation. Smelting the ore ready for shipment was hot work at best and, at worst, dangerous. A whiff of the fumes would send a man coughing and choking out of the blowing house in search of air worth breathing. Farrow didn't really blame Trevorrow for dragging out this diversion, but he sensed that Mr Bolitho would be watching them all reprovingly from the count house window just behind him. 'We can't afford to be still at it when the toffs start arriving.'

Trevorrow and the carter shuffled sideways through the low doorway into the count house cellar, making a great show of struggling with their burden. The cellar had been cleared out the day before and its contents, partly refined ores of tin and copper, were set out in heaps along one side of the building, ready for shipment.

'Why weren't you here yesterday?' he demanded of the carter as the latter emerged, wiping his forehead with a handkerchief.

'Lost a wheel at Tregurney!' the carter complained. 'What you d'call roads round 'ere aren't fit fer Christian commerce. I shall be glad when I'm safely out of it. There's the rum and some gin still left to unload, if I'm not mistaken.'

'You're right about the roads, they're disgraceful in all conscience.'

Both men looked up in surprise at the speaker, a horseman who had ridden up quietly over the soft turf. He was sitting easily on a tall horse that had something of a thoroughbred to him. The broad blue lapels of the rider's coat proclaimed him a gentleman.

'Zackly so, Mr Gurney,' agreed the carter, doffing his cap, 'but I meant no disrespect for Tregurney.'

'No need to apologize for speaking the plain truth,' said Gurney, patting his horse's neck reassuringly. The animal was made restive by the nearby engines. 'If only more people had listened to John McAdam years back we'd have proper roads and Cornwall would be a civilized country.' He dismounted lightly.

'You there, Trevorrow,' the clerk called to the workman whose face appeared sheepishly in the doorway, 'get hold of Mr Gurney's hoss and take him across to the stable. See he gets oats aplenty. Shall I inform Mr Bolitho you're here, Mr Gurney?'

But Gurney wasn't listening. He had already walked away towards the stamps and the other engines. Farrow hastened to complete the unloading and paid the carter.

'Looks like this'll be an account day to remember, from the amount of liquor you've ordered,' said the latter, pocketing the money. 'The adventurers'll be pleased as Punch with their shares in Wheal Fortune. Never in my born days 'ave I seed so much copper,' he gestured towards the ore piled up beside the count house, 'and I've seen plenty. And to think, if it 'adn' been for one man's persistence – But there's no knowin' the ways of the Almighty. Good day to you.'

Farrow hurried up the steps into the count house. Its interior had been changed out of all recognition. Stiff white linen cloths covered the long central table. A trestle sideboard was laden with wine, walnuts, cheese and other provisions. The table itself was laid with the Wheal Fortune plate, fashioned of purest tin, emblazoned with the Gurney arms and recently burnished so it shone like silver. Two Windfall women were doing the rounds, putting a final shine on the crystal goblets with their dusters.

'Are we ready to receive company yet, Mr Farrow?' asked Hector Bolitho, bustling towards him from the desk where he had been leafing through the cost books, memorizing details.

'We've drink enough for a regiment, if that's the yardstick.'

'It would've been a poor account dinner without it,' said Bolitho drily. 'I've never known the adventurers to stint themselves in that direction and today's meal is by way of being a celebration.' He leant close to his clerk and murmured, 'And be sure to see that Wyatt Kitto's glass never gets empty. That's a recommendation from you-know-who.' He jerked his head towards the engine house in explanation.

As he did so, he saw that the other adventurers were already arriving. Two had just dismounted. One was Wearne, an ironmonger from Liskeard who was a small investor. The other was Kitto, a florid-faced, mutton-chop-whiskered shipowner.

'Is it true what they say about Kitto?' asked Farrow. 'Was he really a blackbirder?'

'Ask him yourself,' replied Bolitho, 'but be sure he's well-oiled and smiling. You could injure your health, if you cross him.'

More adventurers rode up and dismounted. Trevorrow,

who had appointed himself ostler, led their mounts off to the stables. There was a bulky, red-nosed clergyman on a hunter: Rector Adams from Tregurney. A sedate, high-collared banker called Rowe looked out of place in his well-cut, dark worsted. These, and a few late arrivals, formed a series of small groups beside the ore heaps, picking up samples and looking knowledgeable.

'There's thousands here, thousands,' said Wearne, 'never thought to see the like of it, never.'

'Wheal Fortune's always paid off our investments very well with tin,' said banker Rose, 'but now copper – that'll be gilt on the gingerbread.'

'All very fine if Silverton Gurney do let us taste it!' said Wyatt Kitto, sourly kicking a lump of ore from the nearest heap. 'If he don't fritter the profit away on his damned inventions.'

'Good afternoon, gentlemen!' called Bolitho from the top of the steps where he emerged quickly, anxious to put a damper on such discussion. 'You'll be wearied with travel, I expect, and in need of a little refreshment. If you'll step this way, we'll do our best to accommodate you. And the books are here. The books are open.'

Within a minute or so, the banker had his nose buried in the books, with Wyatt Kitto looking over his shoulder. The rest of the company were strolling about chatting, while Farrow and the two women helped them to wine and porter brought up through a hatch from the cellar.

'I say, Bolitho, didn't I see Curnow at work by the shaft?' asked Rector Adams in his booming voice. 'Wasn't he the one who was blinded?'

'That's so; he serves as tallyman – I know what you're getting at – his boy does the checking. But you needn't lose any sleep; I'm not paying twice for the one job, I'm paying the father.'

'Smells very like paternalism to me. It's too easy to be generous with the adventurers' money.'

'I'm one myself,' Bolitho reminded him. 'Curnow has a wife and family. They'd be a burden on the parish.'

While Bolitho was speaking, one of the serving women stepped forward and poured port into the glass Rector Adams was holding, topping it up until it ran over and stained his white breeches.

'Goddamit, woman!' he cried, with a threatening gesture that spilled even more wine on his cuff. 'Are you blind or something?'

The woman made no reply, but took her napkin and began rubbing the stain into the fabric. Bolitho put a handkerchief to his mouth and turned away to hide his smile of amusement. Perhaps it had been a mistake to pick Mavis Trerice as one of the servers, but she was the most presentable of the bal maidens and, if the truth were told, looked distinctly handsome in her starched cap and apron. If the Rector knew of her role in Curnow's appointment, he would be doubly furious. Bolitho hoped she knew enough diplomacy to hold her tongue on the subject.

'So, gentlemen, are we all here? I hope Hector's seen to it that you're well provided for.' Silverton Gurney spoke from the doorway where he had appeared unnoticed while attention was focused on the Rector.

'Welcome to Wheal Fortune.' He reached for a glass. 'I give you the Cornish toast: Fish, Tin, and Copper!'

'Fish, Tin, and Copper!' echoed the adventurers raggedly. For the most part, they drained their glasses.

'Fellow adventurers,' Silverton Gurney continued, 'we meet in auspicious circumstances. The new lode, exceptionally rich in copper, has already justified the cost of driving the adit. But that's not all: the tributers are all swept away with the excitement, they're all digging like badgers. Wheal Fortune's on the brink of a new era. I think we can sit down to our account dinner with considerable satisfaction. I hope everything's to your liking.'

'These accounts are encouraging, most encouraging,' remarked the banker, slipping his glasses into his waistcoat pocket, 'we're starting to see a healthy return on our investment.'

'Healthy return be damned!' blurted out Wyatt Kitto. 'Begging your pardon, Mr Rowe. What about all that ore outside? What about all that copper? What I want to know, Mr Gurney, is this: when're we going to see the money – No, no, don't answer just yet, let me 'ave my say. Now hark to this: the word's got about that all the good money that comes o' that copper is to be wasted on engines and such. Now there's more'n one of us here that would like to voice an opinion. We'd prefer to see it in our pockets.'

'Mr Kitto,' said Silverton Gurney smoothly, 'I can assure you the money won't be wasted. But this isn't the time to be backbiting. It's time to get down to serious business. I've just been to the engine house to inspect the roast and it's good and ready. They're bringing it over – If you'd be so kind as to be seated, we'll see if our stokers are as good at roasting as they are at steam-raising.'

As the adventurers shuffled to their seats, the roast was brought in: a huge round of beef, still smoking on a massive tin platter. The Rector sniffed appreciatively and tucked his napkin into his collar. Mr Farrow contrived to insert himself between Kitto and the banker, intercepting the former's muttered complaint as he did so: 'If he thinks he's heard the last of the question, he's mistaken.'

If Silverton Gurney heard, he showed no sign of it, but turned back his lace cuffs and began carving. The serving maids went round with the plates while Bolitho tipped the wink to Farrow to pour liquor for all in reach of him.

'What's the name of the cove to whom we're indebted for our new good fortune?' asked one of the half-dozen petty adventurers who had remained silent up to that time. 'I 'ear 'e's no tinner at all, but 'ave come from up the country.'

'You've heard right, Mr Poldark,' replied Bolitho. 'Welland Halt's not Cornish. To tell the truth, I don't know much about him. He's not over-talkative. Keeps himself to himself, perforce to some extent; the tinners have never taken to him. Now that he's·doing well, they have added reason to give him the cold shoulder, they envy him. Maybe you saw the new house he's been building when you were on the way here.'

'Didn't I notice that you were paying out nineteen and six tribute on the ore he's been winning?' inquired banker Rowe innocently.

'Trust a man of your profession to sniff that out!' Bolitho laughed. 'But not for long, I promise you. Next setting day, he'll be down to something more modest. All I ask you to do is think, Mr Rowe, think of the incentive to the other miners when one of their number picks up a windfall of this nature. Nothing you could imagine would make them work harder. Welland Halt's prosperity is worth a mint to Wheal Fortune. I propose a toast to him: to Welland Halt, gentlemen!'

'Welland Halt!'

Glasses clinked all round the table. Farrow was quick with the bottle.

'I propose we call the new lode after him,' said Poldark, 'a miner can do with a memorial.'

'I second that,' said Silverton Gurney. 'To the Welland Lode, gentlemen, fellow adventurers, may it run forever!' Soon the table was a-buzz with minor conversation and the champing of jaws. The serving women were kept hard at it, fetching drink from the cellars and recharging platters. Like other count house dinners, this one stretched out into the late afternoon. When Silverton Gurney considered the adventurers were sufficiently mellow he passed round the cigars and tobacco. Bolitho signed to the women to pour more brandy. Silverton Gurney rose to speak, supporting himself on a straight left arm posed upon the table.

'Look out of the windows, gentlemen. What do you see? – Mules and donkeys, and why are they here now? We all know that: they've come to carry off our ore to the smelter. Well, it's a disgrace, gentlemen, and a slight on Cornwall that we haven't the roads to take wheeled traffic. But that's going to change, gentlemen, take my word for it, just as Wheal Fortune's going to change, adopt new machinery, become more productive. Take the bal maidens over there, what could be more archaic than hand spalling? This time next year, they'll be gone for ever. Steam will take over – and do the job better.'

'And what's to become of the maidens, Mr Gurney? What's to become of the boys at the buddles?' The woman's voice took them all by surprise and the adventurers at the foot of the table craned round to see her.

'And what concern, pray, is it of yours?' answered Silverton Gurney in his smoothest voice. Bolitho felt uncomfortable: there was trouble in store for him that evening when they got home to Tregurney.

'I'm a bal maiden myself.'

'What's your name, young woman?'

'Mavis Trerice. All my friends are bal maidens. Who's to earn the money when the mine's gone mechanical?'

Silverton Gurney hesitated a moment.

'Why, the tinners – the tinners will earn it in higher wages.'

'Pigs might fly!'

'You're a saucy piece. But I'll try to forgive you: I know I can't expect a woman to comprehend the principles of economy.'

'A woman can understand hungry faces at a cold hearth.'

'I'll see to it the men earn enough for their families,' said Gurney peevishly. This woman was beginning to annoy him.

'And if a bal maiden's a spinster, what's to be her income?'

Silverton Gurney looked her over, noting the absence of rings on her fingers. He smiled inwardly.

'She should make haste and marry – if she's as handsome as you are, she'll have no trouble. To be serious, I won't be browbeaten on this. There's no argument on earth that can justify the continued employment of young women and children in the mines. It's uncivilized and the sooner it's done away with the better.'

'Done away with, Mr Gurney?' Wyatt Kitto had risen to his feet and was rocking unsteadily. 'And who's to replace 'em?'

'Why, machines, Mr Kitto, machines are the bill of release for the slaves of the nineteenth century!'

'And who's to pay for these machines, Mr Gurney?'

'They'll pay for themselves with profits.'

'What you mean is, your fellow adventurers will put up the capital by forfeiting their fair share of the profits. There's more'n one of us here –' Kitto paused and looked round his end of the table, expecting support. It came in the form of nods, but timidly. 'More'n one of us here who's sick and tired to death with all the money going for hare-brained inventions: steam this, steam that, and steam the other! We've had all we can stand, we won't stand it!' and he banged on the table with his clenched fist, making the glasses tremble.

'You have one ally, you'll observe, Miss Trerice, who will help you stand in the way of progress. Perhaps you know Mr Kitto's expedients for furnishing cheap labour.' Silverton Gurney was at his most restrained, his most insidious best. He turned to Wyatt Kitto. 'Since you're so disaffected, Mr Kitto, may I inquire of you what you plan to do about it?'

'Why, take a vote on the matter, o' course. We're all equal, we're all adventurers. I'm damned if we'll pay for your steam notions.'

'Is that so, Kitto?' Silverton Gurney surveyed their faces as he spoke. There was certainly support for Kitto's proposition; not many men would prefer to put off the day when the pounds reached their pockets. Poldark for one was restive; he was always skint. Gurney watched him out of the corner of his eye as he continued. 'I hope you're familiar with Wheal Fortune's articles of association? You'll have read them when you were thinking about investing, won't you, Mr Kitto? You'll recall that voting is not *per capita*, but *per partes*, according to our share holdings, Mr Kitto. You are, I believe, proficient at simple arithmetic.'

'That's lawyer's talk,' exploded Kitto, 'it's piracy!'

'You're the best judge of that, Mr Kitto. All I can do is advise you, if you're dissatisfied with your shares in Wheal Fortune, to visit my solicitor in Liskeard who'll relieve you of them at their face value as is provided for in the articles.' He paused and scanned all the adventurers' faces. 'And that goes for anyone who thinks that Wheal Fortune's a bad investment. Now, sit you down, Kitto, and enjoy your dinner. Pay yourself in beef, pay yourself in brandy, take all you can carry away with you.'

For a moment it looked as though Kitto might rush down the room and strike Gurney, but he deflated and subsided into his chair, still scowling. The dinner broke up not long after. Several of the adventurers had to be helped into the saddle. They lurched off through the yard which was still crowded with pack animals. Gurney waved them goodbye from the steps and lingered to speak with Bolitho.

'By God, I near lost my temper with that Kitto fellow,' he confided, sinking the last of his brandy. 'D'you think he'll sell out?'

'It doesn't matter much either way, you'll do as you please, Silverton. You always contrive to.'

'When'm I going to get a look at this Welland of yours? He intrigues me.'

'You'll have to hang about a lot later than this to catch him. He's working the lode like a madman, winning all he can before setting day. But you'll see his new house while leaving; it's up on the right before you come to the church. Our Welland doesn't do things by halves: he's had it built of ashlar masonry. It must be about finished.'

Silverton Gurney was barely listening. Another idea had occurred to him. He walked the length of the room to where Mavis Trerice was passing down dead bottles to her companion in the cellar. She stopped in mid-gesture and faced him.

'It's the sack, I suppose. Well, I'm ready,' she greeted him. Silverton smiled wryly. 'I understand your arguments well enough,' she added, 'thank you, and you're right about some things, but I mistrust your motives.'

'What is it they say about the rich man and the eye of the needle, Miss Trerice? You make the eye damned small for me. Perhaps you'd prefer to deal with Wyatt Kitto. He'd keep you at work, all of you – for a pittance.'

'I've said my piece, Mr Gurney. I don't think I'll sway you. You're too high and mighty to think things through and see the results for common people.' She stopped and there was a long silence. 'Well, I've blotted my copy-book this time for sure, haven't I?' She wiped her hands on her apron. 'No use going on, is there? But I'll expect my wages.'

Silverton Gurney raised a hand and stopped her.

'I like a woman of spirit, Mavis Trerice. You're a handsome creature when you're angry.' Mavis flushed and her eyes wavered. 'Let's hear no more of your leaving. There will be a place for you at Wheal Fortune while I'm in charge here. Another thing, if ever I can be of service to you, you know where to find me.'

He bowed slightly and left her. The woman below stairs waited until his footsteps had receded the full length of the building before she whispered, 'You've made a touch there, my lover, fer certain.'

'If so, more's the pity,' murmured Mavis. ' 'Tis none of my seeking.'

In the golden evening light, Welland and Ruth went arm in arm to inspect his new property. The house stood a little apart from the rest, on the first slope of Carnwartha. The sharpness of its rectangular outline contrasted with the dumpy tinners' cottages with their dishevelled thatch. Here all was order: row upon row of regimented slates, two upstanding chimneys, dressed granite walls, dripstones, sills and lintels.

'Well, what do you think?' Welland paused a few yards off and smiled at his daughter.

'It's lovely, ever so handsome, very like the place we –' She stopped in mid-sentence, silenced by his frown.

'I hope you haven't –'

'No, Father, believe me, I've told no one.'

'You know, if you did, all this would be wasted.'

'Of course I do.' She pressed his arm. 'Now show it to me. I've been very good, I've kept away so you could surprise me.'

'Open the door then. Here's the key.'

She turned the key in the stiff new lock. There was a smell of fresh plaster. She found herself in a hallway with stairs ahead of her and rooms opening off to right and left. The recently planed floorboards were tangy and firm underfoot as she stepped into the first of them. Instead of a fireplace, there was a cast-iron stove, of the kind the Cornish called a slab. It was set in the wall and its recessed top already supported a pot and a cast-iron kettle. It was still unlit, brand new, and its brass knobs and drying rack could have done with a polish to make them presentable.

Behind was a scullery, in a lean-to room across the back. It contained a large copper, with a grate underneath, ready to take their washing. She unbolted the back door and flung it wide. It opened on the wild moor. Heather and grass came right to the house, trampled where the masons had worked, but already reviving.

'Let me show you upstairs.'

Welland led the way and his daughter was briefly aware of his limp as she followed him. That was part of the sadness, the things that came down from the past and could not be remedied.

Around the landing, there were three bedrooms, not leading one into another as was usual in cottages, but each with its separate entrance. Ruth peeped into all three, then ran into one and stood at the window that overlooked the church and Carnwartha.

'This one is mine! Tell me it is, tell me I can have it!'

'It's all yours, my dearest. Take what you want of it.'

'It's *ours*, Father, ours! But you've worked for it.'

She twisted round and clung to him. He leant his cheek on her rippling hair. 'I've done so little,' she whispered, 'but I will, I promise.' She was still so young, so in need of protection, despite her seeming maturity. He was looking over her shoulder at the open moorland.

'There's something I've been meaning to say to you, to ask you – I've seen all the flowers you bring home, I can't but notice – and you know so much about them. You must be collecting them with someone. Don't you think you ought to tell me –'

'No, Father don't press me.'

'But there *is* someone, there must be! Who is it?'

'If I told you you'd only forbid it, and it means so much to me. It's a kind person, ever so kind, though you won't believe it. Don't you trust me? – You must. I'm a young woman.'

She was sobbing. Her tears traversed his shirt. He was on the verge of anger, baffled by her appeal to him. He knew his Ruth. He had trained her well to hold her peace. Without violence, he would get nothing from her, and there had never been violence between them.

'All right then,' he murmured, 'not for now. But you'll tell me soon, won't you?'

She nodded.

'I'll tell you when you've seen you were wrong and there's nothing to worry about.'

Mavis Trerice was the last to leave the count house. Hector Bolitho had stayed on until the last of the pack animals was loaded and had trotted away.

'Here's three shillings,' he had said as he left her. 'Mr Gurney said two, but I've added another. You'll get the count house spick and span, won't you? I'm sorry you have to work on your own; Mrs Trevorrow has to make supper for her children. I've given her part of the roast. Help yourself to the remainder. Lock up carefully. I'll call for the key in the morning.'

She had a napkin full of cold meat under her arm as she removed the key and paused before descending the steps from the building. Mavis was looking for someone. She had hoped to see him come out of the shaft, but he must have slipped past while her attention was on the cleaning. It was late, even Curnow had left his post at the kibble landing. She was about to leave when she saw his son emerge from the engine house. Curnow himself soon followed. Mavis hurried to meet him.

'Have you seen Welland?'

'Welland? 'E went 'ome long since. Come up early. Wanted to show 'is new 'ouse to 'is daughter.'

'I had something to tell him – about Ruth – about the person I've seen her walking with on Carnwartha. Well, I suppose it can wait till tomorrow, if I remember –'

8

THE PIT

When Welland halted at the lip of the pit and looked down at the blur of expectant faces, he found it hard to believe what was happening. The crowd's subdued voices rose towards him with a noise like ebbing breakers scraping over gravel, indistinct and confused as the packed array of spectators whence it came. They crammed the pit's steep slopes from its rim almost to the bottom of its cockpit shape where a pale green pool stared up at the dull sky.

During the past three days, the tinners had terraced the sides of the abandoned clay-pit and carved out a flat area to one side of the pond, dumping the spoil into the water until the apron they had created was large enough for a ring. Welland could see the ring, bleak and empty, far below him. Nearer at hand, he recognized a few Windfall faces, but they were swamped in the mass of strangers who had come from miles around, walking, riding, jammed into carts and every possible kind of conveyance, intent on seeing the sport. Welland still had difficulty in accepting that he was going to provide it.

'What're the odds for Welland Halt?' he heard a burly farmer ask nearby.

'Ten to one against, at least. Mebbe it should be an 'undred,' replied a tinner. Welland held himself in check. While he held his tongue he still benefited from anonymity. ' 'Tes a mismatch, if ever was,' continued the tinner, who was not looking at Welland, 'I'm afeared 'twill be soon over.'

'What's it all about?' asked the farmer. 'Why should they two fight when 'tes so unequal?'

' 'Tes the man what'll lose that've wished it on 'isself, calls it a question of honour, though revenge would be a better description.'

Was that what it was – revenge? Welland had not stopped to examine his motives; he had been too preoccupied with Ruth. It was for her sake he was here, preparing to fight, wasn't it?

'Never paid no 'eed to 'is daughter,' said the tinner's wife, pulling her own child close to her. 'If 'e 'adn' been so took up with money grubbin' 'e'd've seen what was comin'.'

' 'Twould've been better fer that Ruth if 'e'd sent 'er to work at Wheal Fortune with the other maidens,' said the tinner, 'but that Welland's too 'igh and mighty fer that, 'e d'think 'isself better'n us Cornish.'

Welland remembered what he had heard Hilda Trerice saying a quarter of an hour ago, just before he slipped out of his house to join the long line of late-comers who were still shuffling towards the clay pit.

'What's the use of a girt big 'ouse like that fer just one man and a maid?' she had demanded of all and sundry. 'Didn' us 'ave to sleep four in a bed, all in one room? That were all right fer we. And what do a man want with a slab and an oven to cook with? That's what 'e've put in there! That's all very fine fer the gentry's kitchens, but a trivet 'ave allus been good 'nuff fer a tinner.'

If Hilda Trerice was anything to go by, there was no way for a stranger to win the tinners' affections: they had despised him when poor and now they distrusted him when rich. Walking towards the pit, Welland remembered the moment when good fortune had been thrust upon him three months ago.

'Where did this come from?' Angove demanded, coming up behind him unannounced at the end of the level. Welland had swivelled round to see the captain only feet away, with a lump of pyrites glittering in his hands: the same worthless stone he had kicked aside two days ago.

'That? That's fool's gold?' Welland had laughed, proud of his new knowledge, but with an edge of bitterness to his voice.

Angove stopped him, saying, 'Either you're a fool yourself, Welland Halt, or you're a wiser man than I took you for. Where did this come from? Is there more of it?'

Welland pointed at the heap of killas beside the face.

'Help me clear that out,' ordered Angove, setting to work immediately, throwing the rubble aside with feverish energy until the lode was exposed and a vein of golden crystals winked back to his candle. 'Why didn' you tell me you'd found this?' he demanded angrily.

'Didn' think nothin' to it,' Welland replied, lapsing into Angove's Cornish manner of speaking. ' 'Tis worthless old trade: just iron pyrites, not a speck o' tin in un.'

Captain Angove rocked back on his heels and banged his knee with his fist.

'Chalcopyrites, you mean. Mr Bolitho's goin' to be vicious when 'e 'ears 'bout this. Nineteen and six, by God!' He banged his knee again. 'Nineteen and six indeed! 'Tes more'n my job's worth to tell un.'

'Tell him what?'

'Tell un you've struck copper, just by chance, day before the settin', tell un you didn' know what 'twas, tell un I comed by and never seed nothin'! Think 'e'll believe it? D'you think Hector Bolitho'll like payin' out nineteen and an 'arf shillin' in every pound fer good copper?'

Welland had knelt silent. He was too overwhelmed by the implications of the captain's outburst to think properly. Angove took him by the shoulders and shoved his red face forward to within an inch of Welland's.

'Us is in this together,' he asserted. He paused. 'D'you know how to keep a still tongue in your 'ead? I think you do. Well, listen 'ere: say nothin' to no one and 'old over drivin' this level fer a day or so. No one but us d'know where your pitch started 'zackly, do they? Don't show no one this stuff;

keep it covered over. When the time's ripe, I'll tell Bolitho you've just comed upon it. This lode's almost pure copper. If it goes on like this, you're a rich man, Welland, and I 'opes you'll remember your friend Angove.'

That was how Welland had learned of his good fortune. It had meant three months' unprecedented prosperity. The new house was the visible sign of it. He looked over his shoulder and felt a pang of remorse.

' 'Tis a judgement!' Hilda Trerice declared, somewhere ahead of him. 'I allus said that Welland was a ne'er-do-well. Now 'e've proved it, leavin' that poor young critter to 'er own devices. Didn' need a prophet to foresee what 'appened, now did it?'

Welland's eyes glazed with tears. He stopped in his tracks, staring back at the house while the strangers surged past him. He saw himself approaching the door with his month's tribute jingling in his pocket. He had hurried up the final stretch and stepped inside joyfully. It was dim in the kitchen: Ruth hadn't lit the candle yet. He turned to the window-seat, expecting to find her there, reading. There was no sign of her. Her book lay on the floor where it had fallen. There was no smell of cooking in the air. He put his hand on the slab. It was cold. Ruth must have forgotten to stoke it.

'Ruth?' he heard himself calling, suddenly uneasy. 'Where are you?' There was no reply. Had she gone to the mine and missed him while he was drawing his money from Mr Farrow? He didn't think so. He had looked round the sheds before starting homeward. Was she out walking on Carnwartha? She wouldn't have left the door ajar, would she? And she had never been this late. Already, in his bones, he knew that there was something wrong.

Today, as he stood on the edge of the pit, it was still wrong. Nothing he could do would change it. He remembered his boots thudding on the stairs. He remembered pushing open her bedroom door. She was there, crouched on her bed, her body strung tight, like a drawn bow.

'What's happened?'

She had said nothing. Her uneven breathing was racked by suppressed sobs, her face averted.

He had seen the clues: the broken fingernails, the mud and tear-stained cheeks, the torn dress, the bruised thigh.

'Who? Who was it? Who did this to you?'

Still she said nothing. For three days, she had stayed silent. Welland remained at home to care for her. She would not eat. She kept her face to the wall. He feared for her reason. He talked to her softly. If she heard, she gave no sign.

When she fell into fitful sleep, he stole away in search of her aggressor.

'There 'e is!'

A woman's voice roused Welland to consciousness of the present. The woman, Hilda Trerice, was pointing up at him from where she stood half way down the pit. 'That's Welland Halt! God save un, though 'e 'aven't the grace to ask fer protection, too proud, that's Welland.' The crowd fell silent, examining him with cool curiosity. Close by, a child buried her head in her mother's blouse, fearfully. That was how they saw him: a foreigner, a man presumptuous enough to try to bring up his daughter alone. Now they had all the proof they wanted that he was not fit for the task. He had tried to be all in all to Ruth and he had failed her.

One last look back: a party of men surrounding a cart that swung out from the Tinners' Arms was fast approaching. Upright in the cart, arms folded, bare-chested, disdainful-lipped, stood his adversary. It was almost time.

Under the crowd's unfriendly eyes, Welland began the long descent to the ring at the bottom of the pit. He slithered on the white clay path. It had rained that morning and the clay was slimy, like an eel's skin. As he strove to keep his balance, he heard them laughing at him, laughing at his awkward leg. They were still making wagers against him. Well, they were probably right: he had precious little in his favour. It was a hopeless task, a futile gesture, a stab at dark

144

old biblical justice. He had not sought it: it had come to him, begotten of hot anger when he learned the truth. If only he had been told a day earlier.

Welland looked for Curnow in the crowd. He needed the reassurance of a friendly face. Curnow was not there. What would it profit a blind man to attend such a spectacle. But it had been Curnow who set him on the way here.

'Mavis Trerice 'ave been looking out fer 'ee,' he had confided as soon as he heard Welland's voice in his kitchen. 'Said 'twere summat to do with Ruth.'

'What? What was it, Curnow?' Welland grabbed his arm urgently. The blind man's face was infuriatingly bland. He wanted to force some expression into it.

'Don't know no more to it,' protested Curnow. 'Ask 'er yourself, you're 'urtin'.'

Welland ran out into the street and set off towards the Trerice cottage. Mavis was outdoors, tending some flowers in a little patch of garden.

'Curnow said you had something to tell me,' he blurted out breathlessly. Mavis straightened up, brushing crumbs of soil from her dress. A strand of hair hung across her eyes, and she pushed it aside with the back of her hand. Her look was concerned, but not agitated.

'I've been meaning to speak to you about Ruth. It probably isn't important; you'll probably blame me for interfering.' She hesitated.

'Well?'

'You know I often go walking on Carnwartha – I've seen your Ruth up there – she was with someone – someone much older –' Her voice trailed away, seeing the wildness in his eyes, his hands clenching.

'Who was it? His name, I must have it.'

'Why, what's the matter?' A hand went up to her mouth. He nodded. 'Oh no!' she gasped. 'Oh no!'

'His name?'

Mavis had glanced over her shoulder at the cottage door in

145

case her mother were spying on them. She pulled Welland close and whispered to him. His face darkened. Moments later, he was running back towards the Tinners'.

'Magor! Magor!'

All the pit seemed to be shouting his name. The cry brought Welland back to the present. His adversary was arriving. Magor stood at the top of the path and shook his linked hands above his head.

'Magor! Magor!' came the roar. He was the crowd's man; that much was obvious. Even at that distance, Welland could see the ripple of his great biceps and the shine of the broad gilt belt he wore across his midriff. Magor was a prizefighter, the local champion. He paused to wave acknowledgement to the spectators who shouted his name.

Magor had made no pretence of denial when Welland had confronted him outside the Tinners'. He had folded his arms and looked down at Welland complacently.

'Led me on, she did, young slut,' he jeered. 'Takes after 'er mother, I fancy.'

A circle of tinners had formed already, curious to know the reason for the quarrel. They sniggered at Magor's brash assertion, guessing it had struck home when Welland flushed before enunciating slowly and tensely, 'I'll kill you!'

The tinners shook with mirth at the idea of the short, lame foreigner threatening the towering smith.

'Go on, Towzer!' called one of them as if to a terrier. 'Up and at un! Get them teeth in!' This was real sport. They crowded closer.

'What's going on there?'

It was Mr Bolitho who had reined in his dog-cart behind them.

'Bit of a disagreement, Maister,' the same voice piped up. ' 'Tes Tom Magor and Welland Halt. That Welland's just threatened to kill un.'

'We can't have that, now can we?' Bolitho's voice had come to him over the assembled heads unctuously. 'We can't go to

146

such lengths in Windfall. Come now, clear the way, I'll talk to them.' He waited while the knot of men pulled apart until he could see the antagonists. 'Now then, Welland, what's your quarrel?'

'Magor's dishonoured my Ruth. I want justice.'

Mr Bolitho smiled a thin smile. There was no mirth in it.

'Have you witnesses?'

Welland shook his head.

'No need o' that,' interrupted Tom Magor. 'I'm not denyin' it. Led me on, she did. And when she didn' like what I showed 'er, when she played the shrinkin' violet, I learned 'er a lesson.'

'I'll teach *you* a lesson,' shouted Welland, beside himself, 'you great oaf, you shan't live to boast of it.'

'Very well then,' said Bolitho firmly, 'if that's how the land lies, you shall fight it out, but not with knives in some dark corner, with one of you dead and the other one up before Bodmin Assizes. You shall have it out, out in the open, with your bare fists, like men. What say you, Magor?'

Magor had merely grinned and rubbed his left palm significantly across his knuckles.

'And you, Welland Halt, will it satisfy you to meet this man in single combat? Will you make your own justice?'

Welland looked up at the smith; he knew his reputation, he was a pugilist, an unbeaten prizefighter, a much heavier man than himself and remarkably agile for his bulk. To think he could beat him in a fair fight seemed pure foolishness. Welland turned to Mr Bolitho and nodded once, slowly.

'So long as there's no interference, no quarter.'

'That could work against you, Welland.' Bolitho was concerned; he wanted no death as the outcome.

'I'll chance it,' Welland insisted quietly.

'I'll give you three days to cool off – come to a composition if that's possible. Otherwise, next Sunday then, at the clay pit, at two in the afternoon, will that suit both of you?'

That had been on Thursday and now the time had come.

147

Welland was climbing over the crudely built fence into the ring. The fence was made of off-cut elm board slats nailed and tied to a number of posts driven into a platform the tinners had cut into the pit's sloping side. The platform's floor was smooth white clay and the material excavated on one side had been cast out on the other into the deep, circular lake at the pit bottom. The edge of the platform sloped down steeply into the cloudy water. The pool was devoid of life: its abrupt banks had neither bush nor grass on them. It would be years before nature reasserted her way over this wilderness. Welland saw it as something biblical: a Dead Sea.

He felt a hand on his shoulder. It was Angove, the underground captain.

'Could you use a second?' asked Angove with a bit of a smile. It was wan but genuine, not much of a smile but it would have to do. Nowhere else in the crowded amphitheatre which hemmed him in did he see another. The closest ranks of spectators had little time for him: a covey of gentry in autumnal frock-coats and silken waistcoats sat on chairs and benches, fingering silver-headed canes or sipping at port. Bolitho looked up and offered Welland a noggin in his hip-flask cap. Welland shook his head.

'So this is your man,' one of the gentlemen teased Bolitho, between nibbles at a chicken bone from a hamper. 'Looks as though he needs something red in his veins. He'll soon spill plenty, I fancy.' The speaker was a wavy-haired, full-lipped buck who spoke in a provocative off-hand drawl. Bolitho was clearly embarrassed.

'He's not my choice, Silverton, you know that. This is a mismatch if ever I saw one. All the same, this Welland will give a good account of himself, better than you expect.'

'Are you ready to match your confidence in the challenger with a small wager?' asked the gentleman, picking at his teeth with a fingernail before tossing the drumstick into the nearby jade green water which closed over it instantly. Welland looked him over with frank interest. So this was Silverton

Gurney of Tregurney House, owner of Windfall, principal adventurer in Wheal Fortune, M.P., and proprietor of the vast Gurney estates. Silverton avoided Welland's eyes, ignoring him and grinning superciliously at Bolitho. 'Not to win, mark you,' he continued, seeing the latter hesitate, 'just to stay on his feet. Ten minutes we'll give 'im, shall we? He looks a tough little cock. Shall we say ten guineas? If he's still capable of standing after ten minutes, the money's yours, Hector. What's the word, will you match my bet on him?'

Whatever Bolitho's reply was, it was lost in another volley of cheering as Magor reached the enclosure. His arrival distracted Welland from the resentment building in him at being discussed and disparaged as if he were some piece of spavined horseflesh. High above Magor, an enterprising farmer was selling cider from barrels on a wagon. Near at hand, womenfolk were unwrapping lumps of fuggan and handing them round to their children. A girl in a purple velveteen dress with a white lace collar reminded him of Ruth until she looked round and he saw that she was smiling.

Ruth had not smiled once since the evening when he discovered her cataleptic; neither had she spoken. Her sullen face appeared before him now, masking Magor who was rubbing his knuckles in his corner. Welland saw her as he had left her in the house, lying on the bed.

'My lords, ladies and gentlemen!' The beginning of Hector Bolitho's announcement roused Welland to awareness that the trial was about to begin. 'You are about to witness a contest of pancratium – of pugilism combined with wrestling – between our renowned champion, Tom Magor –' he was interrupted by a bout of shouting and cheering, 'and his challenger, Welland Halt.' Another cheer, ironic this time, straggled round the terraces. It was clear there was little sympathy for Welland, though the spectators must know of his daughter's wrong. Welland felt another wave of loneliness, a fear of being trapped in this pit, among a hostile crowd, under an indifferent heaven. 'The contest will be referee by Mr Hawkey.' Bolitho ushered a burly, black-haired mine captain into the ring. 'Rounds will be of ten minutes' duration. Whenever a contestant is felled by a blow or has his shoulders pressed to the ground by a hold, there will be a count of ten. The contest will end when one or other of the fighters fails to come up to scratch.'

There was a mood of quiet expectancy in the arena now. Magor removed his gilded belt and passed it to his second. He bobbed up and down, shadow boxing in his corner. His skin had been carefully oiled and glistened over the rippling muscles. Welland removed his shirt: his own skin was pallid after months in the mine, but his arms were long and sinewy. Bolitho leaned over the rail and whispered to him.

'I hope you'll give a good account of yourself, Welland. I'm betting on you.' Welland looked him in the eye.

'For the first ten minutes, you are.'

'You'll be lucky to hold out that long!'

'Can I have Magor's job if I beat him?'

Bolitho looked him over, pursing his lips and cocking his head back.

'You're a cool one and no mistake. If you'd picked on someone your own size, I'd have backed you for the winner. But you can't be serious; you're doing too well on tribute.'

'That's all over, you'll beat me down this setting. And I want to work in the open air and get home in good time to look after my daughter.'

'You're not going to win, you know that. You've less chance than a snowflake in hell. Why bother?'

'But will you agree to it?'

'I suppose so. And, Welland –' he took him by the wrist as he spoke – 'for what it's worth, good luck. My sympathies go with you.'

The referee was calling Welland to the centre of the ring and he obeyed numbly. Why bother? It was a good question. Close up, his adversary looked even more massive and powerful. Victor of more than half a dozen prize-fights which, so Welland had been told, were all short-lived affairs, he was quite unmarked.

'Let's get it over with,' Magor grunted, wiping his thumb across his nose in a derisory gesture. The referee, after holding their bare fists in his hands for an instant, stepped back, leaving them alone in the centre of the ring. Welland could hear his own breathing, so deep was the hush that had fallen. He heard the quiet shuffling of Magor's hobnailed boots as the smith settled them firmly in the clay. Magor had taken up a pugilist's stance, the old-fashioned one with the right shoulder forward and the left arm across his body. He towered above Welland who stood balanced on his toes, keeping well back out of respect for the big man's formidable reach.

'Kill 'im, Tom, don't keep us waitin'!' a voice drifted from the rim of the pit.

Magor blinked, wiggled his shoulders and threw a punch; not a right jab as Welland had anticipated, but a wild swing with his left arm that had him wrong-footed. It skimmed the side of his head and left his ear burning. An inch or two to the left and it *would* have been all over with him.

But Welland reacted swiftly, ducking forward inside the swing and counterpunching with his own left, planting a stinging jab close under Magor's heart. But his fist had slipped on the oiled skin and he doubted if he had hurt the champion significantly. The only evidence was a puzzled frown and a sharply indrawn breath on his opponent's side.

Magor reverted to jabbing with his right, shuffling forward slowly, trying to pin Welland into a corner. For all his ox-like manner, he had some real ring craft and Welland was afraid he would succeed in trapping him. For the time being, his own best chance was to get the bigger man to expend his energy punching empty air.

Not all of Magor's blows fell wide, however. Welland's left arm ached already with the hits he had parried with it and the constant footwork necessary to keep him out of range was tiring him. If he was going to make any impression at all on Magor, he would have to get to grips with him momentarily.

The pit was already buzzing with subdued talk as the spectators weighed up the two adversaries. The gentry were passing the port bottle and discussing Magor's form. They were impatient for some quick action, but it was obvious that this was too much of a mismatch to last long as a slogging contest. Hector Bolitho stole a glance at his watch; he still had a chance of winning the ten guineas, but the minutes were creeping by slowly and just one good punch from Magor, while still fresh, would be enough to fell Welland Halt. The gentleman who had talked Bolitho into the bet observed his action out of the corner of his eye and called out to Magor, 'Hurry up, man! We haven't got all day!'

It was the chance that Welland had been waiting for: it broke the champion's concentration when his eye strayed to identify the speaker. Welland acted instantly, leaping forward on the other man's right, his blind side, under his right arm and protected from his left. He struck him once with a long uppercut to the kidneys from his own right, followed it with a second, shorter blow to the same place, and jabbed upward at Magor's face as the man turned towards him, flailing with his own left.

The third of Welland's blows had extended him to the full extent of his reach and hardly bothered Magor, but the other two had taken their toll. The big man wilted; his fists drooped and his eyes glazed. Welland tried to exploit his advantage, pestering him with a series of left jabs, but was kept at bay by wild swings. Magor had abandoned his scientific stance and was advancing behind a barrage of hooks. His pain was evident, but it hadn't stopped him and Welland knew he had to do more if he wanted to succeed.

From the moment Welland hurt Magor, the pit was full of yelling, excited people, the women's shrill voices clamouring over the men's. The sound and the tension enveloped the two fighters like a thick mist: they saw one another, but all else was blurred. Suddenly, Welland found himself cornered. The yelling rose to a crescendo. How had he allowed this to happen? He keyed himself up for a supreme effort to break out, but even so, he was taken almost completely unawares by Magor's next move. Feinting a punch with his left fist, the blacksmith kicked out with his right foot. Although Welland ought to have been expecting something of the sort, he had been lulled by the sportsmanlike formal pugilism of the bout's early stages and was unable to dodge the kick completely. If it had struck home, it would have broken his leg. As it was, the heavy, metal-shod boot hit his shin a glancing blow and went on to shiver the lowest rail of the fence behind him. The pain was exquisite, but he had to ignore it. Magor was momentarily off balance from the kick and Welland hurled himself from the corner, forcing his way to the champion's left and regaining the centre of the ring.

Magor followed him. By now, Welland was wondering if his earlier success with blows to the body had done more than pester his adversary. The man seemed as strong as ever and the less predictable way he was fighting made him even more redoubtable. They circled the ring, Welland hobbling backwards, Magor pursuing, throwing punches, some of which landed. Luckily for Welland they did not have the same power as at the outset of the encounter, but Magor had blood on his knuckles from a cut he had opened in Welland's cheek. Both men were breathing heavily. The crowd were egging them on. Hector Bolitho nudged his neighbour.

'That's ten guineas you owe me,' he told him, exhibiting his watch dial.

'I suppose so,' said Silverton Gurney tartly, 'but don't expect him to last much longer.'

A moment later, as Hawkey signalled the round's end, Welland was flat on the floor. Magor had lured him into another lunging attack and tripped him as he passed. Welland was more winded than hurt, but what irked him most was the knowledge that the round was over and the one-minute break would allow Magor to recover completely.

The pit was in pandemonium. Many people thought Welland had been knocked down, stunned by a punch. He raised himself cautiously, wary of a sudden attack, but Magor was in his corner, consulting with his seconds. His own second beckoned him over and wiped his head and shoulders with a damp cloth.

'You're doin' 'andsome,' said Angove.

'I wish I thought so myself,' mumbled Welland through bruised lips. A large patch of drying blood stained his trouser leg where the skin was broken. His shoulders ached with the persistent pummelling they had endured. What was the point of going on? Magor was as hard as the Rock of Gibraltar: he could never beat him.

The referee was calling the two men up to scratch again. Welland thought of Ruth and hobbled forward. Evidently Magor had received fresh advice in his corner for he had abandoned his boxing stance and was advancing, knees bent, body leaning forward, in the manner of a Cornish wrestler. He would be even more difficult to avoid now. Once wrapped in those massive arms, Welland doubted if he could escape.

Magor was manoeuvring him again, slowly but surely trapping him in a corner. Welland tried a few left jabs, but he was out of range. The smith's red eyes were tracking him inexorably and the ghost of a smile was playing round his lips. In a moment, Welland would be locked in the corner. A desperate ploy was all that was left to him.

He threw a tremendous right. First he stopped his dancing retreat, allowing Magor to close in slightly, then he struck out with all his force, straight from the shoulder with all the power built into his arm and back by months of hammering in the mine. Magor's chin was too high for a stunning blow, his temple was even higher. Welland struck him over the heart, in the centre of the rib cage. The jarring shock that returned through his arm told him he had struck home.

Magor stopped and wavered like a poleaxed steer. His breath came in sudden short gasps. And yet, Welland knew his powers of recovery; he had to deliver another decisive punch if he were to take advantage of the smith's weakness and finish him off. He leapt in again with a jab to the chin.

It was a mistake. Instantaneously, Magor's arms locked round him like great branches. The smith leant on him with all his weight like a huge uprooted oak bearing down on a strut. Welland felt his legs going. The smith's oily body pressed against his chest and the sweaty smell choked him.

'I'm going to get you for that,' Magor whispered loudly, 'I'm going to slaughter you!'

Welland's arms were pinioned. He was being driven back on to the fence. If his legs buckled under him before he got there, Magor would fall on top of him and he would be unable to rise. He was desperate. Although the smith was still weakened by the blow to his heart, he was a dead weight, a suffocating net dragging him down.

As if in a dream, he heard Curnow's voice, speaking urgently from far above him. A deep hush had fallen on the pit and the blind man's words came to him clearly.

'You've got 'im beat! 'It 'im again, Welland!'

Welland twisted his head and saw Curnow lurching down the path towards him followed by his son. He was slipping and sliding, but people on either side were reaching out to guide him, passing him from hand to hand.

'I can't,' Welland gasped, 'he's got my arms.' He was weakening and, all the time, he could feel the strength returning to the smith's body: the arms were clamping tighter around him. But he was still standing, braced against the fence, his muscles shuddering. Curnow was blundering through the rows of gentry, stumbling towards him. He felt the blind man's fingers on his shoulder and rising to recognize his face. He felt lips pressed against his ear and heard an almost inaudible whisper.

'Give the bastard your knee! 'It un with your knee!'

How could Curnow see his predicament? How could a blind man pretend to advise him? But his strength was ebbing. What else was left? With all the residual power in his body, he brought his knee up into Magor's groin.

Magor gave a shuddering sigh and slipped to his knees. Welland's arms were freed. A shout of amazement rose from the crowd.

'You've got 'im. 'It 'is 'ead!' Curnow instructed, but Welland hesitated a split second too long. Before he could deliver the decisive blow, Magor keeled over and the referee stepped between them. The round was over. Would Magor recover again in the minute before the next one? Welland returned to his corner to be wiped off. Magor's smell was still on him.

When he looked round, the smith was rising. It was hard to believe, but he was already rising from his knees. He was certainly weaker, but he hadn't given in. Welland had been foolish to expect it. The man was a bull, blindly determined and unable to envisage defeat.

They fought on. Sometimes Welland got in a good blow. Sometimes Magor seemed to be winning. The crowd grew tense. Now that Magor had been hurt, it was a closer match. He was slower and the depth of his rage made him wild and ineffective. The minutes dragged by. After half an hour, it began to rain. The raindrops washed some of the blood from their bodies. The clay underfoot became slimy and treacherous. Welland was in constant fear that his adversary would catch him in a wrestler's hold again. He kept him away by punching, but only rarely did he land a worthwhile hit. It seemed impossible to wear Magor down or break him.

Welland slipped on the clay and fell, striking his head on the fence. Before the referee could interpose, Magor was on him. He picked him up bodily, with a roar of triumph, brandishing him aloft like a doll and threw him out of the ring into the rows of gentry. Welland was stunned and weak, but he was still sufficiently conscious to see Magor coming after him. Scrambling to his feet, among the gentlemen who shrank from his blood and slime-stained body, he lunged up the slope through the spectators, hoping to keep out of reach until his head cleared. No one lifted a hand to help him. A scattering of boos saluted him as he passed. Finally, two thirds of the way up the side of the pit, he turned at bay. He was winded and could climb no more. Magor was right behind him, but the slope had taken away most of his height advantage. Welland waited for just the right moment, then hit him with a savage right cross to the jaw.

Magor crumpled. There was an instant of silence when Welland could hear the blood rushing through his own temples, and then a roar, a roar like the acclamation of a gladiator. He closed his ears to it. Without thinking, without looking at the fallen man, he staggered away. All the anger and hate had left him now. Magor was a limp rag. He had been punished enough. Though he had vowed to kill the smith in revenge for the shame he had brought on his daughter, he was not ready to carry it through. It was enough that Magor had been humbled. Welland went sliding down the slope to collect Curnow and go home.

Something about the way the crowd was acting made him look back. It was impossible: Magor was on his feet again, lumbering downhill. So Welland still hadn't won. It wasn't over. The referee was waving him back into the ring and he complied, moving like an automaton. How much longer could this go on? How much longer could *he* go on? He looked down at his body, spattered with bruises showing through the streaks of mud and clay. He felt a terrible lethargy creeping over him. Where was his will to survive, to win?

Both men were at the end of their tether. They circled each other, exchanging occasional, ill-directed blows. Their breath came in long rasping sobs. How long had the fight lasted now? An hour? More? They no longer looked like men, but more like cumberous antediluvian creatures, struggling in some primeval slough. The crowd watched their every move, shouting with glee when Welland connected with Magor's nose and made it spout blood.

But still he kept coming on, shuffling, ponderous, menacing. There was no longer any pretence at chivalry. His whole shape, its inflexible, shambling determination meant one thing: death.

At last they paused, as if by mutual consent, on either side of the ring. Magor was thinking hard. Welland could see the wrinkles on his brow. He was casting about for some final solution that would rid him of his small tormentor.

When he acted, it was with surprising speed. Turning his back on Welland, he tugged at the rope that held the fence boards in place. It took Welland a few moments to guess his intention and, by then, it was too late. The smith had wrenched a board away and was swinging it round his head. The nail-spiked end whistled close to Welland's head. He sprang back and it came round again, even closer. Why didn't somebody stop Magor? There seemed to be a commotion among the gentry, some of whom were shouting at Hawkey to intervene, but the referee had retired from the ring and was too scared to go near it.

Welland dived despairingly under the hissing board, striking Magor's legs below the knees and driving his feet from under him across the slimy clay. Magor dropped the board which skidded out of the ring before either man could grab it. They scrambled to their feet, panting. Magor lunged forward and grabbed Welland by the hair, forcing his head back, trying to break his neck. Welland was almost finished. The fence was digging into his back and his body was being arched over it. His sight was blurring. His last clear impression was of Curnow close behind him, shouting something unintelligible. With what remained of his strength he hit Magor again. He struck him in the solar plexus with a short chopping blow and was astonished at the instant result that came of it. Magor let go.

Welland coiled himself up and than butted him under the chin with the top of his head. Magor was wavering, but still he refused to fall. He swayed like a great oak undercut by the woodcutters. But he did not fall. He spat a broken tooth from his mouth and came tottering forward, groping for his tormentor. Even now, if those hands caught him, Welland knew the outcome might be changed decisively. He swerved backwards, conscious of the weight of his limbs. He slithered almost uncontrollably. Then he remembered the board. If he could get at it first, hit Magor again from a distance, that might finish him off.

The board had slipped under the fence on the side nearest the deep green pond. It had tilted downwards with its nailed end caught in the bottom rail of the fence. The top rail was missing. That was where it had been until the smith wrenched it loose. Magor must have followed his glance and guessed his intention, for he too shambled towards it.

Welland got there first and hauled the board feverishly towards him, but he could see he would not have time to pull it free. Magor had accelerated and was charging towards him. All Welland could do was throw himself clear.

Magor grabbed at him, but missed. His impetus carried him against the low fence and he hung there momentarily, arms flailing, until his boots slid backwards and he toppled forward on to the steep slope that led to the water. His nails dug into the clay, but they failed to hold and they left long scratches as he slid slowly downward. Welland saw his eyes widen in sudden horror as his feet touched water.

'I can't swim,' he croaked.

Welland looked down at him without pity. The bank was too steep and slippery for him to climb down and save Magor, even if he had wanted to.

'For Christ's sa –' Magor was imploring him as the water reached his chin. Then he was gone. The green skin closed over his head and hands with only a bubble or two to show where he had been. An unearthly hush fell on the pit as the crowd waited to see if Magor would reappear.

'There he is!' cried a voice as a hand broke surface a few feet from the bank, then the other followed, with Magor's face, terrified, between them.

'For God's sake, Welland,' he gasped in the brief moment before he went down again, 'forgive me.'

Welland's mind was blank, blank as the jade water before him. All his outrage and anger had been burnt away in the heat of combat. Magor was beaten. What further punishment would it be to take his life now? He had lost face, he was no longer the champion. Let him live with his conscience and shame for ever. Despite his vow, Welland was no executioner. He noticed the rope that the smith had untied to free the plank he had used as a weapon. He stepped across and tossed it into the water. It wasn't that he wanted to save Magor, but he wanted to give him a chance. He didn't want it to be cold-blooded murder.

As he crossed the ring and threaded his way among the gentry, the clamour grew. Silverton Gurney offered him Magor's gilded belt, but he thrust it away.

'Well done, Welland!' cried Hector Bolitho, pumping his hand furiously. Welland did not respond. He climbed the path doggedly, with Curnow and his boy close behind him. His eyes were so puffed up by bruises that he could hardly see. The blood throbbed in his head. Twice, he staggered and fell, but helpful hands buoyed him up.

They were cheering. The crowd were cheering. He didn't know who they were cheering at first. The cheers swelled slowly, but increased until they were like a gigantic breaking wave. He stopped at the brink of the pit and the cheers reached a new crescendo. The cheers were for him. He had trouble realising it, but it was true. There could be no doubt about it.

'Wel–land! Wel–land!' they were shouting rhythmically. Far below, Magor was scrambling out of the water, but no one was bothering with him. Only Curnow had a half-whispered question.

'Did you kill un?' Welland shook his head, but said nothing. Curnow took his boy by the arm and shook him. ' 'E didn', did a, Frank? No, I thought so. Well, more's the pity.' Welland was not listening. All the hundreds of faces were upturned towards him. They had taken to him: he had broken through. They were treating him like a hero. Some threw their caps in the air, others toasted him with mugs of cider.

The change was too sudden after the long months of ostracism; Welland could not absorb it. He felt weak, drained of all emotion. His one aim was to get home to Ruth. Not that he intended to glory in his victory. He was concerned about her, alone in the cottage for so long with only her black thoughts for company. Why hadn't he arranged for Ellen Curnow to take her in and look after her?

He took a long last look at the crowd in the pit, all yelling and waving, and set off. The rain was still falling gently and the leaves on the elder bushes to either side of the track were beaded with sparkling drops of moisture. They were fresh and green as if newly made. Even the roofs of Windfall were washed clean and glistening under the sun which was breaking through from the west. Welland turned his face up to the sky as he walked, letting the last of the rain soak into the blood and dirt. The road he walked was familiar, so familiar that he had no need to care where he trod, but something had changed.

There were shouts behind his back. The tinners were running after him. Behind them, the crowd was emerging from the pit like a dark stain in front of the spoil heap's white pinnacle. In the ensuing hours, they would disperse into all the hamlets, villages and farms for miles around. With them would go the stunning news that Tom Magor had lost. And there would be a new name on their lips: Welland Halt.

Welland did not know this yet. Mingled with the last of the

rain, slow tears crept down his cheeks. He was coming home. Battered, exhausted, stained with the marks of battle, he was coming home.

The first of the tinners overtook him. Pushing Curnow and his boy aside, they hoisted Welland aloft and chaired him towards the village. The crowd surged round them.

'To the Tinners'!' they shouted. 'Long live our Welland! Us'll drink to that!'

Carried away by the flood of a human river, Welland's figure bobbed and nodded over the rippling heads. Yes, all had changed. He had left his house that morning alone and a stranger. Now, with the cheering tinners all round him, he was coming home.

'Drink up, friend Welland,' cried Jack Lugger, the landlord, 'all you want, on the house!'

'To friendship!' pledged a miner who had always ignored him.

'To Fortune!' smiled Captain Angove, putting an arm round Welland's shoulders. 'You've just won 'Ector Bolitho ten guineas, you'll be 'is white-'aired boy from now on.'

'For 'e's a jolly good fellow,' chanted the Windfallers and Welland believed them. He was so triumphant he forgot their past indifference, their coldness. He was so triumphant he forgot his aching frame, his loneliness. He was so triumphant for the while that he forgot his Ruth, his happiness. When he remembered her, he tried to disengage himself.

'Not leavin' so soon, Welland. You can't. 'Tes a night fer rejoicin'!' Angove protested.

'My daughter,' mumbled Welland, making for the door, 'I must go home to her.'

There was a light burning in his kitchen. For a moment, as he reeled towards it, he dreamed that it was Ruth, that she had come to herself and was waiting for him, but when he entered he saw that it was Mavis, seated at the table.

'Where's Ruth?' he asked thickly.

'Where you left her.' Her voice was cold, disapproving. She rose and gathered her cloak about her. 'Now I'll be leaving.'

'What's the matter?'

'The matter? You're drunk, disgustingly drunk, that's what's the matter.'

Welland swayed on his feet. She was right. The realization made his head spin. He felt like retching. He held on to the doorpost, blocking the way out.

'I beat him,' he announced thickly.

'You're a man,' she answered, 'you think you can make matters right by fighting. You ought to have stayed by your Ruth, not gone off prizefighting.'

'The prize was honour,' he mumbled.

'Honour!' She laughed at him. He felt himself crumble. Had he fought for nothing? A pall of weariness fell upon him, his body ached, it was failing him, he thought he was falling.

9

CARNWARTHA HILL

'Well, do I have it then?' Hector Bolitho looked up from his count house desk to see Welland planted in front of him, his arms straight, gripping the desktop on either side. When he realized what Welland was asking for, he leant back, appraising him over the top of his glasses.

'Not satisfied with what you earn from copper?'

'Would you be content with three shillings out of twenty? That's what I'll get at the setting, isn't it?'

By now, Bolitho rather liked Welland's directness. He was tough, straightforward, pugnacious: a man's man. Hadn't he just won ten guineas for him? Welland's face was still dark with bruises. One eye was almost closed. There were scars of cuts on cheek and eyebrow and lip. But he wasn't just tough. Bolitho suspected he was clever.

'So you fancy yourself as a smith?' Welland nodded and Bolitho put down his pen, sat forward, and made a tent out of his fingertips. 'I know you can fight, Welland. I've seen that. But I've yet to see if you're half the smith you say you are.' Welland's brow clouded and his knuckles whitened where he gripped the desktop. Bolitho became conciliatory. 'Don't worry, I'm a man of my word.' Welland relaxed somewhat and smiled a thin smile. Bolitho stood up and went to the window overlooking the stamps and the engine house. 'The thing is, Welland, the man I'm going to need here soon will have to be more than just a smith. There are changes coming to Wheal Fortune, big changes. Squire Gurney has been touring the country, looking into the benefits of machinery, he's completely taken with it. Steam's the thing, so he tells me. We'll be investing, fitting new machinery, building another engine house, installing a high-pressure boiler and engine to haul the kibbles, maybe another to drive the stamps. Mr Trevithick will be coming to oversee it. He'll need an assistant: someone who understands mechanics.'

'You'll need to pay good money for that kind of assistant, they don't grow on trees,' said Welland drily. Hector Bolitho held back a laugh.

'Can you do it?'

'Try me. But what's the pay to be?'

'You'll do better than ever you did stoping and that wasn't half bad, now was it?' Bolitho took out a fine linen handkerchief, breathed on his glasses and polished them with it. 'Now, if you'll excuse me, I must get back to my figures.'

Welland remained at the window, looking out at the stamp houses where the troughs at the end of each stamp in turn were filling with water from the sluice. As soon as each trough was full it canted the balance beam down on that side, raising the heavy stamp at the other. At a certain angle, the water spilled out of the trough and the stamp crashed down. The water sloshed into the trough and the procedure began again. It was simple enough if you had a head for that kind of thing; in fact it was primitive and, when Trevithick had come and gone, it would be swept away, replaced by machinery altogether more urgent and powerful. Where would the bal maidens and the children be then? Steam and iron would steal their bread away from them. They had no inkling of what was in store for them. It was croust time and the other bal maidens were laughing and joking with Mavis Trerice.

Mr Bolitho glanced up from his work. 'Still there, Welland? Didn't I tell you? Tom Magor is indisposed today, a little off colour. Perhaps you'd be good enough to take over the smithy from him.'

Welland nodded, half engrossed in some private dream, then made for the door. As he grasped the latch and pulled it towards him, Bolitho cleared his throat significantly.

'Yes?'

'Your daughter Ruth, how is she faring?'

'As well as might be expected.'

'Is she being cared for? She shouldn't be left alone. I hope you don't think I'm meddling. I'm genuinely sorry it had to happen.'

Welland's lip trembled, he was struck by Bolitho's sincerity. 'And there's no real redress, is there? What can ever rebuild a shattered dream, a young girl's innocence? Still, you did what you could, you beat him.'

'I blame myself,' muttered Welland. 'I blame myself. I always shall. It should never have happened. Perhaps if I hadn't shamed Magor in his smithy –'

'You made but one mistake, Welland.' Welland raised a questioning eyebrow, and the purser continued. 'You should have let him drown. A man shamed is a snake in the grass. What does it say in the Book? "Thou hast bruised his head and he shall bruise thy heel . . ." '

Welland shrugged and stepped outside. He walked with a new jaunty step. A passing tinner grinned at him and tipped his hat. The music of the stamps was like a triumphant march as he crossed the open space towards the forge. He paused to speak to Mavis, shouting over the hammers' racket.

'Ruth's better – a little – she talked this morning.'

'She's not alone, is she?'

He sensed the hostility in her question. He was still at a loss to know what he had done to deserve it.

'She's at the Curnows'. I had to come here. A man must make a living.' What was it in her that put him on the defensive? 'There's something I want to tell you – '

'Grass captain's watching!' she interrupted. 'I have to get on with my job. A woman must work too, while she has the chance, that is.' She turned back to her spalling. She was right to doubt the permanence of her employment. She was wiser than she knew. Wearily, he proceeded to the forge.

Mavis was too much for him. Although she had helped him when he first arrived in Windfall and had maintained an interest in Ruth's welfare, she rebuffed his own advances. Was it his limp, his gracelessness? That answer was all too plausible, but it was too easy. There was something deeper. Mavis Trerice was a woman and that, for want of a better, must be reason enough for the enigma. His experience with that gender had not been encouraging.

The fire in the forge was cold. The tools were in disorder. The bellows boy was playing marbles in a corner.

'On your feet, lad,' he called, 'let's get moving.'

Welland thought, through work, to blot her image from his consciousness, but he was not successful: her intense dark eyes, her full pouting lips, her waving chestnut hair, haunted him like an obsession. She was not as prim and proper as she pretended. He had his own proof of that, though he doubted if he would ever dare confront her with it. He stoked the fire and drove the boy to blow it to white heat so he could punish iron. The forge soon rang to his hammer's clang. He worked until he saw the boy begin to droop.

'Sorry, lad,' he muttered, patting him on the shoulder, 'you'll be thinking you've swapped one bad master for another.'

'Me 'eads ringin',' the boy complained.

That morning, Welland's head had been ringing too. When he awoke a voice was calling him. He thought it was part of his dream; he had been trapped in the rock, his limbs refused to respond when he willed to move them. Was this the way to death? He felt a coolness on his brow, and heard a whisper,

'Father! Father!'

It was Ruth's voice. She needed help. He must break through to her. When, at last, his eyelids rose, he found her bending over him, a damp cloth in her hands, her eyes full of concern for him. He was lying, fully clothed, on his bed, though how he had arrived there, he had no recollection.

The last thing he remembered was his quarrel with Mavis in the kitchen. Someone must have got him up there. He pushed himself up, grateful that his limbs responded.

'I must go to the mine,' he had muttered. 'Will you be all right, Ruth, if I leave you with Ellen Curnow?' She nodded. 'I must see Bolitho and claim my employment. What time is it?'

'Ten o'clock, Father. You ought to rest longer.'

Welland had caught her to him.

'Thank God you've come back to yourself,' he murmured.

'You needed me,' she had replied, 'Mavis said so,'

'I do, I do,' he told her. It had been easy to think that Ruth needed him, but equally he needed her.

'D'you need me?' the bellows boy was asking. 'Can I sit down a minute, I'm knackered.'

Welland came back to the present. He nodded. The boy slipped off to his corner. Welland set his hammer head on the anvil, linked his hands over the end of its haft, rested his chin on them, and pondered. He had achieved his objectives: he had built a home for himself and his daughter, he had won acceptance in Windfall, and now he held the job he had asked for. Three things, however, lurked in the back of his mind to disquiet him: he had won recognition and his new work by beating Magor and, from what Bolitho had said, he should fear his resentment. His other disappointment was Mavis's attitude. One part of his mind was continually tracking her through the woods, glimpsing her beautiful body as it rose from the water, standing entranced by the laughing eyes that shone through her hair. The other, rational, part of his mind reminded him she had always rebuffed him. Was it something to do with her mother? The old woman had always been hostile. And yet, he could not avoid the conviction that there was something wrong with him, something she found unattractive. The third was Ruth: how could he work and still care for her properly?

Through the doorway, he could see the nodding stamps,

the bal maidens, and Mavis among them. It was a harsh picture, but the future was harder. Trevithick was coming. There would be new engines. That way of life would be swept away for ever. He had heard of Trevithick; what miner in those days had not? He wondered what sort of man he would be to work for.

'There's some 'urts even a pellar can't 'eal,' Hilda Trerice muttered as she bent over Tom Magor whose slack body lay across her table. ' 'Urts to the body's one thing, 'urts to the 'eart's another. If you don't 'ave no 'eart, Tom Magor, 'Ilda Trerice can't 'elp 'ee.' She paused, palpating his limbs before continuing. 'No bones is broke, but what about your spirit!'

'I know when I'm beat,' mumbled Magor.

'Beat? You're not beat. You're a man, aren't you?'

'*You* aren't the one to fight! 'Tes easy fer a woman to say "No surrender!" but she don't 'ave to take the blows,' he protested. ' 'Tes your fault, 'Ilda Trerice, if I'm in this state. 'Tes your fault I've lost me champion's belt. 'Tes your fault I'm a smith no longer. You put me up to it. Look where it've got me.'

'Pah!' exploded Hilda Trerice. 'If you believe that, you deserve the medicine that Welland've made 'ee swallow. Weren't 'e out fer your job, first off? 'Ilda Trerice didn' 'ave naught to do with that now, did she? But 'tes real enough. That Welland'll leave 'ee poor as the day you was born if you don't stand up fer youself, if you don't stop un.'

'I'm beat, I tell 'ee.'

'You've lost a battle. But don't you fret, I'm not tellin' 'ee ter fight un again, that's not the way you'll 'ave un, that's not the way ter get even.'

'Then what is it?'

'The law. One day you'll 'ave the law on Welland. E's a man with a past. Sooner or later, that past'll catch up with un. If you bide your time, if you keep your eyes and ears open, you'll 'old un in the palm of your 'and like a nut. Mark

169

my words if you won't. You'll just 'ave ter squeeze when the time comes. Now, drink this, 'tes a dish of 'erbs that'll make 'ee better.'

While Tom Magor sat and sipped at the drink she handed him, Hilda Trerice examined him closely. He had been about to give in, but now she believed she had fuelled his resentment and given him hope of revenge.

'I owes Welland me life,' he announced unexpectedly.

'E didn' want your death on 'is conscience. 'E wanted you beholden to un.'

Magor nodded. He was beginning to see reason.

Dapper Richard Trevithick rode into Windfall the next Sunday afternoon. He sat perched in a fashionable new phaeton, a cheroot clamped between his shining white teeth and a stove-pipe hat pushed back on his head. When he blew out puffs of smoke, it looked like one of his own wheezing engines. His small eyes looked like bright birds' eggs in a nest of small wrinkles. A crowd of boys was waiting for him at the crossroads by the tor. They ran along beside his phaeton, laughing and shouting, though more than a little disappointed he had not driven up in one of those fabulous steam-carriages they had heard he had invented. The village dogs, disturbed from their dozing in the middle of the dusty street by the horses' hooves pounding, sprang up and followed, yelping.

Mr Trevithick installed himself in the best room at the Tinners' Arms, making a face at its dinginess and its lack of amenities.

'This ale of yours is cat's piss,' he told the landlord, and sent his servant down to fetch a bottle of claret from the boot of the phaeton. The meal brought up by the landlord's wife was predictably half cooked and indigestible: leaden dumplings submerged in stringy mutton stew. He drank several glasses of claret in quick succession to protect his stomach and then sat down to study the drawings from his portfolio.

Late at night, when the sounds of roistering in the taproom below had subsided, he left for a brief moonlight walk, picking his way carefully along the rough, rubbish-infested road, fearful of scuffing his gleaming patent-leather boots. His cheroot glowed in the dark, illuminating a sharp, pensive face. He heard the old Smeaton engine's distant panting and sniffed in disapprobation.

Next morning, Mr Trevithick drove up to the count house at nine a.m. precisely. Hector Bolitho hurried out to greet him and took him on a tour of the mine buildings. He was impressed by Trevithick's fastidious, almost dainty manners, the smartness of his turnout, and the gloss on his patent-leather boots. He had expected an engineer to have rough mechanic's hands with grime in their pores and black under the fingernails. Richard Trevithick was not a bit like this; he spoke in a low-pitched voice, with neat grammatical phrases and just a tinge of a musical Cornish lilt, but the drift of his remarks did not please Bolitho. He complained that the inn was a disgrace and intimated that, if steps were not taken to improve his accommodation, he would remove himself from Wheal Fortune to a mine whose owners were more appreciative of his needs and sensible of his genius.

'I'll have a word with Jack Lugger the landlord about it,' muttered Bolitho, 'but don't expect miracles. This is Windfall, not Peru.' He was not sincerely sympathetic. After all, Trevithick wasn't a real gentleman. His father had been manager of Dolcoath mine, but had none of Bolitho's own connections. He had picked up ideas above his station. He ought to know how to put up with a little hardship without complaining.

'I don't think you've adequately caught my drift, Mr Bolitho,' Trevithick insisted, with an edge of exasperation. 'What I'm trying to get over to you is that, if you don't take steps to see that I am lodged in a suitable fashion, I shall take myself off immediately. Your Silverton Gurney has ordered the machinery from the foundry; he didn't baulk at putting up money for that; he knew it was a sound investment. Now, through you, he's cheeseparing over the expense of accommodating the engineer. If you think he's so unimportant, I suppose you're prepared to undertake the installation of the machinery yourself. Even in the wilds of Peru I've had better treatment – '

'You must excuse me,' Bolitho interjected, trying to keep the sarcasm out of his tone, 'we have never had occasion to lodge persons of your importance in Windfall. You are the first to complain of the standard of hospitality at the Tinners' Arms, but rest assured, I shall go there immediately and remonstrate.' Fleetingly, he had even considered offering Trevithick the hospitality of his own home or asking the Gurneys to put him up at Tregurney House, but had dismissed the idea. All said and done, the man was a mechanic – a brilliant, versatile, visionary thinker – but a mechanic none the less. 'And I'll have suitable food sent up from Tregurney. Your room shall be improved at once, but the Tinners' Arms is the best we can offer in Windfall, and you'll be wanting to stay in the village to keep on top of the job.'

'Aye, I'll be wanting to stay on top of it, as you put it, if only because I'm anxious to quit this godforsaken dump as soon as possible. Now let's meet this assistant feller you've been praising up so much. I hope he doesn't turn out as much of a disappointment as everything else round here.'

'What d'you know about engines?' Trevithick demanded of Welland when they were face to face in the forge.

'I know a high-pressure boiler when I see one,' said Welland.

'You do, do you? I see the fame of my inventions runs before me. And a cataract valve, can you describe that?'

'As the fluid runs out, it operates steam and exhaust valves.'

'You've got an unusually clever smith here, Mr Bolitho. I hope he's not going into competition with me,' laughed

Trevithick. Bolitho studied Welland. There was more to this man than met the eye.

'Do you know anything of that chap Halt?' he asked Trevithick when they were out of earshot.

'Can't say I do. The name means nothing to me. Why, what's the problem?'

'He and his daughter just turned up here one day, out of nowhere.'

'And you think he's got a skeleton in his cupboard, do you? Haven't we all? Well, he's left his behind him and I, for one, don't intend to disturb it. Let's get down to business. When are boiler parts from Harvey's arriving?'

Over the ensuing weeks, the wagons rumbled into Windfall, bearing the strange iron contraptions constructed at John Harvey's foundry in Hayle, shipped round Land's End by water to Fowey and hauled up the long wooded valleys from the head of navigation past Tregurney House where the ladies taking tea on the lawns wondered at the toppling metal masses, and feigned horror at the carters' oaths.

'What's Silverton up to now?' asked the squire's wife. 'I suppose *you* know. My husband honours yours with his confidences. Those infernal machines must be his doing.'

'Hector tells me he's ordered the last word in machinery for Wheal Fortune and he's brought Mr Trevithick to Windfall to fit it. The adventurers were pretty glum at the news, though, they wanted a share out.'

'Well, Janet, I don't blame them. We are all starved of cash so my husband can have his playthings. The engine we have has served us well enough. I hope and pray this steam mania of his won't drag us all down to bankruptcy and ruin.'

'I don't think you need touble your pretty head over that, Diana, my dear. Hector tells me that Richard Trevithick is most capable, a bit conceited perhaps, but eminently capable.'

'How many times must I tell you I can't bear that "pretty

head" expression of yours. I resent your condescension. I'd like to be credited with the ability to think as well as you and Silverton. It isn't as though he really understood those steam contraptions: he has to rely on men like Trevithick to construct them for him.' The porcelain cup rattled in her saucer as she spoke. 'And I think it's disgraceful of him to have skipped off to London again on some pretext or other, just when he ought to be here, keeping an eye on things.'

'He knows he can rely on Hector for that,' smiled Janet Bolitho, picking up her sewing. 'As for what calls my brother away from Tregurney so often, you must satisfy your curiosity by questioning him directly on that. Or perhaps Mr Trevithick could enlighten you; he's seen him in Town quite recently. I hear Trevithick's a most personable fellow, not so young as he was perhaps, but then, none of us are, are we, Diana? And well turned out, quite a dandy, I think you might find some consolation in a visit to Windfall.'

'I'm sure he's more to your taste than mine, dear Janet,' rejoined Diana distantly, a smile of disdain on her lips, 'but I suppose anyone married to someone quite as stodgy as Hector Bolitho can be excused for having an urge to flirt with the Mr Trevithicks of this world. I myself haven't come down to tradesmen.' She picked up her skirts and sailed off towards the mansion with all the dignity she could muster.

If she had been introduced to Richard Trevithick that morning, she would not have taken him for a dandy. After the first day of Wheal Fortune, he had abandoned his patent-leather boots, rolled up his sleeves, and got down to business. But he had not abandoned his grand manner. Despite that, the miners respected him. Nothing mechanical seemed beyond his grasp. When the massive boiler arrived, strapped to a special low-slung four-wheeler, it puzzled them how he would swing it into the engine house, but he immediately set them to work rigging up sheerlegs and, within the day, it was hoisted and slung on a web of tackles that carried it into the new building. All the time, he was egging the men on.

'Call yourself Cornish!' he taunted them. 'I've seen it done quicker by ignorant savages. Let's see what you're made of.' The tinners grumbled a bit, but they put their shoulders to the wheel. Trevithick was a Cornishman like themselves, his coat was off and he would haul on the fall of a rope when needful.

'Is it true you was over to Peru and Costa Rica?' Trevorrow asked him.

'True enough, and to tell you the truth, I often wish I was back there when I realize what it's like to be here in Cornwall. But come on, brothers, 'tis no time to think of might've beens, we still have to install this engine. Another week at that Tinners' Arms will be the death of me.'

The tinners soon realised that he had another compulsion: Trevithick was working against time, he couldn't wait to see his engines working. From dawn to dusk and after, he lingered at the mine, putting his ideas into execution, pestering Welland to make modifications to the parts that arrived from the foundry.

'Can't you stay a bit later tonight?' he begged him.

' 'Tis late enough already,' said Welland. 'There's always tomorrow.'

'Not for all of us.' Trevithick's face glowed with what appeared to be ruddy health in the light from the forge where Welland passed most of his time making up parts for the engines. 'I'll see you're rewarded. There'll be a special bonus for you when it's all over.' Welland shook his head. Trevithick cocked a quizzical eyebrow. 'There must be something that draws you home, something more magnetic than my conversation. And you're never in the Tinners', are you? D'you have a spirited young wife there? That's it, isn't it? It must be love, only love can compete with money –' Welland shook his head again. 'What, do you deny that too? Well, I'll not press you further, though I'm sorry you can't see your way clear to stay back and help me. You're a good man, Welland, a great help to me, the only thing about Windfall that hasn't been a disappointment. It's never been my lot to have a better assistant, one who could work metal the way you do. In fact, I suspect at times you know more than your master. You haven't been a smith in these parts all your life, have you? Bolitho said – '

'Bolitho knows nothing,' cut in Welland. 'Anyway, it isn't worth the telling – but I can tell you why I don't linger of an evening. I've a young daughter, my Ruth, and I don't care to leave her alone more than I must.'

'What about her mother, can't she look after her?' asked Trevithick innocently. He had heard a rumour or two about Welland, and the story of his fight with Magor was still going the rounds in Windfall. There was a chance he would learn more by feigned ignorance.

'Her mother's gone.' Welland pursed his lips and a shadow clouded his eyes an instant.

'I'm sorry to hear it,' mumbled Trevithick automatically.

'No need for that. 'Tis all long gone, before we came here.'

'I've been over-inquisitive, forgive me.'

'You're a good man, Mr Trevithick, and I'd like to help 'ee. Tell you what, I'll talk to Ellen Curnow and see if she'll take Ruth in for a few evenings. You shall know tomorrow.'

Trevithick was delighted, his face glowed with satisfaction and he clapped Welland on the shoulder.

'This Ruth of yours, she must be a beauty, otherwise I'd've been introduced to her. I don't blame you, old chap. But don't worry, I'm practically past it: too old for cradle-snatching. Now, back to business: the last of the castings are on their way, we should get some tomorrow. Within the week we'll have them in place. Thanks to you, we're getting along splendidly. But it's late already, isn't it? Off you go, home to your daughter.'

Trevithick fell ill. He said it was the dampness of his room at the inn, but the doctor diagnosed some obscure tropical ailment and said he should be bled. Trevithick refused, but he was light-headed and weak. The doctor applied his leeches anyway. Even the drinkers in the taproom lowered their voices when they heard how bad his condition was. Hector Bolitho scurried over solicitously, afraid the engineer might be carried off before he was able to fulfil his contract, but Trevithick's servant turned him away at the door. Late at night, the last of the wagons rumbled down the street. If the carters had looked up, they would have seen a watcher, white as a ghost in their swaying lanterns' glare, standing at his window in a nightshirt, with frail arms braced on either side of the frame.

Next day, he was back at work. The miners looked at his parchment-yellow face and shook their heads. When he arrived in Windfall, three weeks ago he had walked with a youthful step. Now he looked old and frail. He leant heavily on his servant's shoulder as he dragged himself from one project to another. Hector Bolitho gave him a cheery wave from the count house, but he did not raise his hand in reply. Every so often, a shivering fit took him and he retreated to the forge where he stood by the fire's glaring eye, trying to absorb its heat and drive out the miasmas of Costa Rican jungles from his agued bones.

When he felt better, he discussed progress with Welland. None of those around could follow their conversations. They were all about bronze and iron, loads and pressures, cylinders, valves, governors, cog-wheels and cranks, blast pipes and flywheels. Sometimes they would discuss a certain quality of steel for ten minutes at a stretch while Welland forged special parts for the engine which Trevithick was continually modifying.

At long last, everything was ready to fire up the boiler and give it a test. It was late in the evening when Welland tightened the last bolt and wiped his hands on a piece of rag.

'Are we done then?' asked Trevithick. 'Is it really all over?

Fire away then!' he instructed the stokers who were waiting in the shadows. 'I suppose, by rights we should wait for Squire Gurney to be present to observe his new toy in action,' he confided to Welland, 'but we can always have another start-up tomorrow when he gets back from his travels – I've heard he's expected – he won't know any different.'

The first furze bundles were already flaring into life. Within minutes, they were shovelling sea-coal into the fire-box and the glare from its open door illuminated their half-naked bodies. The fire roared through a tunnel in the heart of the boiler, then doubled back and shot up through the stack. As the temperature in the engine house rose, Richard Trevithick relaxed and appeared much better.

'With training like this, Hell should have few terrors for us,' he joked.

'You play the part of Lucifer with conviction, Mr Trevithick,' chimed in Bolitho, poking his head through the doorway. 'I was at the accounts and saw the fire. I guessed something was happening. You're testing?'

Trevithick nodded. It was dusk and the engine house entrance was crowded with curious faces: miners just off the ladders at the end of their core, kibble landers, horse-minders from the whim, some of the bal maidens. The fire's roar had subsided to a dull rumble now, with only a brief whoosh when the fire-door was opened for fresh coal. Trevithick was concentrating on a gauge at the top of the cylinder, waiting for the vent valve to blow. When the first steam jet shot out, several onlookers jumped back in alarm.

'Try a working stroke, if you please, Mr Halt,' Trevithick requested politely, but before Welland could act, another voice stopped him.

'Before you do that,' said Mavis Trerice from the back of the crowd, 'I've a question for you, Mr Trevithick.'

'Out with it, we can't stand about waiting.'

'What's that engine going to be used for, and the other one you'll be installing?'

'They'll power the pumps, haul the kibbles, work the stamps, probably a man-engine into the bargain.'

'And what's going to happen to the kibble landers, the men who work the horse whim, and the bal maidens? Will their jobs continue?'

'No,' said Trevithick crisply, 'and I don't see why they should.' He fixed her with a firm stare. 'Look here, Miss Whoever-you-are, I've been installing these things for thirty years, they've taken away work and they've created it. If it weren't for steam, Cornish miners would still be scratching at the surface instead of showing the way to the world as they are now.'

'We're wasting time,' said Bolitho. 'Mr Trevithick is right. You'll see that in time, Mavis. As for the rest of you,' he scanned their anxious faces, 'Squire Gurney'll look after you, he always has, hasn't he? Do you want to get his back up by striking?'

'Us don't want to stand in the way of improvement,' said Trevorrow, 'but us don't want to be driven abroad fer work neither.'

'We should wait till the Squire comes home, we should get his promise,' said Mavis, thin-lipped with anxiety.

'I don't know what you're going on about,' said Bolitho suavely. 'You have his promise. Hasn't he promised *you* employment whatever happened?'

'Yes, but that's not true for all these others, is it?' she snapped back, and instantly regretted it. The tinners were looking at her strangely. 'One and all, isn't that the Cornish motto?' she added, but they were no longer with her, she sensed it.

'Oh well,' said Trevorrow, confirming her impression, 'if you're all right, Mavis, us others don't need to worry. Let's get on with it. Comeason, Welland, do what Mr Trevithick d'want.'

Welland hesitated a moment, as though making up his own mind, then pulled a lever, allowing steam from the boiler to enter the cylinder. The piston rod slid through its guides and the beam rocked for the first time. There was a gasp of admiration from the crowd, and a small cheer led by Hector Bolitho. The engine settled down to a pattern of panting strokes. Welland relaxed and smiled. The tinners watched for a while and then began to drift away. Only Trevithick showed anxiety. Something was wrong, but he couldn't place it.

He snatched up a lantern and began to examine the boiler casing. The onlookers stopped leaving and waited to see what he was searching for. Finally, he halted at the extremity of the casing where a ring of large rivets held the flanges together. Whatever it was he saw, it was imperceptible to any other eye than an expert's. When he held the lantern close, it showed intermittently, fitfully but unmistakably, like a small flame. At other times it was so hot and dry as to be almost invisible. Trevithick bit his lip. It was there, damn it. It was unmistakable. A thin tongue of steam was emerging.

'Let her out,' he snapped at the stokers. 'We'll have to cool 'er down if we don't want to be blown up among the angels. That'll be all for tonight.' He turned to Welland. 'Some damn fool carter has cracked the flange. I can't believe it's Harvey's. Now we're held up. It'll take weeks for them to send us another.'

His face was jaundiced again: all the colour that had animated it while the boiler was being stoked up had ebbed away. Abruptly, he turned on his heel and walked out into the night.

'Reprieved,' said Mavis quietly, 'reprieved, but not pardoned.' She too departed, leaving the ring of solemn faces. Only one man smiled: Tom Magor, who had been relegated to tending the pumps at the foot of the shaft. Trevithick's despair and Welland's consternation amused him. He too had heard the steam escaping, but had said nothing.

Soon, everyone but Welland had drifted off into the night and he too was anxious to leave, but felt it his duty to wait until the boiler cooled and the steam leak had died away. Ruth would be impatient to come home from the Curnows'. She did not adventure out alone now. At last, the pressure dropped to a safe level. Welland had already raked out the coals to speed up the process. As he did so, his mind kept repeating the parting words Trevorrow had spoken: 'That'll be the last engine Trevithick'll build, I reckon. 'E'll be lucky to see the end o' this un.'

As if to confirm his prediction, Trevithick failed to come to the mine next day. The energy to face up to the unexpected setback was not forthcoming. He did not come the next day either and his servant went off in the phaeton in search of claret from Liskeard. There was no claret in Liskeard, but plenty of good Fowey brandy. Trevithick sat in his bed and drank hot punch. His hands were dry and feverish. Hector Bolitho paid him a call, pushing past the servant in the doorway.

'What's to be done?' he demanded as soon as he saw how the engineer was looking.

'Wait for a new part from Harvey's.' Trevithick took a gulp of punch and a rivulet dribbled down his chin.

'It's disgraceful,' said Bolitho, 'poor workmanship, we shall have to sue them.'

'You know what's disgraceful?' grumbled Trevithick, pulling himself up on a pile of soiled pillows. 'What's disgraceful is that a man in my condition, at my time of life, should have had to come to a hell-hole like this to make a living. I ought to be receiving money for the patents on my inventions. The first steam tramway, that was me! The high-pressure internal flue boiler, that was me! The steam threshing machine, that was me! The Euston Square railway, that was me! The road locomotive, that was me! And what do you see me reduced to? Reduced to petitioning Parliament for a reward for my inventions. Reduced to taking on an unprofitable contract with skinflint adventurers! You know what's disgraceful? It's having to put up with visits from people who only turn up when you're ready to keel over and leave them adrift without a compass, people who've never thought to invite you home because you weren't quite a gentleman. Well, don't worry, I don't intend to give up the ghost in your precious Windfall. I'm too proud to leave my bones in a place like this. Now, pass the toddy and get out!'

'You're unreasonable, Trevithick, damned unreasonable.' Bolitho's blood was up. It was unusual for him and he was trying to restrain himself. 'If you were half as clever as you say you are, how the Devil did you allow so many people to get round you? Anyway, I should make it quite clear to you that there are two sides to every contract, and I've the distinct impression that you're malingering. I expect to see you at work tomorrow, next day at the latest.' When he was gone, Trevithick let out a whistling sigh of relief.

Perhaps there was something in the Fowey brandy. It was fiery enough and had never seen a customsman. Trevithick sweated through the night. In the early hours he felt slightly better. Someone was scratching at the door. Perhaps it was only a dog, it was so tentative. After a while, he roused himself to speak:

'Come in.'

The door swung back and Welland's face appeared round the edge, dishevelled and concerned in the light of the tiny oil lamp that Trevithick kept burning.

'Are you well enough? Can you get up? Can you come to Wheal Fortune? There's something I'd like to show you.'

It was not yet dawn. Cold stars glittered through the window and it felt as though there had been a frost. Trevithick shivered, regretting Costa Rica's caressing warmth. But he agreed. Welland wasn't the sort of man to drag him out for nothing. He dressed hurriedly, wrapping himself in a long greatcoat, and they set out for the mine. The roadside grass was stiff with white rime, the ruts were frozen hard and the plates of thin ice between them crackled under the walkers' feet.

'Just like Peru,' mused Trevithick quietly, 'cold like this, open like this, barren like this. A Cornishman should feel at home there. The only difference was, there were real mountains all round the Altiplano, great pink peaks with the light on them before sunrise, not like that piddling little sand-heap over there. People here think they know about the world because they've read about it in a book, but they've never seen real mountains. Imagination isn't enough. There are things that need to be seen, and even then, we can't comprehend them. Do you know, I've seen oyster shells in the rocks on top of the Andes? How do you account for that?'

Welland looked at him sideways, wondering whether he really expected an answer. Trevithick seemed to be wrapped up in a private dream, living in a far-off land that was more real to him than his present circumstances, a country where he cut a figure, a landscape where dream had become reality.

'They had gold there once,' Trevithick resumed, 'great treasure. The Dons came and took it away. All they have left is tin and copper, but they have mountains of it, great nuggets waiting to be dug out and carted off. It will be the death of this industry here in Cornwall. The miners, the Indians, they work for nothing, near as makes no difference. They chew coca leaves all day to keep out the hunger and cold. They're resigned. A skilled Cornish miner can make a fortune out there as a captain, but it's cold up high in the Andes, you can't imagine how cold.'

They reached the new engine house and Welland pushed him inside, feeling his arm shaking through the thick cloth of his coat. The contrast was overpowering. The furnace door glowed cherry-red. Steam was hissing from the escape valve. There was a smell of hot metal and a whiff of oil. Trevithick cocked his head on one side, looking at Welland quizzically. Welland grinned sheepishly and asked, 'Shall I start 'er up?'

Trevithick was streaming with sudden perspiration. He felt a momentary weakness, but there was something he must do. He picked up the lantern and examined the place where the steam had been leaking. It was dry and quiet. Not a breath disturbed the small hairs on his knuckles when he risked passing them across it.

'You know a thing or two, don't you, Welland? You didn't learn how to do that hereabouts. That's more like magic than blacksmithing. I've always thought there was something special about you, something familiar. At first, I thought it was the way that you walked, but it's more than that. I can't place it.'

'Plenty of smiths have a limp: they get kicked by horses,' said Welland gruffly.

'It's not that. It's not the name either. It's something about the way you do things. You haven't worked in Newcastle, have you? Or Stockton? Or London? Or Swansea? There was a man in Gloucester once, or was it Bristol; he could handle metal like you. He had a knack, a special understanding. You couldn't put it into words.'

'If we'd met before this, I'd have remembered it, even if you didn't.'

'I suppose so.' Trevithick sounded disappointed. He was trembling again, but his eyes were sparkling. 'I don't often thank people; I don't often have much to thank them for. I've done the work and they've reaped the credit like Gurney. But in this case, I've a debt of gratitude – let's put it this way: if ever Parliament votes me the money that's due for my inventions, I'll use it to go back to South America. I'll take you with me, Welland, I'd like to. You're not Cornish, but I think we could get along together.' There was a short silence while Welland pretended to do something with the crank mechanism. He didn't want to face Trevithick, for his eyes were wet. 'I know what it is,' the engineer went on, 'it's your daughter. You must bring her along. She'd have wider horizons; she could live like a lady.'

'Shall I start 'er up?' Welland repeated with a catch in his voice.

'It's not realistic, is it? I suppose that's what you're thinking,' Trevithick muttered, 'but we need our dreams, don't we? We all need a country to go –' His voice tailed away, then with fresh assurance, 'Go on then, start 'er up! We're not finished yet, not by a long chalk!'

Welland pushed over the lever and gave the beam a push with his other hand. The engine gasped and then settled down to a steady series of panting strokes.

'Regular as a chronometer,' Trevithick exulted, 'best piece of machinery that ever came out of Harvey's.' Welland still couldn't face him. Trevorrow was right, these *were* his last engines.

But Trevithick recovered. The improvement was dramatic. In a couple of days he was once more the sprightly, slightly foppish fellow who had driven into Windfall at the outset. The work surged ahead: Trevithick's first engine began to haul kibbles up and down the shaft and the sleepy boys who used to tend the horse whim circling the capstan had to be found new jobs underground. The second engine was being set up alongside a new bank of heavier stamps. Another week and everything would be in working order.

On the Sunday morning, Welland left Ruth with Curnow's wife, making bread in the slab oven, and walked alone on Carnwartha. In the ordinary way, he might have taken her with him, but now he reasoned that she was better off with plenty of company. Curnow's house was always alive with children, the fire was always warm, and there was frequent laughter. She was better there or at home with Ellen than out on the moor where there were many bad memories. That was his conscious reason for walking alone on the moor, but his real, unavowed purpose, was different.

Around him, the bracken had turned listless. Its stems had been broken in the equinoctial gales and their shattered tops stuck up like the masts of a fleet, half shot away in some deadly engagement. Between them, abandoned spiders' webs were strung like parted rigging. The bracken patches stained the hillside with a rusty iron hue, interspersed with the green of sheep-runs and the grey of ancient rocks. This wilderness, beyond the last cottage, beyond the last attempt at a garden, was fairy and pixie country, ghost territory where timeless spirits lurked among the stones. Ahead of him, where Carnwartha butted into the sky, the last wraiths of mist contorted themselves into nothingness. An air of melancholy, pungent as the scent of an abandoned orchard, clung to the land.

Welland fought it off. He climbed with a firm step, his boots swishing through grass wet with overnight rain. The bracken spears dug into his ankles, but he paid them no heed. His attention was fixed on the heights where the sky was brightening, minute by minute.

As he approached, the summit's structure became more evident. At some time, long before history books or chroniclers, men had been at work here, ditching and walling, throwing up earthworks in a labyrinth whose pattern was perceptible only from within. The exterior dyke offered a smooth front on all sides of the crown of the hill, broken only in two inconspicuous places where carefully contrived openings brought the intruder face to face with a blank inner wall. Some distance along this inner ring was a further cleft opening on to yet another wall. Because there was no central commanding height from which a bird's-eye view of the whole could be obtained, the purpose of the fortress was understandable to the imagination alone. Its original history was already forgotten when roving tinners camped within its walls. Some of them quarried the dykes in search of buried treasure. Their works were mere scratches upon its surface: a pit, a few rotten posts, a hearth, a heap of turf and stone that was once a hut.

The centre of this vast enclosure, so private that only the larks and buzzards could see into it, was ringed by a circle of gigantic stones. Askew and tottering, they were a source of wonder to the rare visitors who came there. What disturbingly primitive cults had our ancestors celebrated in their shade? What dark ceremonies were performed around the enormous altar-stone at the hub of the wheel?

Welland had thought of these questions just as he had marvelled at the geometry of Carnwartha, but there were no answers, only speculation. There was another magnetism that drew him here and kept him peering ahead over the swell of the hill as he climbed and later, scanning the earthwork's curving vistas, thinking he saw, momentarily, a retreating figure, vanishing into the heart of the maze. He knew who it was, or was nearly certain. No one else came here so often. Even so, when he passed the final cleft and surveyed the enclosure, he was not sure he had seen anyone. Perhaps he had been led on by a trick of the light, the shadow of a tiny cloud, a figment of his imagination.

Standing there, he had the brief illusion that one of the distant standing stones was a person. He surveyed the circle again meticulously. There was no movement. No movement: no life. According to legend, these, like other stone circles, were Merry Maidens, petrified in punishment for Sunday dancing, a perpetual reminder of the reward attending the sin of frivolity. The circle was dead and empty. A mood of deep disappointment gripped Welland, an unspeakable loneliness. He felt vulnerable, uneasy, ready to run away.

'You followed me!' The voice came from high on the slope behind him. 'It's not the first time. I've seen you. Don't try to deny it.' He knew the voice, but the tone was not the one he had hoped to hear. It was hard, accusing, dismissive.

She was standing on the earthwork ridge above him, seeming taller than in reality. She stood straight, with the breeze moulding her dress against her body. Despite the rigidity in her pose, there was enough womanliness showing through the drapery to remind him of that other time, the time he could never avow, when he had seen her naked.

'I wanted to talk to you.'

'Here? You see me every day in Windfall.'

'You're not easy to talk to anywhere.'

'If you care to know, I come here for a little peace, a little solitude.'

'I'm sorry.' If she felt anything for him, he knew he ought to admit to himself, she would not be so cold, so dismissive. He felt acutely conscious of his crippled body, his gracelessness. He noticed she had a book under her elbow, clasped against her breast. It had a black cover. 'You read the Bible up here?'

'The New Testament,' she specified.

'I didn't know you were religious.'

She laughed at this and he wondered if she were mocking him. He had not thought to say something amusing.

'Did I say something foolish?'

'If reading this is what you'd call religious, then I'm religious. But if it's churchgoing or chapelgoing you're after, then I'm a proper heathen.' She was laughing again and this time he was not so sure she was laughing at him. 'I can safely leave that to Mother, can't I? She'll pray for both of us. She's got the Law and the Prophets at her fingertips.'

This was a side to Mavis he had never suspected, but then how little he knew her. She was a puzzle to him as she was to many. If she had been like the other bal maidens, she would have married years ago while still in her teens, and have a tinner husband and a houseful of children.

'What was it then?' she was asking him. For a minute, he was bemused, until she continued, 'You said you had something to tell me.'

'Oh —' he stumbled. Suddenly all the phrases he had rehearsed in his head were irrecoverable, as if they had tumbled to the bottom of a deep well. 'Why do you have to make it so hard?' He had to force the words out, one by one. 'Why are you always so distant from me?' Did her face soften slightly? 'I tried once to tell you how pleased I was about getting Tom Magor's job. You wouldn't let me.'

'When?' she was frowning with concentration as she descended the slope towards him. 'Oh, that day at the mine!' she answered the question herself, remembering. 'Well, you needn't have bothered. You got it by fighting, didn't you? There's no merit in that.'

'What other way was there?' he blurted out and regretted his question at once. The answer was in the Book under her arm, it was in the gently chiding look in her eyes, though he could not really accept it. '*You* stood up to Bolitho, didn't you?'

'That was not for myself. There was no violence.'

'I suppose not.' Why did every conversation have to take a hopeless turn like this. 'But it wasn't for that I fought Magor, and you know it.'

'You said you did it for Ruth, or was it "honour"?'

Stung by her disapprobation, he hurried on.

'Well, whatever the cause, I've a good job now, more of an engineer than a blacksmith. I'm making good money.'

'I'm glad someone's benefiting from Trevithick's engines. They say you're a clever man, Welland.'

'I'll make more. I'll make enough for a good home for Ruth and –' He stopped and bit his lip.

'–and,' she prompted.

'I'm a clever man. I can bend iron, but words won't heed me.' If only she would relax, soften towards him, then perhaps he could speak freely. 'You're not courting, are you?' The boldness of his question shocked him.

'No, not courting.' Her reply was serious, but a barrier had suddenly fallen. A wry smile seemed to haunt the corners of her lips. For the first time, he could look at her directly.

'I wanted to tell you what Mr Trevithick said to me the other day. It's a secret. You'll keep it to yourself, won't you?' She was looking straight at him. She wasn't really smiling, but the hardness had gone. 'He said he wanted to take me with him to South America. He said I should take Ruth with me.'

'Then go, Welland,' she answered with hardly a pause.

'Something holds me here. Or I thought perhaps that you –'

The wind blew a strand of hair across her eyes and she brushed it back with an impatient hand, at least that was what she seemed to be doing.

'You're a married man, Welland. At least, you were before you came here. There's Ruth. There's my mother. I can never leave Mother.'

'She doesn't deserve it. She's a terrible woman. Everybody knows that.' How had he managed to say something so wounding, so personal?

'She's a terrible woman: she's vindictive, she's vicious, she's full of hate, and she's lonely. Marriage made her so. And she's my mother. She says it will happen to me when I leave her. She says it's in the blood. She's a hard woman, and she sees clearly.'

'Your life, she's eating it away!'

He regretted the words immediately. The tears were unmistakable. Her hand went up to her face, her lip quivered, and suddenly she was gone, running, running across the earthworks. He scrambled after her, but she was far ahead in the labyrinth of ditches. He shouted her name, but there was no response, no echo. He cursed his hobbling gait; he ran too slowly; he would never find her. And then, at last, he glimpsed her as he reached the last rampart. She was far off, hastening down towards the village. He caught his breath; he had been close to her.

The earthworks at his feet stretched away like the last wave of a rolling sea. Much farther off, glinting in the rays of a steely sun, was the Channel itself, a broad stretch of it and a distant horizon. Beyond the horizon was more sea, oceans, and beyond the oceans, land: Peru, mountains, bleak uplands, fabulous mines. What had Mavis told him? Go,

Welland, go! He clenched his fists. No, he would not give in; he would not accept it: he would struggle on in Windfall.

Closer at hand, in the fold of the hills, the Wheal Fortune mine buildings looked diminutive, homely, dependable. The new engines were working. Puffs of steam were emerging from their windows. Smoke was trailing from their chimneys. Some kind of carriage, probably Trevithick's phaeton, was standing outside the count house. There was no bright colour in the village, no elegant architecture. No, this Windfall was not Peru. Welland sighed and began the long walk homeward.

Outside the engine house, Trevithick was talking to Hector Bolitho. He was wearing the patent-leather boots again and smoking a cheroot. Nearby, his servant was wiping mud-splashes from the phaeton's dashboard. They would leave on the morrow. Trevithick was a young man again, confident, alert, enthusiastic. You had to look close to see the greying hair and the crows' feet round his eyes. A bumper of claret had put colour in his cheeks.

'No hard feelings?' he challenged Bolitho with a winning smile.

'You're not the easiest of chaps to get on with: you have to admit it,' grumbled Bolitho.

'Well, you'll be rid of me tomorrow. The machinery's running: I've fulfilled my contract. I've waited long enough for Silverton Gurney to come and inspect it. What the devil's become of him?'

'The last I heard, he was at Yeovil or Mere, somewhere like that: some kind of breakdown. He's bought one of those steam-carriages up in London. Why a man can't be content with a nice carriage and pair, I can't imagine.'

'Never heard of progress, Bolitho? Your Silverton may be a bit of a dreamer, but he's headed in the right direction – made a big mistake though – if he'd had any sense, he'd've got me to design his steam-carriage. If he had, he wouldn't be stuck in the wilds of Wiltshire. Give him my regards when he gets here. Tell him I've left him a couple of first-class engines.'

'I will.' Bolitho held out his hand. 'I'll not detain you. I'm sure you have other projects to attend to.'

'Goodbye then.' Trevithick's eyes were already taking on a faraway look. Bolitho couldn't help feeling oddly sorry for him. He was pretty sure Trevithick had no other commission available. 'Another thing,' Trevithick called as he swung up on to the phaeton, 'that fellow Welland Halt – in case you didn't know it – he's good, too good for Windfall, worth far more than you pay him. God knows what brought him here. God knows what keeps him. But treat him well, make sure you do. You'd be a fool to lose him.'

❦ 10 ❦

TREGURNEY HOUSE

Tregurney Feast was the greatest event in the Windfall calendar. If St Winwalloe's Feast had once been marked by rejoicings, that distant day was long forgotten. But Tregurney Feast drew revellers from miles around. By order of Silverton Gurney, the mine was closed for the day so that the tinners and their families might come and enjoy the sport. They were glad enough to quit Windfall and walk the few miles to the nearby parish.

Quite early in the morning, Mr Nichols the Curate harnessed up his trap and led the long procession of his parishoners up the hill, past the carn, and down the valley towards the great house at Tregurney. He was as eager as any to quit his sad vicarage and exchange the Spartan pleasures of his own parish for the sybaritic charms of Tregurney village. For a few brief hours, he would be able to enjoy polite conversation on the terrace at Tregurney House, take tea with Squire Gurney and his pretty young wife, and hear the latest ecclesiastical gossip from the Rector of St John's who, when he wasn't hunting, spent all of his time in London or at Exeter, buttering up the Bishop.

My text this morning, is taken from the Book of Exodus, thought the Curate, allowing himself a secret smile, and I am Moses, leading the children of Israel out of bondage, across the desert, and into the Promised Land. And indeed, Tregurney Vale did seem close to Paradise that summer morning: the meadows sang and the cornfields held up their heads and laughed. At his back and gradually overtaking his slow stepping pony, the Windfall folk, all in their

Sunday best, were pressing on, intent on making holiday.

'Can I offer you a ride, Miss Halt?' he called to the serious-faced girl as she came alongside him. How grown-up she looked: experience had aged her. In a sense, she was a fallen woman, no longer virginal. That ought not to make him any the less charitable towards her.

'No, thank you, I'll walk with Father.' Her reply was polite, but he sensed a coldness. He had been wrong to ask. There was no bridge between him and these people. Thank God he would soon enjoy a brief respite with his own kind at Tregurney.

From time immemorial, the feast of St John, patron spiritual of Tregurney Church, had been celebrated on the twenty-first of June with all the pomp and circumstance the village could muster and its present patron temporal, Silverton Gurney, J.P. and a Member of Parliament, was determined that each succeeding revel should be more lively than the last. To this end, he threw open Tregurney Park on that day and no other, allowing the common people to take their diversions on the meadow habitually devoted to his deer, and encouraging them to pray in the old church which flanked the great house and whose crypt was crammed with leaden Gurney tombs.

But Silverton Gurney did not incline to dwell too heavily on the divine aspect of Tregurney Feast. Far better, he thought, for his servants and tenants to dwell on the tangible pleasures of frolic and good cheer. For weeks past, they had been preparing the sideshows and amusements that were traditional and now he stood watching from the head of the terrace steps, near the door in the Queen Anne façade which had been added to the earlier Elizabethan structure when its two wings were demolished and rebuilt in a more enlightened manner. Long tables with white cloths were being set out under the direction of his wife of a few years, Lady Diana, ready to receive the provender his tenants would contribute. She was badgering the kitchen maids, having a cloth straightened here, a table moved there, with the cool confidence that came of her Greville breeding. Diana was, she never tired of reminding him, to be a countess in her own right, and he, a mere commoner, had been lucky to catch her, doubly lucky for she was one of the beauties of Bath and an heiress to a title to boot, 'when dear Papa leaves us'. Was it that conscious superiority that had made him indifferent to her, or was it her vacuousness? He transferred his attention elsewhere on the fairground.

In the midst of the meadow, a troop of men was busy erecting a tall sycamore pole and building up a bonfire of fifty large furze bundles around it. Close by, the course for the foot races and the wrestling ring were being marked out. The crossbar for the sheaf-pitching contest was rising on pulleys between its two high posts. There was a bowling alley, a fortune teller's tent, a tinker's stall, an ox-roasting pit, the brewer's dray pulling alongside the marquee, all this and more was Silverton providing for his tenantry's delectation. But his particular pride was the strange contraption being unloaded by a pair of outlandishly dressed Dutchmen: it was a steam organ, surely the first ever to play in Cornwall. He smiled as he imagined the crowd's amazement and enthusiasm when first they heard it. 'Steam Silverton' they called him, and he was pleased to live up to his nickname: young Gurney was enamoured of everything that had to do with steam, he had bought steam-engines for his farms, steam-engines for his mines, not to mention his latest project. 'Steam' was a compliment; it placed him in the vanguard in progress. It was a matter of deep regret that delay on the road and an unavoidable detour to Bath had kept him from home while Richard Trevithick was at Windfall. He would have liked to converse with him, for all that Hector Bolitho had called him a swank and a fop, but the man had put in some good engines, hadn't he? His brother-in-law Hector was inclined to be an old sobersides. They wouldn't have blended well together.

He fished in his French waistcoat for his hunter and checked the time. In half an hour the lodge gates would be opened and the people would flood in. There was no time to lose, he must hurry round to the stables and see to it that his new steed was ready. He planned to ride out and meet the arriving Windfallers. He could hardly wait to display it to them: their faces would be a study. The like of this had never been seen in their village.

Mr Nichols flicked his whip at his pony's ear to liven it up. He had just caught the first glimpse of the pinnacles of Tregurney House through the trees and couldn't wait to get there. He noticed some tiny figures, a small group of men on the ridge overlooking the mansion and wondered what they were doing. Then he recalled: they must be preparing the 'holes' – yet another pagan tradition, no doubt, like the bonfires, but it didn't bother him. It was those spoil-sport, long-faced, killjoy Nonconformists who were doing their damnedest to wipe every trace of jollity from the face of merrie England. Hadn't they put their ban on guise dancing? Didn't they call the St Columb hurling sinful sport? And the Padstow 'Obby 'Oss? And all such harmless survivals of a pagan past, mere folklore now? Wasn't there a Society for the Suppression of Drunkenness in Bethel already, and talk of starting one at Windfall? That old woman Trerice was behind it. What sort of life would it be for the tinners if they had to forgo their distractions and make do with psalm singing and hellfire sermons?

Around him, the Windfall folk had fanned out into the heather on either side of the roadway. Most of the men had sprigs of flowering broom stuck in their hats. 'My Plantagenets', the Curate laughingly called them, recognizing the ancient badge, the device that set them off as Windfallers among the men of Tregurney. They too laughed and sang as they followed the little brawling stream in its wildwood covert, down towards Tregurney church whose bells were pealing in welcome, sending the rooks showering out of the elms like fireworks exploding. Every man Jack was there, save the few deputed to watch over Wheal Fortune, leaving Windfall as desolate as the Roanoke Colony. Last of all in the Curate's holiday retinue, came Curnow and his family, with Ruth and Welland.

Welland had bought a new coat for himself, a wideawake hat, new nankeen trews, and calfskin shoes. For Ruth he had bought a poke bonnet and a nut-brown dimity dress. As they walked along, he stole occasional glances at her face, framed in the stiff taffeta brim. He was concerned to know whether she shared her companions' exhilaration. As the months rolled by since that traumatic incident with Magor, he had hoped that the smith's defeat would somehow exorcise the sullen spirit that possessed her, but the expectation proved largely vain. He had spent freely of the good wages Mr Bolitho was giving him to buy her trinkets, shoes, a parasol. She remained withdrawn: not all the gold in the Indies would buy her laughter. She walked through life like an entranced funambulist. Welland feared to wake her, lest she fall. And yet, it seemed that all that was required for her recovery was a charm, a rite, a prince's kiss.

'What's that? What's 'appenin'?' Curnow was asking excitedly. Welland took notice. There was a commotion on the road ahead. A thin column of black smoke mingled with bursts of sparks was shooting up from a dip, clear of the holidaymakers' heads. There were shouts. Mr Nichols's pony reared in its shafts and had to be held down by a couple of tinners. A woman screamed.

The column of smoke seemed to have stopped in a place where the road dipped down to a ford. There was a sporadic belch of vapour and a burst of laborious panting. People scattered in all directions across the moor. Children were crying.

' 'Tis one of Squire Gurney's contraptions,' said Welland reassuringly. 'Naught to be afeared of. I'll go and take a closer look at un.'

He hastened forward, momentarily forgetting Ruth in his eagerness to inspect the cause of the disturbance. From the brow of the dip, the whole thing was clear as crystal. A strange contrivance was canted over, half in, half out of the ford, with one if its drive wheels intermittently spinning. At the front, clinging to the driving seat, which was set up like that of a four-in-hand, were a gentleman clad in the French fashion, and his liveried groom. The gentleman, who was struggling with the controls, gave them a fierce wrench: there was a roar of steam, the heavy flywheel spun furiously, and the left-hand driving wheel bit into the bank. But the cleated wheel only dug deeper into the shingle and the vehicle tilted at a crazy angle. The knot of brave spirits who had approached the machine leapt backwards in alarm as hot red cinders showered down on them. There was an abrupt crack and the remaining drive wheel stopped moving.

'That's torn it!' lamented the driver as soon as the steam and smoke had subsided. 'Well, don't just sit there,' he told the groom shrilly, 'get down and see what's wrong with it.' The latter clambered reluctantly down, with dubious looks at the muddy water which soon covered his buckled shoes and stained his yellow stockings. Pushing back his hat, he scratched his head.

'Don't see nothin',' he muttered as Welland approached quietly, curious to examine the steam-carriage closely.

'It's these goddam roads, not fit for packhorses. I'll never rest until they bring the turnpike. Look closer, you nitwit.'

So that was the steam-carriage, and that was Silverton Gurney. Welland had seen him a few times at the mine and in the crowd when he fought Magor, but 'Steam Silverton' had never vouchsafed Welland more than a nod on his rare visits to Wheal Fortune.

'It's beyond me, your honour,' whined the servant, 'and I'm ruinin' the gilt on this jacket. I can't do no better.'

'I didn't expect you would,' said Silverton Gurney, screwing up his lips in pique. 'Well, here's something you *can* do:

run home to Tregurney and harness up a pair of draught horses. We won't get out of here otherwise.' After the groom had scurried off in evident relief, Silverton Gurney settled himself and became aware that a solitary figure had remained close by and was staring at his vehicle. 'What d'you think you're looking at?' he demanded querulously. 'Who are you anyway?'

'A cat may look at a king,' said Welland whose face was hidden in the shade of his broad-brimmed wideawake hat.

'If I had a horsewhip on this, I'd flog you for your cheek. Won't you leave off gloating? You know nothing of these inventions; they're the way of the future; country's just not ready for 'em; only fools stand grinning.'

Welland seemed to ignore him. The wry turn of his lips did not change. He slipped off his shoes, stepped into the stream and crouched on his haunches, examining the mechanism where the water swirled around the rear axle.

'Looks like a few sheared bolts in the drive,' he announced, 'nothing too serious.'

'What makes you say that?' Silverton Gurney stared at him narrowly. Who *was* this fellow?

'Well, it's broken free at the crank coupling. Come down and look if you don't believe me.'

Silverton Gurney hesitated: he was in a foolish and precarious seat on the carriage, but he was reluctant to wet his silver-buckled shoes.

'If it's broken, it's broken. The horses will be here soon to tow it.'

'If you've tools on board and a spare bolt or two, I think we could fix it,' said Welland, confidently, tossing his hat on the bank. Now Gurney recognized him. He made a swift decision. He would enter into the spirit of the thing. A boyish grin spread over his face as he rose to his feet, flung off his French coat, and leapt down into the shallow stream. Next minute, the two men were kneeling by the back wheels, discussing the problem excitedly. 'See that broken coupling?' Welland was asking.

'What's the next step?' Silverton Gurney was asking politely.

'Find me the tools; you must know where they're hiding. If you're game to muck in, we can bodge this up before your chap comes back with the horses.'

Silverton Gurney unbuttoned his sleeves and rolled them up. He had already forgotten his embarrassment, this was a real adventure. Fighting wasn't the only thing this Welland was good at, he seemed to know something of engines. He was inclined to like him.

Mavis Trerice turned into the beech avenue that led from the lodge to Tregurney House just as the church clock struck noon. Responding to the signal, a line of white puffs shot up from the skyline ridge above the trees, followed by the bangs of sharp explosions. Beside her, the Curate's horse shied again and Mr Nichols's knuckles showed white where he gripped the reins. He ought to have been ready; it was the miners shooting their 'holes', a set of primitive mortars dug in the rock, full of sound and fury, in celebration of the commencement of Tregurney Feast. Mavis reached across and took the bridle, blew in the pony's nostrils and calmed the beast. She was sorry for Mr Nichols; his discouragement was writ plain all over his face. Even at the Feast, the taste of happiness eluded him. His eyes were damp and pathetic in their thankfulness.

'Where is your mother, Miss Trerice? I do not see her anywhere. I trust she's well,' he mumbled.

'Mother's gone on ahead. She has some kind of sideshow.'

'May I offer you a ride to the end of the avenue?'

'Why not?'

The Curate was rather confused by her acceptance, but enjoyed his brief summer warmth of her sitting beside him.

'Remember,' he told her as she alighted, 'the door of St Winwalloe's is always open.'

'I'll remember,' she told him with a quiet smile. 'It was, once before, wasn't it? But you shouldn't be over hopeful on my score. I have better things to do with my Sundays than churchgoing.'

She left him and made haste to the tables that were now loaded with fuggan, lardy-cake, seedy-cake, and saffron. Burnished bowls of scald cream stood among them. There was buttermilk too, and bowls of junket. Behind the tables stood the plump, rosy-cheeked dairymaids from the Tregurney farms. You could tell the Tregurney folk at a glance: they were portly, well-fleshed, ponderous peasants, with hayseeds in their hair, unlike the spare, sharp, hungry Windfallers. Although superficially amicable, there was no love lost between the two communities. In the eyes of Tregurney's farming folk, the tinners were fearsome barbarians. But this was Feast Day and old hurts were best forgotten. The two communities mingled in a single, jostling, laughing crowd around the tables. The choicest morsels were soonest swallowed.

'Come on, I'll treat you!' Mavis cried impulsively when she came upon Ruth, standing irresolute in front of a pile of sweet-smelling saffron buns, her parasol hooked over her arm.

'Have you seen my father?'

'Don't worry about him; he can take care of himself. Come on, we're going to have a splendid time!'

On Tregurney House terrace, Mr Nichols was insinuating himself gently towards the tea table where he hoped to engage Lady Diana in conversation. He fancied that she, like himself, was a delicate flower, who found it hard to bloom in these crude and rustic surroundings. Unfortunately, he happened to jog his Rector's elbow and transfer a dollop of scalding Lapsang Souchong from the latter's cup to the belly of his favourite bloodhound.

'Goddamit, Nichols,' snapped the Rector. 'Wha'd'you think you're up to? Feller's not fit to be let loose in polite society,' he announced to all and sundry. 'Must be the company he keeps up there in Windfall. Rubs elbows with them tavern hussies and bal maidens, I'm certain.'

'I'm sorry, I didn't mean to – ' faltered Mr Nichols, blushing furiously. Rector Adams must have seen him arrive with Mavis Trerice seated in the trap beside him.

'Then say you're sorry!' interjected the offended cleric. 'No, not to me, dunderhead: to him, to Redeemer there!' pointing at the slavering animal which had risen to its feet and was panting vigorously. 'Go on, pat his head, the poor beast needs sympatthy. Oh, he's a sensible soul: that animal's got more feeling than a dozen curates. Go on, pat his head; he'll not harm you.'

Mr Nichols, much against his better judgement, was extending a timid hand towards the drooling monster whose flabby jowls, rolling eye and lolling tongue spoke of anything but sweetness and refinement of nature, when he was providentially reprieved by a cry of distress from Lady Diana who, by virtue of her exalted station, claimed instant and absolute attention.

'What has become of him?' she wailed, clutching at the table for support and pressing her forearm against her severely knit brows in a gesture worthy of Emma Hamilton's famous Attitudes. 'What *has* become of him!'

Her guests looked at one another in alarm. Had she lost her cat? Her little terrier? Her Brazilian cockatoo?

'His carriage has exploded! I know it! He's hurt, poor darling! I know it, I tell you: I feel it here!' she cried and boldly transferred her expressive hand to her left breast which was but lightly imprisoned in her *décolletage*.

'Don't be a goose,' grumbled Hector Bolitho, 'he's gone hundreds of miles on that thing. He gets stranded often enough, but there's no disaster.'

'There is! There is! I just saw his groom run back to the

stables. Why didn't he come to the house? There's something he's afraid to tell us. To be widowed so young: what have I done to deserve it?'

Lady Diana's audience stood transfixed, overwhelmed by her wild surmise and sudden emotion. Mr Nichols lowered his eyes and clasped his hands in silent prayer while Rector Adams gazed at her heaving bosom with frank admiration. She wavered, reached out for support, and seemed ready to swoon. Only an unkind soul might have noted the fierce look she gave her brother-in-law, Hector Bolitho, when he half led, half carried her off to the privacy of the drawing-room. If his eyes had met hers, her Gorgon look would have petrified him, but he was a past master at ignoring her.

'Damned women, always fainting,' grumbled the Rector, putting down his tea and fishing for the brandy flask in his cut-away coat, 'no stomach for anything. If they had their way, a man couldn't do anything that gave a bit of excitement. They're trying to put an end to bull-baiting and cock-fighting. What'll be next? Fox hunting? Well, at least there's still the wrestling to afford a man a little enjoyment.' He took a long pull at his flask. 'Coming, Nichols?' The Curate shook his head vigorously. 'No, I thought not — lily-livered,' and he stumped off towards the meadow. Mr Nichols waited for his departure with eyes still averted, delving within his soul for sufficient charity to add a prayer for the Rector to those he had already soundlessly uttered for Lady Diana and her husband.

Down on the fairground, the sports were well under way. There was bowling for the pig, climbing the greasy pole to snatch a chicken from its top, foot racing, sheaf-pitching and wrestling. As usual, a keen rivalry between Windfall and Tregurney folk was developing. A string of broom-trimmed hats surrounded the wrestling ring where the Tregurney champion, a muscular, lanky, red-whiskered farmhand, was challenging all comers to a bout of Cornish wrestling.

'Who's first? Where's that girt fighter o' yourn?' he was

taunting. 'Didn' I 'ear you'd found a man that could beat Tom Magor? Don't tell me 'e's afeared o' Bill Cock?'

'Well said, Billy boy!' shouted the Rector provocatively, pushing his way through the throng to the ringside. 'These Windfall chaps are full of big talk, but they're lily-livered, yellow as the flowers in their hats. Now, here's a guinea for the man who can take Bill Cock to three falls.' He held up the gold coin, making it flash in the sun before placing it ceremoniously on one of the ring-posts. 'Let's see some sport, you pale-faced men from the underworld! Who'll be first? Won't anybody stand up to him?' The miners shuffled their feet: they all knew Bill Cock. Only Tom Magor had been able to stand up to him and Tom was stuck at the bottom of Wheal Fortune, tending the pumps on Hector Bolitho's orders.

Nearby, the sheaf-pitching was in its early stages. One by one, the farmhands sidled out of the crowd, grinned at their sweethearts, spat on their hands, jabbed the two-tined pike into the heavy wheaten sheaf that lay on the ground behind them, and swung it up towards the crossbar. Most of these early contenders were very young, or clumsy inexperienced louts. The real contenders, the men who habitually pitched sheaves from the harvest wagons to the rick builders, would come in later. They were capable, some of them, of hurling a sheaf clear over a high rick. Now they waited, smiling at the antics of the shamefaced youths who failed to reach the crossbar at fifteen feet. They themselves would come in at their own level, each having three tries with which to establish himself.

The pig grunted and snuffled in its wooden cage alongside the bowling alley. Small boys leaned over, tormenting it with straws, jabbing them at its small frightened eyes until it squealed as if being dragged off to the slaughterhouse. In the alley, the wooden balls bounced along between the hessian walls towards the skittles, setting them flying in a clatter. Would the pig have been happier to know that its torments would soon be over when the highest scorer took him home and prepared him for supper?

Mavis Trerice winced at the pig's screams and guided Ruth away towards the foot race enclosure. They paused to watch the fat-stained boys hauling themselves up the greasy pole towards the chicken which had toppled from its perch and hung, with barely a twitch, from the twine around its claws. One by one, the boys shinned up the lower part of the pole where the grease was thinnest, slowed in mid course where their arms weakened and the pole became slipperier, and slid back with yelps of chagrin when still ten feet below their prize.

Mr Nichols, left alone on the terrace, had settled himself into one of the gilt French chairs beside the table and, having waited in vain for a servant, was pouring himself a cup of cold tea. He wanted to rush indoors to Lady Diana, pat her hand, murmur condolences, but felt inadequate, inferior, confused and shy. The shout he heard from the foot of the steps compounded his confusion.

'Where *is* everybody? Where's Jacques? Tell him to come immediately.' Anxious servant faces blossomed from windows all over the façade. 'And, Hilda, fetch some boiling water to my room, plenty of it, we're both filthy. And tea, make some tea, we'll be needing it. You there, Nichols, where's everybody gone? Where the devil's my wife, Lady Diana? I want her to meet my new friend Welland. He knows all about engines.'

Curate Nichols was horrified. Only with difficulty could he bring himself to turn his head and confirm *de visu* the evidence his incredulous ears transmitted to him. It was all too true: Welland's figure was unmistakable, so was Silverton's. Both men were indescribably dirty, but Silverton was smiling and had draped his arm round Welland's shoulders. Did he know what sort of low fellow he was consorting with? He struggled awkwardly to his feet, making a low bow and trying to catch the Squire's eye so that he could warn him.

'Lady Diana's unwell. She was concerned about you,' he mumbled.

'Concerned about me! You must be joking!' scoffed Silverton as he swept into the hallway, leaving a trail of muddy footprints on the parquet.

'You'll stay to tea, won't you?' the Curate heard him say as he vanished upstairs, still dragging the limping smith. Mr Nichols subsided into his seat with a loud gasp.

'I'm afraid I can't, Mr Gurney,' Welland's voice was heard replying, 'my daughter Ruth is at the fair alone and I'm neglecting her.' Mr Nichols heaved a sigh of relief at this intelligence.

'You must fetch her over. She must meet my sister Janet; she loves to encounter young ladies. What are her favourite distractions? Music? Embroidery?'

'She loves to read, Mr Gurney.'

'Good, tell 'er we've got a whole library here. It's at her disposal. And no more of that "Mr Gurney"! To you I'm Silverton, or just plain Silver. You're a mechanical genius. I knew it from the first. There must be no ceremony between us.' Mr Nichols put his hands over his eyes in despair. He would have covered his ears too, but he feared to miss what followed. 'We're going to be partners,' Silverton's firm voice filtered down to him from his dressing-room amid sounds of splashing, 'Halt & Gurney – Gurney & Halt, Steam Car Constructors, how does that sound to you? With your mechanical skill and my money and business sense, we'll soon be famous.'

'Gurney Steam Cars will suit me better,' Nichols heard the smith protesting, 'I seek no fame, but I'll help you if you desire it.' Sly dog, thought the Curate, pretending to be disinterested like that – surest way of ingratiating himself. This whole conversation was unbearable to listen to, but he could not avoid it.

'This coat's too grand for me,' Welland was insisting, 'I couldn't possibly wear velvet.'

'Fetch 'im another, Jacques, something more sober to put on while his own things are sponged and ironed. We'll make a gentleman of you yet, if we can find the right outfit. Clothes make the man, you know.'

'Is that the same as a wolf in sheep's clothing?'

Their laughter tumbled down from the upper room and fell like lead on the embarrassed Curate. Mr Bolitho must have heard it in the drawing-room, for he came to the door with a quizzically cocked eyebrow.

'No need to dye all your wardrobe black, Lady Diana,' he called over his shoulder, 'not yet, if the voice I hear is anything to go by.'

Mr Nichols crooked his finger and beckoned him over urgently. He must be told immediately about the Squire's impropriety in consorting with Welland.

A quarter of a mile away, loud shouts rose from the meadow. Rector Adams cheered with the lustiest. Blood was flowing! One of the Wheal Fortune tinners, egged on by taunts and jeers, had taken up Bill Cock's challenge and now his nose was broken, butted flat by the crown of the Tregurney champion's head. There was general laughter as he stumbled from the ring with his bundled shirt turning scarlet as he pressed it to his face.

'Who's next?' called Cock, in a voice that rang with grim resolve. A silence fell. The Rector fumbled in his coat, produced another guinea, held it up and challenged:

'Now, which of you fine felows has a little pluck? Who's going to earn this second guinea? There's two of 'em now for the man who will stand up to Bill Cock. What, are you all yellow? Well, if no one's man enough to climb into the ring with Bill Cock, the money goes to him. How's that, Billy? They're yellow, ain't they? Yellower than this golden guinea!' and he placed the second coin alongside the first on the post. The tinners looked at each other. Who would be next to take a beating?

'Where's Welland to?' they murmured to one another. The Tregurney men, grouped behind their champion, laughed outright.

Welland heard the mocking laughter in the distance as he crossed the meadow in search of Ruth. If the mirth had been nearer at hand, he would have believed he himself was the butt of the laughter. He glanced down at the fine fabric and extravagant cut of the coat he was wearing and hastened to lose himself in the crowd. In this rig-out, even his best friends would make fun of him. Things were easier in the jostling press of revellers: no one paid him any particular attention, the free flow of ale from the marquee saw to that. He was inconspicuous in the crowd, but Ruth was untraceable. Several people said they had seen her with Mavis at the racecourse, but when he went there, they had moved on. He stood irresolute, wondering where to go next, when a figure emerged from a small tent somewhat detached from the general flow of people. In the tent gable above her head was a round panel, ringed with cabbalistic signs. The woman looked scrawny and old, but her identity was concealed by a soft chamois mask that covered her face from the brim of her hat to her wrinkled chin and throat. Only the tip of her nose and her eyes' sharp gleam showed through it. She was dressed with gipsy extravagance, brocade skirt over green petticoat, purple shawl flung over bony shoulders. The woman was summoning him with a bejewelled hand. Still he hesitated and the woman called him even more insistently in a cajoling, croaking voice: 'Come on, me 'andsome, I've something to tell 'ee. Don't be afeared, my lover, I shan't 'urt 'ee.'

Welland did not respond, he even half turned away to depart, but the old woman forestalled him, scurrying forth and laying a compelling hand upon his sleeve. It was like a bird's claw, knobbly, with long talons digging into his flesh through the borrowed coat.

' 'Tis 'ere, what you d'seek, my fine gennulman. I've

watched 'ee castin' about. No need to look further.' She was
dragging him towards her tent door. He still resisted, but
more feebly, half-believing that Ruth might be there, or
some message. And, when all was said and done, what harm
could a feeble old woman do him?

Before entering the tent, the woman paused on the
threshold and made a gesture like the sign of the cross with
her free hand, then reached up and spun the wheel, watching
it turn till it stopped dead before ducking through the
door-flap. Welland followed and found himself in a small
obscure space with purple hangings that, once the flap fell
shut, was completely dark but for the glimmer of an oil lamp
on the tiny table. The woman pushed him down onto the
chair at the near side of it and seated herself at the other. She
still gripped his right forearm, but now she manipulated his
hand, flattening the fingers and laying it out, palm upper-
most, beside the lamp. Its dim glow, projected upwards,
gave a sinister cast to the old woman's masked features and
Welland shivered involuntarily. He told himself to be rational: he had no love of omens; superstition exasperated him.
The contrived drama of this setting made him want to pull
away his hand and escape, but the woman held fast and
began to chant in a peculiar dreamy voice.

'Today I see you rise – Fortune's Wheel turns, and you rise
– from the depths of despair, the Wheel snatches you up –
you tell yourself you do not believe in the Wheel, you think
yourself master of your fate, but blind Fortune picks you up
by chance encounter, gives you a new habit, sets you on a
journey across the water –' Welland laughed at her. The way
she was exploiting the clues his appearance afforded was
pathetically obvious. 'Do not mock, foolish man,' she continued. 'Fortune knows all secrets and in her own good time,
reveals them all, even those you most wish hid. The Wheel
turns, you rise, you have your heart's desire, money you
have, and love, and respect, the land resounds with your
name, you are happy,' she broke off, panting quickly as if

breathless, 'you are happy,' she repeated, 'soon, you have your heart's desire.' She paused again and, as much as the mask revealed, she seemed to be smiling. 'And the Wheel turns!' her voice suddenly loud again, exultant, 'You feel nothing at first, but it turns. Them that the Wheel hoists high, them does it dash down. The Wheel rides over them.'

'There are other wheels than yours, woman, wheels we turn ourselves. Now free me. I must find my daughter.'

'He must find his daughter. What, has he lost her? Lost her mother more likely! Where is she? Find the mother first, the daughter'll look after herself.' The old woman cackled with fierce laughter. 'No, never fear for your daughter. That maid will outlive us all, and still she'll hold her tongue, save one secret. Them that keep secrets seldom laugh or speak. She'll laugh when you cry, though; I can vouch for that.' Welland saw the glint in her eyes. What did she know of him and Ruth? Why the malevolent glee?

'I'm leaving. I'll get no sense here.'

'Cross my palm with silver and you shall go,' wheedled the woman, still gripping his arm tightly. 'A man with a fine coat like yours should be able to spare something for a poor gipsy.' Welland sighed with frustration, then dug into his trouser pocket with his free hand and flung a shilling on the table. 'Goodness gracious, what a kind, generous gentleman! I must tell 'ee more for that, mustn't I, me 'andsome?' She bit the coin between her yellowed teeth, affording him a fugitive glimpse of her lower face, before dropping it into the bodice of her dress. Her index finger swept down to trace the lines on his palm. ' 'Tis a 'ard 'and,' she enunciated carefully, as if reading from a book, 'an 'and made for 'ard labour, the 'and of a maker. The line of the 'ead is long. Aye, but the 'eartline's broken. I see two women, two loves, the latter short. And the line of fortune fades when it meets the heartline. What did I tell you? 'Tis all written 'ere! See now, the line of life, look 'ow soon it ends!'

Welland felt her long, sharp nail stabbing into his palm

where the line ended and was shocked by the rejoicing in her voice.

'Everyone's lifeline has an ending. There's always an end.'

'But not there, not so soon! Look to thy soul, my lover, be sure 'tis ready.'

'I've nothing to repent of, old woman. 'Tis you should repent of your evil tongue.'

'You'll have cause to repent,' she screeched as he shook off her slackened grasp and pushed his way out into the light, blinking as the sunshine dazzled his eyes. 'You'll take your pleasure. Then, when the deed is done, you'll repent.'

'Hold your wicked tongue, damn you!'

'Repent! Prepare thy soul! Repent!' she leant out after him, shouting. She reached over her head for the wheel and gave it a vicious twist, making it squeal as it spun on its pivot. 'The Wheel of Fortune turns, the Wheel returns, what's up comes down! Repent! Repent!'

Welland was gone, plunging into the crowd, hardly remembering his search for Ruth in his haste to remove himself from the aura of hate surrounding the fortune teller's tent. Who was the malicious woman who had vented her spleen on him! He thought he knew, but it made no difference. He moved in a world gone mad: the inane, grinning faces all round him were like masks in a carnival. His spell in the tent had alienated him from the prevailing mood of frivolous gaiety. The yellow sheaf rose behind the crowd and fell tumbling like a tattered doll. The pig's squeals set his teeth on edge. The fowl at the top of the greasy pole flapped feebly. When he discovered Curnow and his wife Ellen, it was initial relief that changed to anxiety when he saw that his daughter was not with them.

'Where's Ruth?'

'Never you fret about she.' Curnow was slightly tipsy, his bland moon-face was flushed and a wide smile split it at the sound of Welland's voice. Ale slopped round as he gestured with his tankard at arm's length. 'Your Ruth's away with

Mavis Trerice, 'avin' some sport, and so should you. This is the finest Feast I ever did see! 'Ark to that music! That there's a steam organ. A blessing on the young Squire for leavin' us to 'ear un. Tis 'andsome. All that good provender, all this good ale, what could be better this side o' 'Eaven? Look around 'ee, boy, tell me if 'tiddn' 'andsome.'

Welland did as he was told, trying to change his mood and see things as Curnow saw them. Why wasn't he grinning like Curnow? The crowd *was* happy; Tregurney House and the flag-topped church *were* splendid; the sky *was* virgin blue, and the hills behind *were* plump like folds of flesh under a matron's dress. If it were not for the gash, the red stain that spilled down the slope, vanishing behind Curnow's head, all would be perfect. But the stain was where the adit emerged from the mine and the water pulsed out by Wheal Fortune's pumps left its blood-red mark. This reminder of where the two of them had blasted their way into the light, Curnow would never see. Neither would he see the borrowed coat that Welland wore, lent to him by the very man who had been strolling on the lawn that fateful day. These thoughts still saddened him, but he could not speak of them, Curnow was too content.

'Goos on, admit it, boy: you never did see nothin' so brave!' prompted Curnow, but before Welland could frame a reply, he was pulled away by a band of tinners.

'Where've 'ee been to?' they demanded as they dragged him towards the wrestling ring. 'Us needs 'ee!'

While they were hustling Welland through the throng, the pig, goaded beyond endurance, smashed its way out of its cage, screeching as it took flight. The boys gave chase. It doubled back into the crowd when they cut off its escape and vanished in a forest of legs. There were shouts of alarm as it blundered through and then a new hue and cry on the other side. Everyone, it seemed, was after it now. Welland watched dully as women threw stones, boys grabbed at its ears and tail. Its screams rose to a new pitch of anguish as grown men thundered in pursuit. They snatched up staves that had marked the foot race course. They lashed out at it unmercifully. When it stumbled and fell, they kicked at it. These were good-natured country folk, gentle enough in ordinary times, but now the hunt was on, their blood was up. At last, a burly farmhand struck the pig a stunning blow across the snout and the chase was over, leaving the crowd scattered and breathless all over the meadow. Welland glimpsed Mavis in the distance; she had her arm round Ruth and appeared to be turning her away from the spectacle.

'Tremendous sport!' Welland heard the Rector cry as the tinners lugged him the last few yards to the ringside. He took in the situation at a glance: they wanted him to champion them against that hulking great yokel who was swaggering around the ring, head thrown back and arms folded across his barrel chest.

'Is that him?' asked the yokel superciliously. 'Is that the best you can find? D'you expect Bill Cock to fight a runt like that?' The Tregurney men dissolved in laughter.

'Three guineas, it's three guineas now to the winner,' announced the Rector adding another coin to the pile.

The crowd, which had dispersed during the chase after the pig, was suddenly densely packed around the ring, sensing coming excitement. Welland studied the faces, seeing the well-marked factions from each village. The Tregurney men's eyes were cold and disdainful. Those of the Windfall men were encouraging and full of hope. He was their white-haired boy now, wasn't he?

Then he saw Mavis and Ruth again. What were they doing here in the front row, wedged among the Tregurney people? Ruth's look was as distant as usual. He felt Mavis's cool eyes full upon him as he was shoved forward into the ring. What was she thinking? No doubt she was condemning him out of hand, just as she had the last time. What did she expect? He was a man, wasn't he? She knew what was expected of him. How could he back down?

'Give us that coat,' shouted one of the tinners, ' 'tis too fine for this sport.'

'Look lively, lads!' called the Rector. 'We haven't got all day. What's it to be? Cornish wrestling? Pugilism? The choice is up to the challenger.' There was a long silence while Welland thought, then he made his announcement.

'I won't fight.' Standing firm and foursquare, he waited for the storm to break.

'Won't fight! 'E's even more of a chicken than the rest o' that Windfall trade,' came a shout from behind Bill Cock. It was followed by others. Men spat in the ring. Welland looked at Mavis. Her eyes were glowing, but there was still doubt in them.

'What'd'ye mean, "won't fight"?' insisted the Rector in his booming voice. Welland turned round with apparent deference.

'I've made a vow, Your Reverence, no more fighting, a vow to God. You wouldn't have me break that, now would you?'

'If you'd made a vow to Beelzebub, if you'd made a vow to the Devil incarnate, let alone God, it wouldn't excuse you from standing up for your fellows,' fumed the Rector.

'I'll take him on at something else,' said Welland.

'At what?' shouted the crowd. Welland waited for the tumult to subside.

'Sheaf-pitching,' he announced quietly.

There was a groan from around the ring, but Welland was unflustered. He had the impression that Mavis might be smiling. There was a new complicity between them. ' 'Tis fair enough to challenge a farmhand to sheaf-pitching, I fancy,' he added and set off for the other enclosure, removing his coat and folding it across his arm as he went. After a moment's bewildered hesitation, Bill Cock followed.

The sheaf-pitching contest was officially over. The winner had gone off with his prize, the sheaf lay abandoned and battered, the pikes were stuck in the ground. But the crossbar was still hoisted as high as the last contestants had left it. It seemed impossibly high.

'I 'spose you'll want to start lower,' said Bill Cock tauntingly, 'work your way up, like. I'll wait for 'ee.'

Welland shook his head, then walked across and selected a pike carefully. Bill Cock followed him and grabbed another.

'Let's get on with it then. I wants me three guineas.'

'I'll toss for who goes first,' said Rector Adams, who had appointed himself referee. 'But don't count on winning three guineas for this. It's not sport like wrestling. Now listen, you'll have three tries at each height. The best throw, unequalled, gives the winner. Now, I'll toss a coin.'

'Heads,' called Welland as the penny spun in the air.

'Tails it is,' proclaimed Rector Adams disclosing it on the back of his hand where he had trapped it after catching it. 'Will you go first, Bill Cock?'

'No, I'll come after,' grunted Cock, stepping aside.

Welland walked over to where the sheaf lay on the ground and speared it on his pike. Then he stationed himself half way along the crossbar, close underneath. He heaved the sheaf upward. It tumbled in its flight and fell hopelessly short of the bar. Bill Cock's face creased into a thin smile as he retrieved the sheaf.

Before pitching it, Cock laid it on the grass at right angles to the bar, but towards him, inserting the tines of his pike parallel with the straw, between the butt and the tie. He lifted it off the ground a few inches, testing its weight and balance, settled his feet, left foremost, gripped the pike's haft firmly, with left elbow high, and swung it upward. For such a shambling man, it was a movement of surprising grace. Welland had not expected it of him. The pike's head described a subtle curve as Cock straightened first his right arm, then his left, giving the sheaf a final impetus as it flew smoothly off the curved tines. Instead of tumbling as it had for Welland, it turned slowly in flight, rising in a smooth parabola that easily cleared the bar at its highest point. There was an instant cheer from the Tregurney folk as he sauntered to the side.

Now it was Welland's second try. He had watched Cock's every move, but putting it into practice was a different matter. This time the sheaf climbed higher, but thudded into the bar and fell back at his feet.

'You're too close under the bar!' shouted a Windfall voice. Welland considered a moment, then moved out a few paces to where Cock had stood. He paused again, with the sheaf nicely balanced on his pike, waiting for the shouting to stop. When it was quiet, he took a deep slow breath and his powerful arms went into action. The sheaf shot skyward as if fired by a gun. It soared above the crossbar and hovered at the apex of its trajectory. An enormous cheer burst from all the Windfall throats as it fell beyond the crossbar.

'How much shall we raise it,' asked the Rector, 'one foot or two?'

'Five! – No, put un up ten!' shouted Cock. 'Us don't want to fiddle about, do us?' So he's risking everything on one big throw, thought Welland; he's trying to unnerve me.

'Agreed?' asked Rector Adams. Welland nodded. He didn't want to prolong the contest. He was doing his best. If he won, he won. If he lost, he lost. He took his place for the first pitch. Although it had appeared that his last throw had risen as high as the bar now stood, he could not repeat it. The sheaf-tie caught on the pike's tines just slightly, but it was enough to make the sheaf jerk erratically in the air. It was well short of the bar.

Cock grinned, spat on his hands, and settled himself for his turn. His pitch had the same elegance, but the sheaf struck the bar just below its tie, teetered a moment, and dropped back on the same side. Cock's supporters groaned, but he was still jaunty as he stepped aside.

Welland tried again, taking his time. The watchers were quieter now. There was no need for the referee to call for silence. All around him, the faces were intent as he took his stance, a little further from the crossbar. The sheaf rose in an apparently effortless curve, climbing at least two feet above the bar, but it fell back on the same side without touching. It was Welland's supporters' turn to groan. He had misjudged the trajectory.

Cock's second try also fell short. Perhaps he hadn't taken it seriously enough. He muttered a curse as the sheaf came down. The crowd stirred uneasily. The contest was closer than they had expected. Welland paced about, trying to fix the exact spot from which to try his last pitch. He wondered whether Mavis and Ruth were still watching him, but did not dare look up for fear of losing his concentration. He went through the careful ritual of balancing the sheaf and adjusting his stance. All the Windfallers were willing him to win; he could feel it. Now for the supreme effort.

The pike snapped. It's handle broke between his hands, right at the beginning of his swing. There had been a flaw in the grain. Welland stood there, hopeless and bewildered, wondering what he could do. Rector Adams came up and handed him another. There was a buzz of talk. It was hard to regain his composure. He inspected the new pike; there was no obvious flaw in it.

It was his last chance, he knew that. All his fellow villagers were counting on him. A mere game that he had refused to take seriously was suddenly all important to him. He closed his eyes to concentrate. He saw the Wheel of Fortune turn. It's rising, he told himself as he revived and flung the sheaf at the sky. He didn't even bother to follow its flight. He knew it was good: he had done his best, now it was in the lap of the gods. There was no need to look up. The shouting told him all. Hats flew in the air. Tinners jumped round him, pounding him on the back. He shook them off.

'Not done yet,' he growled.

This time, Cock took infinite precautions. He tested the wind to be sure a gust would not spoil his throw. He loosened his belt and tied his kerchief round his brow. He stood more than a minute, poised, flexing his muscles gently before he threw.

The sheaf floated upwards, kissed the bar gently, pivoted on it and hung in equilibrium. All eyes were fixed on it as it vacillated, undecided where to fall. It fell on the far side.

The Tregurney folk went wild. More hats flew in the air. There was kissing and screaming.

'I'll take the money, said Cock when the tumult subsided. ' 'Tother chap 'ad four goes, countin' the broken pike, so 'e's disqualified.'

Welland bridled in sudden anger. Would he have to fight after all to obtain justice?

'I think not,' came a quiet voice from the back of the crowd, 'if Welland's throw is called into question, he might question yours. Is it not customary that the sheaf must pass clear over the bar without touching it?' The crowd parted and Silverton Gurney stepped through it, elegant, self-assured, imperious. 'I declare this match a draw, a most desirable result. I'll add a guinea to the prize money, we'll split it and make the prizes equal. Now, shake hands and we'll proceed to further business.' He held up a silver ball he had been concealing under his elbow. 'How about hurling to country? Let's see if you Windfall men can carry this to St Winwalloe's. And let's see if our brave Tregurney lads can stop 'em.'

There was a burst of cheering as he flung the ball high and far into the field with the men rushing after it. Squire Gurney knew how to please his people. He turned to Welland.

'You've been an unconscionable time finding that daughter of yours, Welland. Where is she? Lady Diana's quite out of patience with us. And where's the coat I lent you? Don't say you've lost it.' Welland squirmed in embarrassment. 'No, Welland, don't say you're sorry. I was only chaffing. I saw what happened. A man has to stick up for his own. Now hurry, where is she?'

For a moment, Welland feared that Ruth and Mavis had slipped away again, but he glimpsed them and plunged into the crowd to catch them.

'You're required to take tea with Lady Diana, young Ruth,' he told her.

'My, aren't we grand!' said Mavis. "Required for tea", just fancy. Quite a gentleman in our fine coat, aren't we all of a sudden, no time to pass the time of day with a friend either.'

Welland studied her, trying to judge her seriousness. Her face was a mask as usual. Suddenly, she grabbed him by the shoulders and kissed him.

'What's that for?'

'That was a fine thing you did, Welland,' she told him. 'I was proud of you.'

Welland could guess he was blushing, but felt unexpectedly bold, clasping her to him and whispering in her ear. She did not repulse him as he still dreaded, neither did she reply to him. Eventually, she stepped back, disengaging herself and he began to wonder if he hadn't made another unpardonable mistake. The eyes that met his were suddenly cool again. Still, what did he have to lose?

'Well?' he challenged.

'What about Ruth?'

'She can go home with the Curnows.' He waited. 'You'll be there?'

'Perhaps – if you're sober.' And she was gone, swallowed up in the remains of the crowd that were left now the hurlers had departed. There they were, toiling and broiling on the steep slope below the adit. They still had a long way to go, over hill and down dale to St Winwalloe's. Even as he looked, a youth from Tregurney snatched the ball and came running back with it.

'You didn't tell me she was half so pretty,' exclaimed Silverton when they came up with him. 'All our waiting has been rewarded. Come, Ruth, let me tell you what a clever man you have for a father. That's if you don't know it already. I hear you're clever too, a reader and a writer. You must visit my library. I'm not much of a bookworm myself, ought to be ashamed of it, but there it is. Who's your favourite author?' He waited, then spoke to Welland. 'She's a shy one. Don't say much, do she? But don't worry, my sister Janet'll draw her out. We must get down to business. I want to show you the workshop in the stables. We're going to talk engines.'

So the afternoon wore on while the young men fought for the silver ball in the bogs and streams, and raced headlong through the gorse until, near sunset, a Windfall boy carried it into the porch of St Winwalloe's. The pig, which had been hobbled in its cage, was carried off to make bacon. The chicken was finally pulled down from the greasy pole by a triumphant climber. The smell of roast ox was wafting over the evening air as the hurlers straggled back to refresh themselves with ale. If they had glanced towards the adit mouth they might have seen Magor who had come there to glower over the proceedings.

On Tregurney House terrace, Mr Nichols was trying to brace himself to address the young woman who was conversing quietly with Mrs Bolitho, but was finding it as impossible as usual. Ruth Halt was strikingly reserved as well as being strikingly beautiful: a sweet child, totally unversed in the ways of the world. How like Wordsworth's Lucy she seemed.

' "She dwelt among the untrodden ways . . ." ' he began murmuring to himself.

'Balderdash!' snorted the Rector who had come up behind him. He had a gun-dog's nose for all sentiment, and the bathos in Wordsworth in particular.

'Mr Adams,' said the Curate, changing the subject, 'don't you think someone should have a word with Squire Gurney? Is he aware that Welland is merely an artisan? How can he ignore it?'

'You don't know your Silverton Gurney, that's certain,' replied the Rector with an unexpected grin. 'Half of that familiarity is put on, just to vex Lady Diana. The rest is cheap enthusiasm, half-baked democracy. It's not the first time by a long chalk. But he'll get over it – he always does.'

Rector Adams's explanations were cut short by Lady Diana Gurney's reappearance. She had thought it time enough to recover from her fainting fit. Now she was in a vile temper. Silverton had not even bothered to ask after her welfare. She pointedly cut Welland's daughter and went to sulk alone at the end of the terrace.

At dusk, Silverton Gurney returned with Welland. Leaving the latter with Ruth, he offered his wife his arm and led the house-party down the steps, across the lawns, to the great bonfire in the midst of the meadow. With an ill grace, Lady Diana Gurney put a torch to the furze bundles which flared into the night while the tenantry cheered. They toasted the Gurneys in deep mugs of ale while the flames soared higher and the heat drove them back. One of the sun's swings was over, another had just begun.

Welland found the Curnows munching beef and preparing potatoes to roast in the embers when the fire died down. He entrusted Ruth to their care for the long walk home and slipped off into the dark, hurrying down the beech avenue to the Windfall road, past the place where the steam-carriage had stuck in the ford. He was glad to be wearing his own clothes again, though his hat had vanished somewhere during the cleaning.

A noise behind him made him stop in his tracks. With a crackling roar, a string of blazing tar-barrels came spinning down from the ridge above Tregurney.

Excited shouts rose from the park. Welland wondered whether he were not making a ridiculous mistake, leaving the Feast when all was jollity. But a stronger compulsion than merrymaking drove him on. He left the road and followed the tinkling stream, threading his way between the furze bushes which loomed dark and menacing under the rising moon. Beyond them, he sought a way through the wild wood, feeling the silence close in on him and his skin prickle with primeval fear.

The stream's quiet music led him on. He found its bank and twisted his way upstream along the semblance of a path. Everything was unfamiliar. He felt lost. Perhaps only the packman could find this glade. No, if Johnny Fortnight could discover it, so could Welland Halt. It was here somewhere and he *would* find it.

Silence ahead told him he was almost there. There was no chuckle from the water flowing over stones. A few more cautious steps and he saw the sheen of moonlight on the pool. Around it, the clutching boughs made a tight circle. The water was still, so still it reflected the moonlit leaves. It was deserted. There was no laughter this time, no splashing, no naked flesh, no packman either. Only spirit-haunted solitude. He leant against a tree, his heart still pounding, and gave himself over to melancholy. It was a wild-goose chase. He ought to have known.

Out of the darkness at the far side of the pool came a ripple. It was followed by another. They spread deliberately across the surface and lost themselves in the reeds. An otter? He was afraid to find out, but he had to know. Stepping back into the trees, he stripped off his clothes and hung them on a branch. The open moonlight made him feel his nakedness as he approached the water's edge and he was glad to slip into its concealment. Welland was at home in the water: his lameness disappeared as he swam gently forward without a splash, feeling the currents caress his body. The shaded part of the pool was only a few strokes away. Soon he would know. Her mother was a pellar, an evil-minded witch. She too was a witch, an enchanting, irresistible, beautiful witch.

The dimness closed around him. He stopped swimming and hung suspended between heaven and earth on a carpet of reflected stars. Another slow ripple rocked the pattern, and then another, as though in harmony with gentle breathing. This was where she had stood and frolicked with the pack-

man. Even now, the memory made him hot with embarrassment, shame, jealousy.

He had dared to give her a whispered tryst here. Would
she come, or would he see her only in his imagination?
Already, he saw her smile, white teeth gleaming in the
dimness under the trees. Her eyes seemed to gleam above
them. Wafting himself forward with slow-moving hands, be
breathed her name. Was that the breeze in the leaves, or a
quiet answer? Through the cool water, he divined her flesh.
When he closed his eyes, he could feel their lips touching. He
sensed her eyes still smiling at him from under the archway
of her hair.

THE TENT

'Praise the Lord!'

At the sound, Welland Halt looked up from his work and across Tregurney Park to the turnpike where a man in a billycock hat was striding purposefully towards Windfall.

In those days, a little man was walking through Cornwall. Short, stocky, a miner among miners, yet following where Wesley trod, this man had helped unloose the wind of change that was blowing through the county. And change was coming: there were stage-coaches rattling down the new turnpikes, more ships in the ports, new goods in the markets. Yet the biggest change was not in wealth, but in men's minds. It was a revulsion against barbarism, a groping for order, a vision of grace. Paradoxically, it was the wild, irreverent miners, enmeshed in the cog-wheels in their churning industry, and living in the valley of the shadow of desolation, who responded most eagerly to the bringers of good tidings when they brought promise of another life and the grace of redemption. Exchanging hymns for oaths and sermons for drunken maunderings, they lusted after righteousness, joined voices in the new harmony, eschewing present pleasure in return for the promise of sunlit uplands beyond the grave.

One man more than all other, a simple fellow in a billycock hat, a man of little schooling, but wise in the workings of the human heart, spoke to the tinners in the tongue they knew. Inspired by inward grace, his words could charm the birds from off the trees or make the very stones sing hymns of praise. Downright, devout, radiant with the joy of certified salvation, he marched from place to place, drawing great crowds as a magnet draws iron. Cornish among the Cornish, humble beside the poor, lionlike defender of the meek, leader of the lost, exegete of their universal book: his name was Billy Bray.

'Praise the Lord!' he shouted as he walked joyfully towards Windfall. 'Hallelujah! Praise the Lord!'

They had his promise, the chapelgoers who walked the long miles to Bethel each Sabbath. He would be with them soon. They knew that Windfall was in need of grace, and of a shepherd to lead their flock towards green pastures. They prayed for his arrival as if for the second coming of Christ himself. Postponement only served to whet their eagerness.

First, he was coming at Michaelmas, but he was building a chapel with his own hands near Camborne, and the work went slow. Billy worked his daily core in the mine and preached thrice on Sundays. Then it was Christmas.

'I'm took sick,' the message reached them. 'You'll see me Easter.'

'I pray to God he'll not delay,' cried Hilda Trerice when she heard the announcement in Bethel chapel. 'There's great wickedness in Windfall. Us do need an archangel to come with a rod to put to the backs o' the ungodly, us do need a whip fer the wicked. There's too much gamin' in Windfall, there's too much drinkin', there's too much whorin'. I pray to God fer the souls o' my bretheren and sisteren. May God preserve 'em from the sins o' flesh and from the evil of atheism!'

Welland was well aware of her uncharitable charity, but he shrugged off her disapproval. Now that he was prosperous and befriended by the Squire, he felt secure. Each day, he drove down in a trap to the stables behind Tregurney House where a forge and a workshop had been set up so that he could construct his own steam-carriages. He wore clothes that were good quality, but sober. Ruth sometimes spent the day with Janet Bolitho. Welland felt at one with Windfall, at home in Tregurney. He tried to forgive his enemies.

'Why can't Tom Magor have his old job back at Wheal Fortune?' he asked Silverton Gurney one day when they were working together. 'I have so much to do here, I can't get there often.'

'You're more forgiving than I am,' laughed the Squire, 'but you *are* hard put to it to be in two places at once. I'll think about it. We're doing damn well with these contraptions, but we could do better. We'll be pipped to the post if we don't get a move on. How soon can I drive the first one to London?'

'A fortnight, I reckon.'

'Magor shall have his job: then it'll be but a week, won't it? Ah, Welland, we're going to make a name for ourselves, you and I.' Silverton Gurney put an arm round Welland's shoulders and hugged him. 'It's a strange thing, friendship, but we have it, don't we?'

Welland felt the warmth of the embrace and was comforted. No voice, not even Hilda Trerice's would be raised against him. Only the lower orders were subject to such harsh morality. The gentry, who paid lip-service to the Established Church, were beyond its bounds. The Church of England was a broad church, encompassing hard-drinking, hunting parsons, as well as moralists and spiritual dreamers. Had Welland aped their observances sufficiently to attend St Winwalloe's with Ruth from time to time, he might have numbered among the elect, but on Sundays when the Windfall women and a handful of male converts took themselves off to the chapel at Bethel, he stole off to the moor alone, through the overgrown lanes and the bracken-clad slopes of Carnwartha. Sky and moor were his church; the druids' ago-old stones his congregation.

She took another way, gathering primroses as she walked, breathing deep of the warm spring air while the cottony clouds rolled over. He watched her coming, transported by her free strides, exhilarated by her windblown hair, entranced by her dreamy smile. He hid from her, standing behind one of the huge stones, with its rough lichen coat against his cheek, prolonging the pleasure of waiting now that she was there. *She* was the anxious one now. He saw her glance about. Welland always came first. She would be missing him. She turned and took a few halting steps towards the break in the earthwork through which she had arrived. Suddenly, it was his turn to be afraid, afraid because she was leaving. He whistled once, imitating the curlew's cry. She paused. He whistled again. She turned and saw him.

'You shouldn't have done that,' she told him as he took her hands, 'you worried me. I used to feel safe up here alone. Now I feel lonely.' He clasped her to him and stroked her hair. They leant against the great menhir behind which he had been hiding. He lifted her small hands one by one and brushed her fingers with his lips. With her forehead pressed against his, she felt the hardness of the man, his strength. Like the stone behind him, he would endure. After a while, he spoke.

'Well?'

She pulled away from him slightly, looking at the lichen patches on the old granite. Some of the lichen was silver grey, with leaves like seaweed; in other places, it was red, the colour of old blood, spreading in a slow, flat stain. Her conscious mind concentrated on her perception of the lichen.

'Have you decided, Mavis?' he persisted.

She sighed.

'I've told you: we don't need to.' Her voice was flat, almost despondent.

'But will you?'

She stepped from his embrace and walked away slowly, kicking at the plantains that poked through the grass all round her. He followed.

'It's that mother of yours, isn't it?'

She shook her head.

'If it were only that!'

'She never liked me, though what I ever did –'

She shook her head again, more violently.

'I vowed I never should.'

'But why?'

'Feyther.'

'Your father?'

'You don't know what he done to Mother. No, I don't just mean hit 'er, though he did that too.' She stopped speaking as she reached the altar-stone, a low dolmen supported on three half-buried rocks. Then she hoisted herself up on it and sat with her legs dangling while she sniffed at her primrose posy as though to sweeten her remembrances. 'I can't bear to think on it.'

'What was it he did?' Welland's face was full of concern. Mavis did not reply directly. Her face turned hard as she continued, making him think of Ruth's ever since Magor –

'She's bitter, isn't she? Vicious? All the kindness gone out of her soul, squeezed dry. She used to smile, I can remember that, but that was before he – I hated him too. I knew he was evil, yes, evil, shaming her, coming home drunk from the Tinners' with the smell of strange women of him, glorying in it, telling her she was dry as a stick. I hated him. She hated him, but wouldn't run away like I told her to. She said she was married to him, for better or worse. And worse it was. It got so bad us prayed for him to die. Us prayed for the mine to fall and cave in on his head.'

She stopped and her face took on a rapt look, as though peering into infinite distance. Her speech had become insensibly coarser as though taking on her father's character. Welland approached and clasped her thighs in his rough hands, but she did not look down at him.

'Poor li'l maid!'

'He knew, of course, he knew us wanted to see the end of un. He laughed and taunted Mother with it, and only drank the more. I thought she would murder him with the fire irons, but she never could.'

'Did she love him then?'

'She loved him and hated him: he was her husband. One night, she waited up till after midnight. When he didn't come, she barred the door against him. Later, I heard him shout and beat upon it for a while. "Open up! Open up, you bitch!" he cried till all the neighbours were at their doors. Then he went away. He never comed back. Mother never stopped crying, but I was glad, wanted to put on my best clothes in celebration the day they found his body in a winze where he had fallen. Mother wept. She said she'd killed him when she closed the door. I told her no. I told her he was evil. Women can't always submit. I don't know whether she heard me, but she changed. The day they buried him, she changed, never smiled a sweet smile more. Poisoned her life, he did. His spirit's still there in that house, in her, and it's evil, evil!'

'Come away then. You know I'm not like that. Haven't I sworn not to fight!'

She took his head in her hands, staring deep into his eyes as if to fathom out all future intent.

'You're a man, Welland. God knows what you might do.' Then she relented, with a ghost of a smile making her lips tremble. 'No, my Welland couldn't be like that. He's strong, but he's not brutal, is he?'

'Your Welland, aye, I am that. Your Welland wants to stick up for you out in the open, not just meet in secret here. I want to take you out of that house, 'tis no life for you, Mavis. There's evil in that place will poison you. You must leave now. Decide! Decide!'

'And if I decide against you?'

'I'll ask again.'

'It's not just me, Welland. It's you. I know nothing about you, you've never told me. It might be something terrible.'

'It is terrible, though not the way you think. That's the reason I could never speak.'

'But you'll tell me now?'

'If you'll say you'll have me.'

He waited. She sat still as a statue but for the rippling of her hair in the wind.

'For my maid's sake. Young Ruth gets older. She'll need a mother.'

'That's not fair!'

She pressed his face down into her lap and ran her fingers through his hair. How dear he was, how strong, and yet how defenceless. How much longer could she deny him? Gradually, her sight returned to the surface of things. Their isolation was complete, locked in Carnwartha rings' shallow saucer, with the sky's uninterrupted dome arched over and wedded to its rim, an enclosed world like an ocean wanderer's. And yet, though not a single sign of humanity was visible in its whole compass, she felt the certitude of being watched. She shivered. She ought to be full of joy to be so close to the man she loved, but she looked round again and she shivered.

Later that week Welland set off to find Mr Nichols. The Curate was not at home. Welland's knocking echoed hollowly in the dusty recesses of the vicarage. He found him in the church, making a pretence at decorating the pillars with Easter flowers.

'Will you marry me and Mavis?'

'It isn't that easy,' Mr Nichols replied to his question. 'There's the little matter of the banns to be considered, the chance that someone will stand up and claim there's "just impediment".'

'I'll risk that.'

'It's a legitimate curiosity and, to be frank, I share it.'

'You're a just man, Mr Nichols, at least you seem so, and discreet. If I agree to tell you something on that score, enough to satisfy you, will you consider – And anyway, there's never more than two or three in your congregation, hardly a soul in Windfall will know the banns have been spoken.'

'It isn't as though you yourself were part of that congregation,' answered the Curate with ill-repressed pique, 'not even at Christmas, or Easter, or Harvest Festival. If you had merely brought young Ruth for catechism – even those misguided Nonconformists out there, the ones who are putting up the tent for the wandering preacher, still come to the old church for their baptisms and their funerals. If I could think of you as a Christian – Perhaps you ought to address yourself to them in any case; isn't Mavis of that persuasion?'

'Her mother is,' said Welland gravely, 'but she herself is not a Methodist. She's not one for organized religion, but she reads the Gospels.'

'I can only recommend attendance at holy worship – to both of you. Then, in the fullness of time, when I have earnest of your good intentions –'

Welland had been studying him: the pathos of the man in his rusty serge cassock and rumpled white neck-bands checked his urge to make a quick, angry reply. Mr Nichols was not a hypocrite. He seemed a true believer, a man ready to face the cold lash of indifference and the agony of neglect. Though he could not speak the language of common men, he embraced the cross of his solitude uncomplaining and served his God the Anglican way, with ceremonies, with muttered prayers, with hand-picked flowers.

'I'm not a churchgoer, I'll admit that,' he countered, 'but I'm not an idolater, I'm not a drunkard, I'm not a whoremonger –'

'I know all that, Mr Halt,' the Curate interjected quietly, 'but do you have faith, do you recognize Christ as your Redeemer?'

' 'Tisn't that easy: you know that yourself. The more a man thinks, the more he'll wonder.'

'Have you ever considered, Mr Halt, that therein lies the reason for the establishment of our holy and catholic Church? Does not the Church offer the assurance that greater intellects than either of us have wrestled with the problems of belief? Have they not found proofs? Is not the church a rock on which we, poor doubting mortals, may stand secure?'

For Welland, his words had the ring of the Oxford class-room about them and he found them strangely belied by the sad dilapidation of St Winwalloe's shrine in which they stood. Birds flitted in and out of the broken windows to their nests among the beams; green damp grew up the walls; the altar-cloths were jaundiced and rotten; the odour of decay was universal. Yet it appeared that the Curate was unaware of the irony in his assertion. For him, all these externals were transient. Truth was elsewhere – in the City of God. For Welland, the decayed remnants of this once splendid church were all that was left of some man's masterpiece, an express-ion of creative greatness, God's word perhaps, but spoken through Man.

'I may not be much of a churchgoer, but I *am* something of a smith.'

'I've heard it said you're more than that: you're something of an engineer. You've been hiding your light under a bushel; there's more to Welland Halt than anyone here imagined. What brought you here penniless is beyond my comprehension. Aren't you involved in building a steam-carriage for Mr Gurney? He says you're a great crafts-man.'

Welland nodded.

'I was thinking I might use my craft to make something to go in here, a kind of offering – to make amends for being such a doubter.'

The Curate raised his eyebrows.

'There's not much we seem to require. Some things are a little old-fashioned, certainly, but we are well provided.'

Welland wandered off, examining the fittings, casting a critical eye on the altar rails, the candle sconces, the strap-work on the doors. Finally, he came to a halt beside the font, eyeing it curiously, gauging its size, glancing up into the roof above, surveying the space around it.

'I could make you a font cover.'

'A font cover? I doubt if we really need one. We've managed without one for several centuries.'

'No, you don't need one, any more than you need an altar, or bells, or paten and chalice, the font itself, for that matter. But doesn't man's handiwork add to the glory of God?'

'Man's handiwork can express that glory, he can't add to it,' corrected the Curate, 'God's perfection is of the essence: he exists, if only because perfection must exist in order to perfect itself.'

'Let's say I would be expressing it then, acting as an agent for the Almighty. I could make something special, not one of your everyday lids with a bit of curlicue on top, but something like the medieval carpenters used to do, a kind of pinnacle rising up into the roof, like the one at Sall in Norfolk, but different really: Christ blessing. I can see him already, larger than life, with arms outstretched over the font while you performed your ceremony.'

Mr Nichols pondered. Something of Welland's vision had infected him. The shadowy figure of a transubstantiated, grieving, all-merciful Christ hovered there already where Welland's arm was pointing.

'You can't make such a thing of metal. It would be too heavy.'

I can make it lighter than you could ever imagine. You could have it hanging there within three weeks.'

'Within three weeks? That's how long it takes the banns, isn't it?' said Mr Nichols stroking his chin.

'You could call it a coincidence.'

'It smacks of simony.'

'Call it a quid pro quo, an exchange of gifts.'

Mr Nichols already heard himself calling the banns to his empty, echoing church. In charity, he might do it. Jesus

Christ had consorted with a publican. Might He not pardon a poor curate for indulging a sinner?

'You'll send Ruth to catechism?'

Welland looked at him narrowly. What was his motive?

'I'll ask her. She'll come if she wants.'

'If you persuade her, you can call it a bargain.'

'You'll not regret it.'

'No, but *you* might.' Mr Nichols felt that he had done a good deed. Despite his scruples, a strong intuition of having done the Christian thing warmed his heart. Timidly, he shook the hand that Welland Halt held out to him. On three successive Sundays, after the second lesson at matins, he would read the banns.

Outside the church, Welland heard the beetle hammers pounding in the field near the clay-pit where the tent was being erected. He knew what it was for: Billy Bray was coming. But he did not follow the file of curious villagers who were setting off to watch the proceedings; he was hurrying home to Ruth. In his mind he rehearsed the phrases he would use to persuade her to Mr Nichols's catechism. It would be easy. She had a mind of her own, but for his sake she might be persuaded.

Never had such a huge tent been seen in the neighbourhood. It had arrived on a wagon train with its crew of erectors. The poles were like ships' masts, fitting together in sections. The guy ropes seemed a hopeless tangle. And yet, in just a few hours, the tent was pitched, the web of rope stays around the poles was established, the pegs had been driven home, the furled canvas unrolled and laced together, and now it was billowing skywards. The empty tent was like a vast submarine grotto; a greenish light filtered through its fabric roof on to the flattened grass. Its emptiness was a challenge: could it ever be filled? Its silence was a weight that would have to be lifted. No man in Windfall was equal to the task.

But that man was on his way, striding along the turnpike.

Disdaining horse or coach, the little man in the billycock hat was steadily approaching. As he passed the labourers working in the fields, he shouted to them boldly.

'Praise the Lord!'

They looked up in amazement from their hoeing, then whispered to each other.

' 'Tes brother Billy.'

'Look to the weeds each time ye sow,' cried Billy. 'God will be there to count your crop.' Was it madness or sense? They exchanged glances. Billy did not pause. Already, he was receding up the hill from Tregurney, still shouting, 'Praise the Lord!'

'Can we go to hear Billy Bray, Father?' Ruth greeted Welland as he crossed the threshold. 'Mavis is going. Everyone in Windfall will be there.'

'I can think of a few that won't,' muttered Welland. 'The Tinners' is a stronger attraction.'

'Don't be such a spoilsport. How often do I ask you for anything?' It was true: Ruth asked for so little. How could he begrudge her the excitement a revival meeting would bring to Windfall. He ought to be glad that she was interested in something, after the long months of apathy that followed her mishap with Magor. He wanted to talk to her about Mr Nichols, but this was not the moment, that would have to wait.

'Aye, we'll go there, but don't expect me to enjoy it.'

'Quick, let me brush your coat and make you look decent.'

She squeezed his arm and kissed his cheek and he was astonished by the wave of happiness that went through him. Life, for all its troubles, was good. Old woman Trerice had been wrong when she boded him ill: his wheel was still rising.

The wheels at Wheal Fortune spun fast as the tinners came up to grass from the core. Billy Bray was waiting for them at the shaft mouth. As they stood panting from their climb, he approached them with a stone in either hand. There was something comical in his appearance that caused a young tinner to call out, 'Doan' 'urt us Billy, us be too winded to fight!'

The men laughed, but Billy laughed with them. It was obvious he had no fear.

'Fight!' cried Billy. 'Aye, I'm to fight – to fight the fight o' the Lord, brothers. But I'll not 'urt 'ee,' he said softly, mock reassuringly to the young tinner. 'I'm just come to ask 'ee a question. Which one o' these yere's got tin in un?'

The miners craned forward, peering at the two samples that Billy waved under their noses.

'Why, that one for sure,' said the young tinner, pointing one out amid the mutter of general agreement.

'I see you're a fine judge o' good ore,' said Billy. ' 'Tes a great thing to know good from bad. No man makes a proper livin' minin' barren rock, do 'e?' and he threw away the poor sample. 'Now, look at me, I'm a prospector meself, but I'm not lookin' for tin nor copper, not no more. I'm lookin' for the mettle in men's souls. I can tell a good sample from bad. I can show you the difference twixt good and evil, between eternal fire and sweet salvation. Come on over to that tent yonder and I'll tell you the sweet word o' Jesus – just like you showed me where the tin were. Will ye come or no?'

They followed him. Others had come from far. The name of Billy Bray brought men from distant farms. It brought the people of Bethel; it brought fishermen from Fowey, shepherds from Bodmin Moor, tin streamers from Caradon, grocers from Liskeard, and the whole population of Windfall. Only Jack Lugger and Mr Nichols stayed away; the former because he feared denunciation as a publican, the latter because he could not countenance this enthusiastic, schismatic religion.

Old Hilda Trerice was there in the front row. Blind Curnow with his family was there. Even the drunkards from the Tinners' were there, led by Tom Magor, ready for some sport. Welland and Ruth were there. It seemed as though the tent could take no more and yet new arrivals kept crowding in. They sang. Many had been singing along the roads. Now their voices blended in the strong, untutored Cornish harmonies they fused with Wesley's hymns. There was an atmosphere of subdued excitement, slow commotion, and gathering expectancy.

Suddenly, he was there among them, springing in at the door with his hat bobbing above the sea of heads as he bounded on to the platform. He gripped the lectern and tamed the gathering with a fierce stare from under his bushy eyebrows until a hush descended. Only then he spoke.

'You've been askin' yourselves "Where's Billy? Where's Billy Bray? Why's 'e keepin us waitin'?" – I'll tell you. I've been visitin' the wells o' salvation. Yes, 'ere in Windfall! The wells o' salvation are 'ere and ye knew it not! They're yere, under your feet!'

The crowd in the tent wriggled uncomfortably in the pause which followed. Already, Billy Bray had cast his spell upon them. His challenging stare sought each of them out. His tense pose at the lectern had them wondering which way he would jump next.

'The wells o' salvation are deep,' he assured them resonantly. 'I've been down there at the three-hundred-fathom level, and there's deeper yet. There's nothin' deeper than the love o' Jesus Christ, you'll find at three thousand! 'Tes dark down there, with only a small candle, and there's a shriekin' and a wailin' from the pump in fork – or is it the souls o' the wicked? And there I am, and I know I'm burdened by sin. Yes, I'm a sinner! Billy Bray's a sinner! Us is all sinners, whether 'tes in the deed or in the thought. And that sin is pullin' us down into the bog, into the quicksand o' perdition. And 'e's waitin' down there for me, that old Devil, the old Beezlebub, that sly black Satan. 'E's waitin' for Billy Bray's sins to get too 'eavy for un, and make un drown!' Billy Bray stopped speaking. Then he took the thick black Bible and shook it at arm's length above his head.

'Why didn' Billy Bray drown?' he shouted. 'Why didn' the weight of 'is sin pull un under?' He replaced the Bible firmly, riffled through its pages and marked one with a pointing finger.

' 'Tes yere! Writ in this good book, I tell 'ee! Hark! This is what 'E do say: "I am come a light into the world that whosoever believeth on me should not abide in darkness." – There you 'ave it, 'is promise. What could be clearer than that? And there I am, down at three 'undred, wrestlin' with my sin, and I remember these words: "whosoever believeth on me shall not abide in darkness", and all of a sudden, I can feel the weight fallin' off me, and me 'ands are on the ladder and I'm climbin'. And I looks up and I sees the light, but tes terrible small, terrible far off. Still, I 'ave 'Is promise and me faith floods back. 'Tes like a flood o' pure water, more than Satan's pumps can suck. I'll wet my lips with it, so I will, for I'm athirst, and I tell 'ee, bretheren and sisteren, I'm a man transformed. I'm skippin' up them ladders like a boy.' Here he gave over speaking and mimed the climbing of a ladder on the stage, reaching up and stepping high. Everyone watched him until he stumbled.

'There! I missed a step,' he shouted. ' 'Tes that old black Beelzebub a-trippin' me up. I shall 'ave to go careful, shan't I!' And he climbed slower, with his limbs appearing heavier with each step.

'He's behind me, allus behind me, waitin' fer me to weaken so 'e can pull out a rung, and now, to tell 'ee the truth, though I thought when I began at three 'undred I 'ad 'nuff faith fer twenty, now I finds I 'aven't 'ardly got 'nuff fer wan. I can feel that Satan breathin' on me 'eels, ready to draw me back into the pit. And I knaw what 'tes, I d'knaw why I'm gettin' weaker: 'tes pride! 'Tes because I thought I 'ad faith aplenty to come to grass on me own.' He fell forward on the lectern, panting, head lolling, tongue hanging out.

'I can't go no further. I've made it to the two-'undred-fathom level and I can't do no more. Me 'eart's poundin'. I think I shall die.' He stayed still a moment, and there was a great silence in the tent, with all of them watching until he resumed in a small, faraway voice.

'Billy! I 'ears a still small voice callin'. Billy! it calls again. No, I'm not dreamin'. But there's not a livin' soul down there with me. 'Tes all dark, and all rock, and all drippin' water. He calls me again: Billy! 'E calls. And this time I looks up and 'tes terrible bright, too bright fer me eyes to rest on, and I knaw I'm lookin' on the face o' the Lord. And then I knaw, I knaw that that drippin' is the blood o' Christ, and 'E's reachin' down to pull me up, me blest Redeemer.'

Now Billy knelt on the stage, with his head thrown back and his hands together.

'Praise the Lord!' he cried in a strangled voice. 'Praise the Lord for 'avin' remembered Billy in 'is time o' trial and tribulation.'

'Amen!' came a cry from the crowd, and another: 'Praise the Lord! Amen!' One of the voices was like Ruth's, it seemed to Welland, but he knew she was standing close beside him.

'There's no salvation without the Redeemer!' thundered Billy. 'No way out o' the toils o' sin without redeemin' grace! Fool that I was, I thought to be saved by faith, but 'tiddn' 'nuff. I 'ad to find grace.'

He stopped to wipe his brow and began climbing once more, moving lightly and surely so that it seemed he really was pulling himself out of the dark pit.

'Sometimes, when I'd got past a 'undred,' he confided, 'I 'ad doubt. What if I should fall? Did I 'ave the faith to 'old on? Then I'd 'ave to stop and pray fer grace. But there's the miracle, brothers, there's the miracle, sisters, there's always 'nuff. Praise the Lord!'

'Praise the Lord!' echoed round the tent like a thunder-clap.

'Aye, praise the Lord!' continued Billy. 'I'm gettin' closer now. I can feel it! He's yere! I can feel 'Is grace like a shower o' warm summer rain. The light's so bright, I can't look up to face 'Im. And suddenly I knaw I'm saved! I'm up to grass. I was up to me neck in slime and sin, but yere I am, washed clean, free again and walkin' in the sight o' the Lord.'

He danced a little jig all over the stage, his face lit by a beaming smile. He threw his hat in the air, shouting, 'Glory Hallelujah!'

The tent resounded to a broadside of hallelujahs. Immediately, Billy Bray was serious again, severe even.

'Did you see me dancin'? – Where's the 'arm in that? I was dancin' for joy in the praise o' the Lord. But there's dancin' and dancin'. There's dancin' that pleases Satan. That's why I'm come to Windfall. They tell me there's a world of abominations in this place: dancin' and drinkin' and whorin'. They say 'tes corrupt, like to Sodom and Gomorrah. Now, I say unto you, if 'tes true, this Windfall shall be filled with sorrow and gnashin' o' teeth.' He stopped and glared around the tent. 'Now I'm askin' 'ee, is it a fact, is Windfall full o' strong drink?'

'It is!' screeched Mrs Trerice.

'Is it full o' whorin'?'

'It is!' she echoed.

'Is it full o' dancin'?'

'It is!'

'Is it full o' gamin' and hurlin'?

'It is! It is!' She was becoming ecstatic, swaying on her feet.

'Is it full o' swearin'?'

'It is!' came the beginnings of a chorus.

'Then beware o' the Lord in the day of 'Is wrath! If ye don't give over and turn to true repentance, 'E will visit this place with 'Is anger till there's not one stone standin' upon another! Now, I'm implorin' you: put away strong drink!' He waited. 'Did you 'ear me? – Then let's 'ear. Will you do it?'

'Us will! Us will! Us will!' came the groundswell of voices.

'Will ye put away whorin'?'

'Us will!'

Welland was astonished to hear Tom Magor's voice loud in assertion. When he found his face, it seemed to glow with revelation and sincerity.

'Will ye put away dancin'?'

'Us will!'

'Will ye put away sport and 'urlin'?'

'Us will!'

'Will ye put away profanation and swearin'?'

'Us will!'

'Then you're 'arf way to grace already. Praise the Lord!'

'Praise the Lord!' they cried in return.

'But 'tiddn' that easy,' he cautioned. 'There'll be backsliders. 'Tiddn' easy to be a Christian. You'll be mocked, I tell 'ee. You'll be put to the test. Listen 'ere, Luke, chapter twenty-one, verse sixteen:

' "And ye shall be betrayed both by parents, and brethren, and kinsfolks, and friends; and some of you shall they cause to be put to death.

And ye shall be hated of all men for my name's sake.

But there shall not an hair of your head perish.

In your patience possess ye your souls." '

Welland shivered. There was something in this old Bible rhetoric that unnerved him. Was it man's inhumanity to man? Was it something unavowed, something deeper?

'I tell ye, 'tes 'ard,' Billy Bray was continuing when he picked up the thread. 'What does St Luke say? "Some o' ye shall they cause to be put to death." That's not a comfortable prospect, is it, friends? A man's got to stand up and fight for the love o' Christ and so 'as a woman. There's no easy way to salvation. 'Tiddn' in the bread, 'tiddn' in the wine. There's no way but prayer, and faith, and love o' Jesus, and the 'ope o' grace. There will be fasting, there will be discouragement, there will be mockery. Now, who will stand forth and declare for Jesus?' His fierce gaze swept their faces, his knuckles whitened on the lectern's edge.

'I don't want no luke-warm, 'arf-earted Christians!' he thundered before anyone could move, pushing them back with outstretched palms. 'The ones I wants is double-planked, copper-bottomed, unsinkable Christians! Who will stand forth now and declare it?'

There was shuffling of feet in the silence and surreptitious glancing from one to another. First Mrs Trerice raised her hand.

'Will I do?' she asked in a voice full of humility.

'Praise the Lord, there's one!' cried Billy. 'Come out yere.'

Another hand was raised, and another Bethel chapel-goer pushed her way to the front.

'Praise the Lord!' the shout rang round the tent. More hands shot skyward.

'Glory Hallelujah!' cried Billy. 'Standin' up to be counted they are. 'Tes music to the ears o' the Lord.'

Tom Magor pushed forward. Amid gasps all round, Billy Bray greeted him, turning the Bible pages to find chapter and verse.

' "A certain man had two sons; and he came to the first, and said, Son, go work today in my vineyard.

He answered and said, I will not: but afterward he repented, and went.

And he came to the second, and said likewise. And he answered and said, I go, sir: and went not.

Whether of them twain did the will of his father? They say into him, The first. Jesus saith unto them, Verily I say unto you, That the publicans and the harlots go into the kingdom of God before you."

And *I* say welcome, welcome to the repentant sinner, what's your name, man? Say it.'

'Magor, Tom Magor.'

'Jesus do prize 'ee above all other!' Billy reached down

from the platform and clasped both Magor's hands in his. 'Glory Hallelujah!'

'Praise the Lord!' boomed Magor.

As the converts swayed and eddied around the platform, Welland was searching for a familiar face. She had been close to her mother at the outset, but now was lost in the press. He wanted to tell her of his bargain with the Curate. Three weeks was a long, long time, but he had his part to fulfil. The fire in his forge would burn late at night, his hammer would beat without respite, but Mr Nichols would have his Christ before the banns were out. And there was Ruth to talk to about catechism, though this was not the time.

'Have you seen Mavis?' he asked her. He looked around and saw with a qualm she was no longer there. Why had she left him?

Her arm raised straight above her head, Ruth, his daughter Ruth, was forging forward into the ranks of the redeemed. He rubbed his eyes incredulously. A minute ago, he thought he knew her, believed he knew her as he knew himself. Now, all was quicksand. That she and Tom Magor should be standing side by side before Billy Bray was beyond comprehension. Above the clamour and the shouting, the preacher was making himself heard again, reading from the Bible in a voice that rang like a sounding trumpet.

' ". . . now is our salvation nearer than we believed. The night is far spent, the day is at hand: let us therefore cast off the works of darkness, and let us put on the armour of light." '

'Amen! Amen! Amen! reverberated the crowd.

Welland could listen no longer. He needed air; he needed light. He clenched his hands and strode to the door. He had to escape the intoxication of shared guilt and quick redemption. That could not be his way. As he walked into the evening calm, the sadness of that hanging Christ he was to build, the figure he had already structured in his brain,

243

pursued him with a Greek icon's doleful stare.

Welland walked the hills in the falling dusk, while the dew gathered on the leaves and the birds grew still. The revelation that Ruth might have, indeed certainly had, developed a personality separate from his, was a profound shock. Yesterday, she had been a little girl, mirror to his moods, echo of his opinions. Now, she was a stranger to him. As he strode alone through the bracken, tiredness settled on him like a pall. The stars began their slow cortège. Windfall's lights glowed in the dark. That one on the far right shone from the Trerice house. Mavis must be there with her mother, inaccessible to him though he seethed with impatience to tell her of his bargain with Mr Nichols. At the other end of the village, his own cottage window was alight. Ruth was at home then. He wondered how he would find her. Would she be absolutely changed?

She sat facing him across the table as he entered, still wearing bonnet and shawl, her hands on the bare wood top, interlaced and motionless. Her lips seemed to be drawn out with the ghost of a thin smile which vanished as she became aware of him. She might have been praying, but he did not think so.

'About Mother.' Her question startled him as he hung up his coat. 'Was she a bad woman?'

'Bad? What do you want me to say? – Anyway, not at first.'

'Not at first?'

'She changed. Something went wrong in her; it broke, just like a clockwork doll. Why did it happen? I don't know. Perhaps it was partly me.' He leant back against the wall and studied his daughter's face. 'You still miss her?'

'I don't know. I was so young; I hardly knew her. She was what she was and I accepted it. It was my start in life; I had known no other.'

'So you think I was wrong to bring you here.'

'You had your reasons; you must have. – Will you tell me about her?'

244

He felt suddenly old, washed out, exhausted.

'I'll try. Sometime. Not tonight.'

'There never is a time that's right, is there?'

'It's too painful.' How impossible it was to stir the grey ashes of their past into life without producing a searing flame. And yet he must, someday, he knew he must, or he would lose her. If he hadn't lost her already. How grown up she looked, how serious. 'You blame me, don't you?'

'I don't think so, but I don't understand – I thought I did, but there are questions.'

'What sort of questions?'

'Do I take after her?'

He scrutinized her features with a new interest, trying to see a similarity.

'Not much, you look quite different.'

'I didn't mean that, I didn't mean looks. You know what I meant: I meant my nature, the way I am.'

'No, you're different, different in nature too.'

'How do you know?'

'I know you –' He stopped, halted by some almost imperceptible sign: the smallest of gestures, a flicker in her eyes. 'I thought I did – until this afternoon. I don't know what possessed you.'

'Do you blame me?'

'No, but I don't understand.'

'You thought you did. I worried you just now, didn't I, getting carried away by religion like that? I'm sorry. I saw you walk out. I saw the look on your face. It's just that I got carried away. I think I'll get over it. It was exciting. There's not much excitement in Windfall.'

He made himself face her, meeting her candid eyes. Yes, she was grown up. She always had been solemn, old for her years. Perhaps that had been his fault for not having charmed out the child in her. And there was the shadow of that other thing. How could he ever be sure it had lifted from her? However, for all the distance between them, there was something he had to say to her. He was fearful of how she would take it.

'There's something I've been meaning to speak to you about,' he began tentatively. She raised a cool interrogative eyebrow. 'About Mavis.' She nodded gravely.

'I know – I love her too.'

'And I feel I must –' Even then, he faltered, not sure of her inner thoughts. She rose, unlaced her bonnet and paused, candle in hand, at the foot of the stairs. She was less then ten feet away, but the distance between them might have been infinite. If only he could reach out and pat her shoulder, but she had moved too far for that.

'You'll be going ahead then, Father.'

'I hope so, but it's not all cut and dried. To a certain extent, it depends on you.'

'On me?'

'I have a favour to ask you.' When she stayed silent, he continued, 'Mr Nichols wants you to attend catechism in his church. It's a kind of condition. Now, if you're against it –'

'It's ironic – don't you see the irony? You didn't want me to declare for Billy Bray's Jesus – now you're asking me to submit to the Curate's.'

'It's only a form of words.'

'How do you know? How do you know it won't affect me?'

'I'm sorry, I shouldn't have asked. I'll tell him –'

'You'll tell him I'm coming,' she interrupted. 'I'll do it for you, Father, and for Mavis, but there's one thing I think you should know, one thing we'll never alter.' She paused, and her candle shook fractionally. 'I've said I love her, but Mavis can never be my mother. I can't help it.'

'I understand. At least, I think I do. And I'm grateful.'

'Take care, Father. Whatever you do, you will take care, won't you? Now, good night.' Her voice was quiet and her steps receded up the stair. In a moment, she would be seated, brushing her hair, facing her own green eyes within the mirror. Then, as she always did before she slept, she would write in her book.

He sat at the table opposite where she had been and studied his hands. They were good hands. They would make the Curate's Christ. He knew intuitively how he would shape it, without need of a plan.

Welland became aware of the silence. By listening intently, he could hear faint scratchings from Ruth's pen. There she sat, the living link between the past and future, a fragile, deeply implicated witness. Was he being fair in confiding her to Mr Nichols's attentions? Were they entirely disinterested? He feared for her and, for a fleeting moment, he feared for himself. A cold hand seemed to weigh upon his shoulder. He shrugged it off. There was so much hope in his relations with Mavis; so much warmth that it cast out fear.

The scratching of Ruth's pen had stopped. By concentrating his attention, he thought he could perceive the soft rhythm of her sleeping breath. He went to the door and held it ajar, breathed the cool air and scrutinized the constellations above Carnwartha. Cool and distant, if they knew of his future, they told him nothing. It was enough to feel them detached and uninvolved, eternal. He thought of Mavis and the love he bore her. He remembered his hands, the hands that would clasp her, the hands that would carve out a future for her, for all three of them. These hands would do no more violence: that was the vow he had made to Mavis and he would keep it. Tomorrow, he would meet her on Carnwartha and tell her the good tidings, tell her Mr Nichols had accepted. She must share his joy.

'Praise the Lord!'

Faintly from afar, where the road out of Windfall passed the carn, a voice came down to him.

'Amen,' whispered Welland as he closed he door.

'Praise the Lord!' shouted Billy Bray again as he crested the hill and paused to reconsider sleeping Windfall. The echoes rattled among the stones of the carn. A wayward sheep ran off at a scamper. Billy felt no fear. He had reason to rejoice. That evening, in the enthusiasm that followed his preaching in the tent, he had led the converted back to the village and laid the foundation stone for a new chapel. They had been wayward folk, these Windfallers, lost sheep, and he brimmed with joy that he had been given the grace to lead so many of them back to the way of the Lord. They had found grace together and their Redeemer had found a path to their hearts.

'Hallelujah!' he crowed at the starlit night. He felt as if he could run and sing for ever. He had brought Jesus and love to Windfall. His heart was full of the glory of the Lord.

❊ 12 ❊

THE CHURCH

She wept at her wedding. Welland prayed she would smile or laugh, but she wept. He stood stiffly beside her, with Ruth at arm's length beyond her, looking on.

'What's the matter?' he whispered, conscious of the Curate's basilisk stare. Her stare. Her eyes met his a moment. They told him nothing. The tears fell faster. Why she wept she would not say, but he knew inwardly it was not for joy, it was her need to know his secret. He wished he had told her. This was not the time. He had kept putting it off, waiting for the right moment, when it would be easy. Often, he told himself it were better she never knew, but he knew he lied.

She wept at her wedding and the tears ran down into the bunch of wild flowers she held clasped to her chin. Her solemn beauty wrenched at his entrails like an executioner's hand. He wanted her. How he wanted her!

'Wilt thou have this woman to thy wedded wife, to live together after God's ordinance in the holy estate of matrimony?'

It was Curate Nichols addressing him. He felt himself nodding, giving quick jerks of the head. What was it in the Curate's tone that riled him? Was there a tinge of irony?

'Wilt thou love her, comfort her, honour and keep her, in sickness and in health . . .'

'I will!' blurted Welland.

'I've not finished yet,' hissed the Curate with a covert look at the two silent old women who were his sole congregation beyond Welland, his daughter, and Mavis. Their wrinkled faces seemed to be smiling, perhaps out of indulgence, perhaps sardonically. Mr Nichols dipped his head back to his book. '. . . and, forsaking all other,' he enunciated pointedly, 'to keep thee only unto her, so long as ye both shall live?'

'I will,' repeated Welland more quietly and a kind of tiredness blanketed him. Forsaking all other? That was easy; he loved her. Keep himself only unto her? The words had a hollow echo, like memory. Welland came to himself. The Curate was bending towards Mavis.

'Wilt thou obey him and serve him, love, honour and keep him, in sickness and in health . . .' The voice muttered on. Welland watched sidelong as Mavis mastered herself. Her face seemed to stiffen as the Curate came to the final words: '. . . so long as ye both shall live.' Ruth took her by the arm and shook her gently until she replied.

'I will.'

'Who giveth this woman to be married to this man?'

Ruth stepped forward, arm in arm with Mavis, bringing her closer to Welland. Curate Nichols put down his book and took the man and the woman, each by the right hand, joining them solemnly and facing Welland.

'Repeat after me: I Welland take thee Mavis to my wedded wife . . .'

'I Welland take thee Mavis to my wedded wife . . .'

'To have and to hold from this day forward . . .'

'To have and to hold from this day forward . . .'

'For better for worse . . .'

'For better for worse . . .'

Mavis felt Welland's hand tighten on hers as he spoke. His voice was regaining confidence. If only she too could feel it. Another speech still rang in her head. She had stiffened as she heard the Curate pronounce it.

'I require and charge you both,' he had mouthed menacingly – and she had been mesmerized by the string of saliva that strung across between his lips, lengthening and contracting with each syllable – 'as ye will answer in the dreadful day of judgement, when the secrets of all hearts shall be disclosed,' – She tried not to look at Welland; the pain of his secrecy seized her heart and crammed it like a tender fruit in an iron fist. Why could he not trust her? Then the tears had come, unbidden, unrelieving, while the exhortation continued – 'that if either of you know any impediment why ye may not be joined together in Matrimony, ye do now confess it . . .' The Curate had paused, making silence tangible. Mavis waited for a voice. Welland, she knew, would never speak. But what of the old women, friends of her mother's. They had stood in their places on either side of the nave each Sunday these past three weeks, and said nothing. She could not believe it. Silence. The faint cracking of stirring woodwork. And yet what could they know that she herself was ignorant of? Mere suspicion could lay no ban on marriage. 'For be ye well assured,' Curate Nichols informed them solemnly, 'that so many as are coupled together otherwise than God's Word doth allow are not joined together by God; neither is their matrimony lawful.' She had shivered slightly, touched by an inner coldness. It held her now as she came back to the present. She herself was repeating after the Curate.

'. . . for richer for poorer . . .'

'In sickness and in health . . .' he intoned nasally.

'In sickness and in health . . .'

'To love, cherish, and to obey . . .'

'To love, cherish, and to obey . . .'

Oh, she would say anything, repeat anything, promise anything, to get this over. It was destroying her. In a strange, slow movement, like a dance underwater, she saw Welland's hand approaching, with a ring locked between thumb and forefinger. He was fitting it on her, but her own fingers felt huge, distended, awkward.

'With this ring I thee wed . . .' led the Curate.

'With this ring I thee wed . . .' Welland followed.

'With my body I thee worship . . .' The Curate was staring at Ruth, devouring her. He ceased immediately he knew himself detected. Mavis pitied him, despite her grief, his emptiness was greater.

'With my body I thee worship . . .' Welland announced confidently. She believed him. Had she not that faith she could never have sustained this struggle. She was ready to break and it was a blessing to be motioned to kneel beside him.

'Those whom God hath joined together let no man put asunder,' the Curate's voice was final. Why had no one shouted out? A prickling fear still haunted the back of her neck. Was it the same for Welland? It must be. She remembered Curate Nichols apparelled in cassock, in surplice and chasuble and stole, facing down the nave on each of those three earlier occasions and putting the question:

'If any of ye know of any just impediment why this man and this woman should not be joined together in the bonds of Holy Matrimony, speak now or for ever hold thy peace.'

Silence. Her mother had known, yet she had never come forward. She led the upright chapel folk to Bethel, feigning to ignore her daughter's intentions. The old women stood nodding in their pews to either side of the nave like worn-out dolls. It was as though they never heard the Curate's calling. Even now, Mavis expected the door to swing back with a crash. Where was the accusing screech? Where were the burning eyes? But all was dusty silence, a whiff of spent candles, stale incense, the Curate's mumbling drone.

'. . . and so fill you with all spiritual benediction and grace, that ye may live together in this life, that in the world to come ye may have life everlasting. Amen.' Curate Nichols paused and coughed. An audible breath made Mavis steal a glance at Ruth. Her lips were parted; her features set in a strange expression as though controlling a spirit she would not let out. Something told her she was observed and she willed her face into a smile before putting herself to rearranging the wild flower posy she carried. Mavis felt her own fingernails dig into the stems of the posy she herself clutched in her left hand. Ruth had gathered it for her that morning. The dew was still on the petals when she presented it: an offering. Now Mavis was Ruth's mother – her stepmother, rather. Something in the girl's demeanour told Mavis that she would prove difficult to tame. There was a shyness, an indefinable distance, another flesh. And yet, there was no mistaking the child's attempts at friendliness. The Curate's voice disturbed her reverie. He was reading a final passage from the prayer book and directing it especially at her:

' "Saint Paul, in the aforementioned epistle to the Ephesians, teaches you thus; Wives submit yourselves to your own husbands as to the Lord. For the husband is the head of the wife, even as Christ is the head of the Church: and he is the Saviour of the body. Therefore, even as the Church is subject unto Christ, so let the wives be to their own husbands in every thing . . ." '

Mavis looked at Welland. Could she do so? She had been accustomed to wildness, to freedom, all her life, perhaps too long. But his face was strong, without hardness. A faint smile haunted his scarcely parted lips. He worshipped her. If she must submit, if that was the law, she would try – for Welland's sake. He needed her.

As they walked home to Welland's house, Mavis kept the posy up close to her chin. She clung to Welland's arm. Ruth strolled behind them. A few curious faces looked out of cottage doors. There was a stirring behind the new net curtains that had accompanied propriety to Windfall. There was no general celebration, no well wishing. Welland had not sought it.

'Are you happy, Mavis?' he whispered.

'It's done,' she murmured, 'it's over.' Her tears had stopped, but their salt tracks still shone on her cheeks. She buried her nose in the posy.

The smell reminded her of the afternoon on Carnwartha when she had bowed before his passion. There had been another posy: Welland had picked it for her. She recalled the

253

gravity of his expression as he handed it to her.

Later, they had lain on the grass, with the posy scattered and the scent of the tall peppery broom heavy on the air around them. She had broom-petals in her hair, Windfall's flower. They breathed it as his lips met hers, so demanding, so urgent. She became deaf to the larks chattering overhead. Her breast was choked with tenderness for him and a feeling of lassitude, like a diver trammelled in a net, suffocating in the warm depths of her love for him.

Suddenly, he had broken free and turned away from her, with his hands to his face, trembling. She knelt over him and saw slow tears welling between his fingers.

'What's the matter? You can tell me.'

His face flushed, his lips opened, but no words came. She reached down to him, running her understanding fingers through his hair, while his shoulders shook and some secret resentment rushed through him like an angry tide.

'There, there,' she murmured, her voice curiously broken, 'there, there.' He was like a child really. And yet, for so long he had seemed old to her, old and deformed, but now, she saw nothing but beauty. Somehow, he had been hurt. Not just his leg, but wounded internally, like an old soldier carrying a jagged piece of case-shot in his flesh. She knew she was made to comfort him and make him well. 'There, there,' she breathed in his ear, turning him back to face her, dragging him down and burying his face in her breasts. 'There, there. You'll tell me, won't you? Take your time, my sweetheart, but tell me, tell me what's troubling you.' And Welland, choking on the impossibility of saying, raised his head and stared into her troubled eyes.

'Oh, Mavis, if only I could. 'Tis so terrible, so hurtful to remember. I'll try, but 'tis hopeless now. All I can tell you today is this: I love you, love you like the fire in my forge, love you like white-hot iron. I need you, Mavis, or I'll never be quenched.'

He reached across and, with a timid finger, traced the

outline of her parted, tremulous lips. Her eyes closed and she sighed deeply.

'Say it, my dearest,' he insisted gruffly, 'say you'll relent. Say you'll marry me.'

'You know that's not possible,' she heard herself saying. Her voice came from very far off.

'It is! It is! I've spoken to Mr Nichols and he says he'll do it.' He waited. 'You love me, don't you? No use to fight it.'

No – no use to fight it. Her lids rose slowly and her eyes answered him. There was no need of words. But her look was only half happiness. As now, the other half was pain. She had wept then, and kissed him gently. And he had groaned, and struggled up, and kissed her face, kissing the tears from her eyes, stroking her cheeks with rough fingers.

'There, there,' he comforted her, 'all will be well, I promise you. I love you. Ruth loves you. She told me. There can come nothing but good.'

She wanted to believe him. He was so positive, so demanding. Now it was over. She was Mavis Halt. Was that his real name, she wondered. What did it matter. He was striding beside her, with hardly a sign of his bad leg. It was a new beginning.

But the sadness surrounded her like a cloud. It hung about her all the way home. Then, like a cloud, it went away.

'Come on, Mavis, let's bake some fuggan. The pastry's ready,' cried Ruth the moment they crossed the threshold. Mavis found her unpredictable, but could not gainsay her present gaiety. Soon, the cottage was full of the smell of fresh baking and Welland smiled at the sight of the two women in their aprons, bustling about the slab.

'Hold on, I'll get some cider,' he announced. 'I've been saving it. 'Tis the best stuff, not scrumpy.'

They toasted each other. The bubbles surged up in the cups and splashed their eyes, bursting.

'To the future – our future!' ventured Mavis.

'Aye, it ought to be a better one now I'm working flat out

for Squire Gurney. He says I'm to go to the mine but one day a week – watch over things a little. I'm to spend the best part of my time building the second steam-carriage. He's taken the first one to London. Wanted me to go with him, but I wouldn't. Told him I was getting married.'

'What did he say to that?' Mavis couldn't help asking.

'Lucky dog! That's what he said when I told him who 'twas. Said he'd've wed you himself if he hadn't been married already. Look what he gave me.' Welland pulled his left hand out of his pocket, held it out, and disclosed a clutch of golden guineas. 'There's more where these came from.'

'He's very generous,' said Mavis, 'but, Welland, you will be careful. You won't expect too much of him, will you? Oh, I know he likes you and that, but he's far above us. You *will* take his promises with a pinch of salt, won't you? It's all fine talk, but he's Squire Gurney and you're but Welland Halt, blacksmith.'

'Aye. I know that. I've no illusions on that score. But he needs me. He knows he wouldn't have a Flyer without me.' Welland filled their glasses all round. 'But I don't want to talk about that tonight. There will be time enough tomorrow. I want to celebrate. Ruth, will you go fetch Curnow and Ellen. They must share this with us.'

Mavis put down her glass and stepped forward. Her face had clouded with a new recollection. She took her cloak from behind the door.

'I'll go. I'll call in for them on the way back from Mother's. I'd forgotten. I must fetch my belongings.'

'Don't linger, we'll be waiting. The fuggan will be spoilt if you do,' said Welland, reluctant to see her go. 'Shall I come with you.'

'No, it's my cross and I must bear it.'

Her mother sat by the dull fire, stirring a simmering pot. She barely glanced up when Mavis came into her cottage. All Mavis's things were heaped on the floor in the corner.

'You're a fool, Mavis. I warned you. I told you first off

256

you'd do this foolishness. But 'tis bred in the bone and 'twill come out in the flesh – just like your feyther, God rest un. Now you've made your bed you must lie in it. But don't think us don't know 'tis no true weddin'.'

'If you know that, why didn't you speak out? We made no secret. The banns were called in St Winwalloe's.'

'There's knowin' and knowin'. We'll 'ave to wait to find proof. But the truth will out. Never you mind about that, my girl. The truth will out.'

All this time Mavis was stuffing her possessions into a bag. Her mother had cleared the house, all her childhood things, every item that had ever belonged to her.

'I think that's everything,' she said finally as she straightened. 'That's what you want, isn't it? You want me to take all of it. I suppose it's too much to ask if I can take your blessing.'

Her mother laughed, a malevolent cackle. Looking at her crouched at the hearth stirring and stirring, Mavis had difficulty in recognizing her for her mother. Was she really a witch? She played at it, she knew. Hilda Trerice found no difficulty in reconciling the pellar's art with her burning Methodism. Good and evil in her were strangely mixed. On balance, she tended to evil.

'Go your ways, ungrateful child,' she said at last, 'go your ways and don't come back. You've made your bed and you must lie in it. Don't ever darken that doorway again.'

Mavis shouldered her bundle. Despite the hatred, she was close to tears. This *was* her home. This *was* her mother. The silence hung heavy between them.

'You're a bad woman, Mother,' she announced, as calmly as she could. 'You scheme for evil. You made that wrong prophecy to Welland at Tregurney. He told me. It was you, I know it, no use shaking your head, denying. Well, it won't come true. Welland's a good man, Mother. I love him and I'll stick to him. If it means breaking with you, well, so be it. That's not my wish – not my wish to see you die lonely. God

257

help you, Mother. I hope He'll hear you.'

She was gone, out into the street, down the lane, past the Tinners' Arms. Ahead of her, on a knoll, stood Welland's cottage – welcoming – home.

She knocked at a cottage door. Curnow himself answered it. His eyes wrinkled with concern.

'What's the matter, maid? You're all in a tizz-was.' He took her by the arm and held her firmly. How did he know? How had he sensed it?

'Mother,' she said blankly.

'Don't you fret,' he commanded. 'Come on in fer a dish o' tay or somethin'.'

'I can't do that. Welland's waiting. He told me to bring you over to try his cider.'

'That's a better idea yet,' said Curnow, turning back into the house. 'Come on, Ellen, bring that saffron cake, and bring the childer. There's nothin' like childer to liven a weddin'.'

It was strange how a good man could change life in a moment from grief to happiness. As they walked along, it seemed all their neighbours had a kind word. When they were all gathered in Welland's kitchen, her kitchen now, she wept again, this time for happiness when her husband held her, and kissed her, and laughed, and spilt cider all over her apron.

She had wept at her wedding and Welland was troubled, but things were changing. He began to feel comfortable in the village and thought he might leave his bones there. Even Hilda Trerice held her tongue and ignored him. That was blessing enough. He had despaired of her from the outset. The dream of Richard Trevithick and South America faded right away. He was respected at Wheal Fortune. He worked many a happy hour in the Tregurney stables, perfecting Silverton Gurney's steam-carriage. It did not matter to Welland that the Squire would get all the credit. Indeed, that was what he wanted. Welland desired no more than wedded bliss and decent obscurity. There was good food to eat in his house, linen on the table and even, luxury of luxuries, plenty of tea for the pot that Ruth brewed beside the kettle that sang on the slab. He was grateful to her for her acceptance. He thanked Mavis too, inwardly, for having taken him. He thanked Mr Nichols likewise for having united them and, had he known a god to believe in, he would have thanked him also, for all these blessings.

❊ 13 ❊
THE TINNERS' ARMS

No letter for Welland Halt had ever arrived in Windfall, but, by an odd coincidence, one came on the morning of the same day that Squire Gurney drove up from Tregurney with another message. Welland was in the church when the mail-coach, which had only recently begun to use the new turnpike between Bethel and Tregurney, shuddered to a stop outside the Tinners' Arms.

'Is there a Mr Welland Halt lives here?' the coachman demanded of the sullen ostler who slouched out to catch the bridles. The ostler nodded. 'Can 'e pay for a letter, d'you think?'

'Don't rightly knaw,' sniffed the ostler. 'I s'pose so. I'll 'ave to ask the landlord.'

'Get a move on then, I've driven out of my way to bring it and I've passengers inside as can't abide waitin', friends o' Squire Gurney.'

The ostler moved off at his own sweet pace, leaving the coachman ample time to study his surroundings. Since the last time he had been here, half a year back, the Tinners' window panes had been whitewashed over. Its door was kept shut and barred. Drunken tinners no longer lounged in the doorway. The reason was not far to see: just down the street, flaming new in its fresh white paint, its ashlar granite front, and its shiny Delabole slate roof, was the huge new chapel.

You could tell a great deal about those chapel folk, thought the coachman, from the outward appearance of their buildings. That was evidence enough, for it wasn't his way to waste time in them, nor churches neither. Like their new chapels, these Nonconformists put on an austere look when they faced the world. They had the prim faces worn by upright souls enjoying self-denial, though they claimed to belie this with an uncommon generosity of heart. This chapel in Windfall had a range of plain, round-headed windows along each side, above a lower rectangular row that illuminated the basement Sunday school. The only ornament was on the gable end, facing the street, where a half-hearted classical portal opened at the head of a monumental stairway, flanked by a pair of arched windows that lit the gallery. The purpose of this restrained ornamentation was to differentiate the chapel from the Church of England's frivolous gothic. Windfall was certainly changing, thought the coachman, it was getting tame. Before long it would be as civilized as Truro or Bodmin. It was becoming a damned dull place to wait in. Now, where the devil could that ostler have vanished to?

The ostler had found Jack Lugger sipping ale with Tom Magor and a couple of other cronies round the hearth.

'What do I want with a letter for Welland Halt?' complained landlord Lugger. 'He never drinks 'ere. Why should I put out good money for un? Tell the coachman 'e can carry it back again.'

'Steady on! Steady on! Wait a bit!' called Magor as the ostler reached the door. 'Bring that letter 'ere. Then find out 'ow much is owed for un.'

'Didn' know Welland Halt were a friend o' yourn,' said the landlord, spitting into the fire.

'What do the good Book say?' said Magor sanctimoniously, ' "Love thy neighbour", if I'm not mistaken. Us shouldn' shrink from a Christian deed from time to time.'

'I never thought that conversion o' yourn with Billy Bray did last so long,' remarked Jack Lugger. 'Us didn' notice no effects that lasted longer'n it took 'ee to walk back to the Tinners'."

The men round the fire dissolved in laughter.

' 'Tes a mistake to go by appearances,' said Magor, keeping a straight face as he went to meet the ostler who returned with the letter. 'Keep the change,' he added when he passed over the money. There was a moment's silence, followed by a whipcrack as the mail-coach rumbled away.

'Well, I'll be damned,' snorted Lugger in disbelief, 'never thought to see Tom Magor play the Good Samaritan. Come on, Tom, what're you waitin' for? Open un up! That's why you've took un, us don't need second sight to know it.'

'You knaw very well I can't read,' said Magor, as the others dissolved into further chortles. ' 'Twasn't for that I took un. No, this letter might be worth somethin' to Welland Halt. 'E might make me a more'n generous offer to 'ave un.' Magor stuffed the letter into his pocket and drained his tankard. 'Now, if you'll excuse me, gennulmen, I've business to attend to.'

Welland Halt saw the mail-coach come and go, flickering across the leaded panes in the church windows, but it meant little to him. He was busy adjusting the system of tackles he had devised to raise and lower the font cover. If he thought of the coach at all, it was an example of a doomed species, destined to be overtaken by the steam-carriages he had been building with Silverton Gurney. The idea that it might be carrying correspondence for him never occurred to him. He cleated the fall of the tackle under the watchful eyes of a small audience. Half the audience was composed of his daughter Ruth, the other half was Mr Nichols the Curate.

'How splendid! How splendid!' the Curate kept exclaiming while he twisted his wrists round each other in the sleeves of his cassock. 'Perfectly wonderful. There's nothing like it. I keep telling Mr Gurney he absolutely must come and see it. Do you know, Ruth, your father's an artist, a genius? I never could have imagined you'd produce anything like this when you promised to do it. Such workmanship!'

The Curate advanced and ran a finger over the figure's delicate strapwork construction. It was at least life-sized and was poised over the font as though hanging on air. By a cunning disposition of masses, Welland had made it so that it leaned slightly forward, arms outstretched, fingers spread, as if flying forward to bless. It was, thought the Curate, a singular embodiment of Christ's mercy. The light, etherial transparency of its form was delineated by a filigree in strapwork, a cage that appeared to have captured the invisible spirit of the Redeemer.

'Those eyes! That mouth!' he enthused. 'How did you do it?' How, indeed, had it been possible to draw such pathos from dumb metal? Everything about the structure was perfect, down to the smallest rivet, and every inch had been burnished to a peculiar iridescent brown bloom. How could a mere man have created such a marvel without God's assistance? He was forced to look at Welland Halt with new eyes. Atheist he might consider himself, but was he not the unwitting executant of the divine purpose? And young Ruth, did she not partake of the same genius? Was it not his duty to save her from error and set her feet upon the way of truth? Watching her from under lowered lids, he was almost suffocated with emotion as she breathed through barely parted coral lips. The youthful bloom on her skin put him into a trance like that of Teresa of Avila viewing the risen Christ. The odour of violets she wore intoxicated him. Her air of virginal sanctity was like a blow to his heart. Her little feet were made for the way of perfection; her untried heart was the heart of a saint.

Now, months after the wedding, with the tinted light from the leaded panes splashed on to the outstretched arms of his all-embracing, compassionate, sorrowful Christ, Welland felt a tranquillity he had never known before. How had he, an unbeliever, achieved such communion with this man of sorrows and acquainted with grief? Was it safe to inquire?

'Welland!'

The cry roused him abruptly as the church door squealed open and Silverton Gurney bustled in.

'Oh, Mr Gurney,' babbled the Curate, leaving Ruth with whom he had been having a murmured conversation, 'I'm so glad you've come at last to see it. Isn't it splendid, uplifting, inspirational?' He gestured at the hanging Christ, but Silverton Gurney ignored him. Instead, he grasped Welland by the hand.

'Congratulations, dear fellow, congratulations! I'm so happy for you, so glad to be able to share the honour with you.'

'Honour? What honour?' asked Welland flatly.

'I'll come to that. You know I had to beg off attending your wedding. I'm sure you're most happy, your Mavis is a delightful creature, a shy, wild bird of the hedgerows, and you have tamed her. And Ruth,' he continued, turning to the girl, 'how wonderful to be blessed with a kind new mother! And you, Mr Nichols, what a pleasure, what an honour to have celebrated their union. No, had I not been unavoidably called away to London, I should certainly have been with you. But I was involved in something that must ultimately be to your benefit: I was presenting a paper on steam transport to the Royal Society and I had occasion to point out your own valuable contribution.'

'I told you, Mr Gurney, I thought I made it clear, I never wanted –'

'Nonsense, man, nonsense, you deserve all the recognition you're going to get and it's coming, it's coming.' While Silverton Gurney spoke, he was fishing in his pocket for something and eventually came up with a crumpled newspaper. 'Awful dim in here,' he complained to the Curate as he held it up and tried to read the text, 'but you clergymen thrive on gloom and obscurantism, don't you? Come on, let's go outdoors so I can see this properly.'

'But, Mr Gurney, before you go permit me to draw your attention to this incredible font cover that Welland has constructed and so generously donated to St Winwalloe's. There has been nothing like it since the Middle Ages.'

Silverton Gurney glanced up at the hanging Christ, but his thoughts were largely elsewhere.

'That cage thing? Very handsome, I suppose, but out of date, irrelevant. Waste of Welland's talents when he ought to be making something useful, something for the future – I say, Welland, I hope I haven't hurt your feelings, have I? Come on outside, when you hear what's printed here, you'll understand which side your bread's buttered. Cease that frowning at once, d'you hear me?'

They followed him into the street where an inquisitive knot of people gathered to hear what the Squire was about to read. He set his pince-nez on his nose, smoothed the paper and began to read it out loud, with long, sententious pauses.

' "The Bath road is nowadays the scene of the regular passage of a most remarkable vehicle. This magnificent steam-carriage is capable of transporting six inside and six outside passengers from St Paul's churchyard in London to the Pulteney Bridge in Bath, in exemplary comfort, at the unexampled sustained speed of sixteen miles an hour. It is confidently expected by its promoters that a fleet of such vehicles will soon render the present coaching system obsolete and relegate dobbin to the knacker's yard." '

Silverton swung his head, peering over the rims of his glasses to ensure that his audience was paying him proper attention. When he was satisfied, he continued.

' "Mr Silverton Gurney has been gracious enough to accord an interview to your correspondent in which he gave the following intelligence: in consequence of the remarkable success attending the Flyer, he is to form a new company for the manufacture and operation of steam-carriages throughout the United Kingdom. This company will bear the name of 'Gurney & Halt Steam Transportation'. Mr Gurney informs us that the second name in the title is in recognition of the contribution to the Flyer's design and construction provided by his associate, Mr Welland Halt of Windfall in Cornwall." '

Here Silverton Gurney paused again, throwing an arm round Welland's shoulders and waiting imperiously for the ragged cheer that broke out almost spontaneously. He paid no attention to Welland's own reaction which was more frowning and glowering.

' "Little is known of Mr Halt's background, or of his previous contributions to mechanical science, but it is the intention of this journal to devote its diligent researches to a future article on the subject. This is all the more apposite as the Royal Society has decided to award its gold medal to Messrs Gurney and Halt jointly for their pioneering work in the field of steam transportation. Its justification in Mr Gurney's case is his outstanding work on an improved steam boiler of greatly increased efficiency . . ." ' fresh cheers rose from the growing crowd, ' "and, in Mr Halt's case, for his technical and metallurgical inventions that have enabled Mr Gurney's conceptions to be put to practical effects." '

More cheers. Shouts of 'Good old Welland! Long live Squire Gurney!'

Silverton foraged in his waistcoat and produced a bright gold medal on a striped silk ribbon which he handed to Ruth, saying, 'Here, girl, to you the honour of decorating your father.'

The street was suddenly full of cheerful people, chattering, laughing and clapping, while Ruth strung the ribbon round her father's neck and kissed him warmly. Only one person remained subdued and disconsolate and that was Welland himself.

'Now for a celebration!' cried Silverton. 'We must all drink to the health and success of our fellow countryman.'

'Quick, maid,' Welland whispered urgently to Ruth, 'run and fetch your mother. We mustn't forget her.' And, as she still stood immobile with a peculiar smile on her face, he added quickly, 'You know very well whom I mean; go tell Mavis she's wanted.'

Silverton Gurney was rapping on the inn door with his silver-knobbed malacca cane.

'What's this? Locked doors and blind windows? What's going on here? Can't a man buy a drink for his friends when he chooses?'

' 'Tes that 'Ilda Trerice and 'er Society fer the Prevention o' Drunkenness, sir,' came a voice, 'they won't leave Jack Lugger open up but six hours a day.'

'And naught on Sundays!' cried another.

'And the landlord accepts it?' demanded Silverton, flabbergasted.

'Course 'e do,' replied the second man, ' 'e do sell just so much in six hours as 'e did in twenty-four previous. 'E do sleep all o' the forenoon and much o' the afternoon also.'

'Well, he shan't sleep sound today,' exclaimed Silverton, hammering ever more insistently until the landlord's tousled head appeared in an upper window. 'Look here, my man, there's fifty of us here need a glass of good ale to celebrate friend Welland's good fortune. D'ye see that medal? It's from the Royal Society. You wouldn't want to stand in the way of a royal command, now would you? Open up quick and set your spigots running. 'Tis your squire that pays. If you value your lease, you'll look lively.'

Long before the crowd, led by Silverton Gurney and Welland Halt, streamed into the Tinners' Arms, Tom Magor had left by the back door and stolen round the back of the row of houses to Hilda Trerice's cottage. When she saw who was at the door, she tried to keep him out, but he whispered something to her and she relented. Curnow, who was passing at the time, tap-tapping with his stick on the roadside stones, heard the two voices, though even his hearing was not acute enough to tell what they were saying. What can Tom Magor be doing with old woman Trerice? he wondered. Nothing to do with having found religion: Curnow knew very well that Magor had not given up his visits to the Tinners' for all his pretence of faith and joy in redemption. No doubt Magor had come to see Mrs Trerice the pellar. Not a few villagers came to her when they had a wart to be charmed, an ache to be healed, or needed a glimpse of the future. Old mother Trerice would read the tea-leaves for you, she would interpret dreams. Some said she would cast or remove the occasional spell. In no wise did this appear to conflict with her perfervid Methodism. Such were the mysteries of the human soul. Nodding his head and tap-tapping his stick, Curnow proceeded down the street in the direction of the Tinners' where a commotion was occurring.

Though he had never seen the new chapel, the Tinners' Arms was still a clear picture to him. Until the chapel's construction, it had been the most prepossessing building in Windfall, a bulky granite square, strong as a jail, with massive stone lintels over its windows and doors, and thick chimneys poking through a hipped slate roof. There was no sign over the door; never had been; none was needed; even a blind man could tell that such a fine place must be the inn.

The interior, as Curnow remembered it, was devoid of luxury. The tap-room, floored with slate flags, must have been fresh plastered and lime-washed once, now it was brown with smoke. Stale smoke was always in the air: smoke from the poorly-drawing gorse fire, smoke from the numerous clay pipes that were kept ranged upon the mantel. And, mingling with the whiff of tobacco and furze, was the reek of spilt ale from the ranks of casks and firkins that occupied the longest wall, the odour of yesterday's revelry when the long deal-topped table that ran down the centre of the room had been packed with drinkers and card players. The only bits of decoration were a cutlass with a chipped blade and a fox's brush that had always hung over the fireplace. All this was clear as a picture at the moment he crossed the threshold and heard the Squire's voice over a babble of conversation.

'This is uncommonly fine brandy, Mr Lugger,' announced Silverton, sniffing at his glass, 'pray serve my friend Welland another like it and give ale to all the company.

I wonder why I can't get liquor like this in London.'

' 'Tis all captured by us Cornish before it can sail up Channel,' said a wag amid general laughter, 'aren't that so, Jack Lugger?' The landlord smiled a knowing smile. There were differing opinions about his past: some said he had shipped before the mast and fought in many a hot engagement, his stiff right shoulder and chipped cutlass were proof of it; others, perhaps more knowledgeable, hinted that the chip in the blade had flown off in a desperate night-time encounter with the preventive men. Jack Lugger was too canny to deny either assertion, indeed both might have been true. He merely screwed up his eyes, with the ghost of a twinkle at the back of them. He was a gaunt, lank man, with the ascetic face of a Carthusian, not at all the plump, jolly figure you would expect of a landlord. However, whatever his past links with the smuggling fraternity might have been, his present association was an active one. His brandy was cheap and good, far too good ever to have known a gauger's rod and paid the duty.

'Here's a health to the Squire!' shouted the landlord as soon as all glasses and mugs were full.

'And to our esteemed fellow countryman, Welland Halt!' cried Silverton Gurney in his turn once the mugs were lowered. 'But where *is* the varmint?'

Welland was no longer at his side; he was whispering with Ruth in the doorway.

'What d'you mean, "won't come"?'

'She says she won't come if there's drinking,' explained Ruth.

'Come on, man, we're trying to drink your health!' called Silverton, catching sight of him.

'You can see the fix I'm in. Tell her I'll be home shortly,' Welland muttered as he turned back into the room.

'Good old Welland!'

Mugs and glasses clinked, there were more shouts of approval. Men he hardly knew shook Welland by the hand.

Women, for there were a few who frequented the Tinners', kissed his cheek. Jack Lugger topped up his glass and marked the Squire's slate. Jack himself drank little, but the sight of customers drinking could raise his spirits and extract a smile.

'You'll come up to London with me, won't you?' Silverton Gurney was asking. 'Everyone wants to meet you. You'll make a fortune.' Welland stood silent. 'What's the matter with you, man? Come on, don't be such a dog in the manger. "There comes a tide in the affairs of men . . ." surely you know the line.'

'I've tried to tell you. From the very beginning, I've tried to make it clear to you, Mr Gurney, I don't seek public notice, I don't wish to leave Windfall.'

'I know what it is, you sly old fox, but why can't you say it outright? You've gone to ground here with that pretty young vixen and don't want to bring her into the light. Can't say I blame you. Love's labour lost to try and lure you away. But you'll change your mind sooner or later. Bring Mavis with you, Ruth too. They'll be charmed by London.' Welland, he noticed, was smiling a wan smile. 'Cheer up, old chap. What can be wrong with becoming famous? Having your name on everyone's lips? The toast of the town?'

'It's not possible.'

Welland drained his glass and the landlord poured him another.

'Well,' grumbled Silverton, 'you can take a horse to water, but you can't make him drink.'

'I'm grateful, don't think I'm not,' protested Welland, 'but believe me, all I want is to stay here quiet. I seek no notoriety. I'd rather it all fell to you. There's no need for Gurney & Halt: just plain Gurney will do.'

'Your modesty does you credit,' said Silverton in a pained manner, 'but there's no puttting the clock back. There's not a soul in London hasn't heard of Welland Halt. They're all consumed with curiosity about you.'

'Would to God they weren't!' Welland exploded. A scowl darkened his face.

'Look here, Welland, I'm hurt. I only thought to please you. If you take my disinterested generosity this way, I don't know what to say to you.'

'What's done is done, I suppose, and there's no help for it,' continued Welland with evident bitterness. 'I'm sorry I ever got started in this business. I should've known better.'

'I can't understand you, Welland. There's something peculiar about you. Why a man of your ability should have turned up in Windfall like you did is a mystery. To be as cagey as you are, there has to be a reason. If you don't trust me –' Silverton consulted his watch. 'Now, you'll have to excuse me. I've promised to sup with my wife before taking the road for London. I had thought to have you ride beside me, but I see that is impossible.' He turned away with a hard face. Welland was acting so strangely; perhaps Lady Diana was right – for all his manners and skill, he was no gentleman. 'Landlord!' he cried, tossing a purse on to the table. 'Make shift to pay yourself with that. And see if some more of your liquor won't make that dog Welland more cheerful.'

As he stepped into the street, Welland came up with him. He seemed choked, desperate to express something. He caught at Gurney's hand.

'Silverton,' he said at last, 'I'll call you that for once. I'm grateful; I want you to know that. It's only – If you knew my reasons –'

'Out with it, man! Out with it!'

But Welland had seen Jack Lugger watching and listening in the doorway.

'Not now, some other time maybe.'

'There may not be another. If you can't see your way clear to come to London, I must think twice about our partnership.'

Silverton was impatient. He felt rather ridiculous out there in the middle of the street, holding hands with a tradesman, however talented. Shaking himself free, he hurried away from Windfall. Tregurney's lights beckoned. The table would be laid already, the wine brought in from the buttery, Hector Bolitho and Janet would be sipping madeira with the Rector. There would be civilized conversation, even with sharp-tongued Diana, and good food aplenty, just what he needed to help him forget this difficult afternoon with Welland in Windfall. How foolish he had been to imagine he could bring the two worlds together.

Welland watched him leave, waiting till he was out of sight. A wild desperation made him want to return to the inn and drown his sorrows, but he hesitated, knowing that he should go home to Mavis. Perhaps he would have done so had not the landlord called out that Tom Magor was inside, looking for him, with a letter or something. A sixth sense told Welland he could not ignore it. Mavis would have to wait.

Mavis had polished the brass candlesticks and ironed the tablecloth. She simmered the mutton stew on the slab and boiled cabbage and onions. A saffron cake was fresh from the oven. The grate was full of coal and crackling ever so quietly. All of her tasks were done. She had nothing to do but wait. She waited. On the far side of the room, Ruth was reading in the lamplight. Through the window behind her, Mavis had watched the blood-red sunset collapse behind Carnwartha. She wished she were up there. She wished she had the night wind in her hair and its hiss in the heather instead of the sound of the tea-kettle. She wished she were heart-whole and fancy-free again, and she knew it was impossible. Even were she free, she could never be heart-whole again. You were never free. She thought of her mother and the familiar face loomed in front of her, filling the house with bitter laughter.

She pulled up her apron to cover her face and pressed her hands against her ears tightly. Rough hands were scrabbling for the latch to open the door. There were grunts of frustration, squeals from the hinges, the beery breath, the sound of blows, and a woman whimpering, then the rhythmic creaking from the bed until, at last, the shriek in the night, and silence. Inside the apron, the tears coursed quietly down her cheeks. Her mother's martyrdom was over; her own was just beginning.

When she dried her eyes and let fall her apron, Ruth was still reading. Since she had come to live in the same house, she found that the girl had become inexplicably distant. How could she be so unconcerned at this moment?

'What did he say when you spoke to him?' she asked sharply, breaking through Ruth's concentration.

'I've told you already. He said he'd be home shortly.'

'But he's not, is he? I'm worried about him.'

'Father can take care of himself. If you begrudge him a drink with his friends, you should go and fetch him yourself.' Ruth's face was bland, her voice seemed unconcerned.

'I can't do that. It's his choice. He'll come home when he wants to.'

'You must wait then. He'll come home if he wants you.'

Ruth returned to her book and Mavis to the clock's slow ticking.

'Us should let bygones be bygones, aren't that right?' asked Magor. Welland Halt looked at him suspiciously. The sullen smith had never once spoken to him since their terrible battle. Yet Magor seemed frank and jovial enough. 'And you're a better man than ever I took you to be. It've took me whiles to admit it. Will you touch glasses with me, out of kindness?'

Well, thought Welland, a man might as well drink with an old enemy as a new friend. They clinked their glasses.

'Didn't you tell Jack Lugger you had a letter for me?'

'Oh that! I'm sorry, I almost did forget. It come by the mail-coach this mornin' and the landlord wouldn' put up the money for un.' As Magor spoke, he reached inside his shirt and pulled out a letter. It was crumpled but, as far as

273

Welland could see without close inspection, the wax seal looked unbroken.

'How much was it?'

'Nothin' o' no consequence. I ferget now. Why don't you read un.'

Welland was turning the letter in his hands, smoothing it on the table, surreptitiously examining the handwriting in the light of a nearby candle. It was already dim in the taproom; with the windows painted over to keep out the chapel folk's glares, almost no light percolated from the street. He took a long swallow of his drink and sat motionless a moment with the paper in both hands.

'Goos on, read un – may be worth somethin',' Magor insisted.

Welland broke the seal. Magor studied his face while his eyes flicked back and forth, from top to bottom of the page in one concentrated act, before folding it again and sitting absolutely still like one entranced. There was no outward emotion on his face, nothing but a stony indifference, akin to lassitude.

'Well,' asked Magor, 'good news, is it?'

Welland drained his glass before answering.

'Nothing important.'

He took the letter by its corner and held it in the candle flame until it caught light, burning briefly and curling into contorted leaves of fragile grey ash. The red wax softened and dripped on to Welland's other wrist. He seemed unconscious of it at first, but eventually flicked it away, leaving a white patch on his tanned skin.

Welland did not go home. He sat and drank with Magor and the others while the talk turned to poaching which they could discuss freely now that the Squire had gone. When they had finished with poaching, Jack Lugger took down the brush from the wall over the mantel and displayed it to the company.

'Cleverest fox ever I did see was this un!' he proclaimed.

'Squire Gurney and the quality never could catch un. A merry dance 'e led them 'osses, up 'ill and down dale. They never comed near un. Mr Fox took a Tregurney chicken whenever 'e wanted and made off for the moor.' He paused and Welland had the impression this wasn't the first time he had told the tale. 'It looked like 'e would never get 'is come-uppance. But one day 'e took one chicken too many. 'E took un from a tinner's fowl-pen in Windfall. Now, that tinner didn't run screechin' and hullooin', and whoopin' all over the moor, 'e were too clever for that. What 'e did was this: 'e tied a fowl by its leg inside the pen and waited.' Jack Lugger stood smoothing the fox's brush reflectively, staring across the room as if he were the waiting tinner. 'Sure 'nuff, the old fox comed and took the second fowl. The tinner chap followed un, quiet like, with 'is old 'ound leashed in an' muzzled, till 'e found the place where the fox 'ad gone to ground. 'E left 'is dog to watch the place and ran off 'ome to fetch the rest of 'is pare. When they comed over, they just dug and dug, they dug so fast as they could, and tinners d'knaw 'ow to dig, don't 'em? They dug down till they come up with Mr Fox and catched un by this tail.' He waited for the ritual cheer. 'But that's not all: they tinners did come upon a famous lode o' tin where they dug un out – Don't believe me, do 'ee? Well, I can point to the very spot, and so can many another 'ere. Us can take 'ee straight to Balreynard.'

It was an old story and Jack Lugger had improved in the telling of it. Old tales were still the best. Magor chuckled with the others and sipped at his ale before asking Welland, 'What d'ye think to that? Don't pay to cross a tinner, do it? Tinners are like terriers, they don't never let go.'

But Welland was no longer there beside him, nor was he anywhere else in the room. Cursing himself under his breath for having let the man out of his sight, Magor stood up unsteadily and made for the door. Night was falling and the street was empty. Magor hesitated, but only for a moment. If

Welland was responding to the message he had received, there was only one way he could have chosen. Magor set off after him.

Mavis had gone to bed. She had left the table laid downstairs, but without hope of sharing the meal with Welland. The food was all spoiled. In despair, she had gone to see Curnow who had told her that Welland was drinking with Magor. What was Welland thinking? Whatever it was, she could not face him. When she came home, her grief had turned to anger and she was short with Ruth.

'Don't you care?' she had demanded. 'You just sit there and read as if nothing had happened.'

'It's his choice, you said so yourself. He'll come home when he wants to.'

She had taken her book and her candle and gone up to bed early. Now, she lay sleeping in her room across the landing, at least Mavis hoped she slept, but she might just as easily be lying sleepless like herself while the seconds dragged by like hours and the hours like centuries. The only proof of time's passing was the slow swing of the stars across her window, but the clock she felt was the insistent battering of her heart. Her consciousness was attuned to the smallest sound: a cinder falling through the grate, a fox yelping on the hill towards Tregurney, owls' eerie hooting. To wait on was unbearable. She kept telling herself that soon she would dress and go in search of him, but kept putting it off. She had even considered marching into the Tinners' and removing him by main force, but her heart failed her, not because she was unequal to the task, but because she feared he would never forgive her. Now, it seemed, even that project was unrealizable: the drinkers from the inn had straggled home, laughing and shouting as they staggered down the street. It was just like the old days in Windfall and she was glad she was not out there, fighting off their crude embraces. When the last of them had reached home, all was still once more. She thought she heard the faint chime of Tregurney church clock, but could not tell what hour it struck.

Somehow, she must have dozed off into a shallow sleep. She awoke nervously to a clatter in the kitchen. Someone was inside the house. It could not be Ruth, she always moved delicately, but it didn't sound like Welland either. She had left the door on the latch, unbolted, for him. For a few moments, she lay rigid with fear, wondering what to do. Then she sat up and reached for the tinder-box to light her candle.

'Welland?' she called softly. There was no answer. Before she could produce a flame, there were heavy footsteps on the stairs, erratic, stumbling. They did not sound like Welland's. His lame leg was usually unmistakable.

'Is it you, Welland?'

Her candle sputtered into life, filling the room with dancing shadows. The door swung inward menacingly.

He looked done in. The man she saw had been involved in a terrible struggle. His features were drawn, haggard. His eyes were sunken. She had expected him to be boisterous and wild. Instead, he was silent and withdrawn. She was full of concern, but could not hold back the accusation she had prepared for him.

'You've been drinking!'

He nodded dumbly. He clung to the edge of the door, swaying slightly.

'We waited for you. We waited and waited. Your food's spoiled. Everything's spoilt. You've spoilt it. You swore you wouldn't – you told me you'd never –'

'Is Ruth all right? Did she get home safely?' he whispered.

'Asleep. In bed. You worried her too. You scared both of us.'

She watched him as he stepped into the room, treading carefully on the creaking boards. He looked the same, but different, subtly different, not the man she had been expecting. It might be drunkenness, but she did not think so. She should have felt relief, but what she saw brought tension.

'You've been fighting.'

This time, it was not so much an accusation as a cry of despair. He followed her stare to the red stain on his shirt and the tattered remnants where the buttons had been torn away. 'Yes.'

His voice was flat, defeated. There was a long silence. He could not face the pain in her eyes. She could not face the pain in his. 'I could say I'm sorry, but it wouldn't change much, would it? You were right, Mavis. I made a promise, but I couldn't keep it.'

There were tears in his eyes. His twisted body that had repelled her at first, but she had come to love, expressed his grief. She sprang out of bed and stood beside him.

'You're not hurt bad, are 'ee?' she asked, helping him strip the shirt from his back. 'Poor man, poor man,' she crooned as she saw the red weals on his chest and the runs of dried blood that streaked it.

'It's all done now,' he murmured.

'All done?'

'There'll be no more fighting. There's naught left to fight for.' His body was racked with sobs.

'Hush! Hush! Poor boy. Hold still while I care for you.'

She dampened a cloth with water from the ewer on the wash-table and stroked his skin with it. Gradually, his trembling ceased.

'It was for you,' he whispered, 'for you I did it.'

'But who?' she asked urgently. 'Was it Magor again?'

'Hush!' he commanded. 'I'll tell 'ee tomorrow,' and sealed her lips with a kiss. Her gentleness had restored him. There was a compressed strength in him like a coiled spring. As he kissed her again, she felt such a hungry desire in him that she was afraid. He kicked off his boots without bending to unlace them. His hands were busy exploring her body. 'Undo my belt,' he told her, and she complied in a kind of ecstasy. Was this how her father had been to her mother?' No, this was different. Her father had been drunk, bestial.

Her Welland was not drunk. Not drunk on liquor. He was

drunk with desire, desire for her. He had the dust of stars on
him and the animal musk of the fighter after the fight. She
had never known him like this, all restraint forgotten. They
fell across the bed and he held her away from him a while,
studying her face in the light of the candle. His eyes were
deep and penetrating; they seemed to see right through her
head, and still he was not satisfied.

'Tell me you love me.'

'I love you.'

'Whoever I am. Whatever I've done.'

'Whoever you are, whatever you've done, I love you.'

'It was for you,' he told her, 'remember that. Whatever
I've done, it was for you. Because I loved you.'

She did not question the way that he put it, though she did
so after. He gave her no leisure to think, but pinched out the
candle and drowned her with kisses. She forgot the waiting
and the spoiled supper; she forgot the barking fox and the
shouts in the streets; she forgot her fears of his drunkenness;
she forgot her father; she forgot her mother and the venom
she carried; she forgot Ruth, awake and listening across the
landing; she forgot herself. There was only Welland. All the
world was enfolded in their heaving bed. For the time, there
was no other. He was her miner, she his mine, digging,
digging, till he reached the richest lode.

They slept. It was daylight when she heard the tapping. A
white stick was rapping against the window. Wrapping a
sheet around her body she went to investigate. Curnow was
looking up anxiously. He spoke in a loud whisper.

'Where's Welland? 'E's 'ere, isn't 'e? No need to pretend 'e
aren't. Tell un to leave this minute by the back door. Tell un
they're about to come after un. Don't you 'ear 'em shoutin'?
Magor's at the back of it. They'll kill un.'

Curnow was right, there were mounting cries from the
direction of the Tinners'. Whatever it was, it was urgent.
When she turned, Welland was sitting on the bed with his
head in his hands.

'Welland,' she called, 'you heard what Curnow said. Get dressed! Get moving! I don't know what it is you've done, but don't just sit there. Get dressed! Get moving!'

' 'Twill do no good. 'Tisn't no use.'

'Never mind that. If you love me, get moving.'

Outside in the street, loud voices were already approaching.

14

THE OLD MEN'S GROUND

'Have you seen 'un?'

Johnny Fortnight was startled by the cry. A band of men had just topped the rise ahead and were bearing down on him. He was climbing the steep incline out of Bethel on the road to Tregurney and Windfall and his whole attention had been concentrated on his donkey's heels, giving Emma a prod with a sharp stick whenever she slowed, which was often. She stopped again as the band, half a dozen strong, came closer to her, moving fast at a pace between a walk and a trot.

'Seen who?' answered Johnny Fortnight.

'Welland Halt,' called their leader breathlessly.

Johnny Fortnight was about to jab Emma again, but stopped in mid gesture. The men arrived and came to a stop, panting, beaded with sweat despite the early morning chill. Their leader, whom the packman recognized immediately as a tinner from Windfall, repeated his question.

'Welland Halt — 'ave you seen 'un?'

Johnny Fortnight pondered a moment before answering with a question of his own.

'What d'ye want 'im for?'

'Murder!' said the men in jumbled chorus.

'Is 'e the one what builds carriages for Squire Gurney? The one what limps?'

'Aye, aye, 'e's the one.' They were persuaded they were hot on his traces. The packman looked down at the dust and then up again, bit his lip and screwed up his eyes thoughtfully.

'The feller what fought Tom Magor?'

'Aye, aye!' said their leader impatiently.

'Well, I ain't seen 'im.'

'Don't fool with us,' said the leader angrily while his companions looked crestfallen. ' 'Twill go ill with you if you're 'idin' somethin'. How far've you come this mornin'?'

'From t'other side o' Bethel. I've been on the road since daybreak.'

The men whispered together a few seconds.

'Can't 'ave missed un, can 'e?' said one of them.

'Do I look blind?' demanded the packman.

'None o' that clever-dick stuff or you'll feel the weight o' my fist,' growled the tinners' leader. 'Now tell us, are you certain sure you 'aven't seed un?'

Johnny Fortnight shook his head.

'Who's 'e s'posed t'ave murdered?'

'A woman. Tom Magor 'eared un do it.'

'Well, good luck, but I don't think you'll come up with 'im on this road.'

'If us do, I can tell 'ee wan thing, if you've lied about un, Johnny Fortnight won't come selling no more frippery in Windfall!' He turned to his companions. 'Come on, boys, us is wastin' our time jawin' with this varmint.'

They were off again, somewhat disheartened, but still sufficiently determined to carry their search to Bethel and beyond. The packman watched them diminish into the distance and then poked his donkey into motion. Welland Halt, he ruminated, now wasn't he that strange cove who had turned up in Windfall with his daughter? Young Ruth was the one who kept pestering him for books to read. He had something for her at the bottom of his saddlebag at that very moment. And wasn't Welland Halt the one who had recently got married to Mavis Trerice? He wondered how he'd managed to get the Curate to read the banns and go through with it. Strange chap, that Welland, you couldn't help wondering where he had come from. But then, Mavis herself had a touch of strangeness. Wasn't she a wild one, leading the other maidens down to frolic with him in his hidden pool? The thought of her white skin shining wetly in the moonlight still excited him as he completed the slow climb. He'd have married her himself if she'd have let him touch her, even though he wasn't the marrying kind either. The memory of her shrill laughter, leading the other maidens in earthy mirth as he sprang out of the water exposing himself, haunted him still. Well, she wouldn't be laughing now.

On the saddle of land before the descent to Tregurney began, man and beast came to a tacitly agreed halt. Ahead of them, the newly constructed, stone-surfaced turnpike dipped across the open moor, passing close to the granite carn where the Windfall road forked off. This was where the woman who spoke to him at Bethel during the night would have alighted. He had been drawing a drink for Emma at the pump there in the early hours of the morning when the Truro stage rolled in. The coachman had stepped down and gone off on some errand or other, leaving the horses to steam and stamp. Suddenly, a curtain was pulled back, a coach window was pulled down and a pale face appeared in the opening.

'Is this Windfall?' came a woman's voice assertively. It was not a West Country voice, and it wasn't really genteel either, but a kind of combination of several elements, some raffish, some pretentious, that chimed ill with an inside passenger.

'No, it ain't,' he answered shortly.

'Well, where *are* we? Why are we stopped in the middle of nowhere?'

'Ask your coachman.' Johnny didn't like being questioned at the best of times, still less to be treated in an overbearing manner. 'I'm busy.'

'Look, 'ere, I'm sorry. Who else can I ask?' The change in her manner had been dramatic. 'I've been asleep; it's such a long journey. I'm afraid we've already passed through it.'

'Well, you 'aven't. This stage don't go through Windfall, not so far as I know.'

'Good God, 'ave I taken the wrong conveyance? I must get off immediately.' She struggled with the door latch and began to alight. The packman saw she was wearing what looked like expensive, though garish, clothing.

'Not so fast, dearie. I didn't say you was on the wrong coach, all I said was it didn't call there. But what can a fine lady like you be wantin' in Windfall?'

'That's my business!' She was abruptly supercilious again.

'Then it ain't *my* business to tell 'ee nothin'. You can wait for the coachman.'

'Prickly, aren't we? Worse than an 'edge'og!' She was wheedling now. 'You're a man of the roads, aren't you? A tinker? I saw that right off. Well, we're not so different. If you must know, I'm goin' to Windfall to seek my fortune.'

'Good luck to you then. You won't be the first, nor the poorest, but you'll 'ave to walk there. This coach don't leave the turnpike. Ask the driver to set you down at the carn near Morvan. You'll be able to see the place from there. There's an inn, the Tinners', that's unless you're expected.'

'I'm expected.'

'That'll be all hunky dory then. I 'opes you're not disappointed.'

'I shan't be. I shall 'ave me due, don't worry.'

The coachman had reappeared and cut short the conversation. The coach had rumbled off into the night, leaving Johnny and Emma alone in darkened Bethel.

Now, looking back on the conversation, the packman wondered if the woman had had any connection with the Welland Halt business. He had not intended to call at Windfall that day, but go straight to his camp near Tregurney. Now he was intrigued by the man-hunt and the murder accusation. Welland Halt hadn't seemed the kind of chap who would do that kind of thing, but you couldn't go by appearances. He pulled Emma's halter to the left and set her off, trotting towards the Tinners'.

They would be lucky to reach there before the rain overtook them. All across the western horizon, massed like a fleet in line of battle, great, black-sailed rainclouds were fast approaching. The rain would be bad news for Welland if he was out there somewhere in the bracken, he would soon be soaked and shivering. Good luck to him wherever he was, poor devil. Johnny Fortnight's heart went out to the hunted; weren't all the laws of men arrayed against him?

Down in the village he was approaching, the hue and cry had been hard to set up. All the tinners had been abed when Magor raised the alarm and only Jack Lugger showed instant enthusiasm, lighting a lantern in the tap-room and flourishing the old cutlass which he took down from the wall, but he showed no sign of wanting to venture outdoors alone.

It was left to Tom Magor to run from house to house in search of those few of the sleeping miners who were ready to respond to his summons. For the most part, they grunted incredulously and went back to sleep.

Only when Hector Bolitho drove up from Tregurney on the way to the count house was there any substantial action and even then, it was prudent. Magor ran shouting to intercept the manager's trap and he pulled up reluctantly.

'What is it, man? Be brief. I'm in a hurry.'

But he listened attentively to Magor's jumbled account while his horse chomped at the grass and jingled its harness. There was more to this story than met the eye.

'You're certain you're not imagining it? Did you see it happen?'

'In a manner o' speakin', I did.'

'A manner of speaking? I want better than that to keep me from Wheal Fortune.'

'I didn' see nothin', but I did 'ear all right. I 'eard plenty. Clear as a bell I 'eard it, clear as you 'ears me now, your honour.'

'And what do you claim these two people were saying?'

'Welland was for tellin' 'er to go, and she was sayin' she wouldn'. She kept sayin' she'd come to share 'is good fortune. First 'e argued with 'er a bit, then 'e offered 'er money if she'd go 'way again. When she wouldn't 'ave none o' that, when she swore she'd come to stay in Windfall, I 'eard un cuss and threaten 'er.'

'How long did all this last?' Mr Bolitho continued probing with professional diligence worthy of a Justice of the Peace.

' 'Bout 'arf an hour, I reckon.'

'And how did it finish?'

'Well, while they was squabblin' she'd been inchin' 'er way down the Windfall road from the place where 'e met 'er by the turnpike. "Not a step further!" 'e shouts. "Try to stop me!" she cries, "I dare you!" Then there was sounds of a scuffle, and more damnin' cussin' from 'im, and then I 'eard 'er cryin', "You won't do it! You can't do that to me. You'll never rest. It's not in your nature, Welland. I know you too well, you won't do it." "For the last time, will you turn back and leave us?" "Leave us indeed! Leave you to your fancy woman? Never! I've come to share your good fortune, I'll not be cheated." ' Magor paused and licked his lips.

'And then?'

'She screamed.'

'And still you said nothing. You did nothing to save her?'

'I'd come as close as I dared, your honour. I'd learnt to my cost not to cross Welland.

' "You've driven me to it," 'e tells 'er. "No!" she screams. Then she screamed again. ' 'Twas 'orrible. I thought all Windfall must awake. And as she screamed I 'eard a thud, like she was fallin', and the scream went 'ollow and broken like, and then 'twas quiet as the grave till I 'eard un comin'. I ducked down by the wall and 'e walked right past me. I knowed for certain 'twas 'e for I 'eard un limpin'.'

'And where exactly did all this happen? Can you point out the place? Can you indicate it precisely? Show me a body?'

There was still a good chance, in Bolitho's estimation, that the whole story was pure invention.

'I can take 'ee straight to the spot. I went there meself, right afterward, but there was no 'elp for the woman, poor critter. 'Tis the old Gipsy Winze, just this side o' the carn yonder. 'Twas dug for the first Windfall workin's. 'Tis ten fathom deep. She can't be livin'.'

Bolitho sat silent. His horse was still munching contentedly and the sun was just clearing the hills ahead of him. He wanted to catch Magor's eye, stare him out, judge his veracity. But Magor was looking all round excitedly, trying to drum up support among the few onlookers.

'Us should start at once,' he insisted. 'There's no time to lose. That Welland's got a 'ead start on us.'

'All in good time,' agreed Bolitho with some reluctance, but realizing that, sooner or later, the allegation would have to be investigated. 'The first thing we'll do is send a party to the bal for a windlass and kibble. I'll send someone down to see if there's a body. You, Ellis, get over to Wheal Fortune and get Captain Angove to bring the gear and a pare to work it.' When the messenger had gone, he turned back to Magor. 'Now tell me about that other thing you mentioned, the letter.'

'It comed yesterday forenoon and I gived un to un.'

'*You* did? And how, pray, did you come to possess it?'

'I paid the postage. Landlord Lugger wouldn'.'

'You did, did you? Most uncommonly generous! And how did you discover what was in it!'

'I read un.'

Bolitho thought it superfluous to question the ethics of tampering with another's correspondence. Instead he remarked, 'But you can't read, can you?'

'No, your honour, but I knaws wan as can.'

'And who was this person?' Bolitho sniffed. Magor stood silent. 'No, well, I suppose it is too much to expect you to divulge it – honour among thieves and all that. Now, tell me again what you said was in it.'

'It were a woman's writin' – '

'I've no time for that,' interjected Bolitho. 'A man who can't read is no judge of handwriting.'

'Well, any road, she said it were a woman's 'and – '

'She?'

'Her what read it fer me.' He hurried on so that Bolitho could not pursue the question. 'It were a longish letter, but I can remember the best part of un. What she said was 'ow pleased she were to read o' Welland's good fortune. She said as 'ow she'd been proper mazed with grief when 'e went off with Ruth. She said 'ow she'd been missin' un and longin fer a letter. Said she couldn' 'ardly believe it at first when she seed 'is name along o' Mr Gurney's in the newspaper, but she knawed for sure 'twas 'er Welland a-cause of 'is way with metal. Then she said she couldn' wait to see un and share 'is good fortune. Told un she'd be on the Plymouth coach followin', soon as she could borrow the fare and get 'er things in order.'

'And how was it signed? Was there a name to it?'

'It were ended, "Your faithful Freya". I remember that bit particular.'

'Freya? That's not a Christian name. Not many women bear it,' ruminated Bolitho. 'Most interesting. Now, tell me, what's become of this letter? Can you show it me?'

'Sorry, your honour, I gived un to Welland and 'e read un as 'e sat beside me in the Tinners'. Then 'e burned un over the candle.'

'He did? How very convenient! Though if it's true, there ought to be witnesses to corroborate your story. Tell me, did Welland behave in any peculiar way after he read this letter?'

'No, your honour, 'e kept a straight face, just sat quiet like fer a bit, then 'e upped and left when 'e thought I weren't lookin'. Near slipped away altogether, 'e did, but I followed me nose and 'eard un 'obblin' up the 'ill toward the turnpike. I kept well back so 'e wouldn' think I were on to un.'

'Well, these are very grave accusations. They'd better be true – for your sake. There's such a thing as perjury. Yes, grave accusations and they'll have to be investigated. Welland must be found. He'll have to answer to them. But before we get started, there's one thing I'd like to ask you: don't you think you owe Welland the benefit of the doubt? Don't you owe him something? Aren't I right in thinking he spared your own life once, when you were drowning? Another man might have let you go under.'

'That were different,' said Magor coolly, 'that were just good sportsmanship. This 'ere's murder.'

The two women were sitting facing one another across the kitchen when the men broke in. They had not bothered to light a fire. Ruth sat with her hands in her lap, her stare fixed on some invisible object far ahead of her. Mavis had twisted her apron around her own anxious fingers.

'When did you last see your father?' demanded Magor as he barged in closely followed by a brace of tinners.

'Leave the girl alone!' snapped Mavis. 'Have you no shame!'

' 'Tis you should be answerin' that question,' Magor grunted. 'Come on, where is 'e? Where's Welland?'

'Gone to his work like always. What do you want with him?'

'Expect us to believe that when 'e done what 'e've done? Not likely.'

'What d'you mean?' Mavis was feeling hysterical. It was evident that Welland had not fought Magor, the man was unmarked. But he had fought someone.

'Didn' 'e tell you 'bout the woman 'e killed? But 'e wouldn' need to, would 'e? 'Twere in both o' your interests to dispose o' that woman. Now, stop 'edging and tell us: where is 'e?'

'I've told you already, he's left for Wheal Fortune.'

289

'Up those stairs, you two!' Magor ordered the tinners. 'Us can't take no chances. Look in the roof while you're at it, though 'tis almost certain the bird 'ave flown.' He waited for the tinners to leave the room, then spoke more quietly, so quietly that he was barely audible under the racket of hobnailed boots and dragging furniture. ' 'Twill be best fer un to give 'isself up, that's plain as a pikestaff. To go on the run's as good an admission o' guilt as any other. Now, in 'is own interest, tell me, when did you last see 'im?'

'He was here all night. He came home from the Tinners' and stayed here till morning.'

Magor laughed, a dry humourless laugh; he pointed at the unused plates on the table.

' 'Ere all night, that's rich. Ain't you 'eard o' perjury?'

'A wife can't testify against her husband.'

'No, a *wife* can't, but us all knows you're not in that category. Us suspected it, o' course, but now us knows, don't us? Come on, boys!' he shouted up the stairs. ' 'Tis a waste o' time lookin'. Us'll 'ave ter get 'old o' Rector Adams, ask un ter bring 'is blood 'ounds.' He halted in front of Ruth and took her by the shoulders. 'She 'aven't told 'ee, 'ave she, no, nor your feyther neither, who the woman was 'e killed so she shouldn' get 'ere. Well, it don't take much 'magination, do it! If you don't believe me, ask 'er. She's in it with 'im. Birds of a feather.'

And he was gone, and the tinners with him. A long silence descended. Ruth still sat in her place, arms crossed on her breast, and rocking, rocking.

'I lied to him. I had to,' Mavis began, speaking to herself as much as to Ruth. 'But your father didn't tell me. He never told me. Would to God that he had. Would to God we had never come to this predicament. You understand that, don't you: he never told me.'

Ruth said nothing. She just kept rocking back and forth in her chair in the way she had begun when Magor released her. Her arms were still crossed and her fingertips were pressed between her lips. Did her eyes see anything? Would she ever stop that interminable rocking? Did she even hear Mavis's question?

'Why didn't *you* tell me? Oh God!' Mavis burst into uncontrollable tears, tears like the rain that began to tap on the roof and windows. 'Why didn't Welland tell me? Did he think he could hide for ever? They're bound to catch him. Good Christ, let him get away, poor devil. 'Tis the best we can hope for, but if he does we'll never see him more, not ever.'

Outside the cold house, the rain fell in torrents. Sheets of it shrouded Carnwartha. In her mind's eye, Mavis saw Welland crouched in the wet bracken like a fox while the grim beaters, tall and grey as the Merry Maidens, closed in on him slowly. But no, she told herself, her Welland wasn't the man to wait spellbound while the hunters came closer. Welland would run; Welland would trick them; Welland would come through; Welland was indestructible. Then she remembered his lameness, his pathetic, awkward scampering; he was always so slow. And the slow tears welled out of her eyes and coursed slowly down her rigid cheeks, lingered in the corners of her mouth and ran on downward. How could she help him? He was beyond help. What was left? Nothing but the creaking of Ruth's chair under her rocking and the hiss of the endless rain.

Johnny Fortnight was glad to have reached the shelter of the Tinners' Arms before the worst of the rain caught up with him. He had wedged himself into the ingle-nook beside a bundle of furze that he kept kicking so that it flared and spat. Emma was ensconced in the unaccustomed comfort of a stable and he himself had a seat on the stage of an unfolding drama. He listened attentively as Hector Bolitho sent out further search parties. Men had already been to Welland's house, others had set off for Tregurney, Johnny himself had met the group who had gone to Bethel. Now, Bolitho was despatching parties to comb the bracken on Morvan and Carnwartha hills. Within the hour, the Rector of Tregurney, alerted by the searchers, arrived with his bloodhounds and joyfully rushed off to Welland's house to pick up the trace.

'God damn this rain!' he complained when he stumped back into the taproom half an hour later. 'It's washed out the scent completely. Give me a drink, landlord, I'm wet enough outside, I'd better balance it with liquor inside.' 'Any news yet, Bolitho? – I thought not, these gallows-birds get all the luck, the Devil looks after his own, you know.' His thwarted hounds steamed and slavered in the chimney corner.

An air of stagnant gloom settled over the room and afforded Johnny Fortnight quiet satisfaction. Every minute carried the fugitive a few steps further away. Would the Devil look after Welland? He hoped so. God had certainly marshalled plenty of searchers.

Hector Bolitho had his own reasons for displeasure: this hue and cry was keeping the tinners away from the mine; there would be no tin or copper won that day. However, he could see no way to call off the search. Magor had told the truth about the letter; several men had seen Welland read and then burn it. Most damning of all was Welland's disappearance. Although his wife affirmed he had slept at home all night and gone to the mine at daybreak, there was no sign of him at the forge. An innocent man wouldn't have run off like that, now would he?

When the original search parties which had set off on foot returned empty-handed, Bolitho commandeered horses and sent riders in all directions with orders to leave the fugitive's description at every toll-gate on the turnpike. One was to ride as far as Bodmin in the west, though Bolitho doubted that Welland would have gone that way. Others were sent to Launceston, Saltash and Torpoint, where he might attempt to cross the Tamar into Devon. Still more were sent southwards to Fowey, Looe and Par in case he were trying to embark in a ship. Bolitho was methodical, unexcited, exhaustive, and yet, as the hours slipped by, he had the impression that Welland was slipping through his net. Did he care? Did he really want him to answer for the deed of pushing a woman, if woman there were, down a winze? Who was this woman? Even if she existed, what reason could Welland, a restrained, mild man despite his strength, have had to lay violent hands on her? They said that truth lay at the bottom of a well. Well, truth of some kind must lie at the bottom of Gipsy Winze. Bolitho was impatient to learn it.

Meanwhile, Jack Lugger, his rusty sword forgotten on the table, was drawing ale and serving victuals. It's an ill wind, he thought to himself. Who'd have guessed that Welland Halt would have brought him so much custom?

'Nothin' like a man-hunt to liven a place up,' he murmured as he served the Rector his third brandy.

'A man-hunt's no sport when there's no scent to go on. Devil take the varmint! Got clear away by now, he has. Why didn't someone call us sooner? We'd have caught him quick enough, wouldn't we, Redeemer, wouldn't we, Nemesis? Yes, we would, my darlings. We'll have better sport next time, my pets,' Rector Adams grumbled and buried his nose in the brandy.

The hours dragged by and the rain eased, but it was still grey and dismal. There wasn't even much talk of Welland any more. The men played cards or dozed. Only Bolitho fretted, computing all the wasted time. The packman stirred the fire with his booted foot. How many hours' start did Welland have now? Twelve at least. They'd never catch up with him now, not if he was clever.

'They're coming!'

A shout from the street had the whole taproom alive in a moment. In the distance there was more shouting. Johnny Fortnight listened intently. Had they caught him then? He joined the rush that spilled out of the doorway.

Down the road from Gipsy Winze lumbered the wagon.

The pare of miners who had been sent to work the windlass and go down in the kibble were running along on either side, whipping up the horses and shouting in their excitement. The wagon's flat bed was empty but for a white sheet with something under it. As the wagon rumbled past the first cottages, faces came to the windows, children darted out of doorways, forming a shrill cortège. There was barking of dogs and pounding of hooves as the great drayhorses came closer. The solitary driver, standing erect behind the shafts on the heaving bed that rocked like a ship, reined in savagely when he saw Mr Bolitho. The wagon shuddered to a halt and a deep hush fell on the swiftly gathering crowd, broken only by an occasional hoof-stamp and jingle of harness from the horses. All eyes were on the crumpled sheet. What was under it?

'Well, Magor?' said Bolitho finally.

' 'Tis she. Us found 'er, like I said us would,' crowed Magor triumphantly. The silence re-established itself, an uneasy quiet in which the sheet on the wagon assumed a more definite significance. There was the almost irrepressible urge to see what was beneath it, and the chilling, age-old fear of what might be there.

'Was she living? Has she spoken?' asked Bolitho in his careful legal tones.

'Dead!' said one of the tinners. 'She was dead as a doornail when us found 'er!' A rush of whispers circulated among the crowd. So it was true then: Welland Halt was a murderer. Hadn't they been right to distrust him when he turned up in Windfall? And Tom Magor, the man he had dispossessed, the man who had unmasked him, stood vindicated, proud, beside the body of Welland's victim. Hector Bolitho was opening his mouth to tell Magor to drive on when an old woman darted out of the crowd and tugged off the sheet.

Even though they had been expecting it, the sight shook a gasp from the onlookers. It was a woman's body, that was clear enough, but horribly, unspeakably mangled by the fall when she tumbled from side to side of the rugged winze. Her face, or what remained of it, was unrecognizable.

'Look to that! See what that devil 'ave done to the poor critter!' she screeched and Bolitho realized it was old Mrs Trerice. It had taken him a few moments to recognize her, so transformed with hate and passionate accusation was her face. 'Where's 'e to, the one what did it, the one what tricked my Mavis? Where's that Welland? Why aren't 'e found yet? Get on and find un!' she challenged Mr Bolitho. 'If 'is posh connections don't protect un.' Then she turned away, bent over with fury, and beat with her fists on the wagon. 'Justice! Us will 'ave justice!' she screeched, and Bolitho felt a strange knot of fear in his bowels. Thank God it was not his blood that woman was after.

'Justice!' echoed a salvo of voices from the crowd.

'Carry the body away,' said Bolitho with as much firmness as he could muster, 'it can lie in the church until the inquest is over.' He watched Magor anxiously to see if he would be obeyed. Magor was toying with the reins, reluctant to cut short the Trerice woman's diatribe. If he did not put a stop to it quickly, Bolitho knew he could end up with a riot on his hands and be unable to control it. The nearest military were in Bodmin; it would take two days to get them here. He began to wish he had called them already. A great deal could happen in two days.

Bolitho stepped forward, picked up the sheet and threw it over the body. Then, coming back to the front of the wagon, he stared Magor straight in the eye. 'If you value your job at Wheal Fortune, you'll drive on immediately. We're wasting time. Ask Mr Nichols to lock the body in the church until it can be examined by a physician. Take the wagon and fetch the gear from the winze. Take it to Wheal Fortune, then report back to me here. I'll find work for you to do. Now get moving!' To ensure he was obeyed, Bolitho slapped the nearest drayhorse on the rump, setting it shambling forward. To his relief, Magor steered the team up the steep slope to the church. With the focus of attention removed, the crowd began to drift away, but Bolitho was too wise an old bird to imagine he had scored more than a short-lived victory. They would be back when their patience ran out, and, if he didn't lay hands on Welland Halt before long, their frustration would be turned upon him. They were still wild folk, these tinners, under their chapel-going veneer. He turned on his heel, careful to show no emotion, and returned to the Tinners' Arms.

Johnny Fortnight lingered, then followed the wagon. When Hilda Trerice pulled off the sheet, he had pushed forward for a closer look. Death was no stranger to him and he could examine a corpse with cool appraisal. He was curious to know what kind of woman it was who had caught up with Welland.

Despite the severe mutilation of the face, the packman could see she had been a handsome woman. The skull was split and blood had stained her ash-blonde hair. It was the clothes she wore that intrigued him. They were bright, ill-assorted garments that looked like cast-offs from the wealthy. Last night, he had spoken to a woman who was dressed in that manner. Was she the same who had ridden the stage to the Windfall fork to be met by Welland? Later, when all was quiet, he would try to get a closer look at her, for the time he would stay in the inn.

As the afternoon drew on and the evening turned to night, the horsemen returned, tired and baffled, to report their failure to Mr Bolitho. Only one of them had found the slightest indication. The rider who had travelled to Looe brought news of a stranger who had embarked that night on a lugger for France, but his description did not tally with Welland's and the hour was too early for the fugitive to have arrived from Windfall.

The mood in the inn was heavy. Somehow, they were all now convinced, their quarry had slipped through the net. Johnny Fortnight's satisfaction increased as the searchers' gloom deepened, but he took care not to show it. Murderer or no, the man had his reasons, more reasons, no doubt, than those who killed for King and Country. If he had got away, the packman was glad for him. He was sorry too: there would be no end to the man's running. He was draining the last of his ale, ready to slip out and collect Emma from the stable before the landlord had the unfortunate idea of asking him for payment, when Tom Magor burst in.

'Us've been walkin' over the back of un!' he declared to Mr Bolitho, who looked up bewildered from a brown study. 'Walkin' over the back of un! – There iddn' no 'osses missin' from Windfall, is there?' Magor went on excitedly. 'So 'e can't 've travelled far. Our riders've proved that. There's no chance 'e's across the Tamar, or off to France for that matter. And 'e's not in the neighbourhood either. Us've searched the moor all day and there's no trace of un. The bugger can't 've got far on foot; us all knaws 'e's lame and can't walk straight, let alone run. So where is 'e?' Magor paused for effect, letting his audience grope towards his own deduction. 'Now where's the place what Welland knaws best? Where's the place 'e 've worked? Where's the place where 'e could 'ide a week and more till us gives over 'untin 'im? He looked at each man challengingly, but there was still no reply. 'Why, Wheal Fortune, o' course!' he declared, slamming the table so hard with his fist that the old cutlass rattled. 'Didn' Mavis say 'e'd gone there – to put us off, o' course.'

Hector Bolitho nodded slowly. It was a real possibility and they had neglected it. Searching the mine would give the men something to do instead of sitting around muttering. He himself was tired, dog tired, but he pulled himself together.

'Very well, the mine shall be searched, but it must be done systematically. I want the underground captains to meet me at the count house in half an hour and I want the tinners assembled in their pares beside it.'

Now that there was some action, Bolitho felt somewhat brighter. He would see to it that the search was effective. If

297

he had had a choice, he wouldn't be involved in this at all, but be tucked up in bed with his wife at Tregurney. But there was no choice; he must see it through. Someone had to see justice done. If Welland Halt had taken refuge in the mine, Hector Bolitho would seek him out. Then, he would send him to Bodmin for trial at the assizes. If it had to be done, Bolitho would see it was done right.

In the general exodus towards Wheal Fortune, the packman slipped out into the night. He fetched Emma from the stable, but did not set out for his poolside camp immediately. Instead, he tethered her on the moor beyond the vicarage and walked back to the church. With luck, he would find a door or window open.

The fact that the search began in the darkness of night mattered little: below ground it was always night. The tinners, turned out of their beds by Magor's hammering on their doors, were soon at the mine and trooping down the ladders. Half of the captains went with them, instructed by Mr Bolitho to start at a given signal when he set the pump in motion, and fan out into the workings, leaving no tunnel unexplored. The remaining captains were to watch all shafts and winzes.

Although their task was very like their normal employment, the miners became uneasy as soon as they stepped off the shaft ladders, leaving their comrades' comforting presence for the flickering loneliness of the levels. Superstitious men at the best of times, they were ready to ascribe the slightest sound or untoward event to the work of the knackers, even in ordinary circumstances. And these circumstances were not ordinary. If Magor was right, there was a fugitive at large in the mine, a man who had killed already, a man made desperate by his act, a man they knew to be strong and wily, a man who might be waiting to pounce on them at every corner. It was not unreasonable to expect the powers of darkness to be in league with him.

The gurgling shriek of the pump in fork echoed upward

through the main shaft. Soon the pump's noise was muffled as they picked their way in small groups along the winding levels which followed the meandering of the lodes, now broad stoped-out caverns, now narrow passages where they had to stoop and advance in single file.

Whenever they stopped, which was often, the irregular drip from the roof was loud and penetrating. Occasionally, the timbering would give out a groan as the rock shifted and a small stone would come skittering down a scree. The draughts that blew through the winzes made their candles flicker and fail. They advanced slower and slower. The fear of a man with a lethal hammer, waiting, in ambush round the next corner, held them back. The more ground they cleared, the more likely it was that their quarry, if he was there at all, was close ahead of them, listening for their coming.

Up in the count house, Hector Bolitho slept. He had sent a message to Tregurney, telling Janet not to expect him before the morrow and asking her to send him a decent breakfast. Wedged in his chair, with his head pillowed on his arms across the desk, he slept a shallow sleep, mumbling unintelligibly and stirring often.

It seemed to him that someone had just entered the count house. A shadowy man and a girl were standing by the entrance. Who sent you? he heard himself asking. Mavis Trerice. She said you were in need of hands. So it *was* Welland and that must be Ruth beside him. She'll not work here. Life must have better to offer a child than this. Well, she hadn't worked at the mine with her father, had she? I'm a smith, he heard Welland asserting, the best you'll ever encounter. You'll do well to learn to say 'sir' when you address your masters. Come on, Ruth, we'd best be leaving. He might have left then, but he hadn't. Bolitho had stopped him. There's a job for you here. Will you take it, yes or no? You'll not regret it, Welland was saying, but he *was* regretting it, they both were. The stamps weren't working; Bolitho reached out for the lever. Whose fault was it? Curnow's?

Hilda Trerice's? Bolitho ground his forehead into the wood of the desk-top and groaned.

Johnny Fortnight slept. He had found the church barred and bolted and decided to wait nearby till first light in the hope of gaining entrance. He lay under the stars, in the lee of a rock, with his head on his pack-saddle and only a thin blanket for company, but he was not cold; he was inured to it. In his dreams he heard splashings and laughter, and plunged towards the teasing smiles of the dark-haired bal maidens.

Mavis Halt did not sleep. She could not. She had been awake when Magor ran through the village, calling the men to Wheal Fortune. She was still awake now, her mind seething with thoughts. Whose was the body the men had brought back on the wagon? She had always known that a woman existed. She had feared meeting her. Now that would never happen. She left her bed and stood barefoot on the landing listening to Ruth's breathing and studying her recumbent form in the faint starlight that came through the window. Was she asleep? Her breathing seemed regular. Her eyes were closed. Mavis was not reassured. There was something unnerving in Ruth's controlled behaviour, her silence. If only she had wept, there might have been some relief for her. What had she thought of the sounds of passionate lovemaking after Welland came home? She must have heard them. What did she think later when she heard the accusation? Could Ruth still love her? The pale light of dawn was stealing into the world imperceptibly. Another day for Welland, wherever he was. What would she say to him if she saw him? Would she ever have that opportunity? He could never come back, never. If he was lucky, if he was far away, he could take on a new identity as perhaps he had when he came to Windfall. She could not hate him, she loved him, she had married him. But why had he made her do it? They were going to catch him, the idea he might escape was but idle

300

dreaming. In her heart of hearts she was sure he was hidden in Wheal Fortune, sure that Tom Magor was right. If he were, it was only a matter of time before they caught him. And when they did – She must do something. As silently as she could, Mavis dressed herself and slipped out of the cottage.

The first of the searchers were coming up to grass. Hector Bolitho was dimly aware of them grouping in the space between the shaft and the count house. He sat up and straightened his clothes. The men were subdued, blinking in the light, tired with looking. It was clear they had found nothing. Magor stood among them, stooping and dejected. Bolitho didn't know whether to feel sorry or glad. If Welland had been found in the mine, he would have had the problem of protecting him from mob assault and getting him con-veyed safe to Bodmin Gaol for trial at the assizes. If he were not down there, the man-hunt would resume on a wider scale. There would be no rest until the fugitive was disco-vered.

The last pare, two men and a boy, cleared the lip of the shaft. One of the men said something and, instantly, there was a commotion. All heads turned and the tinners were listening intently. Bolitho pulled down the window and the words came to him indistinctly. The elder miner was speak-ing.

'Us found footprints, wan was clear, t'other was draggin'. Us followed em off to the side o' the level, into the old men's ground.'

'Where is 'e then? Why 'aven't you catched un?' It was Magor speaking.

'Never seed un. 'Tis proper angly old ground; us 'ad ter go careful. Us followed they tracks till they comed to a winze. They didn' go no further.'

'And you left off there; you didn' go down un?' said Magor accusingly.

'Rather you than me, Tom Magor. 'Twas smooth as glass, with no proper 'and'olds, and deep, terrible deep. Us didn' 'ave no rope ter git down un. We was lucky to find our way back again.'

'Now's your chance, Magor!' called Bolitho from his window. 'Pick half a dozen strong fellows and go after him. These three will guide you.' He saw their faces fall as he spoke. They were afraid to go back to the old men's ground, afraid of Welland. To have ventured in once demanded courage enough, to go in twice was to invite disaster. But Magor showed no such trepidation.

'Let's go, boys!' he called as he shouldered his way towards the shaft. 'Give us some candles, and a rope too, we'll need 'em.'

'A guinea apiece when you bring him up alive,' added Bolitho. 'We don't want anything to happen to him. He must stand fair trial. You, Magor, I'll hold you accountable.'

He shut the window. It was quiet in the count house, a quietness only accentuated by the ticking of a longcase clock. Welland's hours of liberty were numbered, Hector Bolitho was convinced now. He accepted that the fugitive had gone to earth there somewhere. He sighed.

'What's to be done?'

The voice startled him. He had not heard anyone come into the count house. Turning quickly, he saw that the woman who spoke was still in the doorway. After his initial surprise, he reflected that it was not really astonishing that she should be here.

'You heard what they said out there just now?' he asked quietly. She nodded. 'It's only a matter of time. Magor will find him.'

'But I must do something. How can I help him?'

Bolitho stood and pondered, studying the woman's drawn features and dejected stance before he answered.

'You could try and reach Silverton Gurney. If any man has it in his power to help Welland Halt, it's Silverton. I have no influence. He has plenty. He can call out the military from Bodmin at a snap of his fingers. I only wish I could. When the tinners catch Welland – '

'When?' she interrupted tragically.

'Yes, when, Mavis. They're going to take him, they're bound to. That's when my troubles will begin. I'm far from certain I'll be able to control them, not with that old woman Trerice – I'm sorry, I know she's your mother – inciting them.'

'I'll leave at once.' Already, the decision to act had straightened her shoulders. She was more like the Mavis he remembered.

'Just one question, Mavis, in confidence – Do you think he's guilty?'

'Guilty? I don't know what that means in this context.'

'You've a good heart, Mavis. I remember how you stood up for Curnow. I was wrong then, I admit it. You showed me. God be with you. Now I must try and get hold of the captains and form a party to protect your husband when they've caught him.'

'Thank you!' They had come closer while speaking and now she reached out and took him by the lapel, smoothing it between thumb and forefinger. 'You're a good man, Hector Bolitho.' He saw the tears beginning to form in her eyes and felt that he wasn't far off a similar display of emotion.

'I'll do what I can. Now, get moving. My trap's coming up from Tregurney within the hour with my breakfast. You can ride back with the driver and speak to Lady Diana. She may be helpful. Something someone does might save him. I wish to God that woman had never come to Windfall.'

The dead woman lay on a bier in St Winwalloe's church where the carpenter had just left her after measuring her for a coffin. He had been too busy to notice that someone had slipped into the church behind him. Now, with the carpenter out of the way, Johnny Fortnight emerged from the curtains

303

that hung across the belfry at the foot of the tower. The corpse was once more covered with a sheet and the packman paused before pulling it back. Why was he getting caught up in this engagement? It was none of his business. But there was no denying the curiosity that drove him.

Only the woman's lips retained something of a human shape. The upper part of the face was smashed beyond recognition. Some quirk of rigor mortis had pulled back those lips, exposing her teeth in a malicious grin. The wild angle at which her head lay acoss her shoulders showed that her neck was broken. A jagged piece of bone protruded from the flesh of her forearm. Her hands were clasped, one over the other, with a scrap of striped ribbon between the fingers. He had to kneel down to perceive the innermost fist concealed something metallic. He decided to investigate. The woman's stiffened hands resisted as much as if she still had life. He was obliged to fish in his pocket for an old marlinspike to prise them apart and dislodge the object she refused to relinquish. It swung from his fingers at the end of the torn ribbon: a medal. Now what would she have been doing with a medal? Almost unthinkingly, he slipped it into his pocket with the marlinspike. Now, what other clues were there to the woman's identity?

The packman ran his hands expertly over her clothing. If she had carried a bag of some kind, he had not seen it. At first, he found nothing. Then, setting what few scruples he had aside, he pulled open her clothing. There was a canvas belt about her waist, too narrow to be a corset. He discovered the tie and unlaced it. The belt had been made to hold money, but there was precious little in it now: perhaps one and sixpence. The empty compartments were stuffed with paper. The packman pulled one out. It looked like a newspaper. He tried another, printed on coloured paper. There was a crude portrait in the midst of it, a woman with elaborate, curling locks. What was it?

A small noise from the porch behind him made him

stiffen. Flinging the sheet back over the body, he scurried to conceal himself again behind the curtains. There was no particular reason why he should feel guilty, but he instinctively tried to avoid involvement in other folk's problems.

The footsteps he had heard hesitated outside the church door as if the new arrival were listening for something, ensuring that the church was empty. Then the latch clicked and the footfalls advanced slowly.

It was a woman. When the intruder came into his narrow field of view between the curtains, he saw a cloaked and hooded figure. She wore small black shoes that showed under her grey dress and her body was so slight that he guessed she must be a young woman. She walked with too supple a step to be aged. She held her cloak bunched tight about her, with the hood drooping forward so that it kept her face in deep shadow. It was a grey morning and still dim in the church, almost misty. She moved with a peculiar half-hesitancy, like a sleepwalker, yet never stopped, making straight for the body. Freeing one arm from her cloak, she took a corner of the shroud and folded it away from her, exposing the corpse's head and shoulders. Impatiently, she unbuttoned the bodice and shift, pulling them aside to uncover the breast. She stood a while in quiet contemplation, rocking slightly on her heels. Then, with one finger, she traced the outlines of the face, stark white, but mottled with blue bruises and purple blood, seeming to reconstitute it with care and tenderness. Finally, the visitor leant forward and appeared to kiss the victim's lips or perhaps she whispered something, though her precise action was muffled in the folds of her hood. How long she remained in this attitude, Johnny Fortnight was not sure, a minute at most. A sound from the street seemed to startle her for she drew away and ran to the door. He heard it click shut after her.

Now that this strange apparition was gone, his own urge to escape was overwhelming. He too ran to the door but found it locked. She must have turned the key in parting. Over his

305

shoulder, the half-naked corpse still lay uncovered on its bier. From that distance, its expression seemed to mock at him. Johnny Fortnight was not overly superstitious, but the prospect of staying locked in that church with the dead woman unnerved him.

The noise in the street was increasing. Down by the Tinners', men were shouting about something, he thought he heard the name Welland, but it was too indistinct to hear the message. For a while, he beat on the door, but no one heard him. He was becoming desperate. Johnny Fortnight could not abide being shut in anywhere. Then it occurred to him that, if he tolled the bell, someone was bound to hear him. Still, he tried to put off doing it; he didn't want to be discovered.

After breakfast, Hector Bolitho began fretting again. There was a knot in his stomach that might have been indigestion and then again, it might have been fear, though he wasn't sure which exactly. It seemed to him that Magor should have come up long ago. Perhaps Welland had ambushed him at the foot of the winze. What had he himself told Welland? *You made but one mistake, you should have let him drown.* Yes, Welland could easily have killed him. That was only one of the disasters that might have happened. Magor might have killed Welland. Would that be such a disaster? The fugitive had nothing to hope for if captured, but as fair a trial as the law might afford, and a rope at the end of it. If Magor had killed him, things would be even more messy. To send Magor for trial for a fugitive's murder would be well nigh impossible. Of course, there was still the possibility that the tinners had been mistaken and that Welland wasn't down there. The footprints they had seen might have been left in those remote workings years ago. There was no wind or weather down there to wash them away.

When he glanced through the window, he saw that a knot of

men still stood at the head of the shaft and he noted that
Curnow was among them. Curnow was Welland's best
friend, wasn't he? How much did he know? Had he been
providing the fugitive with aid and comfort? If he watched
him closely, Curnow might lead him to where Welland was
hiding. Before he could pursue that line of thought further, a
change in the waiting men's attitudes showed him that
someone was coming.

First one man came up and then another. It was clear from
their dejected air that they had been unsuccessful. Last of all,
up came Magor, red with dirt and streaming with sweat. But
Magor, unlike the rest, was still defiant. He crossed to the
count house and climbed the steps, flinging the door back
violently.

'Us should've 'ad un!' he declared. 'Only 'e wouldn' come
out like a man, and the place where 'e 'oled up was too small
to get at un. Leastways, too small fer me and t'others was too
frightened.'

'You saw him then?' said Bolitho, still dubious. 'Did any of
you see him?'

'No, but us 'eard un scramblin' about.'

That could be rats, loose stones, anything.'

'I found this bit of 'oggan,' said Magor, pulling a grey
lump from his pocket. ' 'Twas right at the back o' the old
men's ground. It 'ad to be recent. And I found this candle.
The wax was still soft when I picked un up. Ellis will vouch
for that, 'e touched un.'

Bolitho remembered Curnow. Perhaps he *had* brought
food to the mine for Welland. He would deny it, naturally.
'Well, if you can't lay hands on him, what do you suggest we
do?'

'I've thought o' that,' said Magor, smiling enigmatically.
'Well?'

'Flush un out!'

'You mean, stop pumping?'

The answer was simple, obvious, overwhelmingly logical.

Bolitho wondered why he hadn't thought of it himself. Then he realized why. If he did what Magor was suggesting, the mine would be out of action for weeks, months possibly. All that working time would be lost, the underground machinery damaged. Silverton Gurney would be furious. He realized that, up till now, he had not really taken the chief adventurer's interest and possible reaction into consideration. Silverton Gurney was far off in London and the way the man-hunt had begun was so natural, so inevitable, that the fact that the fugitive was the Squire's best friend and new partner had seemed unimportant. To know that Welland Halt was accused of murder would be bad enough; to hear that Wheal Fortune had been shut down while they hunted him out would seem like the final disaster. Hector Bolitho congratulated himself he knew his Silverton Gurney; he hadn't stayed purser all those years for nothing. 'You realise the cost?'

'The cost, Mr Bolitho, if you refuse, will be far greater. The tinners is up in arms and they *will* see justice. Woe betide 'im what stands in their way. If the pumps don't stop they'll break 'em!'

Bolitho sat and reflected. Magor might be somewhat simple and brutal, but he was a rabble-rouser and he had Hilda Trerice on his side. Bolitho himself was alone at the mine. He wished he had appealed to the authorities for armed men but, at the time, it had not seemed essential.

'If he's not there, you'll bear the whole responsibility!' he declared, rising. He took his hat from the peg on the door and threaded his way among the groups of men who were talking excitedly near the shaft. Entering the engine house, he reached up and threw a lever. There was a blast of escaping steam and the beam stopped rocking. The pump-rods came to a halt. The decision was taken. Outside, there was a ragged cheer. He wiped his hand on a rag and set out for the count house. It would not be quick. There might be days of waiting. But Wheal Fortune was a wet mine and, minute by minute, the water level would be rising. If he was in there, Welland was bound to come out. Unless he chose drowning. Bolitho's next task was to organize a close watch on all the shafts and winzes. It was distasteful, very distasteful, but it had to be done.

15

THE WELLS OF SALVATION

Welland's flight had begun with a psalm and a psalm was to lead him to its conclusion. It was a night without recorded time, punctuated by stealthy pattering feet, subdued oaths, distant hymn-singing and the pumps' faint throbbing.

The tinners had descended the shaft singing Crimond. The words of the Twenty-third Psalm were intended to give them a cloak of calm immunity from the powers of evil. Had it not been for his predicament, he might have found their deliberate harmonies inspiring, reassuring.

'The Lord's my shepherd, I'll not want, He makes me down to lie

In pastures green He leadeth me, the quiet waters by . . .'

Their sonorous Cornish voices, falling naturally into harmony and descant, vibrated among the rocks with an organ-like resonance. Yet the psalmist's words gave Welland no comfort: for him they were harbingers of hate, an abomination of desolation.

As they approached, he fled ever deeper into the mine, retreating into the old men's ground where, he hoped, the superstitious miners would fear to venture. He had visited the old workings more than once during his early days at the mine while he was cutting winzes on tutwork. Most of them were deep down, below the two-hundred-fathom level, far deeper than the old men were accustomed to burrow in pursuit of their slim lodes, so deep that he imagined there must have been some other entrance, perhaps driven in horizontally from the bottom of Tregurney Valley. But the old men's works were a warren, a meaningless labyrinth of convoluted tunnels. To find that opening, if opening there were, would not be easy.

He had little enough time to ponder the problem. Clinking of picks and quiet footfalls followed him even here. They must be terribly determined, those searchers. There was no singing now. This was cat and mouse, but with fear on both sides, for the cat was on treacherous, unfamiliar ground and the mouse was reputed a killer.

Once, he let them come close, at the end of a long, fairly wide gallery, so that he could judge their strength and numbers. There were two men and a boy. One of the men was called Ellis. They were folk he had hailed in the street, not friends exactly, but friendly, God-fearing tinners who had to work hard to support prodigious families. What if he were to step out into the open, unmasking his candle? Would they welcome him? Help him?

On the other hand, he could wait where he was, in a cleft with his candle extinguished, and strike them down one by one as they turned the corner. The boy, too – could he do that? Striking them down would afford some respite, time to search the old men's ground for an exit. No, he could not do it.

He turned and hurried on, careful to keep as quiet as possible as he twisted from one gallery to another. Were they still following him? He stood still and listened. What he heard first was his heart pounding. Surely they must hear that. He waited. There was the clatter from a stone falling. Dislodged by a careless hand? All notion of direction and distance was lost. Only one way was left: onward.

His candle blew out. An unexpected gust from an overhead winze plunged him into darkness. Snatching the candle from his hat, he blew on the wick in an attempt to revive it. It glowed faint red, but expired quickly. There was no time to use flint and steel, he could hear footsteps approaching. Blindly, he stumbled on, hands spread in front of him, feeling wet walls and projecting rock masses. Despite the obscurity, he was making some progress. Was this how it always was for Curnow? He could imagine struggling on like this for a while. But a lifetime – ?

What made him pause was unclear. It was as though Curnow had spoken to him, but Curnow was hundreds of fathoms above; he could not be within earshot. And yet, he had a distinct feeling Curnow had spoken to him, given him a warning.

With one hand pressed against the gallery wall for guidance, he stretched out his foot. There was nothing. He swung it about, trying to touch the ground, but encountered only emptiness. He was on the brink of a void. Dropping on his knees, he probed with his hand. As far as he could reach downwards was empty air. He groped for a stone between his feet, found one and let it fall. When he heard it strike bottom, he shivered, realizing the depth of the winze he had almost stumbled into.

But waiting there was out of the question. Footsteps and low voices were still approaching. Leaning yet further forward, he touched the opposite lip of the shaft with his fingertips. He had a choice: he could try to leap across the chasm or he could try to descend it. He decided on the latter. Supporting himself with a hand on each side, he swung himself over and tried for a foothold. There was none, but the winze narrowed quickly. If he arched his body and braced himself with arms and legs spanning the chimney, he could work his way downwards.

As he descended, he wished he had taken the other decision, but there was no going back now. The sounds of his trackers were getting louder. A faint glow from their candles illuminated the gallery above him. Below, all was blackness. He hoped the winze he was descending did not open out into a stoped-out cavern. If it did, nothing could save him from tumbling to injury or death when he lost his foothold. Could his pursuers hear his frantic scrabbling? He could hardly believe they were advancing so slowly. If he didn't get clear of the winze soon, they would be sure to look down and see him.

Then he fell. His right foot pushed into the void. His left leg was too weak to support him and he fell. He felt himself sliding on a shaley slope, tumbling over, and coming to rest against a wall. His elbow was numb and his head was aching, but the thickness of his hat had saved him from serious injury. He felt for his candle. It had fallen out. Where was it? He must find it immediately. It was too precious to abandon.

A faint patch of light made an oval on the scree down which he had just tumbled. The men above must be trying to see down with their candles. They would not be able to detect him where he lay to the side of the chimney. If they climbed down, it would be a different matter. Pulling himself up carefully, he leant towards the hole in the roof in the hope of hearing what they were saying. Their voices came down with astonishing clarity, as though through a speaking tube.

' 'Ow deep is un? The bugger can't 've climbed down there, fer certain.' It was Ellis speaking.

'But there aren't no footmarks over across the winze,' cried the boy. 'There's a pool there and mud, us'd be sure to see 'em.'

Damn that boy for his sharp eyes and wits, thought Welland. Suddenly, a small rock ricocheted down the winze and struck the scree. It bounded away into the shadows and came to rest by the wall. In following its flight, Welland saw a white blur: his candle.

'Bleddy deep,' said the other miner. 'If 'e 've slipped down there 'e's dead as mutton.'

'Us'll go back fer a rope and let the boy down to see,' said Ellis.

'Not bleddy likely!' said the latter.

'Best thing us can do is go back fer 'elp. There's time aplenty. No one could climb out o' there unaided,' said Ellis.

The light dimmed and Welland heard their voices receding. Before he forgot where it was, he must lay hands on his candle. When he held it in his hand, he sat there panting and almost wept. His hands shook as he lit it and surveyed the chamber he had fallen into. There were two tunnels leading out of it. One, not much more than a narrow crevice, climbed up into the rock, probably following a worked-out tin seam. The other was large enough to walk through, barely stooping, and sloped downwards. He decided to explore it immediately in case it led to an exit.

There were several side tunnels branching off it, but he kept to the main downward path. The floor was wet and the wetness developed into a stream of water. If it was running away like this, it must be running out somewhere. He hastened forward. Around the next corner, he came upon a pond. The full width of the gallery, which was now high-roofed and spacious, was submerged in stagnant water into which the little stream sank quietly. With barely a moment's hesitation, he waded in. It deepened slowly, rising over his ankles, then reached his kness and thighs. He stopped. If he went on and it got suddenly deeper, his precious tinder would get wet. Retracing his steps, he removed his jacket and shirt which he folded in a dry corner. His trousers were already too wet to matter.

It was as well he did. As he went beyond the limit of his earlier exploration, the level rose to his chest until he was almost swimming. Then it levelled off. Thirty feet away, a jumbled wall of loose rock rose to the cavern's full height. He sobbed in disappointment. The way out was blocked by a rockfall.

But all was not lost, he told himself, perhaps he could shift it. He clambered up its slippery face and began pulling away fragments of stone, flinging them back into the pool. The air was sweeter here. He was convinced he was near daylight.

Mavis halted just inside the door and tied her bonnet strings with nervous fingers. Her coat of russet serge was buttoned tight and her walking boots were on her feet.

'I've waited long enough for Bolitho's trap,' she announced. 'If I wait longer, I'll miss the stage at Tregurney. I'm going there first, I must speak with Lady Diana. I don't think there's much to hope for in that direction, but we must try everything we can to save him.' She studied Ruth's face uncomprehendingly: it was a mask. The girl sat at the table, still rocking gently. 'Doesn't it matter to you that they're hunting your father? Doesn't it matter that they'll probably catch him? Why don't you speak? You're up to something; you've been out, haven't you? Don't try to deny it.' Acting on impluse, Mavis came back across the room and shook Ruth by the shoulders. 'Stop that rocking! Say something!' The girl still rocked and said nothing. As abruptly as Mavis had hardened, she softened. 'I'm sorry, I shouldn't have said that. It must be terrible for you. Forgive me.' She clasped the stiff girl to her, helpless to bridge the distance between them. It seemed that she had been closer to Welland's daughter before her marriage. Now, there was an added gulf. 'It was your mother, wasn't it? That's what you're thinking. We all are. God help us.'

She picked up her bundle and went to the door. A last look at Ruth's face. There was no reaction.

'I'm going to the Curnows to ask them to look after you while I'm away. You can't stay here on your own, you'll be too lonely.'

'I can.' Ruth's dull tones startled her. 'I'm not alone, I have my memories.'

'So you *can* speak. Wish me luck: that's the least you can do.'

'Luck doesn't come into it. The wheel turns.'

'I don't think like that. I mustn't.' But Mavis could not escape the weight of despair that Ruth's words cast on her. They were still echoing in her head five minutes later while Curnow held her hand and murmured to her.

'I can't see no way to 'elp un. There's precious little chance 'e'll get out safely.' He lowered his voice yet further so that even his own children should not hear him. 'There's only one way I knows of 'e might get out, that they've left unguarded: the adit. I 'eard Bolitho send off the captains; 'e never thought of un. But Welland won't get there; I doubt 'tes possible.'

'Welland won't give up!' Mavis whispered fiercely. 'He won't!'

'No, nor will Magor, nor will your mother. They won't rest till they've catched un. And then – Poor maid, I shouldn' 'ave said that.'

'You'll do what you can to help?' she implored, trying to keep the sobs out of her voice. How had he known the tears had sprung from her eyes; she was sure she had kept her hand steady. She controlled herself. 'I know you will. You're his best friend. No one will try harder.'

'Godspeed!' said Curnow, giving her hand a tight squeeze. 'Make 'aste to find Silverton Gurney. Squire Gurney can do more to 'elp Welland now than ever I shall. If 'e's 'arf the friend 'e 've said, 'e'll come 'ome and pertect un. Ellen and I'll watch over Ruth. Off you go, maid, to fetch Gurney 'ome. God knows, us needs un.'

Mavis set off determinedly up the hill. Windfall was quiet; practically all its inhabitants had gone off to the mine to see what was happening. Somewhere behind her a clamour broke out. Small groups of miners were running to join the men already waiting at each of Wheal Fortune's shafts and winzes, which were dotted all over the landscape, enclosed by low stone walls. She saw a party of excited men run to the Tinners' and heard them shout through the doorway.

'E've gone to ground, Jack, but Bolitho's flushin' un out. Water's risin' already. Us've catched un this time for certain.'

Mavis turned away with a sickened sensation, fearful also

that they would notice her and taunt her. As she strode off again, she heard the church bell tolling erratically. What was that for? She could not spare time for that question. Her only hope was to press onward.

'Marry a vagrant and repent at leisure!' The crackling shout came from her mother's cottage, mingled with spiteful laughter. 'Didn' I say you would? And where are us goin', me pretty? To ask a favour o' Silverton Gurney? Wastin' your time you are, Mistress Halt, 'e'll not be bothered.'

How had she guessed the object of her errand? Did her mother really have the second sight she pretended to, or was she merely giving voice to her vicious wishful thinking? Mavis was so upset that she stumbled on a stone.

'Pride goes before a fall, doan' it, my lady? Better bide 'ere a bit and pray for un, pray for the soul o' that Welland. Nothin' you do'll prosper; nothin'll serve to save un! Just like your feyther 'e proved. I said 'e would, but Mavis wouldn' listen. Murdered a woman 'e 'ave, and us all knows who *she* is. But us'll 'ave justice, see if us don't. Us'll 'ave vengeance! Go if you must, but 'urry yourself, Mistress Halt, or 'twill all be done afore you're back to Windfall.'

Mavis stopped in her tracks and stared full at her mother. Then she spat deliberately in the dust and resumed her journey. Behind her back, she heard gusts of mocking laughter. The bell dinned into her head with a final fit of quick tolling. She began to run. She passed the Gipsy Winze with its circle of watchers and came to the carn where three roads met. With rasping breaths and her frame racked by sobbing, she flew blindly down the turnpike towards Tregurney.

'What's the matter, man, have you seen a ghost or something?'

At the Curate's call, Johnny Fortnight swung round and released the bell-rope he had been pulling. The bell gave one more clang; then there was silence. At first, he was unable to speak, his nerves were so jangled. Perhaps he nodded, he was not in proper control of his actions.

'How did you get locked in here?'

'Just drifted by for a look, that's all I was after.' The packman spoke defensively. He was still trembling. He saw that the Curate's eyes were hard, suspicious. It was evident that he had noticed the uncovered body on the bier as he came in to investigate the tolling and had put two and two together.

'You don't expect me to believe that, do you?'

'That's all it were, God's honour!'

'You know nothing of *that*, Johnny Fortnight. I ought to turn you over to Mr Bolitho; he'd be most interested to know what you have in your pockets. But I don't need to. I think you'll tell me.' He swung the large key from his fingertips menacingly. 'All I need do is lock you in again. I imagine that'll free your tongue a little.'

'You won't do that, Mr Nichols.' The packman seemed almost tearful. 'There's Emma out there, Emma's me donkey. I can't leave 'er.'

'Believe me, Mr Packman, until you tell me what you've been up to, I can and I will leave you.'

'You'll let me go if I tell you?'

'God's honour.' The curate had a wry smile on his lips as he used the expression.

'It was on account of 'er,' the packman began, with a jerk of his head towards the recumbent figure. 'I was curious about 'er.'

'You knew her?'

'I thought I'd met 'er once. Ships that pass in the night, you might say.'

'And you had?'

'In Bethel – she were on the way 'ere. But I don't know 'er name, nor where she comes from. I don't know nothin'. All I did was speak to 'er when she looked out o' the coach.' Now that he had started to talk, the words came more easily.

318

'What did she say?'

'She thought it was Windfall. I told 'er she'd 'ave to disembark by the carn and walk 'ere.'

'What else did she say?' Mr Nichols's questioning was eager, but less aggressive. The packman had the impression that only a few more details would be enough to ensure his deliverance.

'She wouldn't say why she was comin'. I asked 'er and she said it was none o' my business. But she did say somethin': she said she was expected. She said somethin' else, what was it now? – ah, that's it, she said she'd 'ave 'er due.'

'Can you describe her?'

'Not for a court o' law. 'Twas night-time, your honour, I couldn't be expected to see 'er colours. But she wasn't local, I knew that the moment she opened 'er mouth.'

'What was she wearing?'

'She was dressed like 'er, over there,' said the packman and instantly regretted it.

'Dressed like that, eh? Well, someone's been interfering with that woman's clothing.' The Curate's voice was suddenly hard again, his eyes unfriendly.

'I never touched 'er!' lied Johnny Fortnight with all the conviction he could muster, which was considerable. 'Her what comed in did that.'

'A woman was in here?'

'I 'opes 'twas a woman,' said the packman with a shake in his voice that needed no feigning. 'After I'd let meself in – I followed the carpenter in when 'e measured 'er up for a coffin – I'd barely been in 'ere a minute or two when I 'eard someone comin, so I slipped behind these 'ere curtains. Whoever it was let 'erself in ever so quiet.'

'Who was this woman?'

'I never seed 'er face. She wore a cloak with the 'ood up.'

'Why did you hide in the first place?'

'If you was Johnny Fortnight, you'd 'ide too, Mr Nichols. Folk always think a packman's up to mischief.'

319

'And with good reason. Now, something happened, didn't it, that scared you, or you wouldn't have been ringing that bell like blazes?'

'Whoever she was, whatever she was, peeled back the cloth like you see it there. Then she undid 'er dress. Then she stood and looked at 'er. Then she kissed 'er. Leastways, I think so. Then she sailed off; she passed so close I might've reached out and touched 'er.'

'Why didn't you speak to her? You're not afraid of a woman, are you?'

'I was afraid o' this one: she didn't seem 'uman. Then she locked me in with the body. I couldn't face it. I've 'ad enough, I tell you? Can't I go now? You said I could, you promised.'

'Not till you turn out your pockets. I can see you've something in there.'

The packman looked down. There was no denying it. Pulling on the bell-rope had displaced the wad of paper until a corner projected.

'Oh, that,' he said hurriedly, 'that's only worthless paper I found beside the body.' If he admitted to the papers, perhaps the Curate would not inquire further and overlook the medal. Robbing the dead of paper was one thing: gold was another.

'Give it here. I'll be the judge of that.' The Curate smoothed out the sheets and studied them. Johnny Fortnight watched expectantly. 'I suppose you've drawn your own conclusions from these,' remarked Mr Nichols.

'Readin's not a strong point, you might say.'

'It doesn't take a genius to tell that one of these is a newspaper and the other a playbill. Whoever that woman over there was, she was particularly interested in friend Welland's good fortune; the paper has Gurney and Halt all over it. I'm beginning to think that I did him a signal disservice in marrying him to that Mavis girl. If it gets about that the murdered woman was carrying this, it'll be damning enough, without further evidence.' The Curate studied the packman closely. 'You know how to hold your tongue when it pays, don't you? If I were to tell you that a man's life might depend on neither of us saying that woman had this paper on her, do you think you could forget it?'

'I could, your honour, no trouble. You say the other, the coloured one's a playbill. Can you tell me what's on it?'

'Some kind of a music-hall thing, from Bristol.'

'Do it give the name o' the woman?'

The Curate examined the sheet, ruminating as he did so on the propriety of what he was doing: these papers were evidence that, if they came out, might be fatal to Welland Halt. They could also be troublesome for Nichols himself: hadn't he called the banns, read the service, though he had had justifiable suspicions?

'The woman pictured here is called Freya, though I suspect it's a stage name.'

'Freya,' said the packman reflectively.

'You know it?'

'No, you honour, never 'eard of it. Can I go now? My Emma's bound to 'ave wandered off. I'll never find 'er.' If the packman had known the woman's identity, he would not have divulged it. The last thing he wanted was to be mixed up in a murder and he guessed that the Curate's inclinations ran likewise. Oddly enough, the name he had just heard rang a bell at the back of his head somewhere, but he still couldn't place it. But only a fool told all he knew. Johnny Fortnight knew how to hold his tongue when it suited him: none better. If it hadn't been for the state he was in when the Curate came, he wouldn't have told anyone his recent experiences, but he had been desperate to get away from that pale corpse and the memory of its strange visitor.

'You're to stay in the neighbourhood in case you're wanted. In any case, if you run off now, it'll look suspicious, they could try to lay the blame on you instead of Welland. After all, you were on the road that night too, weren't you?

As for these papers, they never existed, understand? It's not a priest's job to bear witness against a parishioner, call it forgiveness, call it Christian charity, call it what you will. Now, be off with you.'

As soon as the packman had scurried off, the Curate went over to the bier and stood with the playbill at arm's length beside the shattered features. *Vanitas vanitorum*, he thought to himself, vanity of vanities, *et omnia vanitas*, all is vanity. A beauty of sorts was gone; did it live in the daughter? And it was this beauty that once charmed Welland; this same beauty that had driven him to Windfall where he met Mavis. How unfathomable are the designs of the Almighty, how devious the workings of the human heart.

Though neither was aware of it at the time, Welland and Mavis had been close together for a few moments. The turnpike passed close to the point where the old men's workings had once surfaced. Only a spring among the boulders might have given a hint to an experienced tinner, but it was lost in a tangle of bracken and thorn and the stream that issued from it crossed the turnpike at the ford. Mavis lifted her skirts as she hurried across it towards Tregurney. Her thoughts were far ahead, rehearsing what she would say when she arrived there.

Welland had worked for more than an hour before he discovered the futility of his task. He had come so close that a faint daylight glow filtered between the stones that he hurled aside with feverish hands. And then, irony of ironies, the final boulders he uncovered were huge, far beyond any man's strength to displace them. Through a crack, he could see green moss and a curling tendril of fern. He was almost free, and yet it was impossible.

Free! The word left a bitter taste in his mouth. Had he been free when he reached Windfall, leading young Ruth by the hand? He had thought so. He remembered the long adventure, the endless roads, the mud, the stinging rain, the empty purse, the curt refusals when he begged for help, Ruth's whimpering, her sad, pinched face, longing to turn back. But he had not turned back, and they had found kindness in Windfall when Mavis discovered them. Her loving face haunted him, seeming to appear in the shadows of the mine just as it had when she met them at the carn.

And there was another face that loomed out of the dark, supplanting her, a face once beautiful, but grown unkempt with the stigmata of selfishness. What had she said? I've come to share your good fortune, I'll not be cheated. She had come and they had shared nothing, no more than they had shared before when together. He tried to see through the face as it was to the face he had first known, the person he had loved. She was gone for ever. The face that remained was not the face of forgiveness.

After wading back through the pond to the place where he had left his clothes, Welland was shaking with cold. And he could not shake off the mood of desperation which that face had cast upon him. Although there were side passages to explore, he was sure they led nowhere. Even if they did reach the open air, what was left for him outside? Flight, only flight, desperate running to keep ahead of the hounds of justice. At the best, escape abroad, a new identity. The Andes? He remembered the coldness of the Altiplano as Trevithick had described it to him. It matched his mood; he would feel at home there. Stark and bare, the imaginary landscape reflected his vision of life without Ruth or Mavis.

Half an hour later, he had tried them all. The winding galleries led nowhere. They were dead ends, abandoned by the old men when each lode ran out. Now he sat under the winze where he had entered, nibbling at the last of the hoggan he had found in a level while descending. He ate in the dark to conserve the stub of candle remaining to him. The hoggan was stale and indigestible, but it was all he had. He felt cornered, alone, a beast in a trap. The winze was so high in the roof of the chamber that he could obtain no grip to begin to ascend it. He chewed slowly, but even so, the hoggan stuck in his throat.

A noise from above made him suddenly alert. New footsteps were approaching. Why hadn't he been prepared for it? They had gone for reinforcements. Where could he hide? To go down to the pool again would be to invite certain discovery and capture.

It was then that he remembered the narrow crevice, probably no more than a stoped-out seam that led off the upper corner of the chamber where he sat. There was a remote possibility that it led somewhere. It was worth a try if he could find it. Hurriedly, he lit his candle stump and stuck it in his hat.

The crevice was frighteningly small. There was no room to turn round in it. After a few yards, he could not even crawl, but was forced to wriggle sideways and upwards, expecting to find it blocked off at any moment. As he was entering this part, a soft thud behind him made him glance back. A rope's end had just landed on the scree behind him. Now, as he inched into the slit, it seemed as though he would be caught with his feet protruding ridiculously from his inadequate burrow. A tight constriction in the tunnel slowed him. Only by stretching his arms above his head could he negotiate it, but beyond this point, the space appeared wider.

As he pushed into this strait, his hat caught on a projection from the roof and his candle went flying. It skittered down the crevice behind him into the chamber below the winze, leaving him in darkness. There was no time to go back and search for it. Someone was coming down the winze. Welland jammed his feet on either side of the slit and heaved.

Beyond the constriction, the tunnel widened suddenly. His exploring fingers told him that he could move forward in a crouched position. The air was much better than he had expected. He crawled on for a few yards until he came to a larger chamber where he could stand. There, he waited.

For the moment, he was not closely followed. Voices

echoed in the winze, then came silence. His pursuer must have gone off down the larger tunnel, but it would not be long before he found it empty, saw the returning footprints in the wet clay and came back. Well, however many came down the winze after him, they could only come at him one at a time here. And, although he had no evidence of it, he knew inwardly that their leader must be Tom Magor. Now, once again, it must be man against man. He had no option but to stand and fight.

They were coming. He heard a scrabbling like rats' clawing paws and saw a faint glimmer through the crevice. There was heavy breathing, muffled curses, then silence.

'Us knows you're in there, my lover,' came Magor's voice cooing gently. 'Us've found your candle and your bit of 'oggan. Why doan' 'ee come out nice and peaceful?' There was another long silence, then renewed struggling in the crevice. 'Tiddn' no use thinkin' you're safe in there 'cause us can't get at 'ee.' For a moment, Welland toyed with the idea of scrambling back to throttle his tormentor, but what good would that do? It would only make him doubly a murderer. He stood stock still and held his breath. 'Won't come out when us asks 'ee nice and friendly, my lover? Then us'll 'ave to smoke 'ee out, you bugger!' Magor's flat tones echoed bizarrely off the tunnel walls, like the prophetic tones of some drugged sibyl. Another silence. Then Magor was gone, clattering back into the chamber at the foot of the winze. In his imagination, Welland could already smell the choking fumes of burning furze curling up through the crevice, making his eyes smart and his breath come in short rasping coughs. If he stayed where he was, they were sure to get him.

More than ever, he knew that he must get out, but the winze was impossible: not only would Magor and his men draw up the rope after them, they would surely mount guard on its upper lip. The only alternative was to explore his present tunnel in case it went further, but to do so in darkness was an impossibility. He felt in his pockets and his

fingers closed round a two-inch stub of candle. It was
precious little and, when it was spent, he would be enfolded
in utter darkness, unable to retrace his steps if the tunnels
branched as often as they had already. It was a terrifying risk,
with the probability that he would be lost in the old men's
ground and starve there slowly, beyond the help even his
enemies might afford him. To go on was a desperate throw,
but a turn of the dice that must be accepted; little Ruth still
depended on him, he must try to reach her.

Ruth sat at the mirror in her bedroom and looked beyond her
present face into another time. She was combing her
mother's hair. Ever since she could remember, she had loved
to comb it. She stood behind her mother's chair and pulled
the comb through the electric ringlets and smiled at the face
that stared back at her. 'I take after you, don't I?' she heard
her small voice saying. The whimsical emerald eyes
answered her with a flicker. 'I know I do. I want to be like
you, Mother. You're lovely. I don't want to leave you, ever.'
Ruth's words tumbled out as she buried her face in the
ash-blonde hair. 'I love you.'
    'If only your father cared as much for me as you do!'
    'Don't say that, Mother! He does, I know he does.'
    'He's wedded to his machines; he lives for rust and iron; he
knows nothing of what matters to a woman. A woman has to
have dreams; she has to have a stage to stand on; she has to be
told of her beauty. Your father won't see it. There are others
who will. I can't be expected to bury myself here for ever.'
    'You'll take me with you, you will, won't you, Mother?'
    'I wish I could. It's no place for a child. But I'll come back
for you.'
    She never had, not then. Ruth had not been able to under-
stand it. Ruth watched her face dissolve, merge and resolve
itself into her own, green-eyed, tight-lipped and solemn.
Yes, she did take after her.

326

Someone was tapping at the door. At first, she ignored it, resentful of the intrusion, but then she heard someone calling from the kitchen. She must have left the door unbolted.

'I let myself in. I felt I had to bring you all the consolation religion has to offer,' explained the Curate nervously as Ruth descended the stairway. While he spoke, his sidelong glances were exploring the room, noting the long cloak that hung behind the door. 'Mavis has left you alone, hasn't she? You must be lonely without your mother.' He brought himself to look at her directly while he said this, but there was no reaction. 'I saw her leaving.' Did her eyes narrow a little? 'These are terrible events you are caught up in, child. You must fear for your father – Why don't you speak? Won't you let me help you?' He tried to put an arm around her shoulders, but she slipped away from him. 'Our Lord Jesus is a very present help in trouble; won't you hear his voice?' Then, suddenly angered by her silence and rejection, 'You're a wilful girl, but you shan't persist in it! You shan't stay dumb! You shan't stay insolent or I'll chastise you! You'll do as you're told for once, you'll learn submission!'

'Get out! Get out! I'll do as I please!' She was beating on his chest with her fists as she spoke. 'I know what I must do, and I'll do it. Get out of here. Don't touch me!'

In his house down the street, Curnow stirred impatiently on his seat in the chimney corner. The whole household was unwontedly silent even the youngest children had been infected by the air of disquiet and melancholy.

'I can't stay 'ere like this, Ellen,' declared Curnow. 'I 'as to do somethin'. Gimme they boots and fit out young Thomas, give un a bag with a pasty and a bit o' 'oggan. Us must find Welland and 'elp un.'

'Every hale man in Windfall's been seekin' of un, all fruitless,' his wife replied. 'Now a blind man thinks 'e can walk right to un. Are you goin' soft in the 'ead, Curnow?'

'I'll find un.'

'I wish I 'ad 'arf your faith, but 'ere's the 'oggan and what's left o' the pasty you pecked at at dinner, there's a good piece of un.'

'One more thing,' said Curnow, taking his stick from its place in the corner and placing his hand on his boy's shoulder, 'so soon as we're gone, get you round to Welland's and see what's 'appened to that Ruth. I've been frettin' about 'er.'

'Which way, Feyther?' asked young Thomas.

'To the mouth of the adit above Tregurney. We'll go across country, 'twill be quicker and no one won't notice.'

Two inches of candle won't last long, thought Welland bitterly as he used his flint and steel. He felt like a doomed man: either he was destined to lose himself in the old men's ground or return to the winze and certain capture.

The tinder took and the candle flared into light. As it did so, he experienced a wild new hope. Instead of burning upright, the flame was being pushed sideways by a draught and the draught was blowing out of the crevice from which he had come. That air must be flowing somewhere and, where the wind could blow, Welland might follow. Thank God! He might cheat the hunters yet.

Twenty minutes later, he was less sure. He had scrambled through half a dozen galleries and climbed two different winzes, always following the direction indicated by the candle flame. But now the draught had slackened and the flame stood upright, giving no guide as to which gallery to follow. And that was not the worst; the stump of wax had burnt away almost to nothing, a sliver of wick in a liquid pool: less than five minutes left.

The singing was faint but unmistakable. At first, he thought it might be a hallucination. He held his breath and listened. Muted by distance and distorted by the convoluted passages of the mine, the familiar tune was like a lighthouse beckoning him across an angry sea but, like a lighthouse, its beam could equally well fetch him to a safe haven or lure him on to reefs and into danger. Some words he heard clearly, others his memory supplied,

'Yea though I walk in Death's dark vale, yet shall I fear
no ill,
For thou art with me and thy rod and staff me comfort
still.'

The tinners were singing again for comfort as they mounted the shaft. Welland was standing at the junction of three tunnels. Now he chose the one from which the singing seemed to come. Within twenty yards, he was sure he had been mistaken and turned back to try another. This time the sound persisted longer, but died inexplicably a little further on. He was getting flustered. Slowing deliberately, he returned to the junction and cast about slowly, palping the rock with his hands. Then he found it. On one side, high up in the wall, an oblique crack in the rock appeared to lead into another gallery. When he squeezed through, he realized at once that he had stumbled on some modern workings. Tools were scattered about and there was a smell of burnt powder. There were even a few stubs of candle. Lighting one and cupping it in his hand, he set off towards the singing in the shaft.

Well before he reached there, he came upon a tramway and began to follow its tracks. The singing had died away now and that was providential. Where there was singing, there must be men. All men now seemed his enemies.

Welland was regaining confidence. It was as if an unseen hand was leading him to safety through all underground perils. Close ahead of him, squealing in their guides, were the pump-rods. Their sound grew louder as he approached the shaft. He masked his candle carefully in case it gave him away. When he got there, he could look up and see if it was day or night. If it was night, he would try to slip out immediately. If it was day, he would wait. The shaft was near now, very near. He feared he would stumble into it.

They stopped. At what precise moment they stopped, he did not know, so carefully was he concentrating on his footsteps. The significance of the pumps' quietness came slowly, but when it did, it was devastating. There was no longer any question of waiting for the night. Magor had tricked him. They were not going to smoke him out; they were employing a more radical, infallible method: they were going to drown him or drive him upwards. Without the pumps working, the lower levels would fill quickly.

He felt timbering under his hand; it must be the shaft cladding. He leant out and looked upwards. It was still day. Which day? How long had he been down there? What did that matter? The pin-head of light was so small that he knew he must still be close to the three-hundred-fathom level. There was no one about. It was dead quiet apart from the eternal dripping and splashing of the water spilling out of the levels. What should he do?

There was only one practical decision. He took it quite calmly. If he could climb up to the two-hundred-fathom level undetected and reach the adit, there was a good chance of slipping away. It was certain they would be watching all the shafts, but the adit mouth was far away. They might not think of it. Once he got out of the adit, he could run down the hill to Tregurney House and ask for shelter. The sooner he took that route the better, before the tinners thought of it.

As he climbed the ladders, he thought of Billy Bray. What had he called the mines? Wells of salvation? As Welland approached the two-hundred-fathom level, he was impelled to thank God for his protection. Even if it was conceivable that he had come this far by his own unaided efforts and his faith in himself, it was tempting to believe that some higher power was helping him onward, enfolding him in its grace.

Perhaps it was a form of grace that there was no sentinel guarding the adit. He stepped off the platform into the familiar tunnel he had cut with Curnow. It was still a long way to safety, but he was full of hope. As he made his way down the muddy slope, the last lines of the tinners' psalm kept echoing in his head.

'Goodness and mercy all my days shall surely follow me
   And in God's house for evermore, my dwelling place
shall be.'

Up at grass, Mr Bolitho was still ensconced in the count house, trying to write a report to Mr Gurney detailing the compelling reasons he had had for shutting down the mine. As he wrote the cool words on the page, he doubted if they would do justice to the mood of vengeful anger that gripped Windfall's population. Yesterday, Welland had been their hero, now they were hunting him like vermin. How would Silverton Gurney feel about Bolitho's participation in the man-hunt for his friend? Another thing, if Welland were caught down there, would Bolitho's team of captains prove adequate to protect him from bodily harm and get him out of the parish so that he could be transferred to Bodmin for trial at the assizes? Bolitho nursed no illusions on the trial's outcome, but it would be fair, it would be justice.

All the time he was writing and thinking, water was trickling into the mine. Drip by drip, then in gushing jets, the water was entering through myriad channels and cascading to the lower levels. Already, the pumps must be submerged and the long pumps-rods were being swallowed by the rising tide. What was happening to the man down there? Was he drowning in some dead-end at the top of a rising level? Was he battling through a siphon, beaten against the rocks like a rag-doll in the darkness? He dipped his quill in the ink, but was unable to go on writing.

Magor was striding impatiently back and forth between the shaft and the stamps. The water was rising too slowly for his liking. He glared around angrily. Suddenly, he stopped walking. He was engrossed by something he saw in the distance and a sardonic grin spread slowly across his features.

'Why didn' I ever think o' that meself?' he murmured. 'Thank you, Curnow, fer puttin' me up to it.' Instead of being hunched with frustration, he was erect and decisive. 'Come on, boys!' he shouted to the tinners warming themselves at the engine house fire. 'Us've work to do. Fetch a pig-net from the village, quick as you can. Us 'ave a fox to catch, over Tregurney.'

Johnny Fortnight was safe in his camp across the turnpike. From his look-out in the gorse, he had watched the search parties speed past. Johnny himself was in no hurry. He had a sailor's patience: a few minutes more or less made no real difference to a landfall. It amused him to judge the passers-by by their rig and speculate upon their errands.

He had seen Mavis go by. She had been running and looked troubled, like a ship in distress running before a storm. For two pins, he'd have called 'Ahoy!' and offered her shelter, but he guessed her purpose and was sure she'd refuse him. She was bearing dispatches for Silverton Gurney. Half an hour later, he saw her ride by on the coach in the opposite direction. Her face was lined and set. The packman doubted she had obtained much satisfaction.

All went quiet for a while and he was about to return to the pool and take care of Emma when he noticed two figures coming over the shoulder of Morvan. Even at that distance, he had no trouble recognizing them. One was a boy from Windfall and the other was poor blind Curnow, though why he should choose so rough a path was beyond the packman's comprehension. Despite his guide, Curnow was continually stumbling and falling. The packman chewed ruminatively at his plug of tobacco, calculating their destination from the course they were steering. Long before they reached there, he knew their objective. It was the adit above Tregurney. He noticed that the usual stream of blood-red water from the pumps was not flowing.

*

332

Welland had been a long time in the adit, though he advanced as fast as he dared on the slimy surface. When he saw the light at the end, he stopped and proceeded with infinite caution. He had to repress his urge to run out joyously into the open air. He took a few cautious steps, froze, then took another, and another, never leaving the side of the tunnel. All the while, he listened for voices. There were none. When he came within yards of the hole he and Curnow had blasted out, he moulded himself against the rock wall and waited. Insects on fragile wings were dancing over a pool in the adit mouth. A robin fluttered in for a drink, cocking its head to one side and sizing him up carefully. From the length of the shadows, Welland could tell it was late afternoon. Although common sense told him to wait a bit longer for twilight, the urge to go on was almost irrepressible. If the robin flew in again, he told himself, that would mean there were no men outside to scare it and he could make a dash for Tregurney. If he moved his head into the half-shadow surrounding the wedge of daylight that slanted across the adit mouth, he could see past the moss and ferns that already softened its harshness. Framed in the opening were the church, tall elms, the brooding mass of Tregurney House. Beyond them, in the fields on the far side of the valley, minute farmhands were following their diminutive teams, harrowing the ploughland. The evening breeze sighed in the ferns and he thought he caught a whiff of the sea. Where had the wind come from? Peru?

Mavis tried to sit upright as the coach shuddered down the hill beyond Launceston. Somewhere ahead, not far now the coachman said, was the Tamar and, across the bridge, Devon. Mavis had never ventured so far from home and the bold, wooded landscape ought to have charmed her, but she found no joy in it. The wheels turned too slowly. Her thoughts kept returning to Windfall and Tregurney. Had they caught him yet? She knew they must, yet could not forbear to hope. Perhaps he was not in the mine; perhaps he was aboard ship already, sailing to safety in another country; perhaps he was somewhere ahead of her, having given his pursuers the slip and crossed the Tamar. But, in her heart of hearts, she knew this was all illusion. The whole world was against him now, her experience at Tregurney House proved it.

'What d'you want here, woman?' an unfriendly voice had called as she entered the courtyard. Looking up, she had seen Rector Adams at one of the windows high in the wall.

'I want to speak to Lady Diana.'

'Wants to speak to Lady Diana, does she? A proper lady is this Mavis! Well, I'll have you know she's indisposed and can see no one. You can tell me the nature of your business.'

'It's about my husband –'

'Your husband!' broke in the Rector with a burst of mocking laughter.

'Call him what you like, Welland Halt is in need of help. If the Tregurneys don't come to his aid, he'll be killed, for certain.'

'Nothing would seem more likely,' said the Rector with relish. She saw him now, his red face beaming at the prospect. 'He'll be hanged within the twelvemonth, mebbe sooner. Richly deserves it – for the wrong he did you too, though you walked into it with your eyes open, you ought to condemn him – we'll be well rid of the varmint.'

'You'll do nothing to help him then?'

'My dear lady,' he had concluded with mock politeness, 'what made you expect it?' As he closed the window, Mavis had seen a woman's pale face behind him: Lady Diana. So there was nothing to hope for from that quarter.

'Then I'll seek out Silverton Gurney himself. He's not a Pharisee!' The clock in Tregurney church had struck the hour. Mavis hitched up her bundle and sped away. She must hurry, hurry. The Exeter Mail would come rolling up the turnpike soon.

What indeed had made her expect help? Mavis herself had never been under any delusions concerning Welland's acceptance into genteel circles. The Tregurneys and Bolithos of this world could never bring themselves to ignore a man's origins. Even Silverton's friendship for her husband, though genuine enough, was rooted in fleeting enthusiasm. But he was the only hope she had. She would press on till she found him.

'Whoa!' The coachman was hauling back on the reins and sniffing the air suspiciously. He dropped to the ground as soon as they stopped and walked round the vehicle.

'What is it?' asked Mavis, jolted out of her reverie.

'Axle's red 'ot. Us'll 'ave to wait till it cools. Slow but sure, that's a good motto.'

'But we'll miss the London Mail at Exeter.'

'Can't 'elp that. There'll be another, allus is.'

Mavis clasped her hands in her lap and tried to compose herself. If the coach did not move soon, she feared she would scream like a madwoman. How many precious minutes must she waste? Before she left that spot, the hanging woods, the bridge, the dreary castle on the hill would be etched deep into her head.

Johnny Fortnight brushed away a bee that flew out of the gorse to settle on his hand. When he looked up again, there were four more men on the skyline. One of them, their leader, was Tom Magor. Strung out behind him as he loped along were three other tinners, two of whom were slowed by a burden. All of them were gaining on Curnow and his son who moved with painful slowness. The blind man was still a furlong short of the adit when something told him of his pursuers. Perhaps it was a thudding on the turf, for the packman saw him turn his sightless eyes in their direction, then murmur to his son. They changed direction and Johnny guessed the reason: Curnow was trying to put the pursuers off the scent. It was a vain hope.

In seconds, it seemed, Magor was upon them seizing

Curnow roughly and throwing him to the ground. The boy pounded their assailant with ineffectual fists. Suddenly, no doubt in response to a command from his father, he ran off towards the adit. The second tinner bore down on him from up the slope and cut him off. His cries, if he cried at all, were lost in the bleating from the moorland sheep that scattered in all directions. By now, the last two tinners had arrived and helped to secure Curnow. His son was served likewise. Then, leaving one of their number to guard them, Magor and the two men with the burden set off deliberately, treading softly on the turf, towards the adit. As they approached, a kestrel which had been hovering there, waiting for creatures to come and drink at the pool, sheered off towards Morvan. The two porters spread their burden, which looked for all the world like a rolled up topsail, across the brow of the adit and waited. Magor waited too, crouched in the ferns beside them. The packman knew their purpose. If he had been closer, he would have shouted a warning. But they were too far off. All he could do was wait, wait and hope that their quarry had chosen another bolt hole.

Ellen Curnow bit her lip as she peered through the cottage window. Ruth was there all right. She had ignored Ellen's persistent knocking. She had taken her marbled notebook from the table drawer and begun writing. She appeared flustered, dishevelled, but resolute. Every few seconds, she dipped her pen in the ink, pursed her lips and wrote, line after line, compulsively, the creak of the nib filling the silence with a sound like a mindless insect's chirping. Ellen tapped on the pane.

'Ruth! Ruth!' she shouted, and beat on the glass until the girl could write no longer. 'Won't you listen! I've come to bring 'ee a bite o' dinner.' Ruth's face turned towards her, but her stare looked right through the older woman as though she were as transparent as the glass between them. 'Come on, maid, open up,' she insisted. 'You must look after yourself, you must let your friends 'elp 'ee.'

The girl made no immediate reply, but tore a page from her book and wrote across it. Then she crossed to the window and held the paper to the pane. Ellen Curnow wasn't much of a reader, but she had enough notions to decipher it slowly.

I know my duty

she read,

dont try to divert me.

Ruth crumpled the paper, threw it aside and went back to the table. She seated herself facing away from the window with her hands over her ears and waited. Short of breaking down the door, Ellen Curnow sensed that there was nothing she could do. The girl was beyond the end of her tether. All Ellen could do was wait for Curnow's return to discuss the matter.

Welland had been allowing himself to relax slightly. As time slipped by with no hint of a guard's presence near the adit, he breathed more freely. It did seem that this way out of the mine had been forgotten.

Abruptly, he froze. There was a thudding of feet on the turf nearby and what seemed like voices. To run back into the tunnel would give him away if there were anyone listening. He shrank back into the dark side of the entrance. His heart was palpitating. Surely anyone nearby would hear it. He pressed his ear to the living rock to hear better. The footsteps were receding. The cries sounded like sheep bleating. Something had scared them off.

Again he waited. His pulse returned to normal. Tregurney House, where he hoped to find shelter, lay opulent and peaceful in the glow from the declining sun. In the stable there was the second of the steam-carriages he had worked on with Silverton. A sour taste came into his mouth. Why had he allowed himself to take part in that project? Pride, pride in his skill had made him do it. If he had stayed a humble smith his fame would never have spread beyond Cornwall. He had been a fool and now he was paying for it. The whole construction of his life with Ruth and Mavis had crumbled. There could be no rebuilding.

The robin returned and perched, side on to a reed, beside the trickle that still flowed from the adit. It looked a shy bird. That persuaded him. If there had been anyone about, it would not have been so daring. When it flew off he would part the ferns and follow it towards light and freedom.

Johnny Fortnight was getting impatient. It wasn't his way, but this cat-and-mouse game was too trying. Part of him kept telling him to go away, set up camp by the pool and forget Welland and his misfortunes. The other part, now stronger than ever, kept him rooted where he was, with his eyes on the adit. His fingers played with the medal in the depths of his pocket. He had been lucky that the Curate had been so taken up with the papers that he hadn't searched further. It was gold, or seemed so, worth a small fortune. Perhaps he would give it to Ruth later. And then again, he might not. How was he going to explain how he came by it?

The packman could not help letting out a warning shout when the figure emerged from the adit. He knew it must be Welland, despite the distance, but it was a jolt that the long wait had ended. It was doubtful if the fugitive ever heard him. What sealed his downfall was that he paused an instant to look around. The two tinners flung their net over him and Magor wrestled him to the ground in a moment. The packman shifted his tobacco in his cheek and spat. That was always the way of it. God help him! He walked dejectedly back to the pool and tried to occupy himself with grooming Emma. Although it was his own supper time, he had no appetite. He knew that sooner or later, he would set off over Morvan to find out what befell that Welland.

There had been another watcher observing Welland's capture from his quarters in Tregurney House.

'Oh, famous! Bravely done!' he exclaimed, hopping from one foot to another behind the telescope he had set up on the terrace. 'I knew something was afoot. They have him.' He clapped his hands with glee. 'The fox is caught.'

'Have whom!' said Lady Diana, biting off a thread in her embroidery.

'Why, that damned murderer, that Welland. Magor has him in a net.'

'I don't entirely share your enthusiasm for man-hunts, Mr Adams, but it's lucky he never reached here as I expect he planned to. It could have been embarrassing, most embarrassing. I told Silverton he was making a mistake, but he never listens to me. Oil and water won't mix. That Halt fellow was no more than a tradesman. I knew there was vice in 'im. He could only masquerade at being a gentleman. Silverton'll learn now, he'll learn how easy it is to stand up for that kind of "friend", won't he, Rector?'

But the Rector was already out of earshot, scurrying across the lawns as fast as his gout would allow, with his hounds barking at his heels. He vanished into the church and, moments later, the bells were cheerfully pealing.

It was those bells that perplexed Hector Bolitho when he heard their erratic ringing, but the reason was soon clear to him when he saw the men come trotting over Morvan with something trussed in a net between them, like a calf being carried to market. From all directions, men who had been guarding shafts and winzes converged with the returning hunters and fell in behind them as they made straight for Windfall across the darkening moor.

So that was it! They had him. Bolitho sighed a small sigh

339

as he locked the count house. Before he left the mine, he must see that the pumps were set working again. Then he must collect his captains and ensure that the murderer was not ill treated. Bolitho knew that he ought to think of Welland as the presumptive murderer, the accused, until tried by his peers and found guilty, but the evidence was too damning. The hangman's noose was all but round his neck already.

🎝 16 🎝

THE CHAPEL

The mail-coach slithered jerkily along in the darkness. Mavis kept peering out into the wet night, anxious to see the lights of Exeter, but what few glimmers shone in the countryside at that late hour were soon blotted out by sheets of driving rain. Opposite her, fitfully illuminated by the carriage lamps, sat a tall gentleman in a greatcoat who had climbed aboard at Tedburn St Mary. Mavis herself ought not to have been sharing the luxury of an inside seat with him, but had been installed here by the good-natured coachman who, when he took over at Okehampton, declared that the top was no fit place for a lady in such weather.

Their advance had been slow, dreadfully slow, as the coach splashed along the tortuous roads that fringed north Dartmoor. Though the axle had been eased, the driver still needed to nurse it if they were not to break down completely. Mavis had a premonition that there was little time, but there was no quicker way, even if there were occasions when she was sure she could have jumped out of the vehicle and walked faster. If only there had been one of Silverton Gurney's swift steam-carriages to ride on.

'A wild night to be travelling alone, is it not, my dear?' remarked her companion after an introductory cough. For the past half-hour, Mavis had sensed he was trying to strike up a conversation. She guessed from the cut of his greatcoat and the starched whiteness of his stock that he was a scholar, perhaps a physician or a lawyer. His slightly affected, fluting voice suggested the latter.

'My brother awaits me at Exeter,' she answered with the

barest hesitation. Although her fellow passenger looked harmless enough, a woman could not be too careful.

'I'm pleased to hear it,' said the man with apparent sincerity. 'A young lady can't be too careful. Why only yesterday – ' he paused and wagged a monitory finger, 'only yesterday, a poor woman, travelling alone, was brutally assaulted.' Mavis sat bolt upright in her seat and said nothing. 'Haven't you heard? It's the talk of all the West Country and it happened down where you've come from. They're tracking him everywhere: a lame fellow, but tough, violent, dangerous. Until he's hanged, the roads won't be safe for the gentle sex, now will they?'

'Until he's hanged?' Mavis was shocked into putting the question. Until she heard it said, she had not allowed herself to consider the possibility.

'What do you expect? At the very best, if there were extenuating circumstances, it might be transportation, but that's too soft for cold-blooded murder. I'm clerk to the assize court in Exeter. We see all sorts of cases. One gets to know which show mitigating considerations. In this case, there are none, there can't be. The man's a monster! – Oh, excuse me, have I frightened you? Here, take my handkerchief,' he apologized, seeing a furtive tear steal down her cheek.

'Is there no hope then?'

'Hope? Dear lady, we commonly hang felons for less. You're far too tender-hearted, far too kindly. Why, if we didn't make the punishment fit the crime, there'd be an end to civilized society.'

The coach had just trundled across a bridge and was rumbling up a steep cobbled street. All the houses were closed and dark, except a baker's shop which gave out a welcome glow and a smell that reminded her she had not eaten. The coachman cracked his whip and the horses' hooves splashed in the runnels. Mavis caught a glimpse of a huge building through an alley: the cathedral? The coach speeded up as the road levelled and a columned portico sped by the opposite window. Then, abruptly, the coachman reined in and swung his team into the archway of an inn.

'Can't a man hope for pity? Can't he hope for justice?' Mavis asked hopelessly as they halted.

'My dear lady, the majesty of the law ignores pity, and punishment *is* justice.' It was a nice turn of phrase and the clerk was rather pleased with it until he realized that the girl was weeping. 'Come, my dear, don't take on so! What can I have said to upset you?' And then, with a flash of insight, 'Who is this fellow we've been talking about? You know him, don't you? What is he to you?'

'My husband.'

'Good God! Forgive me,' said the lawyer and she knew he meant it.

A shout from the coachman broke in on their conversation: 'All change for the Bath Mail and the London Coach!'

The lawyer sat forward in his seat and took her hand impulsively.

'We live in a hard world, an unforgiving world.' He paused. 'But we must make the best we can of it.' He felt the wetness of her tears on his handkerchief. 'Now, tell me, what are you doing here? Where are you going?'

'I'm in search of a friend of his: Silverton Gurney, the Squire of Tregurney. There's a chance he can save him.'

'What, is your husband taken then?'

'I fear he will be.'

'I must caution you not to expect too much from that direction. The law is the law, and he won't divert it. What is it they say? Put not thy faith in princes? This Squire Gurney's his friend, you say? And your husband, is he too a gentleman?' Mavis shook her head.

The coach door swung open and the coachman, sodden with rain, water cascading from his hat, looked in. 'Come on now, all change. We don't go no further.'

The lawyer's face, lit by the coachman's lantern, was

deeply cut with lines of concern. It was not the face of a rake or a ne'er do well.

'You'll breakfast with me, young lady, won't you? Neither coach leaves before daybreak. They serve food at all hours here; you'll feel better with a good meal inside you.' Mavis tried to compose herself. Should she accept? The lawyer had descended the steps and was offering her his arm in a warm and friendly manner.

The inn yard was full of the warm smell of horses and the bustle of ostlers getting them unharnessed and into the stables. She let herself be guided across it to an arched doorway by the stooping, deferential stranger. He seemed kindness itself; she wanted to confide in him. What sort of a world was this if you could trust no one.

'But I was forgetting,' he remarked suddenly, 'your brother, what can have happened to him?'

'I have no brother,' she heard herself saying. 'I lied to you.'

The lawyer paused and a look of pain crossed his face. A suspicion of tears made his eyes glisten as he looked down at her.

'But you do have a husband and are trying to save him, dear lady.' Impulsively, he took both her hands and pressed them. 'My name is Dobwell,' he told her. 'Come on inside now. Tell me all. I'll do all in my power to help you.'

Despite the darkness and the teeming rain, there was a human warmth in him that comforted and encouraged her. For a moment, her head drooped forward and she wept tears of gratitude on the rusty melton cloth of his overcoat. Then she followed him into the inn and ate ravenously while telling him all she knew of events in Windfall. Had she known what had happened there since she left, it would have spoilt her appetite.

When Johnny Fortnight slipped back into Windfall, he remained in the shadows. He had been unable to resist the urge to follow the course of events in Welland's story and had left Emma tied to a tree within reach of pasture while he ran hard over Morvan. The sun set as he crested the hill, showering red fire over the fading sky and gloomy land. There was more rain coming. Suddenly, the iron tongues of St Winwalloe's bells clanged exultantly in answer to the peal from Tregurney behind him.

Torches were flaring and swaying in the deepening dusk when the packman stole between the houses. The roadway was thick with people surging about haphazard, their faces angry red in the torchlight.

'Where is he?'

The voice was Bolitho's. He had just been forced to abandon his trap and was pushing through the throng surrounded by a knot of captains.

'Locked in the Sunday school; 'e won't take off in an 'urry.' The reply came from Tom Magor who emerged from the side of the chapel, flanked by his own supporters who were clearly more numerous than the purser's.

'All right then,' said Bolitho briskly, 'you've caught 'im. Now hand 'im over.' A silence fell after Bolitho's words. The onlookers knew the implications. A battle of wills was engaged between the two men and Bolitho caught Magor casting sidelong glances to judge his support; it looked as though he might crumble. 'Get a move on! That's no fit place for him; it's not secure. Captain Angove will convey him to the lock-up in Tregurney. Go fetch him.'

'You'll do no such thing, Tom Magor!'

All eyes turned to the top of the chapel steps where Hilda Trerice had emerged from the doorway. Her eyes shone like a hawk's and her sharp features stooped towards Bolitho challengingly.

'The suspect must be handed over. Don't try to stand in the way of justice, Hilda Trerice,' Bolitho responded. 'The law must take its course.'

'Justice! Us knows all about that justice,' hissed Hilda Trerice: 'Us 'ave a bone to pick with that Welland afore 'e do leave Windfall.'

'Welland Halt is answerable to the courts; he is not answerable to you.'

'But if 'e chooses –' There was a sly, knowing tone to Hilda Trerice's voice that Johnny Fortnight did not like and neither did Bolitho, from the look on his face.

'What d'you mean, "chooses"?'

'I've spoke to un. Welland 'Alt is ready to stand before Windfall and answer for 'is misdeeds.'

'I don't believe it.'

'Come in and ask un for yourself.'

Johnny Fortnight could see Bolitho hesitating. What seemed to decide him was a menacing movement among Magor's supporters and hostile looks from the other Windfallers.

'All right then, lead me to him. He shall speak for himself – but that doesn't mean you have any right to judge him; that's the royal prerogative.' Bolitho was playing for time, trying to find a favourable moment to spirit Welland away. For the moment, that was impossible. The packman saw him murmur something into a mine captain's ear before he mounted the chapel steps with all the dignity he could muster. Angove and all the captains, bar the one he had just spoken to, followed him closely. The crowd surged after them, jamming the doorway while Johnny Fortnight waited. The captain that Bolitho had sent for help faded discreetly into the gloom and, at first, it appeared that he had left unnoticed, but Magor sent two of his crew after him before he too pushed into the chapel. Johnny himself remained in the shadows until the last villagers were on the steps before joining them. In the vestibule, there was a temporary halt. The latecomers' advance was blocked by the press of earlier arrivals already jammed into the interior. Doors to either side of the vestibule gave on to stairs leading to the balcony. The packman eased his way up one of these.

Once he entered the chapel itself, the light was brilliant. Every candle and lamp was lit and was reflected off the white

346

of the walls and the white of the ceiling. They picked out the gilded fillets on pew backs and cornice. From the packman's vantage point at the back of the balcony, it was like a theatre, but the tiny stage on which the minister stood to preach was vacant. On either side of this stage, with its lectern and pew, were twin doors that probably communicated with the basement. It was through one of these that, moments later, the captive was dragged unceremoniously.

Blinded by the light and dazed by the sudden hubbub, he stood blinking until Magor shoved him sideways into the pit at the centre of the room. From the packed box pews that rose in stages on three sides of the central area, his fellow villagers examined Welland Halt coldly. His face was streaked with blood and dirt. There was more blood on his shirt and chest. No doubt they had been ill-treating him for there were fresh bruises on his arms which they had roped tight at the elbows behind him, making him stumble and almost fall on the steps that led down to the small arena in front of the lectern. No one extended a helping hand; rather the villagers cringed back at his approach as though he carried some dread contagion.

Rough, quarrelling voices rose from beneath the balcony. Bolitho came into view and approached Welland who was swaying on his feet, barely conscious of what was happening around him. Bolitho took him by the shoulders and brought his face close to the captive's.

'You want a fair trial, don't you? You've no need to say anything here if you don't want to. Say the word and Captain Angove will escort you to Tregurney.'

Bolitho waited. After what seemed an impossible delay, Welland shook his head. It was an almost imperceptible gesture, but there was no mistaking it. The packman was as perplexed as Bolitho. It was as if the captive was refusing his one chance of succour. Bolitho cleared his throat but, before he could speak again, the initiative was taken away from him.

Without warning, a woman sprang out of the crowd.

Swinging her angry stare from side to side, she leapt on to the platform and seized the Holy Book on the lectern, turning its pages feverishly until she found the chapter and verse she wanted. It was old Hilda Trerice. Bolitho had thought he knew her, but this woman was inhabited by a strange spirit and her sharp eyes slashed the onlookers like a knife she turned in a wound.

' "There was in a city a judge," ' she read, concentrating her will upon Bolitho, ' "which feared not God, neither regarded man:" ' she allowed the words to sink in before proceeding, ' "And there was a woman in that same city; And she came to him saying; Avenge me of mine adversary." ' Hilda Trerice smiled a crooked smile, bringing her audience into a sort of complicity. ' "And he would not for a while:" ' she stopped to smile her thin-lipped smile, ' "but afterward he said within himself, Though I fear not God nor regard man; Yet because this widow troubleth me, I will avenge her lest by her continual coming, she weary me." ' She halted, shook the Bible in Bolitho's face and spat at him. 'I'll weary you! You'll not leave Windfall afore us 'as our justice.'

'Are you threatening me?' Bolitho was trying to maintain his composure.

'Never a bit,' Hilda Trerice answered with sly diplomacy, 'but you should know, Hector Bolitho, that there's not one tinner as'll work fer 'ee over to Wheal Fortune till us d'see justice.' She turned her glare on the audience and demanded, 'Shall us 'ave justice?'

'Us will! Us will!' they chorused.

'Shall us 'ave vengeance?'

And with one voice the packed chapel responded to her: 'Us will! Us will!'

Hector Bolitho ran his eye over the ranks of hostile faces that ringed the room and he believed her. Welland would be lucky to get out alive and he himself must be prudent to avoid injury.

'What precisely are you accusing him of?'

Hilda Trerice's reply was a laugh, a savage cackle as she pointed a skinny finger towards the doors beneath the balcony, then crooked it and beckoned.

'There's reason enough, there's death, there's murder.'

Four of Magor's men emerged, carrying a gruesome bundle that the packman recognized instantly. They set it down on a table near the lectern and stepped back in obedience to Hilda Trerice's imperious gestures. The crowd was restive, full of whispers. She snapped her Bible shut and sidled down the steps until she could hiss in Welland's face, 'Tricked my daughter, didn' 'ee? Tricked all Windfall! Made out you was clean and honourable, and good, oh, so very good! You bloody hypocrite!'

Welland did not respond. He appeared hardly to hear her. Rocking slightly, he looked ready to fall at any moment.

It was becoming a travesty of a trial, but Bolitho was powerless to control it. He had the impression that, were he to walk out, Welland Halt would have been lynched on the spot. All he could hope was that his presence would temper proceedings until the captain he had sent off to Tregurney returned with a strong body of men to escort Welland out of Windfall. He licked his lips and breathed a secret prayer that they would hurry. Stony faces looked on approvingly as Hilda Trerice taunted the captive.

'Go on, deny it, if you dare provoke God's judgement!'

'God's mercy, what about that?' came a slightly tremulous voice from under the packman's feet.

'God's mercy on *you*, Mr Nichols! If you can get it! Weren't it you what aided and abetted? Weren't it you what afforded 'elp and comfort? Who was it called the banns in secret? Who was it married my Mavis to this wastrel? You'd do best to still your tongue, Mr Nichols, and 'ope; 'ope us'll ferget your idolatry and your givin' cheer to the ungodly.'

Johnny Fortnight could imagine the Curate shrinking under her gaze and that of all the heads that were turned towards him. Mr Nichols ventured one more remark.

'Don't you think you should give the man a chance to breathe?' he inquired as boldly as he knew how.

'Didn' give she no chance to breathe, did un?' Hilda Trerice demanded shrilly, pointing at the body under the sheet. 'Didn' show she no pity!'

Welland shook himself as she spoke this time, glancing about wildly as if emerging from a trance, vainly seeking a friendly face.

'Look to 'is shirt,' she screeched, 'blood all over un!' And indeed, Welland's shirt was red, red with the rusty stains from the mine, but redder still from a darker stain across the chest.

'D'ye see it?' Hilda Trerice insisted, pointing.

'Aye, us do!' The words came from the crowd automatically, like the responses to catechism.

'Hold on there,' interrupted Bolitho, 'that's his own blood, if I'm not mistaken – come from the cuts in his chest.'

'Sure 'nuff! 'ow did they come there? Aren't they 'er nail marks that made un flow?' Hilda Trerice, pulled his shirt apart to show the long thin weals.

'He could have got those scratches in the mine,' said Bolitho.

'And why did 'e run there in the first place? Why was 'e runnin' away? Tell us that, Mr Bolitho. Why was 'e runnin' if 'e weren't guilty?' chimed in Magor, pushing forward.

'He could have run away because you were hounding him.'

' 'E runned away because 'e'd killed a woman, that's what!'

'It could equally well have been you that killed her. You were there at the time, by your own admission.'

'Now why would I want to 'urt that woman? I'd never seed 'er. No, 'tes plain as a pikestaff why 'e slunk out to meet 'er. 'E knawed she were comin'; 'twas in 'er letter. Didn't she say she was pleased 'e'd made 'is fortune? Didn' she say she was comin' to share it with un? That wouldn' suit Welland, not with wife Mavis 'ere already, now would it?'

'We all know you had a grudge against Welland,' said Bolitho levelly, conscious that this was the flaw in the circumstantial evidence surrounding Welland, 'you had reason enough to murder the woman yourself if you wished to harm him. You knew where suspicion would lie. Didn't you have reason to resent him? Didn't he beat you in a fair fight and win your job from you? What could be neater than to kill her yourself and make him pay for it?'

Johnny Fortnight was all admiration for Hector Bolitho: not only was he standing his ground like an officer on the quarterdeck, coolness under fire was a virtue an old sailor appreciated and Bolitho had it, not only that, but he was giving as good as he got: his argument had struck Magor like a cannon-ball between wind and water.

'I never touched 'er!' blustered Magor. 'I swear it! Before God I swear it! That Welland did it. I 'eard 'em fight. Then I 'eard 'er scream. I shall never ferget that scream, 'twas terrible. Welland killed 'er! Oh, yes, 'e killed 'er; I swear it!'

'Let un deny it!' broke in Hilda Trerice, sensing that Bolitho might manage to turn sentiment against Magor. 'Let Welland deny it. Before God and 'is Redeemer, let un deny it!'

The stares of more than a hundred folk were full on Welland's face, but that face remained unmoving, the lips set as though chiselled in stone. Only the eyes moved slowly, scanning the sea of onlookers for a certain face. Ruth? Mavis? Did he feel they had deserted him? Johnny Fortnight had seen Mavis riding on the coach towards Bethel, she might have been fleeing, and then she might have been seeking help for Welland. Whatever the reason, neither appeared to be there to give him comfort. A kind of lassitude or indifference overwhelmed Welland and his gaze dropped to the floor.

'There, see, 'e don't deny it! 'E don't deny 'e killed 'er!' exulted Mrs Trerice, while the crowd murmured agreement. 'Killed 'is own legal wife, 'e did; waited for 'er and killed 'er in cold blood when 'e knowed for sure she would come to unmask un!'

'And what proof do we have of this woman's identity?' demanded Bolitho. 'How do we know she was connected with Welland?'

'The letter, o' course. 'Twas in 'er letter,' said Magor.

'And where is this letter? Can you produce it?' asked Bolitho, rejoicing in the knowledge that this particular piece of evidence no longer existed.

'I've told you already, Welland burnt un. Us saw it 'appen. There's men in this room what watched un.'

A chorus of agreement swept round the chapel.

'But we have only your word for the contents,' said Bolitho, 'and you're illiterate.' This was a telling point and Bolitho paused to let it sink in. Without proof of motive, or identity, the case against Welland might still crumble. But he was doomed to disappointment.

'There's not a word of a lie to what Tom Magor 'ave told 'ee,' shrilled Hilda Trerice. ' 'Twas 'is wife as wrote to un. Just like Tom said, she wrote she would come on the coach to claim 'er share of 'is fortune.'

'Ah, I suspected all along it was you that read it for him!' Bolitho swung on her aggressively, then encompassed the room with a belligerent stare before he continued. 'I'll have you know there's such a thing as perjury. There's also the crime of conspiracy. This woman Trerice had her own reasons to want to contrive Welland's downfall. Didn't she hate him for marrying her daughter? You all know that. You've got to admit it.' He paused again and drew himself up authoritatively. 'I'll grant you there's evidence enough to make a case against Welland Halt, but it's evidence we should treat with caution. We'll see clearer in a few weeks' time when he comes up before a judge at Bodmin Assizes.' The packman sensed that Bolitho was gaining control over the audience. He breathed more freely.

'Evidence! Evidence! Isn't this evidence enough!'

screamed Hilda Trerice, tugging at the shroud that enveloped the body. 'What more do we want than this? Didn't 'e run off and 'ide after 'e'd murdered this poor woman?'

'My information is that he went home from the Tinners' and there he passed the night. Was that the behaviour of a fugitive, a guilty person?'

'Who told 'ee that? My Mavis? She would say that, wouldn't she?'

'Her evidence is as good as yours. I'm telling you, I'm telling you all, we should suspend judgement. Isn't Welland Halt a Windfall man? Hasn't he been a good friend to most of you? We know him well. On the other hand, there's this stranger, this woman that only Magor and Mrs Trerice pretend to know about. There's no one else here who can identify her.' Bolitho was toying with his watch-chain, a sure sign of renewed confidence.

'I can!'

The clear voice surprised everyone. Johnny Fortnight knew it at once, so did they all. Even Welland looked up. His face was animated, his lips moved. He watched his daughter make her way slowly from the door at the back of the room towards the table where the body lay under its shroud. Bolitho was in a quandary: it was evident to him that Ruth's evidence could save her father. If she could demonstrate that the dead woman was not her mother, most of the people in the room would believe her and Welland could be led away to stand trial at the assizes. On the other hand, if her evidence went the other way, she would unleash such terrible passions that God only knew what would be the outcome. Her face said nothing; it was the same lifeless mask that had so disquieted Mavis. Bolitho too felt a strange dread of what that mask might cover, but he had no alternative.

'What can you tell us?' he asked quietly and matter of factly. 'Without looking, what can you tell us that will prove whether or not that dead woman is your mother?'

It seemed to the packman that the girl was in a trance-like

state. There was a long lull before she answered the question.

'She has a large mole between her breasts and she is holding the medal Mr Gurney brought for my father.' The words came out slowly, dreamily, and Ruth did not look at her father.

'Let's see then!' cried Hilda Trerice, lugging back the shroud.

Despite the fact that the onlookers were mentally prepared for the sight, it was still distressing. There was a hiss of indrawn breath as the full horror of the woman's injuries became apparent.

'Look!' Hilda exulted. 'There it is! A mole, just where she said it would be!'

Now she bent over the hands, prying them loose in search of the medal. The packman heard her muttering in frustration. He himself was gripped by panic. The medal she sought was in his pocket. He had been in such a hurry to follow Welland to Windfall that he had forgotten to leave it hidden at his camp-site as he had intended. It was too late to drop it on the floor; the room was so quiet that the chink it made would be instantly audible, and he had insufficient time to slip it into someone else's pocket.

'Someone've took un!' Hilda Trerice had straightened up and was looking straight in his direction. 'Someone what sneaked into the church to rob the dead. But I seed un! I seed 'ee, Johnny Fortnight. I 'eared that bell a-tollin' and I seed the Curate let 'ee out. You've took un. Come on, admit it.'

'No, I never!'

'Search un! Turn out 'is pockets!' Hilda Trerice commanded. Within moments, the incriminating medal was glistening at the end of its ribbon by which its finder was holding it up for all to see. 'There!' she crowed. 'What more evidence do us want than that?'

'Would you mind telling us,' the packman heard Bolitho asking, 'how you came by that medal?'

Johnny Fortnight realized what the purser was hinting at.

If he said he had found the medal on the road somewhere, what was to prove he hadn't! It would be his word against the girl's. Another thing, hadn't he removed the medal before the strange apparition, which he now knew must have been Ruth, came into the church. He was opening his mouth to say that he had picked it up near Gipsy Winze when Mrs Trerice forestalled him.

'Tiddn' no use denyin' you thieved un. 'Ere's the rest o' that ribbon, still caught in the poor critter's fingers.' The game was up. Johnny Fortnight knew when he was beat. To be nabbed by an old woman on the strength of a few inches of ribbon, wasn't that poetic justice?

'Were you alone in the church?' Bolitho persisted. The packman was impressed by his perspicacity. The purser had all his wits about him and was using considerable skill to defend Welland. How had he guessed there had been a third person?

'There was someone. There was a young woman. She comed in while I was in church. I 'id meself. She didn't see me.'

'What was your reason for hiding?'

'No one trusts a packman.'

Bolitho laughed at this and a few of the onlookers joined him.

'Quite so. Well, this young woman, did you recognize her? Could it have been young Ruth here?'

'I think so. I can't be certain, but I think so.'

'Good. Now I put it to you, all of you here, that the person Johnny Fortnight saw *was* Welland Halt's daughter. What could have been more natural than for her to go to the church and examine the body, see if it really was her mother? It wasn't easy. Look at it yourselves. It's a wise daughter that knows her own mother in that condition. Now, listen to this: you have to put that statement of hers about the mole right out of your minds. If she has seen the body, and the evidence points to the fact that she has, then whatever she says about it is probably merely the result of her examination on that occasion. It tells nothing about what she remembered of her mother. Now, Ruth Halt, did you or did you not go into the church and look at this body?' Ruth nodded dumbly. 'Well, you've all seen what sort of a state she's in, she's in a fit, she wants to believe that woman is her mother, so she picks out the mole and persuades herself she remembers it. Yes, the girl's in a state; if she weren't, wouldn't she be trying to help her father?' For a moment, it seemed to the packman that Bolitho had introduced sufficient doubt into the tinners' minds to dull their bloodlust.

'Pay no mind to 'Ector Bolitho's quibblin'! Didn' this poor dead woman 'ave the ribbon in 'er fingers? 'Ow else did she get un than by meetin' with Welland?' Hilda turned to Ruth, putting her arm round her shoulders and speaking to her cajolingly. 'Come now, my lover, don't be afeared. Us don't want to 'urt 'ee, us do want to 'elp. Now tell your Aunt 'Ilda, why did you and your father come to Windfall?'

'To get away, to get away from her.'

'And why was that?'

'Father said she was an impossible woman. He said there was something wrong with her.'

'But there wasn't, was there? Was she kind to you?'

'Yes, she was kind. She used to let me comb her hair. It was beautiful, beautiful blonde hair. I stood for hours combing it. I used to look at her eyes in the glass. She smiled at me – Oh God, I can't look at her now – '

'The girl's romancing,' exclaimed Bolitho, anxious at the new turn of events. 'She's just thinking this up, she's un-balanced.' But in his heart of hearts he knew that what Ruth said was true. She and her father *had* fled another city, left another woman, for reasons he could not fathom, and taken the road which led them here, cold and destitute, to Wind-fall. Had Ruth's wandering reminiscences been tender to-wards her father, they might have saved him, but all the pathos was concentrated on the dead mother. Until she spoke, Bolitho had appeared to be gaining control of the crowd, now it was slipping away from him.

'What was your mother's name, dearie?' breathed Hilda Trerice, confident in her ascendency.

'Freya.'

'That's an uncommon name – a beautiful one.'

'Mother *was* beautiful. She used to dance, she used to sing. I wanted to go away with her, but she wouldn't let me.' While Ruth spoke, her father stood mute and the tears coursed down his cheeks. He was seeing her with a terrible clarity. 'I loved her,' Ruth continued, 'I thought Father did too – I don't understand – why did this have to happen to her?'

'Why don't you ask 'im yourself?' cooed Hilda Trerice. 'Ask 'im why 'e murdered 'er.'

'Why?' Ruth whispered, her face just inches away from her father's.

The room was deathly still awaiting his answer. Someone coughed awkwardly, feet shuffled, Johnny Fortnight thought of slipping away, but Hilda Trerice was watching him.

'Happiness – ' Welland croaked.

'Happiness?'

'Our happiness – yours – mine – Mavis's – '

Ruth laughed at that, clear as a bell, like a child at a party. Bolitho had said she was unhinged, the packman thought it was most likely. The girl put a finger to her lips and turned to Hilda Trerice.

'You'll not tell a soul,' she whispered, 'it's a secret, a secret between me and Father. Everyone thought she was dead, passed away, departed, but *we* knew she'd come back – at least *I* did. Wasn't she my mother?'

Hector shrugged, but the evidence was damning.

'You killed 'er! Admit it!' screeched Mrs Trerice, shoving her face into Welland's. 'You killed your wife, a poor, dear, innocent woman. You killed 'er so you could save your wealth, 'ide your bigamy, your adultery!'

357

Welland seemed to be having difficulty in pulling himself into the present; he was somewhere else, perhaps with Mavis on Carnwartha, or following Trevithick across the high plains of Peru, but at last he answered her.

'I don't deny it,' he said in a low, cracked voice. 'I had to do it. She would not let us be.' There was a tiredness in his speech, a resignation that was like a man reading his own death warrant and that, thought the packman, was exactly what it was. Mavis had deserted him, his own daughter had denounced him; what did he have to live for?

'There! E've confessed it!' exulted Hilda Trerice. 'Murdered 'is legal, wedded wife, 'e 'ave – and dishonoured my daughter. There's naught in that Welland but sin and 'e must pay for it. 'Ow shall us punish un?' Her eyes swept the chapel challengingly.

' 'Ang the bugger!' volunteered Magor.

'Aye, 'ang un! 'Ang un!' echoed a hundred voices.

Johnny Fortnight was on his feet with the others, but not in agreement. An ungovernable fury burnt in him and he gripped the balcony rail tight in both hands while he waited for the tumult to die down.

'Call this a chapel?' he shouted. 'Call this an 'Ouse of God? 'Tis naught but a whited sepulchre, and ye are all serpents, a generation of vipers! Call yourselves Christians? Is this your Christian charity? Is this your brotherly love? Is this the message of your blest Redeemer? Is this your loving kindness? I'd rather sling me 'ammock along of a Moorish pirate than alongside you stiff-necked 'ypocrites. I'd expect more mercy from a Moslem Turk than I would from you 'oly 'angmen! Damn your sanctimonious eyes, damn your forked tongues! There's a stench in 'ere that's worse than bilgewater, worse than a round 'ouse. 'Tis the stink o' self-righteousness. If my old admiral were 'ere, your 'ero, 'im what won Trafalgar and loved 'is Emma, 'e'd order up a broadside that'd blow the lot of ye to Kingdom Come!'

'Blasphemy! Blasphemy!' cried Mrs Trerice. 'You're two

of a kind, you and that Welland. Pay no 'eed to un,' she told the tinners, ' 'e's not worth nothin'. What do 'e know 'bout this Welland and the woman 'e've murdered.'

'More than you think,' replied the packman forcefully.

'Away with un!' cried Hilda Trerice, sensing trouble. 'Leave now, of your own free will, afore you share 'is fortune.'

'All right, I'm leavin' – but not before I tells you this. That woman there, on the table, I knew I'd seen 'er someplace, that's why I went to the church for a look at 'er. I'd seen 'er someplace years ago. Until tonight, I couldn't remember who she was or where I'd seen 'er. Well, now I can – ' The packman waited a moment. He was getting the crowd's attention. 'Called 'erself an actress, she did,' Johnny Fortnight winked broadly, 'called 'erself an actress, name o' Freya. All the sailor-jacks in Bristol knew that Freya. What they didn' know was she lived in a big 'ouse up Clifton where she played the lady. Married to an ironmaster, she was. Led 'im a merry dance, made 'im the laughing stock o' Bristol.'

'Liar! Liar!' shrilled Hilda Trerice. 'Us all knows 'ee fer a liar, Johnny Fortnight! Away with un, throw un out of 'ere!'

The crowd jostled the packman threateningly as a pare of tinners marched him out. This was the last of Windfall for Johnny Fortnight; he was glad to be shot of it.

'Wife to the navy, she was!' he flung over his shoulder before they bundled him down the stairs and out into the night. He was sure that no one listened; they could not hear him; their ears were stopped; they thought they knew all the truth they needed. The tinners threw him down the steps into the night and he ran off, but as soon as they closed the door, he crept round to a window to hear the rest of the proceedings.

'Now for this Welland,' Hilda Trerice was shouting, 'deceived my daughter 'e did, and orphaned 'is own, made fools of all Windfall into the bargain. This Welland's a strong man and a sly one and 'e've tried to 'scape already. If us sends

359

un off with Bolitho's men, ten to one 'e'll do so again and never come up afore the assizes. This Welland 'ave wronged all Windfall. Us don't want to be cheated o' justice; us wants it done quick. What say you us should do with un? What is your sentence?'

'Death!' came the shout, and the packman listening outside winced at the ferocity of it. 'The rope!' volleyed a second cry. Johnny Fortnight could see Welland through the window, but he seemed unmoved by it. He regarded his daughter through eyes that bore a veil a sadness. How could a daughter live with the man who had killed her mother, they seemed to say. The bond was born in the flesh: there could be no forgiveness. When the shouting died down, Bolitho had his say, though he knew it to be useless: his own captains, who ought to have protected Welland, had become as hard-faced and loud in their condemnation as the rest. The one he had sent off to Tregurney for help had not returned and he was beginning to wonder if he had failed in his mission.

'I'll have you know I cannot and will not condone this proceeding. It is an illegal act and the law will hold you severally and collectively responsible for its consequences.' The dry legality of his pronouncement was as evident to him as its inefficacy. If it had had the backing of a troop of dragoons' swords, it might have been a different matter. As it was, the angry growl that followed it made him fear for his own safety.

'Tiddn' no use ridin' your 'igh 'oss with we,' said Magor roughly. 'Us've took that cap'n you sent off, afore 'e left the village. There won't be no Tregurney men to stop us.' He jumped up onto the platform and addressed the tinners. 'Do us want to 'ang un?'

'Us do! Us do!'

'Shall us do it now?'

'Us will! Us will!'

Bolitho's face was lined with a bitterness born of man's

inhumanity to man. The crowd's blood lust made his flesh creep. But his horror of the moment was as nothing to his revulsion at the next when Hilda Trerice halted the movement towards Welland with un upraised hand.

'Easy, easy, not so fast! 'Old your fire a minute and listen. 'Angin's too good fer this devil. I've a better idea that'll spin it out and leave un leisure to repent. A clever smith is this Welland 'Alt; 'aven't 'e showed it over to Wheal Fortune mine, 'aven't 'e builded that idol fer Mr Nichols? Let's make un build a cage for 'isself, to be 'ung up in. That'll give un time to repent. What say you, Welland, what's it to be, the rope ere mornin', or will you build your cage and 'ang in it?'

Welland nodded. It was as though he too approved the sentence. Bolitho turned away from him. His resignation was too terrible to behold.

'Of 'is own free will,' Mrs Trerice called to him, 'of 'is own free will, 'e've chosen 'is punishment. Us don't need no 'size court to get justice.'

'Vengeance, you mean, not justice,' said Bolitho.

'An eye for an eye, a tooth for a tooth,' she countered, ' 'tis in the Bible. Vengeance *is* justice – Take un away to the forge, Magor, 'e can start work afore mornin'. I dare say 'e can't wait to punish 'isself. 'E shall 'ang in that cage for a year and a day, or till 'is body's dead and 'is damned soul's departed.'

'What's to become of Ruth?' asked Bolitho. 'She'll have no father.'

'I shall look after the girl,' said the Curate. 'I'll try to bring her the comforts of religion.' He took hold of her unresisting arm and led her to one side while the tinners took Welland towards the doorway. Bolitho saw the captain he had sent for help held captive under the gallery.

It was all over; the Windfallers were spilling out into the night. Johnny Fortnight stole away across Morvan towards his camp. When he crossed the turnpike, he thought of Mavis. Where was she now? Would her heart break when she heard of this night's proceedings? Perhaps it was broken already.

Mavis emerged from the Shepherd Market and made her way uphill. All around her was the unfamiliar bustle of a big city. Coaches, hackney carriages, broughams, handcarts and chariots clogged the streets and the evening air was full of the smell of dung, the cracking of whips and coachmen's curses. One street looked very like another and the directions she had been given in Piccadilly had become meaningless. She would have to ask the way again.

'Can you tell me the way to Charles Street?' she asked the porter.

'Why, you're lookin' at it. New to Lunnon, ain'tcher? Could tell from yer country lingo. Well, you'll soon find friends in Mayfair. There's plenny o' fine gennulmen who'll take care of an 'andsome filly like you are.'

'I'm looking for Mr Gurney's residence,' Mavis told him coldly.

'Silverton Gurney! Well, you won't be disappointed there; Silverton's got an eye for the ladies.'

'That's not what I had in mind. Can you point his house out to me?'

'No offence meant, I'm sure. It's that one up there with the lighted flambeau. Tell Silverton Tim sent you,' he laughed, 'it'll bring me a shillin'.'

Mavis picked up her skirts and hurried to the door the porter had pointed out to her. It was lacquered black, with a shining brass knocker. She struck three times and waited.

'Go round to the back,' said the liveried servant who opened it, after looking her over. 'This door's for the quality.'

'Wait a bit,' pleaded Mavis, unwilling to be put off. 'Silverton Gurney's a friend of my husband's. This is Mr Gurney's house, isn't it?'

'It's 'is 'ouse all right, but 'e's not at 'ome,' replied the servant making no effort to speak with dignity.

'But he must be. He came here from Cornwall. I've come all this way after him. It's urgent, terribly urgent. You must help me. It's about Welland Halt, surely you've heard of him?'

'If that's the case – ' the servant appeared to soften, 'but there's "not at 'ome" when a person's in, and there's "not at 'ome" when 'e's absent. This one's the latter.'

'Oh God!' sighed Mavis in despair. 'Where is he? Will he be home soon?'

'No use waitin'. 'Eaven knows when 'e'll be back 'ere.'

'It's a matter of life and death!' Despite herself, Mavis could feel tears coming. She tried to hold herself straight and not fall into dejection.

'To the best o' my knowledge, Mr Gurney 'as taken 'is Flyer to Bath or Bristol, 'e left 'ere this mornin'.'

'Then I must follow him. Can you tell me where I must go to catch it?'

'St Paul's churchyard, but you can wave it down at the Marble Arch if you're there waitin'.'

'Which way is that?'

'No use your runnin' off there at this time o' night. There's no Flyer till tomorrow.' The servant had softened during their conversation. 'Come on in for a dish of tea and a bite o' supper, there ain't no one watchin'. You look done in; you look famished; we'll feed you up a bit.'

'I thank you, but I can't stand waiting. If there's any kind of conveyance for Bristol, I must take it, I must keep moving. My husband's life depends on it.'

'As you wish, Mrs 'Alt, I'll not detain you.' The servant's attempt at a grand manner was returning. 'But if you'll wait five minutes, I'll send a footman to guide you.'

He stepped back inside and clicked the door to behind him. When he came back with the footman, the steps were empty.

'Perhaps she's gone round to the back,' said the footman. The other shook his head.

'She's gone,' he said, 'she looked like the devil drived 'er, poor woman. All I 'opes is that Silverton Gurney is 'arf the man she thinks 'e is.'

'But will she find 'im?'

'Oh, aye, she'll find 'im.'

17

THE CROSS

'Runned off, she did. Can't say I blames 'er. You led that Mavis a merry dance, didn' you, Welland?' cooed Magor from his seat at the side of the forge where he installed himself while he watched his captive. 'Couldn' 'ardly expect 'er to stand up fer the feller what tricked 'er, 'twouldn' be natural.'

Welland pursued his task with quiet determination. There had been no need to strike or threaten him. Magor had become so accustomed to the man's dumb humility that he no longer feared a hammer blow in response to his taunting. 'Your Ruth 'ave come out of it better, standin' up fer 'er mother like that. Proud of 'er, that's what you must be, she's an 'andsome young woman, 'andsome!'

Most of the time, Magor's taunts appeared to mean nothing to Welland; all his attention was concentrated on mastering metal. It was as though he were at work on his masterpiece. He shaped each part with scrupulous care, taking his time to achieve perfection. Hour after hour, the four stalwart tinners who guarded the door heard nothing but the beat of his hammer and the sizzle of quenching metal. They lolled about easily, confident that he would not attempt to escape from them. It was not that his leg was shackled to the anvil, it was the self-condemnation they sensed in him. Welland was not only their prisoner, he was the prisoner of his own despondent thoughts.

'That Nichols feller'll take care o' young Ruth all right, like 'e promised, I'm sure. Seen the way 'e d'look at 'er, 'ave 'ee? I'd a-took on the job meself if she 'adn' turned soft in the

365

'ead. She was a proper little wildcat once, but I tamed 'er, didn' I?' Magor continued.

Welland set the heavy hammer on the anvil top and turned to face him. There were a few more gasps from the bellows until the boy who worked them noticed the change and stood watching nervously.

'I've said I'll build my cage,' he stated quietly, 'build it I will. I need no watchin'. I need no tongue from you. Let me tell you somethin' – I made a promise once, I swore I'd fight no more – I've broke it already – I'm nought but a man. Now hear this, Magor, don't try me, I tell you, don't try me – if you speak o' my Ruth again, or my Mavis, I'll kill you, I swear it – '

Magor moved uneasily. He appeared to be ready to speak again, but thought better of it. The silence deepened. Finally, he slouched to the door.

'Make 'aste with that cage,' he threw over his shoulder, 'us can't wait to see 'ee swing!'

Within moments, the hammer was clanging again. It beat in Welland's head, a counterpoint of pointless rage to the refrain that epitomized his existence: marriage is the cage, marriage is the cage. He had built it already, built it with Freya. There was to be no escaping, that had never been possible.

And he was conscious of another irony: the cage he now built for himself was like the font cover, the Christ-Redeemer he had made for Curate Nichols, to make another marriage, a marriage of true love, possible, his marriage to Mavis. What had Ruth said of that? 'She can never be my mother.' She had foretold more than she knew. The wheel of fortune turned. Nor God nor man could stop it. Welland hammered through the day and into the night as if eager to complete his task.

A woman in a mob cap opened the door to Mavis. She had discovered his lodgings by pumping the men who ran the

366

Flyer and made her way straight to the prepossessing house in a huge crescent.

' 'E's in all right, but you can't see 'im,' the woman announced in a tired, surly voice in response to Mavis's inquiry.

'It's a matter of life and death. Tell him Mavis Halt is here to see him. I've been all the way to London seeking him.'

' 'E's not to be disturbed, I tell you,' the woman sniffed, and was closing the door when Mavis reacted swiftly, shoving it back and squeezing her way inside, regardless of the former's protestations. She found herself in a hallway with an open door into a parlour on her right. It was midday already, but a glance told her there was no one in there. Ahead was a flight of stairs. She ran up it, reaching a fashionably furnished saloon. It was equally empty. Another flight of stairs led to a landing with a pair of closed doors. She opened the first of them; it was a bedroom.

'What the Devil's the meaning of this intrusion?' cried the naked man who turned to face her. With him on the bed was a flustered young woman, trying ineffectually to hide her own nakedness under a sheet.

'She *would* come in. I couldn't stop 'er,' explained the woman in the mob cap over Mavis's shoulder.

'I couldn't wait. It's about Welland. He's in terrible trouble. He needs you.'

'Oh, it's you, is it, Mavis? I hardly knew you in that get up. Well, out with it! Can't you see I'm busy?'

'Your friend Welland needs your help!'

Silverton Gurney raised quizzical eyebrows and Mavis went on with a rush.

'The hue and cry is out for him.'

'The hue and cry? What's he charged with?'

'Murder.'

Silverton sat silent a moment, then rose and wrapped himself in a dressing-gown.

'Murder? That's a most serious business.'

367

'It's why I came to see you at once. The whole country's after him.'

The Squire paced rapidly across the room and looked out of the window. Without turning, he put another question.

'Who's the accuser?'

'Magor.'

'It's false, of course. Welland's not guilty –'

After a long wait for her reply, he turned to face her. She stared back wordlessly. Her eyes told him the answer. Silverton pursed his mouth into a moue of distaste. He crossed to the dressing table and began to comb his hair meticulously.

'Then there's nothing I can do, is there?' he murmured.

'But you're his friend; you have influence; you're the only one he can turn to. You told me to come to you for help. Now I need it.'

'My dear woman, what do you expect me to do? If he's not caught yet and I help him to escape, it's a criminal offence: aiding a felon. If they've apprehended him already, I can't tamper with justice. He'll come up before the assizes.'

'It's not going to be like that. The tinners are after his blood. Tom Magor's leading them. They're going to lynch him.'

'Come now, dear lady, let's not exaggerate. This is the nineteenth century. You're talking about Cornwall; it's a civilized country. You know the people; they're moral, God-fearing folk. No one will hurt him. He'll get a fair trial at Bodmin; I'll see to that when the time comes. If he's innocent, the jury will acquit him. If not, he'll be punished. What more can I say?'

'But she forced him to kill her.'

'He killed a woman?'

'His wife, I think. She heard of his work with you, his good fortune, and came to claim him.'

Silverton shook his head slowly.

'A bad business, a terrible business. He'll pay for it dearly.

If only he'd listened to me and come to London. If only he'd told me his reasons, I might have helped him. But he was too proud, too proud to trust me. Now he must suffer.'

'Then you won't help him?'

'If you mean, will I interfere with the course of justice, the answer is no, certainly not! It's more than my position is worth to do so. Regarding your other supposition which I don't believe for a minute, how do you expect me to come between a bunch of angry tinners and their retribution, vengeance, call it what you will? He's deceived them, hasn't he? Deceived you most of all, though you won't see it. If I try to stop them, I'll be inviting riot, insurrection, the destruction of Wheal Fortune.'

Mavis held back her tears. Her body was stiff with anger and frustration. She forced herself to kneel before him.

I'm begging you, I'm begging you. Come back with me and try to save him!'

'E said 'e was busy,' sneered the woman on the bed maliciously, 'didn't you 'ear 'im?'

Mavis ignored her.

'Well?' she demanded, struggling to her feet.

Silverton shrugged his shoulders expressively.

'Then you're no true friend of his, never were and never will be.'

'A murderer has no friends, you should know that by now, dear lady.'

'Don't you "dear lady" me. Damn you for your heartless condescension,' said Mavis in a cold, dead voice. 'I pray you'll live to regret it. I pray that your conscience, if you have one, will never give you peace. You're a monster.'

'You've said enough,' spat back Silverton. 'If you weren't a woman, you'd feel the weight of my fist.' He motioned to the woman in the mob cap who was still hovering in the doorway. 'Mrs Atkins, I'll trouble you to see this person to the street.'

He's right, thought Mavis as she trudged back round the

crescent, a murderer has no friends. She wondered about Bolitho; she wondered about Curnow; would they still stand up for him? She wondered how much longer she herself could love him.

Hector Bolitho sat in the count house, nervously stroking his face. Outside his window, the beam was rocking, the engine was sighing, and the pump was sucking water from the mine. Tomorrow, the tinners would be back at work there and the stamps would start pounding. Life would return to normal. It seemed the only solution. He had been home to Tregurney and discussed events with his wife, who had been troubled, and with Lady Diana, who had been dogmatic. She told him not to cross the tinners, but wait for instructions from her husband, Silverton. It wasn't as if the tinners were about to kill Welland, they were only planning to hang him up in a cage, weren't they? It was barbaric, yes, but there would be time enough to put matters right with a proper trial, when their tempers had cooled a little. Welland's hammer still clanged intermittently in the forge. He was putting the finishing touches to his cage. Bolitho had watched him work on it. It would be ready by nightfall, perhaps sooner. Welland had worked without respite, even when Curnow had found a way to persuade his captors to let him see him. Bolitho had seen him slip in sadly and emerge even more dejected just after daybreak. Curnow too must have reached the conclusion there was nothing he could do to save him.

When Curnow entered the forge that time, he hesitated on the threshold. The clanging had stopped as soon as he appeared in the doorway. He could hear the bellows squeak and the sizzle of burning coals. He also heard the bellows-boy's breath and the panting breath of another person. Swinging his stick in front of him, he advanced towards it. When his stick thudded against a boot, he put out a hand, groping for the face above it. His soft fingers explored the features carefully, lingering on the bushy brows, the strong nose and the tensed lips.

'Welland.'

'Aye.'

'I've brought 'ee a pasty, and I've brought some 'oggan. Ellen 'ave baked it special.'

'I can't eat. I thank her, but I can't eat. I'm not hungry.'

'Why doan' 'ee fight?' whispered Curnow. 'You're stronger'n ten o' they tinners.'

'They've chained me.'

'You can strike off that chain in a minute. I'll 'old un fer 'ee. If only you'll run off and 'ide fer a day or two, till Mavis do bring 'elp fer 'ee.'

'Mavis? Where is she? You've seen her?' His voice was less lifeless.

'She've gone after the Squire fer 'elp. Silverton Gurney's sure to 'elp 'ee. Come on, man, can't you see, 'tis your only chance. I've bribed the guards. They'll say you overpowered 'em.'

'You're a good friend, Curnow. I wish I could see it the way you do. But there's no way out, I see that now. I've made my bed and I must lie in it. I've nothing to hope for.'

'What about your Ruth?'

'I've a favour to ask you, Curnow. I know you'll do it. Take care o' my Ruth, if she'll let you. She's been hard served, for she loved her mother.' He paused a moment, breathing painfully. 'Now, give us your hand, Curnow, and let me shake it, one last time before you go, for I have work to do, this cage to make, and the tinners are waiting.'

Curnow heard him sob as he pressed his hand and held on to it a long time, with a grip like a drowning man's, until he abruptly released it.

'Get on home, Curnow. Leave me. I can't work with you watching.'

Johnny Fortnight knew he ought to have left Windfall long

ago. He had pushed his luck by going into the chapel and had been fortunate to escape Hilda Trerice's malevolence. Too many maidens knew of his camp by the pool and he had abandoned it as soon as he could get Emma saddled and ready. For a while, the Windfallers were too preoccupied with Welland to bother with a packman, but they would change soon enough if they saw him. Yet he had not been able to leave the village without seeing how things would end, and he tracked over the moors by night till he reached the old fort on Carnwartha. Hardly anyone ever approached it, and if they did, he would see them coming. But the wait had been long and he had tired of it. Once it was night, he told himself, he would get moving. He curled up in his lookout among the bracken on the earthwork crest and bit off a fresh plug of tobacco.

He must have slept, for he woke with a start. Far off, near Wheal Fortune, a crowd was gathering. There were horses, a wagon, shouts, confusion. Head and shoulders above the tinners stood Tom Magor. Gradually, he established a semblance of order, the wagon was loaded, the procession started moving.

Mr Nichols came to the vicarage door. He too had heard the crowd approaching. He was angry with himself because he did not have the strength to go down the short street and condemn them. With arms folded and head bent forward in prayer, he murmured, 'Father, forgive them, for they know not what they do.'

But no one heard him. The larks still twittered in the evening sky and the clouds sailed over serenely. Why, he wondered, did not the Almighty show Himself, register His displeasure, make the earth quake? Why did He not send a thunderbolt out of a clear sky? Was there no heavenly justice to curb the injustice of mortal men?

'Bread of Heaven, Bread of Heaven,'
sang the tinners as they passed the chapel, breaking into the familiar hymn.

372

'Feed me till I want no more,'
they sang on, and repeated, with an echoing 'Want no more'
above the other, clear as a bell, uplifting, heartrending.

Mr Nichols watched the singing tinners stride past him.
He wanted to look away, but could not. He felt physically
sick. The powerful, frothing drayhorses jerked the wagon
into view. Straight and tall at the reins stood Magor, holding
the horses in check with a harsh bridle. What the wagon
bore, the Curate forbore to look at. His attention was caught
by the girl who walked behind it. Ruth Halt, wildflower posy
in hand, followed the wagon as if to a wedding. Behind her
strode Mrs Trerice, strong-faced, Bible in hand, triumphant. After Hilda Trerice, the whole population of Windfall fell in and followed with shuffling tread.

'Open now the crystal fountain'
they sang,
'Whence the healing stream doth flow,
Let the fire and cloudy pillar
Lead me all my journey through.'

Hector Bolitho, who brought up the rear, looked over his
shoulder at Wheal Fortune. The fire glowed brightly
through the engine house doorway and the smoke plume
from the chimney leapt up into the sky. How like God's sign
to the wandering Israelites, at once a hope and warning, still,
after nearly two Christian millennia, misunderstood. Violence, barbarism, when would they lose their grip on men's
minds? Hope for the future lay in improvements in industry,
creation of wealth and its diffusion, the softening of manners. For that to happen, there was need of places like Wheal
Fortune. Poor Welland's ill luck was to have been in the
wrong place at the wrong time. Today, a whole community's
blind hate was concentrated on him as the scapegoat for their
religion-inspired, collective sense of sin. Tomorrow, Welland would be forgotten, as a nightmare is forgotten, and
they would forget he ever existed.

Hector Bolitho sighed, he had always felt a special bond of

sympathy with Welland Halt. Already, he noticed, he was thinking of him in the past tense, as though already dead. Well, barring a miracle, he soon would be. The man had lost the will to live. He would never escape his tormentors.

'Strong deliverer, Strong deliverer,'
sang the tinners as they breasted the slope above Hilda Trerice's cottage, The refrain came to him softly, muffled by distance,

'Be Thou still my strength and shield,
Strength and shield,
Be thou still my strength and shield.'

If Bolitho had been of the old religion, he would have crossed himself, but he contented himself with a quiet Amen. If the Lord was to be Welland's deliverer, it would be from this life, not in it. That much was certain.

High on Carnwartha Johnny Fortnight brought a spyglass from Emma's pack-saddle and focused it on the wagon. It had cleared the last of Windfall's houses and was climbing the steep and stony road.

'When I tread the verge of Jordan,'
the superb, harmonious voices floated up to him from the column of marchers who were now led by Jack Lugger who marched behind Hilda Trerice like a travesty of the avenging angel, rusty sword in hand.

'Bid my anxious fears subside;
Death of death and Hell's destruction,
Land me safe on Canaan's side.'

Where indeed, this side of Canaan, would Welland Halt find a safe haven? Man would not pardon him, voyage though he might. Only through this shipwreck would he sink into Jordan's cleansing, forgetful river and be swept beyond the bitter shores of hateful memory, to the quiet sea of death.

The packman's telescope picked out Tom Magor, superb and smiling like a charioteer. Behind him, braced erect by a web of rigging, was the jolting cage. With arms outspread, it advanced in bizarre benediction, like an image in a Popish

374

procession: image of redemption, reality of death.

'Songs of praises,'
sang the exulting tinners as they closed with the carn and the place where three roads meet,

'Songs of praises,'
climbing on to that bare, windswept saddle of land where the mail-coaches now passed daily between Bethel and Tregurney, where the cool sea breezes hissed through the heather, where the crows wheeled, and where now the gibbet stood.

'I will ever give to Thee,'
ringing from the singers' throats, then repeated in a lower register,

'Give to Thee,'
and in the ultimate dying fall,

'Give to Thee,'
and the deep, sonorous,

'Amen'
as the wagon came to rest under the gibbets' arm.

Within moments, the cage was shackled to the arm, the cords were cut and the wagon driven away. The crowd remained a while in a circle to gloat and jeer until they grew hoarse and straggled back to Windfall.

Though Johnny Fortnight could see the cage clearly, limned on the evening sky, he was unable to make out more than a shadow in it, a shadow that moved uneasily, and much too far away to hear the single word its occupant was mouthing and the wind plucked from it. 'Mavis – Mavis – Mavis – Mavis – Mavis – Mavis – ' interminably repeated in a mute appeal, a cry from the heart, for forgiveness. He could never repay. Mavis had not deserted him. Even after Welland lost consciousness, her name seemed to be repeated by the creak of the shackle at every swing of the cage.

Johnny Fortnight did not wait for night to fall. An unavowed fear made him haste away from Carnwartha's enigmatic stones. He cared not where. Anything was better than the sinister Windfall scene. Even Emma the donkey seemed to share his sense of revulsion and trotted ahead without prompting until the hateful village was out of sight and they reached their usual camp on the far side of Bethel. There was something stifling in the Cornish air and Johnny Fortnight did not care to breathe it longer than he must. He would cross the Tamar tomorrow and doubted if he would ever come back there.

The night coach rumbled past him in the early hours. He stirred under his blanket when he heard it coming, but did not rise. Mavis, sitting beside the coachman, had no idea the packman was sleeping in the undergrowth so close alongside. She was listening to the cocks crowing and the dogs barking on the sleeping farms. For hour on weary hour, she had been travelling over unfamiliar ground and now at last, near Bethel, remembered shapes were emerging with the coming dawn, but it seemed that the coach was advancing even more slowly. Far off to the left was Carnwartha's wrinkled dome. Morvan was somewhere behind it. She smelt the odour of sanctity from the chapel at Bethel as they passed by. She felt the caress of the ocean wind.

If Welland had been lucky, he would be out there now, dipping and rolling on the languid surge, every hour taking him further from Cornwall, towards sanctuary in a distant land.

But in her heart of hearts she feared it was not so. Ever since her confrontation with Silverton Gurney in Bath, she had been full of apprehension. A grim certitude had increasingly burdened her breast.

She shivered as they topped the rise and began the long descent by which the turnpike dipped to Tregurney. She had not spoken for many miles. The kindly coachman stole a glance at her in the gathering light that was boiling up, scarlet and gold, to the eastward.

'You'll be glad to be 'ome,' he ventured.

'Home?' Her voice arrived from an immense distance, as though she spoke from a dream.

'Us've nearly reached Windfall, my lover,' said the coachman, pointing with his whip.

Mavis sat silent. How could she tell him? On her left, Carnwartha brooded. How often she and Welland had gone there together. Ahead, just out of sight, was Tregurney. She remembered the feast and what followed; she remembered the pool in the moonlight. She remembered Welland.

The coach stopped to set her down. The driver handed over her bundle. She was in the shadow of the carn, the very place where she had first met Welland. The sound of Ruth's plaintive crying came back to her. She recalled her fears as she searched among the rocks. She remembered Welland's belligerence, his revulsion from Windfall. If it had not been for her, he would have passed on and never stayed there. It was cold in the lee of the carn, its rocks were black on the sky, she shook in its shadow.

She stepped out into the brilliance of the morning light. At first, she could not see anything unusual, she was too dazzled. The music of the stamps floated up from Wheal Fortune. Above it she became aware of a strange creaking. It came from a point close ahead of her. Where the three roads met, a thick post, black and menacing, reared up into the sky. Her eyes followed its upward thrust, reached out along its jutting arm, and saw the cage.

Even then, its significance did not dawn on her at once. She walked forward slowly, gazing up at the half-familiar outline in trellised metal, a shape that creaked on its shackle as it swung in the sun's bright rays. The light traversed it in parts, but its interior was obscured by a dark form, imprisoned in its narrow bands.

She circled it slowly, clutching her bundle to her breast, absorbing the terrible reality of it all, knowing the shadow's identity long before she saw the face. She remained unsure if he was watching her, for the visage was barred with iron and stripes of shade, but at least the eyes were open and had a

377

glint of life in them. She halted and spoke to him, enunciating slowly as if addressing a child.

'Welland? Who did this to you?'

Whether he heard was not immediately apparent, but she caught a rasp of his breathing. When he finally did speak, it was in a thin whisper, barely audible above the creaking of the cage.

'Windfall – myself – I brought it on myself.' There was a terrible resignation in his voice that crushed her too. Her eyes had been searching frantically for some lock or catch that she might break to spring him from the cage. There was none she could see: all was hammered iron, a second skin.

'You should have left here. You should have gone to Peru. Trevithick wanted you; you said so once. You should have gone with him. I told you to.' The memory of the moment, among Carnwartha's great leaning stones, came back to her. His pleading face still haunted her. If only he had gone then, not come to this.

'Trevithick's dead, a pauper, near London,' Welland was saying. A grim smile creased her lips at this. Another dream had fled. 'Silverton told me so,' he added.

'Silverton!' she almost spat. She paused, swallowing the bitter taste in her mouth. 'I saw your good friend Silverton. "If ever I can be of service", he once told me. I asked him to help you, his friend, his partner.'

'He's coming?' Welland stirred hopefully.

'Put not thy trust in princes.'

'Ah – then there's no salvation.'

No, there was no salvation. The sun's disc peered out of the cloud and burned on him. Black crows were wheeling. He closed his eyes in anguish. His frame was twisted, his face and limbs already withering. The bold, strong, confident Welland she had known had already vanished, replaced by this hollow-cheeked caricature.

'Is it painful, Welland?'

'Cramps – the light in my eyes – the crows – I'm afeared the crows will pluck 'em if I sleep.' His eyelids fluttered open, then slowly fell. She shared his anguish.

What could she do? There was still Bolitho, wasn't there? Bolitho was a just man, surely Bolitho wouldn't let this continue.

'I'll go and talk to Bolitho,' she announced, hitching up her bundle. She felt relief; she was about to act. 'He'll call out the militia.'

'Save your breath.' Welland's resignation stunned her; she halted in mid-step. 'Listen to the stamps. The moment Hector Bolitho sends away for help, those stamps stop beating. All the tinners in Windfall will stop work. It's more than his job's worth to close Wheal Fortune.'

She listened. The stamps below still beat their dull tattoo. She remembered the moment when she had confronted Bolitho, her arm controlling the sluice handle. She had won then. Things were different now: the stamps were powered by steam; the tinners were against her. Even that, though, would not have baulked her. What stayed her hand was Welland's resignation, his acquiescence in his punishment.

'What can I do?' Her mind seemed half-paralysed, unable to think beyond the terrible, oppressive present. She felt herself sinking into the same lethargy as the man in the cage.

'Nothing.'

'I can't bear it.'

She swung away from him, towards Carnwartha. Its slopes were desolate and lovely in the dappled sunlight. They had walked there once. They had lain there.

'Who was she, Welland, that woman who –?'

'Freya – my wife. She tracked me here.'

'You never told me. Why did you never tell?' There was real bitterness here. 'Why did you want me wed?'

He was a long time answering, seeming to search for words.

'To make things perfect.'

'Perfect?'

'Good was not enough.'

No, she reflected, good was not enough, and to be perfect all must be complete. How had he convinced her? *'For my maid's sake'* – *'She'll need a mother'* – *'And if I decide against you'* – *'I'll ask again.'* In the last resort, it had not been for Ruth's sake, that had been a side issue, but for his.

'Your daughter, Welland, you must live for her.' Surely that was an argument that would quicken him.

'Ruth denounced me.' There was no resentment in this, only understanding. 'She was her flesh.'

'What's to become of her?'

'Curnow will watch over her, he's promised.' The irony of the blind watcher was not lost on her.

'But I –'

'You can never be her mother. She told me once. I did not believe her.'

Mavis stared down towards the house where they had lived together. It stood foursquare and solid, monument to his industry, haven of their hopes. They had lived happy there, but all too briefly. Down the road, outside the Tinners', a familiar figure strutted and swayed.

'Who made this cage? Magor?'

Welland laughed by way of reply, till his cage rattled and shook. 'Magor has not the art,' he told her finally, with tears on his cheeks that might have been tears of mirth. 'It is too perfect. Look at it now! How well it fits! I made the cage myself, out of my head. It was already there. All Magor did was shut me in.'

Yes, thought Mavis, it was always there, though she had only sensed its shadow on her life. Now, at last, she was beginning to understand the resignation that held him prisoner there. There was no place to fly. His cage was in himself.

She turned and studied him. How long did he have to live? How long could he swing and suffer there, in the wind, the sun, the rain? Had he the will to live, it could be but days – if someone fed him. Had he the will to live? That was the question. There was no need to put it. The answer was in the cage itself. All that was left was when.

If someone fed him – but longer life meant only lingering pain. A thought came to her: it might be her call to cut that life short. But she had no weapon to perform the deed. If she ran down to Windfall she might steal Jack Lugger's cutlass from the taproom wall, or slip into her mother's cottage and take down her father's fowling piece that rusted on a beam. She could scent their scorn; she heard it now already, backed by mocking laughter – 'Good morning, *Mistress* Halt.'

She would have faced them; stood up to even that. But there was another who would condemn her. She felt Welland's eyes upon her, loving, reproachful, as if he guessed her thoughts. '*It was not for myself. There was no violence*' – her words came back at her as if he spoke them. He knew her nature. She would not change it. She had not altered his.

'For you, for us, I killed her. I could not help myself. She had no place in Windfall. I did not count the cost. You, Mavis, were always wiser. Now, let me pay, pay for the joy we had together.'

'So it's all wasted,' she managed to say.

'It's all wasted.'

She dropped her bundle. Her hands flew up to her cheeks. Her nails dug into the flesh. She stood there.

'How long, Welland, how long must you hang here?'

'Till death us do part.'

'I can't bear it.'

She swivelled round to face the morning village. The line of tinners was setting out for Wheal Fortune whose chimneys fumed and whence rose the music of the stamps.

'My curse on this place,' she shouted in sudden exaltation, 'my curse on it and all that dwell therein! My curse on them, even unto the third and the fourth generation! My curse on Windfall, place where I was born! My curse on God that made it!'

Welland's cage. She could not look at him. She heard the creaking.

'Mavis – Mavis – Mavis –' it insisted.

'I'm leaving, Welland, I'm leaving – I cannot watch you die – the sight would make me mad – forgive me.'

'Forgive me too,' he whispered after a long silence.

'What's to forgive? You loved me. There's no forgiveness.'

Then she was gone.

Into the morning.

The cage swung in the sea wind.

The crows flapped round it.

The sun rose higher.

✤ 18 ✤

EPILOGUE

Beyond the account provided by the Reverend Fletcher which has formed the basis of this narrative, there remains but the scantiest of documentation to substantiate it and throw further light on the fate of its protagonists. It is as though the archives have been combed and purged of all relevant documents. From internal evidence in the Fletcher journal, it would appear that he derived the greater part of his information from papers and letters specially concentrated in the muniment room at Tregurney House. These were totally consumed in the fire that gutted the great house, in October 1918, the same month that the last young man to bear the Gurney name was killed near Cambrai in Haig's final offensive.

The modern researcher quickly forms the impression that there has been a deliberate attempt to expunge the record and destroy all trace of the savage punishment meted out to the unfortunate Welland Halt by his outraged and God-fearing neighbours. He has to content himself with small items like those afforded by the St Winwalloe parish register that, after being transferred to Exeter at the time of the death of Mr Nichols and the dereliction of the friendless church, was eventually passed on to the Truro diocesan offices and thence to the Public Records Office. Here we read of the burial of a Mrs Hilda Trerice on 21 June 1834 and the Curate has thought fit to give the cause of death as 'a most malignant cancer'. Tom Magor, together with a number of other tinners from Wheal Fortune mine, was buried in the following year, drowned, as his flaking tombstone confirms, when they 'holed into a house of water', breaking unexpectedly into flooded portions of the old men's ground and inundating all the lower levels of Wheal Fortune.

The surviving cost books of Wheal Fortune, preserved in the library of the Camborne School of Mines, record this event and detail the great cost of pumping it dry again. But its resurrection was brief: both the Windfall and the Welland lode (sic) were suddenly exhausted. Attempts to find others were unsuccessful and the mine was abandoned in 1837 following the final examination of the accounts by the adventurers at a drunken banquet in the count house, as the cost book entry of '3 doz. Porter, 3 gal. Brandy, and 2 gal. Rum' eloquently testifies. Mr Bolitho, who penned these entries, passed on to the management of other Cornish mines and election as Mayor of a small township near Falmouth.

Entries in the parish register become sparse after this period, but there are two significant inscriptions. One concerns the burial of Edwin Curnow in 1840, though, in this case, there is no indication of the cause of death, but it is the second which is most pertinent. In the column reserved for baptisms we note, inscribed in the curate's increasingly shaky hand, 'Jan Nicholson, born out of wedlock to Ruth Halt, 1st January 1848.' Are we to assume from this that the timid curate is coyly admitting paternity? Had he, after the death of Curnow and the probable departure of his family, taken the vulnerable and somewhat deranged young woman into the vicarage in the guise of housekeeper and is she the lady mentioned as being the sole member of the congregation in the report written by the bishop at the time of his last visitation?

Concerning her son, Jan Nicholson, we know only that he lived the life of a humble road-mender until his chance meeting with the Reverend Fletcher who, after a careful examination by a physician, had him consigned to the Bodmin Lunatic Asylum where he remained for some months, but was released at his own earnest entreaty, matched by good conduct, and returned to his home in the crumbling vicarage.

Silverton Gurney's riches likewise crumbled away, hastened by the failure of Wheal Fortune mine, the high tolls levied by the turnpike trusts on his steam-carriages, and the law passed by Parliament to restrict their proliferation, enacting that a pedestrian should run ahead of them waving a red flag. He shot himself in Boodle's Club in 1850, leaving debts which forced the Gurney family to sell off most of their real property.

Johnny Fortnight heard an account of Squire Gurney's death without regret. He had not visited Tregurney for several years now, having saved his profits as a packman to set himself up as a supplier and victualler to the naval dockyard in Devonport. He married a rich widow, grew prosperous and respected, and was carried to his last resting place in St Andrew's church, Plymouth, by a delegation of aldermen and prominent Freemasons. Naturally, the name Fortnight does not appear on his tombstone; it was no more than a nickname in the first place and assorted ill with his later, more dignified persona.

Billy Bray never returned to Windfall, he was not the kind of man to forgive the unforgiving. Tirelessly travelling, his pulpit was the count house stairs, his congregation was the collection of rough tinners at the end of their core, and his message was ever the promise in the wells of salvation. He danced and sang of Christian joy until the Lord gathered him to His bosom in 1868.

Of Mavis Trerice, or Halt, there is no further trace, though her baptism in 1810 had been faithfully recorded by Mr Nichols's predecessor. Ralph Fletcher surmised that she might have returned to Exeter and thrown herself on the tender mercies of the good-hearted lawyer she met on the coach at Tedburn St Mary. He tracked him down, only to find that he had died a bachelor. However, the deceased lawyer's diaries provided him with a full account of his meeting with Mavis, together with a letter she wrote to him from Liverpool shortly afterwards. This letter is lost, burnt no doubt in the conflagration of Tregurney House. Did she then, like countless thousands of her fellow Cornish, take the road of exile and emigration, shipping off steerage to Australia, South Africa or some other destination? Did she end her days on some cattle station or perhaps even the high plateaux of Peru? All is speculation.

Why was Welland Halt left to die in his cage? How long did he hang there? Again, we are left to conjecture. Why, the historian may justifiably wonder, did the authorities fail to send a squad of militia to cut down the cage and save Welland for a royal trial and a proper gallows?

We are left to surmise that no such steps were taken because he hung within Silverton Gurney's jurisdiction, and the Justice of the Peace, through pusillanimity and revulsion, stayed clear of the business. Could Bolitho have saved him? Perhaps. Indeed, there is every possibility that the purser did send ineffectual appeals for help, tardily responded to, and that may account for the cage's having been dismembered and buried. In any case, we can safely guess that the authorities were slow to act in the face of the Windfall villagers' obdurate malignancy.

But there is another explanation which, more than any other, explains the consummation of Welland's punishment: he concurred in it. Having realized the impossibility of his dream of escape from the cage of his marriage, he built and entered voluntarily into the cage of his punishment. Bolitho must have sensed this, folded his hands, and let it happen.

What is not in doubt is the sudden and complete downfall of Windfall. Within five years, the industry which was the be all and end all of that isolated community was completely extinguished. The stones of the mine buildings were sold to a wrecker who carried them off to be incorporated in the expansion of Liskeard and Lostwithiel. The walls of the abandoned cottages were used as ballast for the track of a new railway, and the demolished chapel's ashlar blocks were built into a St Austell brewery. In less than a generation, the village had dwindled to nothing, an abode of kites and crows, an abomination of desolation where not one stone lay piled upon another. Is there a curse on the spot? It is all too easy to suppose so. Although sheep graze peacefully where once were streets, and the gibbet and its dreadful burden did not long survive the cruel weather of the high moors, its long shadow still lies heavy on the land. No amount of conceal- ment could keep it hid. The finger of destiny, acting through a simpleton, pointed it out to the Reverend Fletcher who concluded his account with this phrase:

'I am convinced that this abandoned moorland has been the theatre of a tragedy so disturbing, so profoundly repug- nant, so unspeakably horrible, that not only the men and women who participated in it, but God himself would wish to turn the page and blot it out.'

Such is the story that began and ended at Hangman's Cross, the place where three roads meet. Windfall is gone for ever, so utterly obliterated that naught survives, not even its name; you will not find it on any map. And yet it exists. You may stumble on it one day, recognising the carn, the smooth hump of Morvan, the depression where the ruined vicarage stands beside the fragments of St Winwalloe's, and the high fastness of Carnwartha. Climb up there, if you will, and listen, listen to the wind whimpering among the ancient stones and then deny if you dare that Welland Halt and Mavis Trerice once lived, and pledged their troth under that ruthless sky.